Praise for *The Far En*

DO254041

"Kathryn Craft's *The Far End of Happy* had me captivated from page one. A poignant glimpse into the undoing of a marriage. Craft expertly weaves a gripping tale that hits the reader hard and keeps moving briskly to its heartbreaking but hopeful conclusion."

—*Heather Gudenkauf,* New York Times *and* USA Today *bestselling author of* The Weight of Silence *and* These Things Hidden

"Kathryn Craft pulls off a miracle of storytelling, weaving together the initial magic spell of a couple entwined, the sad shredding of their love and family, fueled by alcohol, and the truth of the past binding them—all revealed throughout twelve hours of a tragic suicide standoff."

—*Randy Susan Meyers, bestselling author of* Accidents of Marriage

"The *Far End of Happy* gives us a newsworthy tragedy from the inside out. In sharply intimate language, Kathryn Craft deftly weaves her story out of many stories, some buried in the past, some fresh as a new wound, stories of true love, of families carefully built and then painfully unraveled, of a good man's life ravaged by alcoholism, and of the guilt, anger, hope, and tremendous strength of the women and children who love him."

—*Marisa de los Santos,* New York Times *bestselling author of* Love Walked In, Belong to Me, *and* Falling Together

"A complex and gripping story of broken hearts, lives, and marriages that will tear you apart from beginning to end."

—*Steena Holmes,* New York Times *and* USA Today *bestselling author of* The Memory Child *and* Finding Emma

"In *The Far End of Happy,* Kathryn Craft does not flinch from exploring the deep-rooted reasons for her characters' actions. Compellingly written, the tension builds throughout the book and the reader comes out the other side with more insight, and more compassion, for those who may find themselves on the far end of happy."

—*Catherine McKenzie, bestselling author of* Hidden

"Kathryn Craft is a masterful storyteller, threading beautiful pieces of the past into a present-day tragedy, resulting in a family drama so real and urgent you'd swear it was happening to your next-door neighbors. She weaves a heartbreaking story packed with tension and brimming with humanity. *The Far End of Happy* is an examination of love, mental illness, and family secrets…and the disastrous outcome when the three are combined. A poignant tale that will stay with you long after you've turned the last page."

—*Lori Nelson Spielman, #1 international bestselling author of* The Life List

"An incredibly honest and courageous exploration of a marriage torn apart by neglect and threats of suicide. Craft's ability to tell a tale as beautiful as it is haunting left me in awe. Not one to miss!"

—*Mary Kubica, author of* The Good Girl

"Despite the known outcome, Kathryn Craft keeps the tension edge-of-your-seat suspenseful in *The Far End of Happy*, with deftly woven backstory and alternating present-day hourly narrative. She creates a story that is unflinchingly honest and hard-hitting. A superb insider's look at the ripple effect of clinical depression and suicide."

—*Kate Moretti, author of the* New York Times *bestselling* Thought I Knew You *and* Binds That Tie

Praise for *The Art of Falling*

"Strikes universal chords in all of us who yearn, who love, who fail and fall, and struggle to find our way back home."

—*Elizabeth Benedict, author of* Almost, Slow Dancing, *and* The Practice of Deceit

"Unfolds with grace and truth…refreshingly and piercingly honest."

—*Kelly Simmons, author of* Standing Still *and* The Bird House

"*The Art of Falling* is a story of friendship and personal growth, and a helluva good read."

—*Elizabeth Zimmer, dance critic, Metro New York*

"Craft presents her mesmerizing characters with depth, understanding, and ethos."

—*Lana Kay Rosenberg, artistic director, Miami University Dance Theatre*

"Beautifully written and strongly emotional, *The Art of Falling* will move readers deeply. Kathryn Craft has penned a winner!"

—*Jane Porter, national bestselling author*

"In her engrossing debut, *The Art of Falling*, Kathryn Craft takes her long-damaged heroine on a quest for healing and truth—true self, true family, true friendship. Craft's sharp and refreshing narrative will leave you pining for more."

—*Julie Kibler, author of* Calling Me Home

The
far end of happy

The far end of happy

KATHRYN CRAFT

sourcebooks
landmark

Published by Sourcebooks Landmark, an imprint of Sourcebooks, Inc.
P.O. Box 4410, Naperville, Illinois 60567-4410
(630) 961-3900
Fax: (630) 961-2168
www.sourcebooks.com

Library of Congress Cataloging-in-Publication Data

Craft, Kathryn.
  The far end of happy / Kathryn Craft.
      pages ; cm
  (softcover : acid-free paper) 1. Psychological fiction. I. Title.
  PS3603.R338F37 2015
  813'.6--dc23

                        2014042684

        Printed and bound in the United States of America.
                VP 10 9 8 7 6 5 4 3 2

To my sons, Jackson and Marty

7:00 a.m.

ronnie

The pages felt thick with life as they flipped through her fingers. A long-suffering friend, this journal, taking everything she'd thrown at it. The questions. The tortured answers. The pros. The cons. Moments rich with beauty. The long slow death of a dream.

At the top of each page, she'd centered her name: Ronnie Farnham. On the lines below, she'd centered herself.

Ronnie sat on the guest room bed, propped a pillow against the wall behind her, and waited for the jostle as her shaggy little dog, Max, repositioned himself against her thigh. She pressed her pen to a cool, fresh page. Today, more than any other, in these last precious moments before her sons awoke, Ronnie needed the ink to offer up its ever-flowing possibilities.

Her pen stalled after one short sentence.

Today Jeff is moving out.

She would not have predicted this day in her marriage. Its impact was impossible to fathom. How could she write beyond such words? Ronnie shut her journal. Only one sentence, but it was a good one. Full of hope, but also one of the saddest she'd ever written. She'd have to sort her feelings tomorrow. Today was a day for moving forward. She capped the pen and placed the notebook onto the growing pile of journals beneath the bed.

At least she felt rested. If she'd tried these earplugs weeks ago, she could have avoided the inexorable pull of Jeff's late-night pot banging, she thought as she pulled them from her ears.

She heard voices from downstairs—loud voices—and she could swear one of them was George Stephanopoulos.

Max bolted through the door and raced down ahead of her as she went to investigate. Their kitchen was devoid of life, but beyond it, the living room was fully lit. The terse *Good Morning America* theme trumpeted another day's tragedies while no one watched. She turned off the set, shocking herself with the sudden silence. Her family had never turned the TV up so loud. The set was hot. Had she slept through another of Jeff's attempts to coax her into late-night conversation? Or was it the boys?

Ronnie headed up to their attic bedroom to check, Max on her heels. Will's covers still bound him mummy-like, the way she'd left him the night before. In Andrew's bed, limbs and sheets were tossed like a salad. Both faces were puffy with sleep, their breaths even.

Back on the second floor, Ronnie passed the guest room as she stole toward the bedroom she'd shared with Jeff for twelve years. He'd taken to sleeping with its door open, a standing invitation. She didn't really want to see him in their bed. It was too confusing, his face all boyish, lips relaxed and kissable.

But her desire for an explanation for the blaring TV made her risk a peek.

The bed was made, the room empty.

Maybe Jeff couldn't bear a scene with the boys and had moved out last night. He had trouble with good-byes.

Tiptoeing into the room, as if the very walls would call her out for prying, Ronnie checked the floor on Jeff's side of the bed, where she would be sure to find yesterday's work uniform in a clump.

Nothing.

Since she was wearing the same clothes as yesterday, she scooted around the bed to pull on a fresh sweater and jeans from her dresser and finger-combed her hair. Last night she'd been too tired to tame her curls.

Returning to this room gave her the sense she was being watched. When she spun around, she tripped over the dog. She stopped just short of kicking him. "Damn it, Max, why are you always underfoot?"

The dog backed up a few feet and sat, looking up at her, whining.

"I didn't let you out yet, did I?" She patted the dog on the head and closed the bedroom door behind them.

Downstairs Ronnie let Max out the kitchen door, one of the perks of living on a farm set back off the road. In the windbreak on the other side of the berry field, a gusty October wind tugged at the branches of a stalwart maple. Despite the beauty of the leaves releasing in a splashy swirl, it hurt Ronnie to watch its branches swinging back and forth in violent indecision. She knew how it felt to be torn between standing firm and uprooting. She called Max, fed him kibble from a low cabinet, and started a pot of coffee.

A black plastic container sat beside the coffeemaker. Drying beef and gravy stuck to its sides. Odd. She and the boys had eaten stir-fry the night before, and she'd never seen Jeff resort to eating a frozen dinner.

On the kitchen table, stuck between the bananas in the fruit bowl, stood a short spine of folded twenties. The wad was thick between her fingers.

Twelve-hundred-dollars thick.

This was not the house she'd closed her eyes on the night before. Something had gone haywire. Shifted.

She pulled the pot away and let the coffee drip straight into her mug as she struggled to order her thoughts. On their own, each of the morning's oddities could be explained away. Max could have sat on the TV remote, inadvertently turning up the volume. Maybe Jeff, hungry after a bartending shift at two a.m., couldn't find a restaurant serving dinner. Or he'd stockpiled tips and accidentally left the money on the table. But together...

Jeff was trying to tell her something, and, as usual, he wasn't using words. Her hand shook as coffee overflowed the edge of her mug.

She glanced at the clock. Ten minutes till the boys' alarm went off. She crossed to the basement door, shut it quietly behind her, and headed down to her office so she could make a call in private.

At her desk, Ronnie reached for the receiver—then froze when she saw the note with Jeff's handwriting stuck to it:

*I see you called Kevin again last night. *69, remember?*

Kevin. Really? Jeff was tracking her interview calls? Ronnie couldn't help but look around the room, even through the door and windows that overlooked the hill and farm store down below, to see if Jeff was watching her now. She crumpled the note and dialed the phone.

"Jeez, Ronnie, the birds aren't even up yet." Her brother Teddy's voice croaked from interrupted sleep. Back when she was twenty-six, she too would have still been in bed, although she already would have nursed and changed Andrew and settled him back to sleep between her and Jeff. Back when a snuggle solved all problems.

Ronnie added up all the odd details for Teddy. Before, her brother had provided a comforting echo of the denial Ronnie had clung to over the past year. *You two were meant for each other. Marriage takes work; you're just in the work part. He's so scared of losing you he's lost his composure.* But such notions were getting harder and harder to cling to. Especially today.

"Do you think Jeff would really do it?" she said.

"No. He's just trying to rattle you."

Just rattling her, yes. Jeff was used to calling all the emotional shots—and was damned good at it.

"You're overreacting, Ronnie. Frozen food, unexplainable cash, a loud TV—those are first-world problems," Teddy said, intoning new perspective he'd earned that summer while providing dental treatments to children in Honduras. "Compared to the rest of the planet, we have it good here."

She hadn't called for a lecture from Teddy. Just this once, she'd needed him to hear her and affirm her sense of alarm. She couldn't simply ignore the crackle of tension that had stolen the calm from her old Pennsylvania farmhouse.

Ronnie heard footsteps overhead. "I hear the boys. Gotta go."

"I'm here if you need me. Hi to the boys."

Yes, if she needed him, he was there—in Baltimore, one hundred miles away. As she climbed back up to the kitchen, each stair pressed the yoke of worry heavier onto her shoulders.

"It's mine! Let go!" Andrew said, his hand in the cereal cupboard.

"I touched it first!" Eight-year-old Will punched his older brother in the arm.

"Boys, what's going on?"

"There's only a little bit of Honey Nut Cheerios left, and I touched it first," Will said. Andrew, ten, looked stony-faced.

"And what do you think I'm going to say about that?"

Will huffed, then poured the remainder of the cereal into two bowls so carefully he seemed to count each Cheerio. The boys sat in front of their ridiculously underfilled bowls, too proud to admit they'd fought their way toward an unsatisfying breakfast, and added a splash of milk from the carton. Ronnie did the same with her equally small portion of Raisin Bran and, for the sake of her children, pretended she had the stomach to eat it.

Though she'd checked the whole house, Jeff felt very much here, his angst clinging to every word, dragging on every effort. She glanced toward the stairs, still thinking he might appear any moment. How many months had it been since she'd been able to relax in her own home?

"Mom, did you get me those markers and poster board?" Andrew said. "The game I made up is due tomorrow."

Another dropped ball. Another emergency. Yet she couldn't

berate Andrew for procrastinating; she had an *Organic Gardening PA* article due today that she hadn't yet written.

"Remind me after school."

Ronnie gulped her cooling coffee, awaiting its jolt. After today, she'd drink caffeine-free tea and return to the simple pleasures of raising her boys.

Will slurped the sweet milk from his cereal bowl.

"Don't forget your instrument," Ronnie told him. "I put it by the door." Will hadn't known what a viola was when he signed up to take lessons, but he did so because his older brother took violin. The show of brotherly one-upmanship Will displayed every time he laid that big viola across his narrow shoulder always brought a smile to Ronnie's face.

"Did you finish marking my form for the reading contest?" Will said.

"Sorry, ran out of energy. I'll do it tonight."

"It's due today!" Will's chair skidded back as he stood. "I could win a day tubing up at Bear Mountain this winter, and you don't even care how hard I worked!"

"That's not true—"

"And now Dad's going to leave, and who's going to be left to think about me?"

The silence was abrupt. She was still assembling a careful path of words when Andrew, her peacekeeper, jumped in.

"Let's go brush our teeth," he said.

"Hey." Ronnie grabbed Will's wrist. "You're right, I've been busy. And distracted. Big changes are going on around here, and it's hard for all of us. But I've seen how much you've been reading. Bring the contest form down, and I'll drive it over to the school later."

"Promise?"

"Promise. Now scoot."

The pounding of sneakers receded on the wooden stairs. Trying to set right what she could, Ronnie tossed the mysterious frozen food container in the trash, slipped the wad of money into her purse, and reached into the fridge for the boys' lunches.

Max hopped from the stairwell onto the deep kitchen windowsill to bark at something. What, at this time of the morning? The boys' sneakers pounded back down the stairs as they raced to the window to investigate. Ronnie rested her hands on their shoulders as she peered out.

Jeff was pulling his Nissan sedan around at the top of the driveway.

"I thought Dad was upstairs," Will said.

"Guess he went out this morning," Ronnie said, infusing her voice with false cheer. No need to share that it looked like their father hadn't slept in the house last night and might just be getting home.

"But his car didn't come up the drive. It came from behind the barn."

Clearly Will had that detail wrong. Jeff must have regretted his decision to slip out without saying good-bye to his sons and returned to do so.

"Brush your teeth and you can go out and give him a hug." She'd send them out alone. She couldn't bear to witness this five-hanky farewell. The boys would miss the bus, of course. Maybe they'd want to miss school too, and Ronnie couldn't blame them. Unexpected as this early good-bye was, the entire day would be better once it was behind them.

Her sons, their summer blond all but gone with the last cut, now stood at the door, looking through its twin panes of glass. "Boys. I said to go brush your teeth."

They didn't move.

"Will, Andrew," she said, joining them. "Why are you just standing here?"

Ronnie looked out. Jeff's car faced downhill, and he was staggering around the trunk to the near side of the car.

"He's drunk," said Will.

Ronnie saw no point in arguing. Jeff had been drinking more

in recent months and not hiding it as well. Even though Will had never seen his father drunk, he had just finished drug and alcohol resistance training in school and knew the signs.

"What's he doing?" Andrew said.

Oh god. Jeff bent over, pulling a length of tubing from the exhaust pipe of the car.

Ronnie flipped the dead bolt shut. "You two stay right here, you hear me?" She squeezed their shoulders to be sure they'd paid attention. "I'm going to call Grandma Bev."

Waiting for the bus wouldn't do. Ronnie needed to get her sons away from this farm. Now.

beverly

Beverly Saylor scrolled through the new rental listings as both a real estate agent with a commission at stake and a mother whose heart was breaking. Her laptop perched on a wobbly TV table, she dutifully checked for a place big enough to accommodate a woman with two growing boys and a dog, in their current school district, within Ronnie's budget. But she couldn't envision her daughter anywhere but in the house she and Jeff had so beautifully tailored to their needs (where else would she find a butcher block counter at perfect kneading height, with an overhang that would allow a pasta roller to be clamped?) and on the farm they'd revived, where they had planned to raise their family.

An adorable two-bedroom, one-bath, over-the-garage apartment popped up. The wood floors would be a plus with the boys' allergies. Beverly could almost pretend it would be fun to help Ronnie decorate it. But no dogs. No point mentioning this one. Leaving the dog with Jeff was not negotiable, Ronnie had said. When she adopted Max, she had committed to caring for him for his entire life; she would not leave him behind.

The listings proved what Beverly feared: her thirty-five-year-old daughter simply wanted too much.

The knot between Beverly's shoulders loosened. One more day without a workable solution was one more that kept Ronnie and Jeff in the same house, where they might find a way to address their differences. That may be the biggest help she could offer.

Lately it seemed Ronnie was more dedicated to her dog than she was to the husband she'd vowed to love for the rest of her life. And she'd done so before God and a church full of witnesses, a snag Beverly had cleverly circumvented with her own marriages, one officiated at sea and the other two in front of a judge. Still. Beverly looked down at the ring with the tiny diamond she'd never removed from her hand. A promise should mean something.

Beverly had been emotionally invested in Ronnie and Jeff's relationship from the start. The summer after her college gradua-tion, Ronnie had been so depressed that Beverly splurged for a nice dinner out for the two of them. Ronnie's degree from Fordham had her ready to "take the world of journalism by storm"—whatever that meant—but left her unprepared to find a job that would pay for the smallest of New York apartments. How could any of them have known that in four short years, the college major offering an on-ramp to a career highway would dwindle to a narrow path as articles that once garnered income were now posted on blogs for free? Ronnie's return to Beverly's apartment, and full-time work at the Valley View restaurant, was a one-way street heading the wrong way.

When surf and turf failed to cheer her daughter, Beverly thought it would be a kick to take her over to have a drink at the hotel bar Jeff tended. Back when Ronnie was a child and Jeff was in college she had adored him, and she hadn't seen him in ages.

The hotel was busy that Friday, and she and Ronnie had taken the last two stools at the big U-shaped bar, watching Jeff locate every bottle by muscle memory. He opened coolers, poured drinks, tapped beer, slid napkins, and pocketed tips without one wasted movement, all while looking debonair in a tux shirt and vest. He was only five years younger than Beverly, she'd once realized, although since he was her best friend Janet's son, she had always thought of him as a generation removed. He was lonely, she knew, since his first wife had left him. Not that Jeff ever mentioned it. It was something in his eyes. She'd seen that same look once before in a rescue shelter, and Beverly had taken the little dog home with her.

"Hello, Bev." When Beverly had showings in the area she often stopped in; Jeff set a Manhattan in front of her before she even ordered. He then slipped a napkin in front of Ronnie. "And what would you like, ma'am?"

"I'd like you to recognize me, for one thing," Ronnie said.

Jeff had cocked his head, thought a moment, then flashed her his broad, gap-toothed smile. "No—Little Ronnie?"

"Well, no one calls me that anymore."

He allowed his gaze to dip. "I can see why not."

Beverly hid her smile by sipping her drink.

Her daughter's face had pinked right up, but she'd kept her gaze steady.

"Been back in town long?"

"What town?" They'd both laughed. Both Bartlesville, where Jeff lived, and Potts Forge, where Ronnie was staying with her mother, were rural post offices more than towns. "I'd heard you worked at a grain brokerage, selling corn to chip companies or something."

"I did, but this hotel has a busy banquet schedule. The money was too good to pass up." Jeff had leaned his elbows onto the bar and gazed into her eyes. "Keeping tabs on me, are you?"

Okay, maybe he didn't do the elbow leaning—Jeff was nothing but classy and professional behind the bar—but that's how Beverly remembered it. And just as she'd hoped, she solved her daughter's blues. Within a year, she was walking Ronnie down the aisle and into Jeff's arms.

Since then she'd been watching Ronnie's marriage from the stands, first cheering then biting nails, hoping her team would go the distance. And what better team to root for than her brilliant daughter and her best friend's son? Those kids were so in love they'd even made their mothers happier people.

After all, people meant to be together should not be separated.

Beverly felt enough regret for all of them on that score, as might several of her husbands. *If only Ronnie could see Jeff safely through whatever personal crisis he's been going through lately*, Beverly thought while shutting down her computer, *there would still be hope.*

For Jeff—and for them all.

Beverly's smartphone vibrated in her back pocket, prodding her from her chair. A request for a second showing, she hoped. She kept telling her clients the housing market was looking up yet was still waiting for evidence that this was true. But no, it was her daughter's ever-smiling face that popped up.

"Hello, Sunshine."

"Mom, I need you to come to the farm right now."

The panic in Ronnie's voice gripped her. "Okay."

"Jeff was going to leave today, but it isn't going right and I've got a full day at the store and the boys will miss the bus and—"

"I'm on my way."

"I don't have time to explain—"

"Ronnie. Let me get my jacket. I'll see you in fifteen minutes."

8:00 a.m.

ronnie

R onnie hung up the phone and heard the flip of the dead bolt.
Andrew yelled, "Mom!"

Ronnie rounded the corner to see Will, skinny and determined, push through the door.

"Will, get back here!" Ronnie shouted.

"We can't let him drive!"

For some reason, after Jeff shut the trunk, he had not come to the house but was weaving his way toward the driver's side door. Will was right—they couldn't let him drive. One swerve and he'd bowl down children arriving at their bus stops.

Ronnie burst through the door and chased after Will, who stood outside the open car door, saying, "Give me the keys, Dad." Jeff ignored him—ignored his own frantic son—and started the car. Ronnie thrust her arm past Jeff, intent on pulling the keys from the ignition. Her hand was inches away from a small cooler, a large bottle of vermouth, a larger one of whiskey, a spilled carton of cigarettes—and a shotgun leaning against the seat.

Oh god, no. Had Will seen all that?

Jeff put the car in drive and let it roll forward. Ronnie moved along with it, hit the gearshift, and threw it in park. Booze sloshed in plastic mugs in the cup holders. Jeff's head bumped against hers, but Ronnie was able to extract the keys. Jeff lurched from the car to take them back and soon Ronnie, Will, and Jeff were pinching and scratching to get ahold of the keys.

Andrew stood on the front porch, as still as one of its columns. "Mom, what should I do?" he shouted.

Ronnie answered, "Call 911 and tell them your father's trying to drive drunk."

She had to put an end to this. Ronnie clawed at Jeff's eyeglasses and threw them, hoping he was intoxicated enough that the vision change might disorient him. In the moment when Jeff watched his glasses skid across the top of the car, Ronnie smashed the back of his hand against the door frame. He released the keys.

"I've got them. Will, run inside!"

When they reached the house, Ronnie pushed Will through the door, causing him to stumble on the threshold. She heard Jeff on their heels. When he lunged for the screen door, Ronnie looked back at the man she'd vowed to love forever and kicked him in the ribs.

Jeff stumbled but steadied himself against the open screen door, his blue eyes looking up at hers in shock. As if she'd shot him, and he'd seen his own blood. *Kick through the board*, she heard Andrew's Tae Kwon Do instructor say. She kicked again, harder, and down he went. Ronnie slipped through the door and threw the dead bolt.

Ronnie and Will stood inside the door, facing Jeff. What the hell had she just done?

"Fuck you," Jeff said, flipping Ronnie the finger. "If you won't let me drive, I'll kill myself right here." He strode back toward the car.

Ronnie pulled Will back, knocking over the viola case. His body heaved with shivers, as if he'd been submerged in icy water. She turned him toward her and warmed his face in her palms. "Will? Are you okay, baby?"

He pushed her away and ran to the window by the stairs, still trembling so hard Ronnie was shocked his legs could move. She followed and saw Jeff rooting in the car. Behind her, Andrew said, "Mom, they want to talk to you." Ronnie pulled Will from the window and into the kitchen, where an L-shaped bank of cabinets would keep them out of sight.

"Mrs. Farnham? I'm the 911 dispatcher." The man spoke in a firm, steady voice. After Ronnie verified their address, he said, "Your son has reported a domestic disturbance. Help is already on its way. I understand your husband is attempting to drive while intoxicated. What's going on right now?"

Ronnie relayed what had happened so far, panting for air. When she got to the part about Jeff pulling tubing from the tailpipe, Will tugged on her arm.

"I saw out the window. When he drove from behind the barn, the tube was hanging out of the tailpipe."

"He's suicidal," Ronnie said into the phone, rubbing her ribs as if she too had been kicked. "And he's pissed as hell."

"And so you fought for the car keys," the dispatcher prompted in that level tone. "What makes you believe he was intoxicated at this time of day?"

It was only eight. Ronnie hadn't even fed the horses yet. She explained about Jeff's wobble, the booze in the car.

Will tugged on her arm again. "His breath made me sick to my stomach," he said.

Ronnie held him close, kissed his forehead, and whispered, "You were so brave." Each time he spoke, his shaking lessened. When school started last month, he'd told her that since he was in third grade, there'd be no more hand-holding on days she picked him up from school, yet now he made no move to extricate himself from beneath her arm.

Andrew stood on her other side. "I didn't know what to do," he said. He would not have engaged. How many times had she heard his Tae Kwon Do instructor tell him the smartest way to win a battle is to avoid the fight?

"You did what needed to be done," Ronnie said and kissed him as well. The three of them stood pressed together in the heart of the house.

Her head buzzed on two frequencies. Even as she told the dispatcher that she'd kicked her husband and locked him out of the house and that he had a gun, the part of her that abhorred such words replayed the memory of walking toward Jeff at their wedding, his bright eyes and enchanting smile pulling her ever closer to a true sense of home.

Will you have me?

The voice, low and steady, had come from the phone. "What?" Ronnie said.

"Will has the keys? Or you?"

"Why does it matter who has the keys!"

"Ma'am, let's stay calm," the dispatcher said in his ridiculously measured way. "Focus on one detail at a time. Who has the car keys?"

"I…I put them on the rack by the door."

"Is this where your husband would look for them?"

"Yes."

"I've pulled up an aerial view of your home. Looks like you have a second floor?"

"Yes."

"Could you explain the layout?"

"It's a typical farmhouse—two long rooms on the first floor, and four square rooms on the second. You have to go through a sitting room at the top of the stairs to get to the others, and to access the stairs to the attic. The sitting room and the bathroom face the back, where we fought with my husband. The two bedrooms face the road."

"Is there an extension on this line in one of those bedrooms?"

"Yes."

"Okay, good. I'd like you to take all the car keys off the rack, move upstairs, and pick up that other line. Keep the boys and the keys with you, and stay away from the windows."

"Should I come back down and hang up this phone?"

"That's all right, ma'am. Leave this line open. Go on upstairs. I'll hold. I'm with you until help arrives."

On their way to the stairs, Ronnie slipped three rings of car keys off the antique hotel key rack that Jeff's mother had found at a flea market and shoved them in her pockets.

Ronnie and the boys climbed to the bedroom where Jeff had slept alone for the last six weeks. Already this morning, up and down, up and down, the verticality of the house one more reminder of the challenges of their marriage. The boys climbed onto the bed and Ronnie let them turn on the television. Max flopped down between them. Ronnie picked up the cordless.

"Mrs. Farnham?"

"Yes."

"Can you see where your husband is now?"

On one side, the bedroom windows overlooked the yard where Max had been romping that morning. On the other, they overlooked the farm store on the road below. No movement in either direction. The car was hidden from view.

With the phone still held to her ear, she said, "Boys, I'm going upstairs to get your blankets."

"What should we do?"

"Just stay here and watch your show. Be right back."

Ronnie shut the bedroom door and headed toward the attic, the only room that had windows looking onto the driveway. She kept the phone plastered to her ear.

On the way to the attic door, Ronnie heard a loud pop.

She ducked; her head jerked toward the windows. Birds lifted from the trees. "Oh no. I–I may have heard a gun." She looked behind her toward the bedroom door, but it stayed shut, muted music the only sound. Outside, a frightening quiet.

"Where are you now?"

"I'm in the sitting room. Facing the parking area at the back of the house."

"Can you see the car?"

Ronnie ran up the attic stairs to peer out. From this vantage point, she could see straight down through the windshield and into Jeff's car. During their scuffle, the car had rolled into the narrowest part of the driveway, between the house and a briar-filled bank.

"Yes, but Jeff isn't in it."

"And how about the gun? Can you see it?"

Ronnie inched forward. The shotgun had been propped against the passenger seat. She should be looking right at it.

"It's gone."

"Okay." Silence. "You mentioned you locked the kitchen door. Are there any other doors that might be unlocked?"

"There's a home office in the basement with a door that opens out onto a patio, but I leave it locked all the time."

"Not a bad idea. And you checked it today?"

No, she hadn't checked it today. Why would she? It was locked all the time. Unless Jeff… Her stomach turned hard as stone. "Should I check it now?"

"At this point, ma'am, just stay away from the windows and get back to your sons. Then lock the bedroom door. Help is about ten minutes away."

From beneath their pillows, Ronnie grabbed the soft blankets the boys slept with—Andrew's red, Will's black-and-white Holstein. They had replaced the sanitized lambskins she'd gotten each of them when they were born to help them settle at night. As a baby, Andrew would rub his face on his from side to side until he'd made a nest; Will would work his little fingers into the deep fluff. After repeated bouts of bronchitis and ear infections prompted a trip to a pediatric allergist, she'd learned that among many other things on this farm, the boys were allergic to wool. The very objects she had offered as an extension of her love and comfort were hurting her children—and she had to take them away. Ronnie had been as sick about this as if the doctor had said her sons were allergic to her.

Recently the boys had left their replacement blankets tucked away during the day, but to hell with that. Even if it was tenuous, today she'd connect them however she could to the notion of safety. When she rejoined her sons, she handed them their blankets and locked the bedroom door.

Ronnie thought of the other "safe" choices she'd made in her life. Marrying a man twelve years her senior, a kind, even-tempered man whose family she'd known her whole life thanks to their mothers' friendship. Living on land his family had owned for more than a hundred years. In this house that had needed loving care, yes, but whose bones had for generations withstood the cycles of hurricane and blizzard, birth and death, hope and despair. On this one door alone, she'd spent hours stripping, sanding, staining, and tracking down period hardware. For what? It wouldn't protect her from a crazed husband in this remote location, its wood all of an inch thick, with a latch that barely caught.

She was ashamed to think how afraid she'd been at the thought of going down to lock her own office. Ronnie had never been one to watch horror movies, but she knew that obligatory scene where the woman goes down to the basement—could already hear the pulsing bass in the score—and she did not want to star in that scene. She'd rather hole up here with her sons. Pretend it was Saturday morning, with the kids piled in for snuggles and cartoons.

"Okay, ma'am, the police dispatcher reports we now have police on the scene. They're on foot. If you look out the windows toward the road, you'll see some men in the yard across from yours."

Ronnie didn't speak—she didn't want to disturb the boys—but let her gaze drift through the window to the Schulzes' yard. The canopies of their Japanese maples were aflame with color against the evergreens that dotted the hill. It took her a few moments to find the officers skulking around the trees. Squatting, crawling, peeking—and holding guns.

Earlier that month, after she finished the barn chores on one of the last warm evenings in October, Ronnie had stood out in the yard watching beams of light crisscross that same hill as the boys played flashlight tag with Brandon Schulz and his cousins. Every now and then, their silent game would be interrupted with laughter or a shouted negotiation. With the moon full, Ronnie could sometimes see them darting across the yard between the spruces. Her chest flooded with warmth to know that while she and Jeff were driven to complete their house renovation, someone had taught her boys to play.

Now all warmth evaporated as she watched a few of the policemen cross the road, inching around the corners of their farm store.

"We have a development," said the dispatcher. The line seemed to pinch shut.

ronnie

W hat? Hello? Don't leave me—"

"I'm here, ma'am. Hold where you are. Police are intercepting a vehicle trying to come up your drive."

Ronnie strained to see, but the farm store blocked her view. "Is it a tan Chevy Blazer?"

"One moment."

The wait felt interminable. The room seemed to shrink. She glanced over at the boys. Andrew's leg was tossed over his brother's at the ankle, and Max had his paws and nose wedged between the boys' hips. Will rubbed his blanket on his cheek. Movement in her peripheral vision. A few of the men on the Schulzes' hill dashed to cover behind closer trees. It was eerily quiet. On any other day, the Schulzes' Jack Russell terrier would have been nipping at their heels. Even the leaves, so recently whipped by the wind into frenzy, now clung to their branches as if listening.

"Confirming here—Beverly Saylor is your mother?"

Relief invigorated Ronnie. "Yes, she's coming to get the boys."

Down below, movement. Her mother's car pushed up the drive, its familiar decade-old grille like a smile.

"An officer is in the car with her. One more minute here…"

Another minute. How many more would there be? She needed this to be over. She looked at the boys, who were laughing at Wakko's antics on the screen.

"You're okay to move, ma'am. Go down to the door facing away from the road—"

"The kitchen door."

"Yes, and let her in."

Ronnie told the boys she'd be right back—for herself, more than for them, as they continued to stare at the TV. The boys had inherited her "extreme focus," she liked to say. Jeff called it disrespect, but Ronnie understood the occasional need to escape to another world.

Down in the kitchen, she opened the door to the backside of a police officer. Beside him stood her mother. Determined to be the bright spot in any situation, Beverly was wearing a red velveteen jacket with metallic gold flowers sewn into it, her dyed blond curls a living flower blooming through its neck. But her face was drawn. One hand twisted the ring she always wore.

Ronnie pulled her inside. "Are you coming in too?" Ronnie said to the policeman, using her foot to hold back the dog.

"I'll stay here," he said.

Unsure of how to greet her mother in the odd circumstances, Ronnie let Max do the work, wriggling and snuffling at Beverly's knees.

"Come away from the windows." Ronnie pulled her mother deeper into the kitchen.

"Where's Jeff, honey?"

Ronnie shook her head. Shrugged. Tried to hold back the tsunami of emotion threatening to engulf her.

"Are the boys okay?"

Ronnie couldn't keep her lip from quivering. "They're upstairs watching cartoons."

"Is this…another suicide threat?"

Ronnie blew out a deep breath and tried to hold steady. "Not sure it's just a threat this time."

Beverly reached out and patted her daughter's arm. "Well. At least he doesn't have access to a gun. This will be okay." She looked around the kitchen as if taking comfort from its familiar inventory. Sink, stove, refrigerator. "This will be okay."

Ronnie didn't speak. Couldn't.

"You brought me the guns. This will be okay, right?"

Choking out each word, Ronnie said, "He had one in the car. A shotgun, I think. I must have missed it."

Her mother turned away and put her hand to her face.

"Ma'am? Ma'am?" came the muffled voice from the phone.

"Mom, I have to stay on the line with the 911 operator. Can you go up to the boys' room and pack a bag for them? Use Will's sports duffel. They'll tell you which toothbrushes are theirs."

Beverly nodded. Once on the step, she turned. "For how long?"

"Ma'am?"

"I'm here," Ronnie said into the phone. To her mother she held up a finger. One day. Then held up a second. A third. She shrugged. Ronnie had no clue what today would hold. But her mother would see to the boys, the police would see to Jeff, and soon enough this nightmare would be over.

"Police cruisers are pulling up your driveway." Ronnie could hear the distant sound of doors shutting. Lots of doors.

A knock on the kitchen door startled her. Beyond it stood several police officers.

"Thank goodness," Ronnie said when she opened the door. "Can you have everyone back their cars out so my mother can leave with the boys? They're almost ready."

"That wouldn't be advisable," one of them said and took the phone from her to sign off with the 911 dispatcher. Her lifeline, severed. No chance to thank him or to say good-bye.

"I hate to be a burden, but I'd really appreciate it," Ronnie said. "I made arrangements for the boys to leave so they wouldn't have to see any of this."

"Our main concern is for your safety," a different officer said, as if the first had already run out of patience. "Your husband is intoxicated and armed. We can't take the time—or risk the exposure—to move all those cars. We're going to evacuate all of you."

Beverly arrived on the stairs, Adidas bag in hand, the boys cowering behind her. Each boy clutched his blanket; the tip of Will's thumb had found its way back to his mouth.

Ronnie couldn't protect them from what horrors the day held. It was too late.

She struggled to order her thoughts in light of this new plan. "But the horses are still out. I haven't fed them yet." As if she wanted to go out to the barn. The words immediately sounded stupid.

They filed down the staircase to Ronnie's office, Max scrambling after them. The house was set into the hill so that the office door opened onto ground level. Full-size windows faced the store and road, allowing Ronnie to see that the driveway could no longer contain all of the cruisers. Taking into account the part of the road obscured by the farm store, dozens of additional state police cruisers must be snaked down the length of the road. One sat directly below, in the driveway that ended beside the farm store.

Ronnie, Beverly, Andrew, and Will stood huddled on the tile hearth of the walk-in fireplace in Ronnie's office, surrounded on every side by stones pulled more than two hundred years ago from the fields of this very farm. Hatchet marks were still visible on the exposed beams and rough-hewn mantel. This room had once been a summer kitchen where a woman had stirred the stew that would welcome her husband home from the American Revolution, Ronnie had always imagined. Now, several uniformed police officers stood between them and the back door.

Thwack, thwack, thwack. The chop of a low-flying helicopter. Really low. She felt its thrum in her bones. Max came over and sat on Ronnie's foot.

"You can set down the bag, ma'am," one of the officers said to Ronnie's mother. "We don't want any encumbrances."

Beverly set the Adidas bag on the low windowsill by the door and returned to the huddle with her arms wrapped defiantly around her purse. Andrew looked over at Will, speaking to him through the silent understanding that passes between brothers. One at a time, as if knowing today would require manlike courage, each boy approached the duffel and laid his blanket on top.

One of the officers spoke with the helicopter pilot via walkie-talkie. A voice squawked: "I have a good view. Clear."

Before she realized they would be separated, a policeman picked up Ronnie's younger son and set him on his hip. Will was still wearing shorts—it was always hard to get him to part with them at summer's end—and the pale flesh of his thigh pressed against the butt of the officer's holstered gun. Will looked at Ronnie with that sweet, stoic face, only his eyes revealing his panic. There was no time to speak. The officer ran through the door with her son, across the patio, down the grassy hill, and past the farm store into the awaiting cruiser. After he and Will climbed in the backseat, the cruiser sped away, taking part of Ronnie with it.

Another cruiser pulled into its place.

A policeman grabbed Andrew by the hand and waited.

"There's still dew on the hill. Be careful," Ronnie said. The pair ran without regard to dew or incline, got into the waiting car, and drove away.

"Clear." Ronnie's mother was next. Strong at fifty-two but with knees battered by her active lifestyle, she would need to take the hill slower. Two policemen, one at each elbow, supported her as she picked her way across the grass.

That left Ronnie. "Where we're going—can I take my dog?" With the thrum of the helicopter, the cars, the strangers, and the palpable tension, Max, who had never once flinched during a thunderstorm or fireworks display, was quaking with fear.

"No."

She couldn't bear to think of him alone in the house, surrounded by strangers, not one of whom would care to take him out. If it were safe to go out.

Ronnie lifted Max into the recliner. Beside it was the windowsill with the Adidas bag, the boys' blankets on top. All things abandoned. She held his floppy ears and looked into his trusting brown eyes. "Be brave."

"Clear."

The policeman took her elbow and rushed her down the hill, his other hand resting on his weapon. The cruiser's tires squealed against the road as the driver pulled away.

"Why did you have to separate us?" Ronnie said.

"To minimize loss if any shooting started."

The policeman accelerated down the hill until he passed the edge of the property. He soon pulled over beside an empty field not visible from the house due to the way the road curved through the woods. Beside several police cruisers stood an ambulance.

"What happened—"

"Everyone's fine," he said. The ambulance's back doors stood ajar. "Check inside."

When Ronnie peered into the ambulance, she found her family, huddled on a bench built into one side of the vehicle. There was no gurney. Sitting on the other side was her seventy-five-year-old neighbor, Mr. Eshbach. Seeing Mr. Eshbach mowing his lawn, clearing his roof gutters, or fixing their constantly vandalized mailbox cluster was common enough. But sitting still? He looked embarrassed to be caught doing so.

You could tell the days of the week by this man's habits. Today was mopping. Ronnie knew because one Monday that summer, when Andrew had cut himself and she'd needed to borrow some gauze, Mr. Eshbach had removed his shoes to venture into the house to retrieve it. Now every Monday, when Ronnie went down to open the farm store, she looked for the comforting presence of the overturned bucket draining by his side door.

As she climbed into the ambulance, it was hard for Ronnie to look him in the eye, with their chaos splashed all over him.

"I'm sorry about your floors," she said, sitting beside him on the bench.

"Got half done."

"Still. You had plans."

"Well." He shrugged. "That was then, and this is now."

Beverly put an arm around each of the boys and pulled them close.

Ronnie fidgeted. She should be calling in to the school. Her boys would be marked absent; the school would be trying to reach her. Amber, the sole employee at her and Jeff's farm store, would be showing up soon for work. On her desk, Ronnie had left interview notes for her *Organic Farming PA* article on aquaponics, a system that combines edible fish production with the growth of food crops that thrive in water. The speaker was coming to a nearby town this weekend; it would be too late for her editor to reassign the story. She had wanted to tweet a teaser of her upcoming *Psychology Today* feature on resiliency, featuring the interview with Kevin that had riled Jeff so. Her laundry room was covered in dirty clothes she'd whisked from the attic floor last night with the hope of cleaning the boys' room later. Their allergies were the worst in the fall. She had to stay on top of it.

How was she supposed to stop her life midthrottle?

Her mother twiddled that ring, always that ring.

"Mom, would you stop?"

"Stop what?"

"Twirling that ring. It's driving me mad." If not for the twiddling, no one would notice it; unlike the bold red button earrings she wore today, the tiny, colorless stone did not live up to Beverly's usual splashy statement. It was just a dime-store trinket, her mother had once told her. If it bothered her so, why did she wear it?

After they waited in the ambulance for an uncomfortable stretch of time, an officer informed them of two things. First, a command post had been established at the Bartlesville Volunteer Fire Station, a mile from the farm, and that the ambulance would take them there shortly.

Second, in the area surrounding their property, the manhunt for Jeffrey Farnham had begun.

9:00 a.m.

janet

J anet Farnham brushed the crumbs from the bust of her Hello Kitty sweatshirt. She'd swung wide of the local haunts to find this little Pennsylvania Dutch diner, telling herself there was nothing better for the soul than a drive out to the country to enjoy the autumn foliage—and a breakfast of pumpkin pie. She ordered coffee as well, and after the waitress turned her back, Janet improved on its contribution to her morning from a bottle she carried in her purse.

She checked her watch. Ten till. Over at the Y, Tai Chi for Seniors would soon be over. Earlier in the year, she'd promised to take an exercise class to satisfy, in some small way, her best friend's crusade to transform her life. "You don't go to the doctor. You don't eat well. You don't exercise," Beverly had said. "That has got to stop. If you don't stick around, who will I spend my golden years with?" January had been just a day old when Beverly had staged a private intervention, making Janet swear with her hand on a vegetarian cookbook that she would "embrace current scientific evidence on the health benefits of a meatless diet and daily exercise."

Since then, Janet hadn't exactly disavowed Beverly of the notion that she'd followed through on her promises. Beverly's heart was in the right place. What was the harm in letting her think she'd been helpful? Especially now, as they tiptoed around each other, feeling so impotent with their kids poised for divorce, both fearing what it meant for their friendship. But fitness was Beverly's thing, not Janet's. Beverly was constantly extending invitations to play golf and walk a 5K and join her tennis league—it would be fun, she said—but you couldn't just pick up sports at sixty-five. Janet had arthritis to think of, and this roll on her belly. She wished she'd never told Beverly she feared it was cancer, but that horrid story in *Reader's Digest* about the woman who thought she'd simply been gaining belly fat got her thinking. Now Beverly was a ready source of unwanted, "anticancer" recipe links with foreign-sounding ingredients.

No doubt about it, the healthy approach worked for Beverly, who still entertained a string of suitors. But Beverly was a special breed of middle age—full of pizzazz, single by choice, and still fantasizing that some white knight would come sweep her off her thinning bones. Janet, on the other hand, had accepted her plight. She was a widow getting by the best she could as she looked out over a stretch of lonely years, unless the cancer got her first, and she wouldn't deny herself the few small pleasures life still offered.

Janet went to the register, paid her bill, and left a ten percent tip. Damn waitress hardly lifted a finger.

Out in the parking lot, Janet put the window down a few inches and took a deep breath. She loved autumn, with its fresh-pressed cider and hearty stews, sweet breads with butter, a two-box ration of candy corn, and a spooky birthday cake for her Halloween baby—Jeffrey, the one thing she'd done right in her life.

Janet took back roads all the way toward the kids' farm store. She loved these hills, so picturesque with their short strings of houses and colorful windbreaks accenting big parcels of farmland. She drove past her own place and admired the way it sat tucked into the side of the hill, untouchable by rising waters or the ravages of wind. Somewhere along the way, she passed the invisible boundary between her land and Jeff's.

Before she could make the final turn up to the farm store, Janet saw a commotion ahead. Flashing lights. Black-and-white cruisers.

It wouldn't be the first time a car went into the woods here. Folks zipped along too fast on these country roads, and more than a few heading downhill couldn't make the curve at speed. Janet lowered her window more and peered into the woods for an overturned car but saw nothing.

Two officers were setting up an orange-and-white-striped barricade. One was Karl Prout's boy. Ed? Fred? Back when Karl's wife was dying of stomach cancer, Janet babysat the kid. Janet put her hand to the roll on her belly. The woman had met an ugly end.

Janet leaned out the window. "I'm trying to get to the farm store. Up ahead, on the left. Can I get through, or will I have to go around?"

"New Hope Farms?" said the second man.

"Yes."

"You're not going to get there at all. We have an ongoing disturbance on that property."

"Like a car accident?"

"I can't say more."

Lingering tastes of cloves, cinnamon, and almond liqueur soured in her mouth. "You can certainly tell me. I own the property you're parked on. That's my son's place. Let me speak to the Prout boy."

"Sorry, ma'am, we're new on the scene and don't have all the details. The family has been relocated—"

"Goodness, where?"

"Hold on, let me check."

Janet let her head tip back against the headrest. They didn't need any more problems.

Who on earth would have caused an "ongoing disturbance"? The boys were so levelheaded, and too young to cause any real problems. And certainly not Ronnie and Jeff. That couple never fought. Even now, poised for divorce, Ronnie was so damned civil about it that Janet wondered why she even found it necessary. Ronnie wouldn't hurt Jeff. Ever since grade school, she'd been crazy about Janet's son.

A red-tailed hawk swooped down into the field beside Janet's car and lifted off, a wriggling mouse in its talons.

Wait.

There was that time when Ronnie was depressed after college. And hadn't Jeff mentioned that Ronnie was seeing a therapist? Yes—one determined to break them up, he'd said, because that's when all this divorce talk started. Then the ranting about Jeff's alcoholism and his need for medical intervention. And Ronnie had a spending problem, Jeff had told her. That sort of thing had a clinical name… oniomania. She saw it on *The View*.

Janet recalled how ashamed Jeff had been when he came over. When was it, the beginning of September? He admitted to overextending himself to make his wife happy. Oh dear, it was all coming back to her now—how worried he'd been about Ronnie lately, that she'd taken on so much work that she was coming undone. Janet hadn't made much of it, because truth be told, her son could be melodramatic at times. But his love for Ronnie, and his deference to Janet, had summoned her dormant maternal instinct back to life. And for the first time since his wedding, Jeff had wrapped his arms around Janet and thanked her. Janet felt plugged in. Important. Capable of making a difference.

Where was that damn Prout boy?

For the life of her, she didn't know why Ronnie wasn't as keen to accept help. As if Janet would draw the line at helping them financially, when they already lived in a house on property subdivided from hers. Janet would have given Jeff that fixer-upper for free if her lawyer had let her. Had she hoped the fifty thousand from her brother's will might have seen them along a little further? Of course. But kids these days didn't know how to stretch a dollar.

The important thing was that Jeff had asked her for help when he needed it. Janet loved Ronnie, but that girl was just like her mother when it came to money—didn't have a clue—and Janet certainly wouldn't let Ronnie tell her how to deal with her own son.

It would be his money anyway, once she died. Who knew? If this roll on her belly was cancerous, that might be tomorrow. So Janet had slipped him a check two weeks ago. That's what family was for.

What if the way Ronnie had been lashing out at her son lately had really been a reflection of her daughter-in-law's own instability? By focusing on her words, had she missed the subtext of Ronnie's plea for help?

Just thinking this way made Janet's brain ache. She was ill-suited for the role of counselor. Emotions were a messy business. She'd been a business teacher, everything in its place: A-S-D-F, J-K-L-semicolon, always beneath the same fingers. What could she offer Ronnie now, when their lives were such a mess? Her heart started to race. She took a long pull from the bottle in her purse.

An *Action News* van nosed up to the police barrier. Right behind, an ambulance pulled into the field downhill, its wheels fitting perfectly into a set of tracks already visible in the long grass. A *second* ambulance?

Why would—no. What if Ronnie had hurt herself? Some people resorted to such measures. Even Jeff had spoken of it when he was younger. Janet couldn't bear it. Losing Ronnie to this divorce was bad enough. It was as if Janet's own daughter sought emancipation. But losing her to self-harm would be a knife to the heart. Adrenaline prodded Janet's memory. Genetics, if you believed in such a thing, were not on Ronnie's side.

Janet reached into her purse for another bolstering draft but pulled her hand out when the man she had queried before returned. "Please," she said. "You've got to tell me what's going on."

"The family is down at the firehouse. You can find out more down there."

The car stalled as Janet turned the wheel. "Don't die on me now," she muttered. The engine coughed a few times, then kicked back to life. The twenty-year-old Ford Escort wagon had rolled past 100K two times, but why worry about it; she'd go before it would.

Janet pointed her car downhill and coasted to the firehouse, her need to know barely outweighing her need to avoid knowing. She could hardly think by the time she pulled up to the brick building. She parked in back, where you had to watch not to mow down families when picking up your barbecued chicken dinner during the twice-yearly fundraisers.

Today, the lot was all but deserted.

She went in the back door and walked down the hallway beside the fire truck bays. A policeman greeted her at the bottom of the familiar metal stairs that led up to the bar and second floor social hall. She and Beverly were both social members; their dues had helped purchase a secondhand ladder truck one of the larger companies was replacing.

"I'm told my family is here," Janet said. She wondered if she shouldn't turn around and go home. Mind her own business and let Ronnie deal with the consequences of her own rash actions. But the boys. And Jeff—she pictured her soothing arms around him. "I need to see them."

"May I have your name, please?"

"Janet Farnham. Jeffrey is my son."

"Do you have ID?"

Janet tilted her large purse away from the man and pawed through it. Between raw nerves and light-adjusting lenses that never seemed to change fast enough when entering a dark building on a bright day, she could barely see and had to feel for her wallet. "Where's Everett? He knows me—"

"Jan."

Beverly appeared at the top of the stairs. Janet abandoned the cop and climbed to meet her.

They threw their arms around each other and at the same time, each said, "I'm so sorry."

Janet closed her eyes and relished the moment. For all their differences, theirs was a friendship forged in the kiln of shared pain.

It had survived the trauma surrounding Beverly's teen pregnancy, Janet's widowhood, Beverly's divorces, and countless other disappointments. When life required that they surrender and readjust, they'd always had each other. As painful as it would be, she'd be the rock that Beverly and Jeff could cling to as Ronnie swept them into the torrent of her crisis.

But Beverly was patting her back—comforting, not clinging. And why had Beverly said she was sorry? Janet pulled away. Looked at her friend. Looked past her and into the hall.

Calmly conversing with a police officer at an unadorned banquet table, her hair returned to its youthful curls, sat Ronnie.

ronnie

Ronnie followed the policeman's gaze to the door behind her and then rushed to greet her mother-in-law. Janet and her mother were so different: Janet short and unadorned, her thick gray bob like a cap on her head; Beverly taller than Ronnie with every facial feature artfully enhanced no matter the time of day.

"Janet," Ronnie said, stopping a few feet short of an embrace. "I was hoping you'd see that we should be together."

Confusion creased Janet's brow. "I tried to stop by your store to get my broccoli—"

The policeman called Ronnie back to the table. She looked to him, then back to her mother-in-law. "I'm sorry," she said. "I've got to deal with this."

Beverly put her arm around Janet and said, "Come sit with me and I'll tell you what we know."

Her mother led her mother-in-law past the bar, a slab of lacquered oak wrapped around the front left corner of the room. On Friday nights, this was the slick stage on which alcohol could ply its magic, stimulating appetites and loosening inhibitions as social members unwound from their workweek. Today its spirits were secreted behind locked cabinets. The hall was set up for Monday night bingo, with a dozen or more rectangular tables in rows three across, surrounded by chairs awaiting their winners. Before she had kids, Ronnie had come along to play a time or two as a guest, the room so crowded that she and her mother had rushed to nab the last open seats. Even though their footsteps now echoed across its uncluttered floor, the space still felt aflutter with nervous anticipation as if these were the final tense seconds before some lucky stiff shouted "Bingo!"

Beverly and Janet sat together at a table on the far side of the room. The boys, separated at different tables and each sitting with a uniformed officer, waved to their Grandma Jan. If she saw them, nothing registered on Janet's face.

Ronnie returned to the table some thirty feet from the entrance door where she'd been sitting with a police officer.

"The officers at the farm reported in," he said. "One found a spent casing up near a big patch of low-growing plants."

"The strawberry field." She and Jeff had put it in that spring. Their last big project together. Ronnie felt the blood drain from her head. "Was Jeff—did they—"

"They're still searching for your husband. And there wasn't any blood. I only told you because that could explain the shot you heard earlier."

"What do you think it means, that he shot the gun out there?"

He shrugged. "I don't know, ma'am."

Ronnie already wanted to rewrite this story. To edit the cop's words. To distance herself, change "husband" to "the man." The man now staggering around the property with a gun; the man who may already have taken a shot; the man whose angst was seeping into her own nerves. Her husband—the gentle soul she'd married—would never have acted like the man she'd engaged with earlier today.

"Call him Jeff, please," she said quietly.

"I'm going to need you to recount all that transpired this morning with your—" He caught himself. "With Jeff. Leave nothing out. You never know what will be important."

The recitation she gave was devoid of animation. She felt empty and prickly, like an October cornfield in need of nutrients and a long, restorative winter. An evacuation from her home, beneath the cover of a helicopter dispatched from the state capitol, to protect her from her own husband? Ronnie felt as if her family had suddenly been thrust into an unwanted audition for a high-stakes reality show. Every few moments, as she delivered facts, she looked over at her mother, who was speaking quietly to Janet. She wondered if Beverly's version differed. If her mother, or Jeff's, blamed her. Because to them, and the rest of the world, it must look as if Jeff had been knocked off balance because Ronnie had decided to leave him.

It even looked that way to her.

The officer told Ronnie their primary goal was to locate Jeff, since he was armed and dangerous.

"Please don't say that in front of his mother," she said. "Or the boys. Jeff isn't a dangerous person. He's sweet. Everyone would tell you how nice he is. Very laid back." *Too laid back. He never cared enough.* "It's just that we're getting a divorce, and today was the day he promised to move out. He's…" *Drunk off his ass.* "Agitated."

Ronnie rubbed her arms—the room suddenly chilled her. She hadn't thought to grab a jacket. The room's narrow, high-set windows, made of glass bricks, were meant to obscure natural light. This was a room designed to allow sparkles from a mirror ball, gropes in the shadows.

And so what? She was cold. She felt selfish thinking about it, with Jeff frozen all the way to the center of his soul.

"Could you give me a physical description of your husband so we can identify him by sight?"

All that she and Jeff had meant to each other, all the intricacies of their marriage, boiled down to the same physical attributes that had first attracted her to him. "Five foot ten. Dark brown hair, thick, trimmed over ears some might call large." *Soft ears that lay flat against his head beneath her kisses.* "Blue eyes." *Eyes that used to pierce her through with their naked honesty.* "Broad hands." *Strong hands that always needed a project, now wrapped around a gun.* "Forty-seven. His birthday is in eleven days—Halloween." She told the officer that last year she and the boys had written and illustrated a book for Jeff, as a birthday present, about a cat named Trouble.

"I'm sorry. That last part might not be relevant. But he's a huge animal lover. Oh, and he"—she ran her finger down the line between her front teeth but could barely say the words—"has a gap."

"Do you recall what he's wearing?"

"A flannel shirt." Jeff had lost weight and felt cold lately. "A denim jacket. It has tan corduroy here." She touched the collar of her own shirt. "And jeans." *In his pocket, a money clip engraved: "Your love is my treasure."*

beverly

After an officer came over to take down what little Beverly had observed that morning and Janet had excused herself to use the restroom, Beverly pulled her chair around to the end of the table and leaned in toward the officer. She didn't want her inquiry to echo across the room.

"Listen," she began. She looked over at Ronnie, and for a brief moment, their eyes met. The intensity of Ronnie's gaze made Beverly look away. "My daughter doesn't know this, but I was close to someone who committed suicide. So what are the chances I'll know someone else? Slim, right?"

"You looking for comfort, or statistics?"

"I want comfort *from* statistics."

"I'm no specialist. But I do know that someone kills himself every fourteen minutes in this country."

"'Himself.' So these are men?"

"Most of the people who attempt suicide are women, but most of those who succeed are men."

"Why's that?"

"More men use guns."

Beverly clutched her hand to her heart.

The officer gathered up his papers, gave her a pitying look, and left her to her stunned silence.

She felt awful for Ronnie, and for the boys. She'd been young herself, only seventeen, when she'd suffered her horrific loss. She'd given Dominic her virgin heart and all the faith and hope that clung to it—and he'd taken it right to the grave. His death had affected every decision she'd made since.

Beverly knew Ronnie thought she was a lightweight. A flirt. But truth was, she had always hoped she'd find a true, deep love like what she'd witnessed between Ronnie and Jeff in their early years together. Lord knows she tried. With Tony. With Daryl. With Jim. But Beverly just couldn't make love stick. Her love life was like a game of pinball: thrust forward by a lusty pull on a spring launcher, kept aloft by the flipper of determination, and then hitting a variety of bumpers on the way down the drain.

Dominic's beach house had finally lost its allure, and she'd quit going along with Ronnie, Jeff, and the boys. She understood why Ronnie wanted to go; that's where she dreamed of her father. But that's where Beverly had fallen in love with him, and each year it had gotten harder to experience the house exactly as it had stood without being able to conjure his spirit. It wasn't that her wounds still bled; she just no longer saw the point in revisiting her scars.

Beverly hadn't dealt with Dom's loss well at all, but at least she'd had a lifetime to try to get over it.

As would Ronnie, if she lost Jeff today. That loss would hit her harder than Ronnie could ever imagine, but she was young and had presumably started to envision her life without him.

But Janet would feel as if she herself had been shot if Jeff pulled the trigger today. And she'd carry a raw, gaping wound for the rest of her life.

ronnie

A couple of tables away, Ronnie heard an officer ask Will, "So what's your dad like?"

Will shrugged. Until today, Ronnie had still thought of her youngest as only a wisp of a boy, but there was hidden strength in his spine. How quickly he had rushed to his father's side; how bravely he had fought for those keys. Just eight years old and he knew what he was about. The pages of Ronnie's journals were her search for that kind of instinctual knowing and illustrated all too well the dangers of bending around others too long. It broke her to watch him arrange his face into a mask of indifference, like a man with secrets to keep. His swinging feet just grazed the floor. "He's nice."

She felt certain Andrew was not giving a similar account on the other side of the room. Jeff had never understood Andrew. The family would be raking leaves onto tarps for compost, and Andrew, consumed by other thoughts, would inevitably slip into a daydream and then dance off to the house to draw, or organize his rock collection, or add another alien race to his science fiction screenplay. They'd find the rake abandoned somewhere between the road and the front door. Jeff thought of Andrew as a slacker. Ronnie knew that one day her older son would choose to leave the rural life of eastern Pennsylvania for a richer cultural landscape—and half of her would want to go with him.

Will was the one who wanted in on any project Jeff undertook.

Jeff had given him a small tool belt, complete with junior-size tools. When Will donned his work goggles, he was a mini version of his dad.

"Did he ever hit you?" the policeman asked Will.

"Oh no, he's a great dad," Will said. "He'd make up soccer games with me in the side yard." Tucked up against the ceiling, above his head, was an old mirror ball. So many ways of looking at any one thing. Will spun this singular moment of connection as if he and Jeff had played together all the time. She wasn't sure if Jeff had ever done anything one-on-one with Andrew.

The admiration in Will's voice clawed at Ronnie. Once—*once*—he had made up a soccer game with Will. Jeff should have spent much more time with his sons. He'd have to, once the divorce went through and he was granted visitation rights. That was one of the reasons why, six weeks ago, Ronnie had chanced leaving the boys alone with him one weekend. Jeff had to see that he'd need his own relationship with the boys; Ronnie fostering one on his behalf could no longer work.

She wanted Jeff to benefit from relationships with their children the same way she had. At least that's what she told herself to try to ease her distress over the fact that she had left her precious children alone with a man who just weeks later would arm himself and stand off against local and state police. Thank god, *thank god* they'd been all right when she got home.

And this morning she had almost sent her children out to him, again. What the hell had she been thinking?

When Ronnie sat back down, Mr. Eshbach, waddling with his bowlegged gait, wound his way between tables and chairs to join her. His compact stature had suited him well for tucking into the tight spaces required of a plumber. Although retired, he still dressed each day in the navy short-sleeved shirt and navy pants that he would have worn to work. His clothesline suggested he owned seven sets. Jeff's closet was filled with the black pants and white short-sleeved shirts required of his work too. What clothes would fill his closet once the farm store took off and his life at the hotel ended?

If he lived beyond life at the hotel.

Mr. Eshbach pulled out a chair and sat with a long sigh, more emotional expression than she'd ever before heard from the man. Their interactions were mostly limited to waves from the car and incidental meetings at the mailbox, although now that they had the farm store, she did know he had a weakness for beets. His features seemed carved into stone, as if a smile would require heavy lifting.

"I gave my statement," he said. "I could leave, but they won't let me go back to my home just now, and I have nowhere else to go."

"I am so sorry you got caught up in this."

Mr. Eshbach let silence stretch between them. She'd heard he'd lost his wife years ago, before Ronnie moved in. She wondered what the two of them might have talked about.

"What can you do," he concluded, as if they had worked something through. His voice dropped at the end, shutting out all possibility for companionable exchange.

His silence was an empty bowl Ronnie longed to fill. "We're getting a divorce," she blurted. He nodded. After a moment, she added, "The boys and I will be the ones moving out, as soon as we find a place, but for now it'll be Jeff. So you'll know. If you don't see him." He nodded. "Thing is, I love so many things about my life. It's the drinking. If he'd just quit." The words marched out of her mouth until their complete inappropriateness formed a clump in the air.

Ronnie would make a terrible secret agent. Even sixty seconds of silence was enough torture to get her to spill secrets.

It was the same way eight weeks ago, when years of questions, months of waffling, and weeks of hand-wringing resulted in Ronnie's decision to file for divorce. She expected an emotional scene, and Jeff had provided one, pounding his fist against a front porch column, lips trembling, tears welling. And even though the dreaded words had scraped her throat like burnt toast, in the end, the emotional act of leaving Jeff had not required the Jaws of Life. It was more like separating two sticky notes. She had feared telling her children, though. Divorce would destroy their sense of family and home, even though they'd done nothing to cause it. Ronnie had lost enough fathers to know how that felt. But her sons had the right to prepare themselves as she had, so once she'd told Jeff, she hadn't been able to sit with the knowledge for more than a day before she'd told them.

To make sure Jeff wouldn't overhear, she'd taken Andrew and Will out to the side yard, beneath the broad canopy of the mimosa tree. Its hearty trunk and low branching offered accessible footholds for young climbers—and their mom and barn cats as well, as several of Jeff's photos had proven. Swallowtail butterflies and hummingbirds flitted among its fragrant, silky flowers while its leaves, like collections of green feathers stitched into an array of headdresses, caught the breeze. An invader from the south, the mimosa was nothing more than another beautiful weed. Its lifespan in Pennsylvania was typically short. But this one had been here for as long as Jeff had been, he'd said, and when she left the farm, she would miss this idyllic spot. They'd wedged the hammock's stand between the tree's shallow roots, and in rare moments of repose, it was a favorite place to curl up with a book.

Ronnie sat the boys on the hammock before her. But that felt wrong. She needed to be talking with them, not at them. So she climbed into the hammock too, and each of them redistributed their weight to accommodate the new balance. The boys looked at her, the sun dappling their skin with gold expectation. In her rush to remove the barrier of hidden truth from between them, Ronnie had not thought ahead.

When at last the words formed, they came out in a tumble: "I am going to divorce your father."

Ronnie braced for their shock. After all, she and Jeff rarely fought. To preserve the marriage this long, she had fluidly readjusted her expectations and diverted energy toward her and Jeff's one great point of connection—the country lifestyle they shared. She looked around at pears hanging heavy on a nearby tree. Chickens clucked and scratched in the dirt, sun glinting off their iridescent neck feathers. The horses peeked out over their stall doors as if they too were listening to Ronnie's news.

"I suppose you are pretty surprised by this," Ronnie said. She certainly was. Divorce, while repeatedly embraced by her mother, went against Ronnie's beliefs. She was determined to do it better than she had. Give her kids the stability she'd never enjoyed.

But there was no longer anything stable about Jeff.

Will, Daddy's little helper, arranged a blank face. Andrew answered, "Not really."

"Why not?"

"You and Dad don't even act like you're in love."

Hmm. Ronnie had needed several sessions with a therapist to come to this awareness. She'd also plunked down twenty-four dollars for a book that told her that her marriage exemplified the predivorce state. She could have saved her money and asked her ten-year-old.

"Explain what you mean," Ronnie said.

"You never spend time together."

He was right on that point. Ronnie was usually on the run with the boys, and Jeff rarely attended Andrew's Tae Kwon Do events or Will's soccer games. She'd ask other couples at these events: Do you always come together? How do you work that out with your employers? Jeff was never able to clear his schedule. Ronnie joked that when it came to sports, she was a single mom. Over time, it felt like less and less of a joke.

"Plus," Andrew had said, "you are way more creative than Dad is. He'll never understand you the way I do."

No, Ronnie couldn't hold secrets. Not from Jeff, the boys, or, as her conversation with Mr. Eshbach in the fire hall had just shown, her next-door neighbors.

As if he'd needed the time to free each word from rusting vocal cords, Mr. Eshbach told her he knew all about Jeff's problems with alcohol.

"You do?" Jeff had always enjoyed his cocktails, yes, but it had only been during this last year that Ronnie finally suspected his problem, and she lived with him. "How?"

"Oh, it was back before you got together. He'd had that other girl."

"Fay." Fay Sickler. They'd had to track down the divorce papers in order to apply for their marriage license. Jeff had bought the house from his mother for Fay, not Ronnie. She and Jeff had married the year before Ronnie and her mother moved back into the area, when Ronnie was entering high school. By the time Ronnie had graduated from college and moved back from New York City, Jeff's marriage to Fay had ended. Crazy Fay stories had filled her and Jeff's early years with laughter and, by comparison, made Jeff's choice of Ronnie seem so sane.

Because Ronnie had never had to deal with Crazy Fay directly, it was easy for her to pretend Jeff's life had started anew when they married. Ronnie had never stopped to think of what it must have looked like to someone like Mr. Eshbach, who would have watched from his house next door as Jeff swapped one woman for the next.

"He didn't take it so well when she left," Mr. Eshbach said. "One night while I was walking the dog, I bumped into him. He tripped right over the leash. He was so blind with drink, I wasn't sure he'd live the night. Had no clue I was even there, I don't suppose."

Had despair been entrenched in Jeff's life even before they'd gotten together? It couldn't be. One of the things she'd loved about him was that, compared to the high seas of her emotional life, Jeff had always seemed so serene. He was her even keel, she always said. Had his contentment always been an illusion? Or was there some turning point to his decline that Ronnie missed? She couldn't believe Mr. Eshbach had been sitting on the story all this time.

"I've wondered, through the years, what would have happened

that night if I hadn't found him and steered him home." His voice softened. "So, however this turns out, well…"

Ronnie looked at him, eyebrows raised, fearing he had run through his quota of words and was done speaking. "Yes?"

"He seemed real content once you two wed. To my way of thinking, you may have given him an extra dozen years."

Ronnie lowered her eyes. She'd blamed herself so much lately that this kindness threatened to undo her.

The officer returned to the room and headed to Ronnie's table. Mr. Eshbach stood.

"I'm so sorry for all this…this…" Ronnie couldn't find words. *Inconvenience* was an understatement.

The old man, who over the course of twelve years had never encouraged neighborly interaction, reached over and patted her on the hand with his stubby, callused fingers. "Been lonely since the wife passed. After your storm blows through, I won't be a stranger."

Her storm, whose winds were whipping at her neighbors. Like Heather Beam, the young woman who'd stopped in the farm store last week while Ronnie was typing up interview notes for her aquaponics article. Raised in a city on frozen vegetables, Heather had asked Ronnie for a full tour of New Hope Farms's produce. She'd taken one of everything, it seemed, even handfuls of nuts and seeds and copies of Ronnie's shelf tag recipes. Heather and her husband had just bought a place up the road. "I want to taste every new experience country life has to offer," she had said.

Ronnie too had once felt that way. She had planned to meet Heather today so Ronnie could advise her on what she could do now to prepare soil for her own spring garden. The references Ronnie had assembled were sitting under the store's front counter.

What a welcome Heather and her husband must be receiving today. She hoped it wouldn't taint the fresh-faced enthusiasm that Ronnie had found so endearing.

The policeman filled the spot Mr. Eshbach had vacated.

"They've tried the doors to all of the outbuildings on the property, but they're locked."

"I know. For the past few weeks, Jeff has been kind of paranoid. He added locks to buildings that have always stood open: corn cribs, the tractor shed, the barn, the tool shed." Ronnie shook her head. "It's weird. When I met him, he always left the house unlocked at night. He even left his keys in the car out in the driveway." *Why was he now so afraid?*

"Do you have any idea where he might go?"

"You mean to hide from the police? How can you expect me to think like that?"

"Or where he'd go to hole up and consider taking…a final action. A place with a certain significance or meaning."

His woodworking shop? Its hardware, tools, and machinery all poised to spring into service, awaiting only Jeff's imagination and skilled hands to achieve their creative potential. He kept the out-building as organized as a small hardware store—except for the dark corner with the filing cabinets and his desk. Once the boys' allergist had put an end to Jeff smoking in their home, Jeff had moved all of their financial records from the upstairs sitting room out to the desk in his shop so that, on his nights off, he could enjoy a cigarette and a cocktail while he paid bills. His record keeping had broken down until the mess artfully disguised its secrets. From Ronnie, and perhaps from Jeff as well.

But those records were no longer in the woodworking shop.

They were in New Hope Farms. After he and Ronnie had completed their home renovation last winter, Jeff had planned the farm store as another project to work on with Ronnie. It was the perfect confluence of their combined skills, he'd said. Meant to be. It would bring them even closer to the farm they loved and to each other. Ronnie hadn't been as sure. She had more than enough on her plate with the boys, the animals, and her magazine writing. But the project energized him, and after the store was built, he'd moved all their financial records into its office, as if from the dark to the light of day. So he could organize the records while he wasn't waiting on customers, he said, and give her the sum of the credit card debt that she'd been awaiting.

That long-anticipated accounting, which he delivered seven weeks ago on a torn scrap of paper, had signaled the end of their marriage. He'd given it to her in the store office. She'd found him there again, distressed, yesterday.

For two weeks, since he'd agreed on the October 20 move-out day, he'd been banging pans around in the kitchen when he got home from work, waking Ronnie every night. So they could talk. Again. She'd argue for divorce; he'd argue against it. She wasn't getting much sleep. Her therapist had cautioned her to stop entertaining such requests; Ronnie needed to guard her health and make it clear to Jeff that her mind was made up.

Refusing him at night had only inspired Jeff to find ways to monopolize her daytime hours instead, constantly interrupting her writing for help with house repairs. From replacing a water heater coil to securing an unmoored downspout to adding those unnecessary locks, the list of projects requiring four hands had grown and grown.

When they'd taken the air conditioners out of the windows the previous day and stowed them in the barn, it seemed their work together had come to an end. Jeff pulled out a swollen key ring to double lock the barn door, but his hands shook so badly he fumbled several times in selecting the right key. Big tears rolled down his face.

"I've tried to stop drinking," he'd confessed, looking out over the cornfield's stubble. "I can't sleep. I've been vomiting. You know I never do that."

Muscling through on his own—a prospect doomed to failure, and so unnecessary with support available. He looked pale, and thinner than ever. How easy it would be for her to pull him into her arms. But Ronnie knew all too well that her solace wouldn't change a thing.

They went their separate ways.

Finally alone for an hour, Ronnie started to think of chores that only Jeff had ever handled. She very much wanted to be able to manage the place without calling Jeff at the hotel every day to find out how she'd know if the ultraviolet lightbulb on the water purification system needed changing or how often she'd need to add water softener salt, so she collected her questions and went in search of him. Down in the store, Amber was closing up shop.

"Jeff in there?" Ronnie said, nodding her head toward the closed office door.

"Yep. I'm heading out. See you tomorrow?"

"I might be a little late. I've been having trouble finishing an article. I'll try to get here by ten, though. Barney will be dropping off more apples and cider, and we owe him money."

Ronnie knocked once and opened the office door.

"What now?" Jeff had snapped, flipping down the yellow page from the legal pad on which he'd been writing. Covering it with his hand, as if Ronnie might steal his test answers. He lit a fresh cigarette. This fluid, practiced movement, which had ignited pheromones when they met but now suggested *potential lung cancer* and *hardening arteries* and *I don't love you enough*, had taken on a substantial quiver. He took a long drag, then set it in the ashtray.

Beside it sat a drink in a cocktail glass.

The sight of it struck fear in Ronnie. "I thought you had work tonight," she'd said. Jeff never, ever drank before a shift at work. Not even one cold beer with lunch on a hot summer day.

"And?"

And nothing. Soon, such issues would not be hers to worry about.

She tucked her list into the pocket of her jeans. If she could get away with asking only one last question today, it wouldn't be about housekeeping. He hadn't mentioned his offer to move to the hotel for some time. Why would he? He didn't want the divorce.

Ronnie hated like hell to press him. She should be the one to go. He needed this home more than she did, and not just because it had been in his family for generations or because he'd lived there for years before Ronnie moved in. Ronnie had put her share of sweat into this house, it was true, but that sweat had evaporated. She could rehydrate, live elsewhere. But it was as if Jeff bled into the house, and it owned a part of him.

A few weeks without his frantic eyes tracking her every movement and she'd be able to find a place for her and the boys, she was sure of it, and Jeff would be able to reclaim his home.

She'd said, "I'd like to keep the boys up-to-date on what's happening. Are you moving out tomorrow like you said you would?"

Jeff's eyes dropped to the legal pad in front of him. "God, Ronnie. Yes, okay? If you'll let me get some work done here, I'll be ready."

She had her answer and walked away.

Are you moving out like you said you would? Now, sitting in the fire hall, Ronnie could only hope these weren't the last words she'd ever say to him.

Ronnie propped her forehead on her hands.

"I know where he is," Ronnie told the policeman. "He's in the farm store. In the back office."

The officer left the room. The boys, done giving their statements, had noticed a TV remote and asked an officer for permission to watch something on the set situated over the bar. They flipped through the basic network channels, changing every time a news show came on. With few choices, they settled on a *Live! With Kelly and Michael* segment on extreme sports: "How far will we go?" Their grandmothers looked on, as if grateful for the distraction.

While they were occupied, an officer came to Ronnie with new information from the farm. "Our men broke down the office door in the farm store and found Jeff sitting at the desk."

Right where Ronnie had pictured him.

"He was holding the shotgun with its stock on his thigh, pointing into the air."

Ronnie sat taller. "And?"

The police had instructed Jeff to lower his weapon. He had.

He'd held the butt to his shoulder, lowered the gun, and trained it on the officer's forehead.

10:00 a.m.

ronnie

The air stirred as Corporal McNichol strode into the room in a no-nonsense brown suit and black oxfords. She had an energy about her that said she was ready to run a marathon. Finally, someone who could get things done.

"Veronica Farnham?" she said.

Ronnie cringed at the name she'd been saddled with simply because her hormone-crazed mother had hooked up with a man in an alley behind a bar. At least that's how she envisioned it. Her mother had a more romantic version, always delivered wistfully: "I went to the shore and fell in love at Veronica's Grotto." Apparently the man split by summer's end, but his permanent impact had already taken root in Ronnie's mother's womb. Her whole life Ronnie had tried to find ways to bond with her missing father to distance herself from the notion that "Veronica" was simply an unintended souvenir of a vacation gone wrong.

"Everyone calls me Ronnie."

The corporal extended her hand. "I'm the commander of the Special Emergency Response Team."

"What's that?" Janet said. She and Beverly moved toward the woman as if reporting for duty.

"SERT is a team of state police negotiators and tactical officers trained to deal with hostage situations."

"Well, there's no hostage." Janet stood taller and straightened her Hello Kitty sweatshirt. Ronnie explained that Janet was Jeff's mother.

When Corporal McNichol spoke again, it was with a markedly gentler voice. "I've been briefed by the officers on the scene. In a way, ma'am, your son is holding himself hostage. We'd like to get Jeff out of there, safe and sound." She pulled out a chair for Janet and motioned for the other women to sit. "I have an update."

"Is the officer okay?" Ronnie couldn't wait another minute without knowing. "The one who found Jeff?"

"Jeff allowed him to back away and shut the door."

Ronnie shook her head. "This is such a mess." All the years Jeff had kept those guns locked in the house, never using them, but refusing to get rid of them—why? In reserve for this?

"It's not uncommon for a person in this kind of situation to turn his weapon on the police," Corporal McNichol said. "They have a name for it—"

The corporal clearly intended to say more but stopped short. The women leaned in. Ronnie prompted, "Which is?"

Corporal McNichol glanced over to Janet, then back to Ronnie, and said quietly, "Suicide by police."

That must be hard for Janet to hear. Ronnie looked at her mother-in-law, but both of the older women seemed absorbed in their own thoughts.

"When Jeff was located, the situation changed from a manhunt to a standoff. That's why we were called in. At the moment, the situation is stable—"

An angry scream erupted from two tables away. "Stop!"

"I didn't do anything."

"You are kicking me, over and over!"

"Boys!" Ronnie snapped. The boys, Beverly, and Janet all turned to Ronnie, as if each were surprised that anyone else was sitting in this room. "Please. I need you to be good."

"I didn't do anything wrong," Andrew said.

"Neither did I!"

"I know," Ronnie said quietly. "I know."

"Hey, Mom," Andrew said, pointing to the television over the bar. "Isn't that our house? Look—there's the store, and our house, and the swinging tree—"

"And the barn and the tool shed. And the woods," Will said, joining in. To get a closer look, the boys went over and stood on the brass foot rail and clung to the edge of the bar. Ronnie could barely stand watching them belly up to it.

Ronnie moved to turn off the set as the boys identified Mr. Eshbach's home up the road, the Schulzes' across the street, and the woods down below. She was glad to see the boys' natural enthusiasm restored, but she couldn't have them watching this. As she reached for the remote, Will said, "But why are the soldiers there?"

"Soldiers? Where?" Ronnie paused and studied the scene before her, transfixed. This was her husband, their neighborhood, their mess. Now, perhaps, their war. How could she turn away?

"Where the leaves are moving."

"Those are my men," Corporal McNichol said. "Damn reporters. Does Jeff have access to a TV in your office?"

Ronnie shook her head no, never tearing her eyes from the screen. She sensed her mother and Janet drifting toward her, past the nearby table where Mr. Eshbach sat. She wondered if they too were trying to catch a glimpse of Jeff through the farm store office window. Ronnie wanted to rip the lens from the cameraman's hand and zoom in.

"We have breaking news about the footage you are seeing," said the news anchor. Ronnie felt relieved to hear the earnest voice of Rob White, who had so far impressed her with his balanced news coverage. "An armed, despondent man has holed up in the office of his family's business and engaged with officers dispatched from two local barracks, state police, and Special Emergency Response Troops, in what a spokesman is now calling a suicide standoff..."

Do not identify him, Rob White. Please leave us our privacy.

A circle appeared around their farm store. "It is confirmed that the individual in question is Jeffrey Farnham, age fifty. He's the son of deceased Schuylkill Valley Sports Hall of Famer Jerry Farnham, who turned around a losing Potts Forge High School basketball team to win a number of state championships over a thirty-five-year career. Jerry Farnham also developed and administered a countywide summer playground program still in existence today. The younger Farnham has locked himself inside the store on the property, New Hope Farms, which sells organic vegetables in Bartlesville, Pennsylvania. He is armed with a shotgun. The family is safe and under police protection at an undisclosed location. Neighbors who were away when the barricades went up have not been allowed to return to their homes."

It was not lost on Ronnie that White, who still straddled the divide between substitute anchor and weatherman, had been assigned to the story. In the larger scheme of things, Jeff was not important. Even though right now he commanded the community's attention and Ronnie's entire world, it would seem from this report that the most significant thing about Jeff was his relationship to his father.

"Earlier this morning, when Farnham's whereabouts were unknown, officials locked down nearby Hitchman Elementary as a safety measure and canceled recess for the day."

"There's our school!" Will said, pointing at the screen.

"Parents with cell phones will receive texts concerning how this will affect afternoon bus service, and of course we will break into regularly scheduled programming with updates as events unfold. Again, a despondent Jeffrey Farnham has…"

Behind Ronnie, her mother-in-law said, "They've got it wrong."

Ronnie too was already arguing with the report. Jeff would never—*could* never—walk all the way to the elementary school. That was over three hilly miles away. His bad knee would stop him. And he was drunk. He'd more likely curl up somewhere and take a nap.

Janet said, "He's not fifty. He'll be forty-eight next week. I ordered his cake."

Two dozen SERT troops, Will's "soldiers," looking like dull green ants on the aerial view, swarmed onto the farm. Another shot zoomed in on the horrific details: sidearms strapped to their thighs. Pockets swollen with ammunition. Camouflage uniforms whose jackets were 3-D leafy and said *POLICE* across the back. Pants tucked into laced-up boots. All the men wore bulletproof vests, helmets, and goggles. Out in front of the store, troops crouched behind black body shields. Others took cover behind Ronnie's house and outbuildings and trained the telescopic sights of their rifles on the doors and windows of the store office.

Ronnie turned her sons away from the screen.

Will strained to turn back. "What's going on there? What are they doing to Dad?"

Behind them, Rob White announced the return to regular programming. The disbelief Ronnie felt was reflected on the faces of her mother and mother-in-law. Bile rose within Ronnie's throat against the background of Rachael Ray's perky, raspy voice: "So is it possible to cook a delicious meal with items from a dollar store? We'll see! On today's show, two chefs go spatula to spatula—"

Someone on Jeff's side had to take charge.

Ronnie went to the bar, hit the remote, and returned to Corporal McNichol. "You've got to put an end to this," she said. "It's too much. He doesn't stand a chance."

"We aren't here to engage with him. We're here to encourage him to stand down."

"That would not be my guess if I were looking out that office window."

Corporal McNichol laid her hand on Ronnie's shoulder. "We have a lot of experience with situations like this—more than any of us have ever wanted to have. These conflicts can end peacefully. Our negotiators are compassionate people who will do all they can to appeal to your husband. But we have procedures we have to follow."

"Like what? What are you doing?" Beverly said.

"For one, we've issued a mental health warrant for Jeffrey."

"Why on earth would you do that?" Janet said.

Corporal McNichol turned to the boys. "We adults have to discuss a few things here. Why don't you two go play?"

Andrew looked around the hall. "Where?"

"With what?" Will added. "We don't even have a ball."

"Come on, Will, use your imagination," Ronnie said, hoping her son had more creative energy to tap than she did at present.

Andrew circled to Corporal McNichol's side. "Can we have a piece of paper?"

"Sure." Corporal McNichol flipped to a fresh sheet and ripped it off the pad.

"Three would be even better," Will added.

The corporal smiled and obliged. Andrew wadded the papers together and told his brother to go long. Soon they were tossing the makeshift ball back and forth, making the happy sounds of the recess their classmates had been denied during the school lockdown.

"Boys," Mr. Eshbach said, pulling himself to his feet. Ronnie wondered if he knew their names—he even referred to his deceased spouse as "the wife." The boys paused as he waddled over, no doubt expecting a reprimand. He patted his ribs. "I believe I could use some exercise too." Andrew lobbed the ball in his direction. The old man caught it with a deft snatch and a smile and encouraged the boys to relocate the game to the other end of the room.

"Why don't we sit back down?" Corporal McNichol said.

"You mentioned a mental health warrant," Ronnie said.

"Yes. It's for people like Jeff who need immediate intervention because they are at serious risk of harming themselves or others. The warrant allows us to take Jeff into custody, evaluate him, and get him the help he needs."

"That sounds good," Janet said.

"My god, Janet, you sound like this is a new idea," Ronnie said.

"I've been trying to get him help for some time now and you keep acting like I'm hysterical. You only believe it once the state police swarm in?"

"Now calm down, Sunshine," Beverly said. "We're all on the same team here."

Ronnie turned to Corporal McNichol. "There's something you need to know."

Janet said, "That's enough, Ronnie. It won't do any good to air private affairs."

Ronnie deflected the slice of Janet's glare. "This isn't the first time he's threatened to kill himself."

ronnie

Six weeks ago, in early September, Ronnie sought out Jeff to talk more about the divorce. As far as she knew, he hadn't even secured legal representation, and Ronnie, who had already put off this decision way too long, wanted to formalize their separation. But she and the boys were having a typically crazy day. Even the pages of her journal couldn't center her that day, the lists and notes in the margins outweighing the prose: *Finish bulk grain and seed purchase order for store, line up interviews for next article, muck horse stalls. (Why isn't Jeff doing this anymore? Should we sell horses?)* To ensure his sobriety, she invited Jeff along for the ride to the day's activities, round two: after-school Tae Kwon Do, a quick dinner, and parent-teacher night. He was all too willing to oblige.

Baiting him with the pretense of togetherness threatened the inner balance she'd fought for with years of journaling and weeks of counseling, but effective communication was impossible through alcohol's haze. If manipulation was required to keep booze out of the equation that night, so be it.

But Jeff was so good at pulling her off the rails. To get through the night, she needed some small symbol of her commitment to self, something to fortify her through the few hours of playacting required. And so, after a moment of hesitation, she slipped off her wedding rings and left them in her jewelry box.

That evening, Ronnie sat with Jeff and Will in a line of folding chairs waiting for Andrew at Tae Kwon Do. As always, Ronnie watched the class. Jeff, apparently, was watching Ronnie.

"Where are your rings?"

For years he had ignored her in every way that counted; Ronnie was surprised he'd even noticed. She hadn't meant to make a public statement. As kindly as she could, she said, "Let's talk tonight, Jeff. At home, like we planned."

After Tae Kwon Do, they got drive-through burgers and ate on the way to parent-teacher night. Ronnie—and Jeff too, she was sure—pretended to listen to the teachers and look at the projects on the wall, slapping smiles over twisting guts and draining hearts. When they finally got home and Jeff declined her invitation to join in on the boys' bedtime rituals, she skipped reading the boys a book by promising two the next night.

Ronnie rejoined him in the living room. He sat on the love seat; she sat on the couch.

Jeff spoke first.

"I was going to shoot myself tonight."

She wasn't sure she heard him right. He wasn't hysterical. He could have been saying, *I was going to watch football, but the Eagles weren't playing.* Ronnie couldn't focus on the magnitude of what he was saying; she got stuck on the word "shoot."

It only took another moment to add it up: he'd already come up with a plan, and it involved a gun.

"What do you mean, 'I was going to'?"

"I wrote a note at work and put it in my pocket. I thought you'd find it when you did the wash, but it was still there when I put on my pants for work today." All Ronnie could think was, *He thinks I go through his pockets?* Even the kids knew to police their own pockets before putting them in the laundry or face the potential loss of their contents. She didn't have time for such nonsense.

"Come with me," he said, leaning forward but not standing when Ronnie didn't move.

She couldn't. Her spinal fluid had turned into a thick, cold paste. The golden wall color they'd so carefully chosen—"Daybreak"— mocked them as the room took on a darker hue. "Why?"

"I want to show you something."

Ronnie stalled. "How could you think of doing something like that? What about Andrew and Will?"

"They've always been your kids, not mine."

What? She and Jeff had wanted those boys so badly. After persevering through two miscarriages, they'd been so grateful when their sons arrived. And he'd lavished them with attention, changing diapers and cuddling with them and buying them toys they could play with together. When had all that changed?

"The boys will be fine," he said, as if already speaking from the far side of the grave.

"Is that how you would have felt if your dad offed himself? *Fine?*" The air thinned; she panted for oxygen. "My god, Jeff, you gave them life! You're wrong. They would never get over it."

He shook his head, as if she were working from the wrong script. "You'll help them through."

The more Jeff had counted on Ronnie to keep their lives on track over the past few years, the more competent she'd felt—but she couldn't imagine anyone powerful enough to help a child past such a horrific act.

"Let me show you something."

She followed his lead through a living room abuzz with dangerous electricity, out the front door, and halfway down the walk. It was only as they left the yellow glow of the porch light and entered the night's pitch that the hair on the back of Ronnie's neck prickled.

"Where are we going?" she said.

"The store office."

They started down the driveway, but the sudden dark and a light fog distorted her senses. Nothing looked right. For the first time, it occurred to Ronnie that the "something" he wanted to show her might be a gun.

"I'm not going any farther," she said. If Jeff insisted on going to the store office, he was going alone.

Her footsteps crunched on the gravel as Ronnie ran back to the relative safety of the living room. The room for living. Her mind frantic, seeking options. They lived in a dark, secluded area. The pasture light that used to come on at dusk had been added to a fix-it list that was now impossibly long. The boys were up two flights of stairs. She couldn't possibly get them out of the house before Jeff got back. She couldn't think. Was he really violent?

The door latch clicked; Ronnie's heart jumped as Jeff entered the room. He reached into his pocket. She pressed her back against the wall, breath ragged. *Oh god, what if he has a gun?* When he withdrew his hand, he passed her what at first looked like a marshmallow. Two sheets of paper that had been folded over and over like the origami fortune-tellers she used to make as a child that told you who you were, what you liked, and who you loved. The edges were rounded, compressed, and worn—as if they had, indeed, been through the wash. He said, "Read it."

Her knees would hold her no longer. She collapsed into a chair. The paper had grown brittle in the dryer. Tension mounted as she picked at it with shaking hands, carefully peeling back its layers. He stared at her as she read, making it harder to concentrate. The letter said he loved her, that she was the best thing in his life, and to please give his love to the boys. He said he hated his mother. He asked to be buried beside his father...

Ronnie went to the kitchen and got the dusty phone book down from the top shelf.

"What are you doing?" he said.

"You need to talk to somebody. There's a suicide hotline—"

"I'm not talking to any hotline."

"They have people trained to help you." Lines and lines

of numbers—how was she supposed to focus, to find the one she needed?

"I'm not going to talk to some stranger," he said.

"Then call Paco." Paco was the manager at the restaurant where Ronnie used to work, the only person Ronnie had ever thought of as Jeff's buddy. A drinking buddy, when both men were single, and until they'd had kids. He'd stood up for Jeff at their wedding.

"I haven't talked to him in years."

"I go years between talking to some of my old friends too, but we always reconnect," Ronnie said, continuing to flip through the phone book for that hotline. "He'd want you to call."

"I'm not talking to him."

"Jeff, you're hurting." Emotion welled in her throat. Somehow, in strengthening her resolve to leave her husband, she'd found a new reserve of compassion for him. "You need to talk to someone. I know you want it to be me, but it can't be."

Ronnie found the listing. She picked up the wall phone to dial. Jeff tore the receiver from her, then ripped the phone from the wall.

A hole gaped from the sheetrock they had so lovingly hung. Ronnie sank to the floor beneath it. Jeff crossed to the opposite side of the kitchen and did the same. Their backs against the oak cupboards they'd installed when Andrew was a baby.

They stared at each other for several minutes, Ronnie held hostage by choices she'd made when Jeff had seemed a different man. It had already been a long day, and as she sat there, the rush from its surprise ending began to wane.

"We're at a stalemate," she finally said. "Guess I'll have to watch you all night because I will not have the boys tripping over your dead body on their way to the bus stop tomorrow."

Ronnie sat with him for another fifteen minutes or so, not talking. *At least he's not drinking.* Yet as the minutes dragged on, she saw the futility in this approach. She'd never be able to stay awake all night. How long could she guard Jeff? For the rest of their lives?

"Never mind." Ronnie stood. "I'm going to bed."

Ronnie washed her face and brushed her teeth but didn't undress. Who was she kidding? No matter how exhausted she was, she'd never be able to relax into sleep with the threat of violence in the air. Her mind raced. She needed to get Jeff help, but how? She reached for the bedroom phone, but it wasn't in its cradle. After looking all over the second floor, she found it where she had no doubt left it—on the sitting room bed. She tried to turn it on. Dead. Her cell phone was plugged in to charge at the store, where she left it every night. Why bother bringing it inside this fortress, where thick stone walls obscured a signal?

If only she could keep Jeff from drinking. Keep him talking. Distract him some way until she thought up a plan. Wondering what he was doing now, she slipped off her shoes and tiptoed down the stairs—but before she reached the kitchen, she heard the freezer drawer slide open and ice clunk against the side of a plastic mug. Then the front door. Jeff must have taken his drink to the porch so he could smoke.

She had to act fast. Holding her breath as she passed the kitchen window, just feet away from where Jeff probably sat, she descended again.

From her basement office, she called her therapist. Anita also worked at the Women in Crisis Center in Reading; she'd know what to do. Ronnie quickly apologized for the late hour—it was just past eleven thirty—and explained what was happening. Anita told her to hang up and call 911 and say that Jeff had threatened suicide and that she'd seen a note with his burial wishes detailed. "The note is important. Don't forget," she said.

Ronnie had been up since five a.m. With this flow and ebb of late-night adrenaline added on to weeks of turmoil, her vision was starting to blur with exhaustion. She anticipated the relief as she handed Jeff over to authorities better equipped to deal with the situation.

"Call now, Ronnie, and don't leave him alone until someone arrives."

What would she do if Jeff pulled a gun, fight him for it? She called the police and gave the prompted report. To head back up the stairs, she had to summon meager scraps of courage and pretend the rest. She hated to admit that she was afraid of the man who had been her lover for more than a decade. She recalled her brother Teddy's words when she'd told him she was divorcing Jeff: "My god, Ronnie, we've known that family our whole lives. You'd think you'd know him by now."

You'd think.

Ronnie forced a casual air as she walked onto the porch in her stocking feet and flopped onto the squashed cushions of the rusting glider beside Jeff's chair. The way his eyes lit up for a moment, as they always had when she walked into a room, ignited a small explosion in her heart.

"I thought you were going to bed." His words were slurring. How could that be? She'd only left him alone a short while.

"How am I supposed to sleep after what you said tonight?"

They sat for a half hour or so while Jeff added his cigarette smoke to a fog already determined to choke them off from the rest of the world. Beneath Ronnie, the glider creaked a distress signal into the night. Each stared off in a different direction. She still couldn't look at him. He'd see right through her. Ronnie's inadequate acting skills were the reason she never went along when the IRS audited Jeff; she'd trigger a bullshit meter a full block away. Let him try to defend his own shoddy tip reporting.

The lulling rhythm of the glider, the relinquishment of demands to silence, the booze—she wasn't sure why, but soon Jeff relaxed into his chair. On the table beside him, ice cubes melted at the bottom of the mug. Jeff used to make his Manhattans in squat "rocks" glasses, as any commercial bartender would. But for the past few years, he'd been making them in plastic beer mugs "so he wouldn't have to get up as often." Ronnie did the math. Chances were he was drinking nine to twelve shots of liquor on his nights off.

For once, she was glad he was impaired. Ronnie no longer feared any sudden movements. As she looked out into the night, an occasional wing caught the porch light as bats swooped down for bugs.

After a while, she sneaked a sideways glance; he'd let his glasses slide down on his nose. Why didn't he push them up?

Creak. Creak. Each crepitation ticked off another second until help arrived.

Finally, the first pop of gravel beneath tires in the driveway. Jeff leaned forward; he'd heard it too. Soon headlights advanced around the corner of the porch.

"Who on earth—?"

Ronnie felt blame's spotlight seeking her out.

Another moment and the full length of the state police cruiser came into view. An evening that began with the removal of wedding rings had resulted in the arrival of police. Ronnie felt, for a moment, that it was her offense that was actionable.

She finally hazarded a look in Jeff's direction. His eyes were like weapons trained over the top of his glasses. Words sloshed around in his mouth before he spit them toward Ronnie: "I will *never* forgive you for this."

ronnie

Two policemen got out of the car, Ronnie keenly aware of the peaceable scene they'd happened upon: a man and woman enjoying a spot of night air before bed. Ronnie stood and acknowledged that she had placed the call. She could feel the heat of Jeff's presence behind her. One officer asked to speak with her in the house; the other said to Jeff, "I hear you're not doing too well tonight, Mr. Farnham."

Inside, Ronnie's officer explained that separating them was standard procedure in domestic situations. Ronnie told him what had happened that evening and showed him the suicide note.

The officer said they'd take it into evidence. He passed the note through the door to his colleague. The other officer asked, "Is this your handwriting, Mr. Farnham?" She heard Jeff say yes. The officers conferred for a bit, their voices muffled behind the door, before the one assigned to Ronnie returned.

Jeff did not repeat the threat of suicide in front of the other officer, he said, so unless Ronnie was willing to get involved, their hands were tied.

"What do you mean, 'get involved'?"

"Your husband does not want our help, but that suicide note will allow you to commit him to the psychiatric ward against his will for up to five days. To do that, you'll have to come down to the hospital and sign papers."

"Okay. I'll head over first thing in the morning."

"It'll have to be now if you want help from us tonight. Otherwise, we'll have to leave your husband here—"

"No." That much was unthinkable. "But I have two children asleep upstairs."

He shrugged. Not his problem.

Ronnie's mind raced. It was past midnight; she wouldn't be able to get anyone to come over now to stay with the boys.

The officer shifted his weight. Jeff watched her through the door.

"I'll go wake them."

The officers called an ambulance from the squad car and gave Ronnie directions to the hospital. She shivered; the night had cooled, the fog had thickened, and she had never put on a sweater. Within a few minutes, she saw flashing lights refracting through millions of water droplets hanging in the air down by the road.

"We'll walk him down so the driver doesn't have to turn around up here," an officer said.

Ronnie then took in an image so incongruous she could only stare: Jeff, in handcuffs. He didn't look at her as they led him away.

In the attic Ronnie dressed the boys, explaining that their dad was sick. The ambulance had taken him to the hospital, and they had to go make sure he'd be okay.

The boys quickly fell back asleep in the car. Ronnie's thoughts flitted back to when Andrew was in first grade and had learned that some of the kids in his class were in a club called Banana Splits, which Ronnie knew to be a support group for kids from broken families. When at the end of the school year they got to have a banana split party with all the fixings, Andrew was jealous. He was a big lover of ice cream. One night, at a rare family dinner in which both Ronnie and Jeff were present, he said, "I think that next year I'd like to join Banana Splits."

Jeff had laughed along with Ronnie, who believed that those

circumstances would never arise within their loving family. Ronnie had told Andrew, "You wouldn't want to pay the cost of membership."

The fog wasn't as prevalent closer to Reading, and Ronnie found the hospital. It was going on two a.m. and the emergency room was empty. The boys sprawled out on plastic seats in the waiting room, CNN droning on the television above them. She'd hoped they'd fall asleep, but they couldn't get comfortable. They wanted to know what was wrong with their dad. It only occurred to Ronnie then that despite Jeff's consumption of filterless cigarettes and alcohol, the boys had never seen him sick. Maybe the farm store vegetables helped, although he ate that way for frugality more than health, so he could eat in maturation what he paid for in seed.

Time dragged while Jeff was assessed. The boys whined and wanted to know when they could go home. Ronnie told them the doctors were trying to figure that out.

At long last, the social worker called her into a small office.

"Your husband's feeling pretty good right now." *Feeling good?* Was Jeff putting on some kind of act? And was the act for Ronnie's benefit or theirs? "His blood alcohol is 0.20. We can't do a psych evaluation until that comes down."

This wasn't drinking to numb—this was drinking toward coma. How on earth could he have consumed so much?

"I understand he threatened suicide and that you want to commit him, so I've drawn up the paperwork."

The social worker slid the papers toward her. Handed her a pen. Ronnie's stomach quivered.

She tried to hold her voice steady when she asked what would happen to him if she committed him.

"Tomorrow they'll want to reassess him. Until then, we'll make him comfortable so he can sleep it off."

Ronnie remembered the words Jeff had hissed at her: *I will never forgive you for this.* Saw again the disgust on his face as he was led away in handcuffs. The signature line on the commitment paper undulated. The consequences of this decision seemed too massive to pin down.

Then she thought of Andrew and Will, out in the lobby, held hostage by CNN in bucket chairs when they needed to be sleeping in their beds.

The line solidified, bold and clear.

Ronnie took a deep breath and signed.

ronnie

A police officer strode into the fire hall and handed Corporal McNichol a piece of paper. She took some time to look it over.

"What is it?" Ronnie said.

"A list of reporters wanting an interview. Two requests for Janet, and a whole lot more for you."

"Like who?"

"The *Morning Call* in Allentown, the *Reading Eagle*, the *Potts Forge Times*, Channel 69, Maura Riley from *Action News*, and it goes on. Maybe a half dozen more television news reporters."

Corporal McNichol handed Ronnie the paper. "You're free to do what you want, but I worry about the effect that more choppers and vehicles might have on Jeff."

There was a time when Ronnie thought her name would be on such a list. She'd planned to be a journalist, not an interview subject. They'd likely ask, "How do you feel?" In answer, the blank space in her morning journal came to mind. She only knew that extricating herself from Jeff had suddenly become a more complex and wretched story than she could comprehend. And despite a safe physical remove, she was still trapped within it.

It was hard to believe any of them belonged here. How had this happened, when slipping into Jeff's life had been so sweet and easy?

The first morning she awoke at the farm, a few months after she and Jeff had started dating, Ronnie was thinking it was a good thing she'd entered under the cover of darkness or the loud clash between the green sheets, purple blanket, and vivid yellow-and-blue-flowered wallpaper peeling beside her would not have allowed rest. She picked up her clothes from the unfinished floor planks, tiptoed past the kerosene heater in the hallway, and headed for the bathroom.

Protected by the bliss of physical intimacy, she breezed over the orange shag carpeting pieced together on the bathroom floor and got in the shower. Once cold water slapped her awake—it took a few moments of fiddling to realize the hot and cold taps were reversed—she couldn't help but notice the walls' plastic gray tiles and mildewed paint.

When she left the bathroom, Jeff was dressed. "So, this is your house," she said. "Guess I was a little too distracted to see it last night."

He wrapped his arms around her and kissed her passionately. "And I aim to distract you again." He gave her an impish grin. "Come on. I need to show you something."

After crossing the rough subfloor of an empty room, he led her up a charming staircase with pine treads worn from centuries of use. Up ahead, however, she expected bats and squirrels. Before he reached the top, he pointed to the floorboards, now level with their eyes. "When my mother gave me the keys so I could take a look at the place, for some odd reason this floor was completely covered with tar. Even so, I was able to see what you see right now."

Ronnie ran her finger over the exposed edges. "Some of these boards must be eighteen, twenty inches wide."

"I'd never seen flooring like this before. Not outside of preserved historic homes anyway. It made me curious about this house's potential. So I bought it and got to work." He took her hand. "This was the result."

He led her the rest of the way up the stairs and into a handsomely renovated, painted, and completely empty attic.

"Wow." Ronnie took in the fresh sheetrock on the peaked ceiling, the exposed beams. "Why don't you use this as your bedroom?"

"I finished this for Fay, but she still couldn't see the potential in the house." Again, that impish smile. "I thought she could hang upside down from the beams."

The room offered an impressive endorsement of Jeff's handiwork. Into the low vertical walls on one side, he'd inserted and painted plywood cupboards and cubbies; on the other side, he'd built in the drawers and shelves of a bedroom suite. He had even crafted a clever hinged hamper and a closet that fit beneath the eaves.

"So why was there tar on the floor?"

"I keep wondering that myself. The place had stood empty for a while. Maybe because there was only plastic over the window holes when I bought it?"

"How on earth did you remove it?"

"What worked best was a blow-dryer. Once the tar was warm, I could scrape it off."

"That sounds like so much work."

"It did take a while," he said. He pointed to a few places where tar still streaked the wood, which Ronnie would have taken for natural markings.

Ronnie squatted by one of the end windows and looked out over the rolling landscape. Jeff explained that most of the land she could see belonged to his parents, whose house was beyond view on the side of the next hill.

"You told me it's been what, six or seven years since your wife left?" Ronnie said, standing. "Not that the place doesn't have a certain…charm, but if you're capable of doing work like this, why didn't you keep going?"

Jeff pulled Ronnie into one of his soul-enveloping hugs and whispered, "I was waiting to find the person I'd be doing it for. Turns out I may have known her for quite some time."

A shopping excursion that day left each of them proud new owners: he of a matching bed set, she of a little calico kitten Jeff bought her at the pet shop. Later, she tucked the kitten, Cupcake, into the collar of her shirt. She and Jeff lay back on the hammock in the yard, side by side, looking up at the stars through the branches above.

"You think you'll stay in bartending?" Ronnie said. "No other plans?"

"I'd like to start a business someday," Jeff said. "I love tools. Maybe I'll open a rental shop."

"Or maybe we should combine our skills and open a restaurant," Ronnie said.

"There's nothing better than an exquisite meal and fine wine." Jeff pulled her into a deep kiss. "Except maybe this."

"You do know how to keep a customer happy," she said, smiling.

"Or maybe we don't need jobs at all," Jeff said. "We could hole up here and homestead. Milk goats, chop wood, raise food, avoid the tax man." Ronnie laughed. He kissed her again and touched her on the end of her nose. "I feel like I could do anything with you by my side."

"This dreaming is fun, but I got a journalism degree for a reason," Ronnie said, although while looking into Jeff's eyes, and with his fingers tracing her ribs, that reason would not fully form. "Those jobs are drying up. I won't find one near here. I have applications out in New York City I'm still waiting to hear about, and one in Boston that sounds promising."

Jeff dug his foot into the ground to stop their swinging. "You do?"

"Don't worry," she said, reaching into her shirt to pet Cupcake. "Kitty cats can live in New York."

"But what about the horse?"

"I do believe they have laws about apartment horses—"

"Ronnie, I'm serious." He sat up; his voice grew urgent. "Please. Don't take those jobs. Let me call the *Inquirer* tomorrow. We'll find you something you can commute to."

He sounded serious all right, almost desperate. "Jeff, we've only been dating a few months."

"But I adore you, and I can't just up and leave." Jeff looked around. "This is my home. Where I belong."

How easy for him, to know where he belonged. Tagging along through her mother's marriages hadn't instilled the same confidence in Ronnie.

The light from the front porch light glinted off Jeff's face. When Ronnie touched it, her fingers came away damp. "Jeff, are you crying?"

"I love you, Ronnie. I love you and I can't imagine my life without you. Stay here. Marry me. We'll renovate the house however you want it, and we'll create a little piece of heaven here. Together."

Ronnie had never before inspired anyone's tears. She'd never even seen her own distractible mother cry. She hadn't realized how very much she mattered to Jeff. But it had taken all of a moment for her youthful crush to blaze again the night her mother took her to the hotel to see him. And he was so settled, with a home and a life she could slip right into.

Maybe Jeff was right. Maybe this was exactly where she belonged.

janet

J anet was tired of accepting fate and wanted to rail against it. Determined to punish something, she slapped the table.

"If she hadn't committed him last month," she said, tipping her head toward Ronnie, "none of this would be happening. Now my son is surrounded by police. Look at all the trouble she caused."

Her tirade was cut short when a uniformed police officer came into the room. They all watched as he sat at another table to fill out paperwork.

"We don't act based on past behavior, Mrs. Farnham," Corporal McNichol said. "This is about what's happening today."

"Jeff's upset," Janet said. "Our families are so close, and Ronnie wants to divorce him. He's beside himself, that's all."

"I understand that you love your son and feel protective of him," Corporal McNichol said. "But do you see the officer at the table over there? The man who just walked in? He's currently charging your son with reckless endangerment and aggravated assault for turning his weapon on the police. This is a serious matter."

"I've heard enough," Janet said, rising.

"Don't you want him to get the help he needs?" Ronnie said.

"Listen," Corporal McNichol said. "We understand that there are extenuating circumstances. And Jeff has no criminal record. The main reason we're charging him is to force him into rehab. If he doesn't agree to it, he'll face jail time."

Janet looked down at the floor around her chair, as if to collect her things, but she had nothing other than the purse already hanging from her arm.

The corporal added something to her notes. If she were writing about Jeff, or her, Janet wouldn't know—the notes were either in shorthand, a foreign language, or chicken scratch worse than Jeff's.

"So this commitment—does Jeff have a history of mental illness?"

"No," Janet said. She looked straight at Corporal McNichol, wondering whether Ronnie or Beverly would challenge her.

"Does he take medication?"

Janet had finally felt she had this interview under control. It bothered her that she had to look to Ronnie for the answer to this question.

Ronnie shook her head. "His psychiatrist prescribed detox. But Jeff wouldn't go."

"He's worked at that hotel for twenty years," Janet said, directing her comment to Ronnie. "These days, that's as loyal as they come. Why would you go around calling him an alcoholic?"

"Because it's the truth. Someone has to face this problem."

Oh, Janet saw the problem all right. Her son had no way to decompress from all his wife's nagging.

"The only alcoholic I ever knew was a homeless person who'd sleep in the gutters near campus when I was in college," Janet said. "Jeff's not like that. He's made a good home for you and the boys."

"You've met more alcoholics than you know, Mrs. Farnham," Corporal McNichol said. "Probably a third of the people in our country suffer from alcohol disorders."

"I didn't want to believe it was all that bad either," Ronnie said, softening. "I thought we were having interpersonal problems. An inability to communicate. But then he had a really hard time with the changes at the hotel, and there were health problems, and—"

"Goodness, Ronnie, everyone strains their back from time to time," Janet said. "Let it go."

"You must have noticed he's lost weight. He was 165 when we

married, and when we went to the doctor about his back, he weighed 135. And the periodontal disease—"

"What's that?"

"He goes to bed every night with booze on his breath. He's in danger of losing his teeth." The potential loss of that adorable gap-toothed smile to a set of perfect dentures still threatened her composure. "But he won't use the rinse or have the recommended procedure or even brush his teeth before he goes to bed."

"I suppose you think I never taught him to brush his teeth."

"Jeff's a grown man, Janet. I'm talking about him, not you. And I understand you cut a check so you know all too well about the debt. But I took a look around the farm. You might be surprised at what I found."

"You'd find a beautiful house he fixed up for you," Janet said. "Horses he keeps for you and the boys. A farm store he built so you two could work side by side. A cornfield for the maze you dreamed up that's half on my land."

"That's what I'd always seen too," Ronnie said. "Until I started digging, and found items that were a lot more menacing."

"Like what?" Janet said.

"He'd been stockpiling booze."

Ronnie paused dramatically, as if it might come as a shock to Janet that a bartender would keep a supply of liquor. Janet refused to reward her little performance with a show of emotion.

That's when Ronnie added, "And guns."

Janet bit down on the inside of her cheek to keep her pain from showing.

ronnie

Since Ronnie didn't get the boys home until four in the morning after Jeff's commitment, she let them sleep in. She rose with the sun, reached under the guest room bed to pull out her journal, and opened to a fresh page. Too tired to write out a narrative of last night's suicide scare, she resorted to a list of bullets.

- *I feel as powerless divorcing Jeff as I did in my marriage.*
- *I do not want to watch what's happening to him.*
- *I don't think it helps that I've been picking up Jeff's slack.*
- *But I do not want to become a nag.*
- *I do not want to let Jeff manipulate me into staying married.*
- *I don't want to manipulate Jeff either. But.*
- *I worry for the boys.*

Ronnie shoved the journal under the bed, woke the boys, and drove them to school late.

She then went on a mission to rid the farm of booze.

When she and Jeff started dating, they were both working in restaurants, and drinking after work was typical. It was the single life. Ronnie left that behind once they started a family, but Jeff never did. He drank habitually, even during one intestinal flu. When Ronnie questioned this behavior, he'd countered with a smile and a quip: "The alcohol kills the germs." And he'd kicked the bug, so Ronnie wasn't overly concerned. It wasn't like he ever got drunk. While she was growing up, her mother was also a fan of happy hour, sipping a cocktail as she made dinner, and often kissed Ronnie good night with the same sweet vermouth on her lips. To Ronnie, it was the taste of love.

Plus, Ronnie understood that Jeff wanted a variety of bottles on hand for entertaining. Only now did she realize how long it had been since they'd entertained. Or since she'd had any of the scotch from the bottle Jeff kept on hand just for her.

Four at a time, Ronnie took more than a dozen liquor bottles off the kitchen counter and poured the contents down the drain, following suit with the Courvoisier, Amaretto, Bénédictine, and other after-dinner drinks Jeff kept in a living room cabinet. It dawned on her that this might not be the healthiest thing for their cesspool. As it leached into the soil, would the alcohol kill the grass, just as it was killing Jeff?

The worst part was that this was not all the booze.

She grabbed the barn keys from one of the hooks on the antique rack and went out to where Jeff kept the rest of his stash.

Jeff had explained that when people contracted with the hotel for a wedding, they were charged for complete bottles of opened liquor; anything remaining in those bottles could not be resold at the front bar. Until the booze was claimed, the opened bottles were held in a special closet.

Since few newlyweds had returned for it over the years, Jeff had helped himself to that alcohol. Ronnie knew they had a couple boxes of clear booze in half-gallon containers that Jeff had marked with a *V* for vodka or *G* for gin. They'd tapped the supply before, for summer picnics. In an attempt to be thorough, Ronnie headed up to the barn to see if any remained.

Poking around in the clean storage room as well as two dirtier grain rooms she didn't frequent, she couldn't believe how much booze Jeff had amassed. She found box after box full of intact bottles and dozens of half-gallon containers.

No way could Ronnie imagine putting all of that down the drain. Why try? Even if she did get rid of it all, Jeff could easily replace it.

Yet she had the need to make a statement, and the warm September day inspired an idea. She loaded boxes of bottles into her garden cart, wheeled it out to the driveway, and dribbled the booze over the warm gravel to evaporate.

By the time she was done, Ronnie was sticky from the booze, coated with dust from the boxes, and dizzy from the scent of a six-hundred-square-foot evaporating cocktail. She imagined desperate, addicted souls from miles around clawing their way up the drive to lick its stones.

Her hands were jittery; she desperately needed sleep. But the boys would be home in ninety minutes, and she still had one more change she was determined to enact. One that made her feel like a thief.

Ronnie searched the farm for Jeff's guns.

She started in the attic crawl space, where she knew Jeff stowed his handguns. For a dozen years, those guns had created a knot of tension in her home. Yes, they were in a locked gun cabinet; yes, the ammunition was stored separately; and yes, they were hard to see or reach, tucked as they were behind Christmas wrapping paper and luggage. But if Jeff didn't ever plan to use the guns, why did he own them? Andrew and Will slept in the attic, separated from the weapons' violent potential by only a sheet of drywall and a transparent acrylic pane that could be unlocked with a key the size of Ronnie's thumbnail.

On her hands and knees, she pulled luggage and wrapping paper and old college textbooks out of the crawl space, went into its farthest reaches, and inched the gun case toward her. She returned the other items to where she found them and opened the little drawer in the bottom of the case where Jeff kept the key.

Empty.

Maybe she remembered wrong. She went down to the first floor, dragged a kitchen chair over to the coat closet, and felt around on the highest shelf, where Jeff stored the ammunition. She pulled down box after box, looking inside, but found nothing but bullets and shotgun shells of various sizes.

Where would he have put that key?

Then again, the last one to use it may have been Ronnie.

Back before the boys were born, Ronnie had found one of her hens ambling around the chicken pen with her innards dragging along the droppings-encrusted floor.

While she and Jeff loved to say they lived on a farm, neither of them had the fortitude required of livestock farmers. They were "farm pet owners"; not one of their chickens was headed to the stew pot. After Ronnie's attempts to wash and reinsert the oviduct per Internet instructions resulted in no permanent resolution, the hen was facing an almost hopeless situation inviting infection and a painful death.

Ronnie was practical enough to know you don't take a chicken to the vet and pay to have it euthanized. She tried to imagine Miss Scarlett's silky neck feathers beneath her fingertips—the twist and the snap—and could not. When it came to animals, Jeff was neither the doctoring nor the killing sort. He would be no help.

As suitable options dwindled, Ronnie remembered the gun Jeff had insisted on loading to protect them from a dangerous and presumably armed prisoner who had escaped from Graterford Prison, the maximum-security facility some twenty miles away. Jeff had showed Ronnie how to load and shoot a small .22-caliber revolver, about the size of a starter pistol, to keep by their bed.

Because Ronnie would not use a gun in a way that might result in a man's death, after a long tug of wills, he agreed to load it with something other than bullets.

He used bird shot.

She didn't want her farm associated in any way with what she was about to do, so she tucked Miss Scarlett under her arm and carried her onto Janet's land, through the woods to a small clearing. Ronnie set her down and put a hand on her back to calm her—to calm herself—and slipped the loaded gun from her jacket pocket.

It couldn't have weighed more than a can of chick peas, yet she felt its emotional heft.

Then she took her place in a long line of cowards who put a gun between them and the act they were about to perpetrate: she stood up, stepped back one pace, and fired.

And fired, and fired. Bird shot did not quickly kill a bird the size of Miss Scarlett, who was hysterical with pain and fear. She flopped around like the heart in Ronnie's chest. Batting her wings until they were wet with blood, she spun around, seeking her attacker. With two more shots, she finally lay still. Ronnie stood until her breathing calmed and her ears once again adjusted to the rustle of the grasses surrounding them. She sank to the ground beside the still hen and cried for the horror of it all. Later, while burying her, Ronnie thought that euthanizing seemed so much more virtuous when a gun wasn't involved.

That afternoon, she got another red hen from a friend down the street and never told Jeff what she had done.

She did, however, remove the remaining cartridges and put the gun back into storage. And…what had she done with the key?

Maybe she was missing the obvious place. She checked the key rack. It held several rings with all manner of odd keys that probably no longer had a use. She ran back up to the attic with several of the smaller keys.

Not a single one fit, and she was running out of time. With no other choice, she lugged the entire gun case down to her Suburban. But there were long guns as well. Before they'd had kids, Jeff had kept them on the landing by the basement stairs. She narrowed her search to every locked outbuilding that had a clean storage area. She knew Jeff was particular about the guns, because although she'd never seen him clean one, she knew he kept a pair of white cotton gloves in his dresser for this purpose.

She gathered all of the guns she could find and laid them out in the back of her Suburban. There were nine in all, pistols and revolvers and longer guns she did not know how to distinguish.

Now loaded symbols of her husband's instability, Ronnie had hated to touch the guns, let alone drive anywhere with them. A Suburban was nothing but windows, she now realized—windows that would let anyone see these guns. What if she had to stop to get around an accident, or if she was pulled over for the burned-out turn signal she hadn't gotten around to replacing? For all she knew, the cargo could be illicit. She didn't know if Jeff had licenses for all of these guns or if he was even required to have them. She didn't know how to check for ammunition without shooting off a toe or how to arrange the gun so it wouldn't go off when the car hit a bump and blow a hole through the gas tank.

In the end, the enclosed trunk of Jeff's Altima seemed a better choice. Ronnie hoisted the locked handgun case into it, shoving it toward the front of the car as if it were a suitcase, then piled the long guns behind it.

Exhausted as she was, she was in no danger of falling asleep. Her fingers clenched the wheel; her shoulders braced.

Reminding herself to breathe, she drove well under the speed limit the entire ten miles to her mother's house.

beverly

Beverly had been watering the tomato plant on her balcony when Ronnie pulled in the parking lot to her apartment.

"Glad I caught you home," Ronnie said when Beverly met her at the security door. Following along like bait on a hook, Beverly listened to her reel out the story of Jeff's commitment as she took trip after trip to the car for the unthinkable purpose of unloading guns into Beverly's house. Ronnie was on a mission at this point and hadn't noticed Beverly's neighbor come out with his trash. She grabbed Ronnie's wrist to stop her so the guy could wheel his can to the curb without fearing for his life.

"Mom, can you take one end?"

All that was left in the trunk was a display case with clear acrylic sliding doors on the front. Full of handguns. Beverly's feet froze to the macadam.

"It's not all that heavy, just ungainly."

And dangerous. And scary. And deadly. The case was lined with bloodred velvet. "What if they all go off at once?"

Ronnie gave the case a heave—she was so strong, Beverly thought, so much stronger than Beverly would ever be—and headed to the house again. "Hasn't happened yet, so I'm hoping it won't now." Ronnie climbed the steps and said over her shoulder, "Since you're still standing there, could you at least close the trunk?"

Inside, Beverly looked at all the firepower laid out on her kitchen table, now set as if they'd been preparing for some sort of crime family rehearsal dinner. She was glad Janet didn't have to witness this. Ronnie said, "Do you have someplace safe we can store these for a while?"

When Beverly had downsized into this apartment after her last divorce, that was a question she had never thought to ask herself.

"Mom, I've got to get home to the boys."

Beverly's vision blurred as if her eyes had focused in slightly different directions. "The coat closet, I guess." Ronnie dove in, pushing jackets and umbrellas aside. At one point, Beverly's faux fur lined her daughter's back like the hide of a bear.

"I'll do this," Beverly muttered. "I'll do this for Jeff."

janet

J anet knew all about Jeff's guns.

Not a quarter mile from where she sat in the firehouse stood the Bartlesville Rod and Gun Club, where Jeff first attended a shooting demonstration with his father. It was the spring of Jeff's sophomore year, and after a second try had not gained him a spot on the basketball team, Jerry decided to encourage Jeff's interest in the gun club with an air rifle and a three-dollar junior membership. A shooting education class was just forming, so Jerry signed him up.

Jeff took to it immediately. Being such a huge animal lover, Jeff had no interest in hunting, so he soon dropped the gun club membership with its antler- and jerky-crazed members. He was interested in marksmanship. Jerry helped him set up a course on their property that met NRA guidelines, and over the years, Jeff started to amass his Distinguished Expert qualifications.

Jerry continued to inflame Jeff's newfound interest, picking up secondhand long guns at local shows and estate sales that he thought Jeff might be interested in, adding some pistols once Jeff turned twenty-one.

But it was for his eighteenth birthday that Jerry had bought Jeff a shotgun—the one her son was holding now—and Janet wanted to damn him to hell for it.

And, of course, she knew all about the booze too. She'd been helping herself to it for years.

11:00 a.m.

ronnie

Sharing the story of Jeff's psych commitment with Corporal McNichol, her mother, and her mother-in-law had Ronnie all twisted up. It was hard enough to live through the first time. Her bones ached, her abdomen cramped, her head pounded—and all of this was made worse by having to sit on a metal folding chair for two hours. She needed relief. She stood to stretch out the fronts of her hips and realized she was still carrying several sets of car keys in her pockets. She pulled them out and laid them on the table. With Jeff secluded, she alone had the power to go somewhere, yet here she was, stuck.

"Mom, you have any painkillers?"

"I could use some too." Beverly found ibuprofen in her purse, and on their way to the drinking fountain near the restrooms, she shook out two for each of them.

Ronnie could sense the pending relief. Was this why Jeff drank? Was accumulating emotion twisting his body as well, causing pain that only the drink could relieve? Ronnie filled her mouth with water, stood, and popped in two of the painkillers. Maybe she knew something about chronic intoxication. Intimately. Her drug of choice: Jeffrey Farnham.

The way Ronnie recalled it, they had only been home from their honeymoon a few minutes before she and Jeff changed into overalls and started steaming off wallpaper and hacking at loose plaster.

They soon sorted out their roles: Ronnie was the room designer, carpentry crew, and gofer, and Jeff was the mastermind whose carpentry expertise could bring the ideas to fruition.

Ronnie wanted to expose the original wood trim on the second floor. Eager to see what it would look like, they slathered paint remover onto baseboards, windowsills, door frames, and doors and scraped off numerous layers of paint. It was only when they butted up against the stubborn red, green, and brown layers beneath that they learned about milk paint, a turn-of-the-century product farmers would make from ingredients found right on the farm. The wood had absorbed the milk paint into its porous surface.

"We're going to have to sand this off," Jeff said.

"That'll be a chore."

"Yep."

"It'll take a long time."

"Yep." Jeff paused and raised an eyebrow. "But we'd be doing it together."

Ronnie smiled. "I suppose we're wasting time standing here talking about it then."

Jeff unbuttoned her denim shirt, slipped his hands around her waist, and kissed her bare shoulder.

"How long do you think this renovation is going to take?"

He pulled her hips to his. "Mmm. Twenty years," he mumbled, his mouth full of her. "At the very least."

They heard a knock on the door downstairs. Jeff leaned his forehead against Ronnie's. "That timing sucks."

Ronnie giggled and buttoned up her shirt. "Don't worry. I'm not going anywhere."

It was the nurse from the life insurance company. Jeff had wanted to set up the policy right away, one of the many ways he was assuring Ronnie that he would care for her no matter what life threw their way. Jeff easily passed the physical. Yet after filling out the lifestyle survey, the nurse informed them that his premiums would be higher than most. Ronnie had expected the smoking might factor in, but there would be additional costs since both bartending and farming were occupations with elevated suicide risk.

Ronnie and Jeff had looked at each other and laughed. They didn't need risk assessment to prove what they knew in their hearts: love would keep them alive.

The renovation work was rewarding and the twenty-year plan on track as they slowly but surely completed the rooms on the second floor. Ronnie struggled to reframe her career expectations. She did not earn a paycheck or time off, although Jeff effusively praised her efforts; they could only afford to do such an extensive renovation because of all the work she did for free. Each night she would wash a rainbow of dust particles from her skin and blow her nose until its contents ran clear. She worked for a demanding boss, but he adored her, believed in her, provided her with all the materials she needed to succeed, and then took her to bed every night. It was the house, the farm, Jeff, and Ronnie. Life was simple. They were happy.

But over time, the drilling and sanding and sawing drained her, as if it were dust from her own drying soul falling to the floor. Ronnie was learning new skills, but the fact that she was not using her formal education always bothered her. College had allowed her access to such an interesting variety of people who stimulated her socially and creatively and intellectually. Life had been more complex. She had been happier.

Such thoughts would sneak up on Ronnie in the early years of their marriage, and when they did, she would go out and sit on an old concrete slab attached to a mostly collapsed pig barn to entertain thoughts of becoming a journalist in private. She'd tried, once, to share her anxiety with Jeff: she wanted to fix up the farm to create a strong sense of home *and* have a career that allowed her to engage with the world. She'd said, "You make me feel so loved. But sometimes I feel like my mind is wilting, you know?" And he'd answered gently, "I don't have a clue what you're talking about. But you're great, Ronnie, and you're beautiful, and our house will be so perfect. You're going to be just fine." He looked at her with those sparkly blue eyes and his warm smile and wrapped his big hand around hers—and Ronnie chose comfort over answers.

Yet the questions kept returning. Why couldn't she be more like Jeff, satisfied with his day-to-day life? Why did she have to set her sights on some distant future and let its lack of definition devil her? Here on the farm, simplicity surrounded her. Apples and pears filled out until they pulled their branches toward the earth; whatever Jeff and Ronnie didn't pick dropped to the ground for the bees and the groundhogs. The late-day sun caught the red in her horse's mane as its teeth tore at the grass; when its lips reached out, it was for more of the same. Every day the chickens scratched at the ground and dusted their feathers in the dirt.

This pastoral setting was never calm, though. Not really. An ever-present breeze whistled through the outbuildings and stirred things up on this side of their lush hill—drifting snow in the winter, dispersing pollen in spring, spreading dandelions in summer, and scattering leaves in the fall. The wood beyond the property line would not be kept at bay, its vines and bramble and sumac snatching at the fence.

Their little farm represented more bounty than Ronnie had ever dreamed of having at this stage of her life. And it should have been enough. Yet her soul felt as rent as the concrete pad she sat upon, from whose deep fissures slithered the occasional snake.

To accommodate Jeff's growing bevy of tools, they soon built a new structure on the site of that old pig barn. Ronnie lost her decrepit hideout; he gained a workshop. They overlaid rifts in the foundation with fresh concrete that buried her fears. They framed the building, sided it with wood, and lined it, Ronnie straining to hold unwieldy four-by-eight-foot sheets of particleboard over her head while Jeff screwed them into place. Jeff had never been happier than he was when designing this space, choosing with great care the locations of his radial arm saw and other large pieces. He outfitted the building with rolling cabinets to house innumerable hand tools and stocked shelving with boxes of screws and nails. He spent hours out there, organizing and labeling inventory as if it were his personal hardware store, although they would come to laugh at Murphy's law of tool ownership: you always need the item you don't own, requiring yet another run to the store.

"Do we really need a router?" Ronnie said. She hadn't known what one was until theirs was delivered.

"You saw how much custom door trim costs. It'll be cheaper to replace the rotting window trim if I make it myself."

Later they'd buy a cement mixer because it was cheaper than renting one for the number of weeks they'd need to use it. Jeff used his own drill press to make Shaker-style peg racks for the bedrooms because the materials would cost less than purchasing that many prefabricated racks. They saved money on lumber by ripping their own scrap boards on his table saw and cutting them to length on his radial arm saw. They did almost all the work themselves and patted themselves on their stiff backs for their thriftiness.

Hand-fashioning this farm meant everything to Jeff. When a contractor Jeff had hired for the bathrooms suggested they were investing in the property beyond what it could ever pay back, Jeff said, "Why would we ever sell? We're creating the home of our dreams."

Ronnie quietly let go of her own dreams, only half formed, and latched on to the twenty-year plan. She was married now, and Jeff's dreams were big enough for them both.

But at night, Ronnie was often troubled by a vivid nightmare in which her car would break down and she would ask for Jeff's help. Auto mechanics was not one of his many areas of handy expertise, but in the dream he'd nonetheless look under the hood of her car. She'd ask, "What's the problem?" and he'd look back at her with a look so disturbing she'd wake up with a cry. She'd struggle to reorient. Renovated room. Coordinated sheets. Gentle, loving husband. When her breathing calmed, she'd snuggle next to Jeff and allow his

janet

One thing Janet loved about Ronnie: she was never too busy to entertain her with stories about the boys. Each one added more personality and humor to an ever-burbling spring that bathed Janet's heart with its only source of joy. That made a particular call from Ronnie, received the second Saturday in September, one that Janet would never forget.

"Jeff's in the hospital," Ronnie said. "I'm sorry to tell you this by phone, but I didn't have time to come over."

"Why? What's the matter?"

"I guess there's no easy way to say this. Jeff threatened to kill himself. He's in the psychiatric unit at Reading Hospital."

Janet braced herself against her kitchen counter.

"He wants visitors. You need to see him."

"I can't, Ronnie."

"I'll go, because he's asked for me, but I'm the one divorcing him. He needs support from someone else. Visiting hours start at two. I'll pick you up at one fifteen."

The locked unit. The buzzing in. Ronnie wringing her hands and pacing. Janet's heart flopping around in her chest so wildly she thought she might not live to see her son join them in the lounge. She almost didn't recognize him, looking so thin. When had he lost weight? Jerry had kept his athletic physique until his final illness; Jeff looked sunken with his beltless pants slipping down on his hips. Even in this state, though, he hardly registered Janet's presence. His eyes, as always, were just for Ronnie.

Ronnie quickly claimed the only single chair; Janet sat next to Jeff on the couch.

"Thanks for coming," he said, giving Ronnie such a sweet smile that Janet had to focus on the cover of a magazine lying on the nearby coffee table to control her tears.

"How are you feeling?" Janet said, her voice tight.

"Better. Getting plenty of rest. Here. You can give these to the boys."

He reached past Janet with two small wooden animals, a turtle and an owl. Ronnie took them. "We have to do crafts. I painted them."

Their splotchy imperfection invoked the little Jeff who used to run to Janet with his art projects after school. She'd beg him to tell her the story of each painting to hide the fact that she hadn't a clue to its subject. It wasn't until shop class, in junior high, that his artistry began to shine.

Ronnie put the animals in her pocket.

"So," he said.

"Yes?" Ronnie said.

If this were earlier in the marriage, Janet thought, even a few years ago, they'd be touching by now. It had always both humiliated and thrilled Janet to see that her son had the comfort of the physical intimacy that had been missing in her own marriage. Ronnie's reticence now stirred Janet to reach over and put her hand on his. Jeff looked at her as if wondering what she was up to before moving his hand and turning back to Ronnie.

"I wanted to tell you, face-to-face, that pressuring you to change your mind about the divorce was a stupid stunt. It won't work. I get that now. I apologize."

"Okay." Ronnie shifted in her chair and recrossed her legs with the elegance of someone wearing a pencil skirt, not jeans smudged at the knee. "Thank you."

Janet waited, but this seemed to be the end of what they had to say to each other. "Is the food okay here?" she said. A stupid question. Almost any food was better than what she could make. She didn't have a knack for anything beyond her Campbell soup cookbook. That one fact could account for why Jeff worked in a facility with a restaurant.

He looked at Janet. "I didn't mean to scare you."

But he did scare her and was scaring her now. The hills of Bartlesville were full of strange characters, but she knew nothing about the kind of mental illness that landed someone in a locked psychiatric unit. He seemed so calm—more peaceful than normal, in fact—that she still wondered how much of his presence here was due to Ronnie's overreaction.

She really wished Ronnie would say something, but her lips pressed together in silence.

"Jeff, I don't understand why you're here," Janet said. If the divorce had him feeling blue, he should pull himself together and fight for his marriage. Just last week, when she'd given him the money, he'd seemed so relieved. Happier. "If you need more money, say so."

Ronnie leaned forward and put her face in her hand. Jeff smiled and shook his head. "At least you're predictable, Mother."

Shouting came from down the hall, then a scream that had Janet looking for the exit signs. This unit, closed up so tight like the hospital's shameful secret, did not have enough air for her. She needed to get out of this building and have a drink.

She stood and found the patience to say, "I hope you feel better soon, Jeff."

It took Ronnie but a moment to follow suit. It broke Janet's heart the way Jeff looked to his wife for some indication of love. But if she harbored any, it was locked away as tight as her son.

All Ronnie said was, "Good luck, Jeff."

ronnie

Early Sunday morning, the third day Jeff was in the hospital, the boys came down to join Ronnie in the guest room bed. She'd been up and down the stairs with them all night. First Will had random leg pains, which eventually woke Andrew, who then heard scratching that he feared was a bat. Ronnie turned on the lights in the crawl space to show it was nothing, only to find a dried-up bat on the floor, so the first good sleep any of them had gotten was when they had all piled in together.

When Ronnie finally climbed out of bed for good on Sunday morning, she stood and stretched—and her legs crumpled beneath her as the world went black.

Ronnie heard Will's cries as if from afar. "Mom! Andrew, wake up! Mom fell down!"

Soon both her sons were by her side.

"I'm okay."

Andrew pulled her to a sitting position, and Will tried to brace her with his shoulder. "Let me sit here a sec." She sat with her head dropped forward between her legs.

"Did you hit your head?" Andrew said.

"I'm not hurt. Um, my blood pressure may be low." Ronnie rolled to her hands and knees and slowly stood. Her boys needed to believe that someone in this house could hold it together.

"Thanks for your help, guys. Go on down and get some breakfast.

And can you let Max out, Andrew, and feed him? I'm just going to rest here a bit longer."

"Are you sure you're okay?" Andrew said.

Ronnie climbed back onto her bed. She didn't know a goddamn thing. "Yep. Now scoot."

As soon as their feet hit the stairs, Ronnie reached beneath her bed for her journal. She turned to a fresh page and dated it.

I blacked out again today. This time, I scared the boys.

She flipped back through her recent entries. Last week, she'd blacked out while hitching the trailer to the tractor so she could muck out the horse stalls and came to with her rear end planted in the dirty straw. The week before that, she'd woken up at the kitchen table at one p.m., her sandwich in her hand.

Back on today's page, she wrote:

I'm losing it. Maybe I should reserve a room at the loony bin for me.

When Ronnie had started journaling three years earlier, loath to leave the warmth of her husband's side, she'd wait until daylight and bring her journal into bed with them. It only took a few instances of Jeff pushing it to the floor and saying, "Come on, baby, you don't need that while you have me," to realize the opposite was true. Soon she was leaping from the bed at five thirty and snuggling with Max on the guest room bed to invest in this relationship with the page before the kids or Jeff awoke. Who cared if that meant she got only four or five hours of sleep? At long last, someone was paying careful attention to her ideas and feelings. If Jeff felt threatened by that, what could she do? He had relinquished his role.

And once she had entered a relationship in which she was being heard, she was powerless to leave it. That was the great tragedy of her marriage.

She remembered that first day of journaling and how her words flooded the page like an advancing tide that could no longer be sandbagged. She wrote for three hours, and the page listened attentively.

And Ronnie realized: that's what Janet always used to do.

While her own mother flitted off to tend to this or that, Janet was the one Ronnie would turn to when she needed an ear. Janet would sit forward in her chair, her eyebrows raised, her slight smile begging for a story. When they were together, Janet made Ronnie feel like she was the only being in the world worthy of her attention.

And when she and Jeff had first gotten together, Jeff had offered that same focused delight. But when Jeff became the source of the drama instead of the healing and Ronnie reached out to Janet once more, her mother-in-law was no longer as attentive. Her eyes, so like Jeff's, were not as bright. Ronnie worried she might be ill, but when she suggested that Janet get a checkup, her words bounced off her as they had Jeff, making Ronnie feel double the loss.

Ronnie heard a knock on the guest room door. "Yes?"

"Did you sleep enough?"

Ronnie smiled. "Yes, Will."

Andrew opened the door, and Will carried in a breakfast tray. Ronnie set her journal aside so he could put it on her lap.

"There's toast, cereal, orange juice, and an egg."

The toast was perfect, the Rice Krispies milk bloated, and the egg still in the shell. Ronnie held it up.

"I told you it was dumb," Andrew said.

"I didn't know how to fix it, or I would have."

The egg already had her tearing up. She could only point to the glass that held a bunch of purple asters and one saucer-size Queen Anne's lace. Her favorites. Her sons knew her so much better than Jeff did. Her soon-to-be ex had plunged them fifty dollars more into debt for a dozen long-stemmed roses for her birthday last week, leaving her angry and bewildered.

"There were still a few left at the side of the driveway," Andrew said. He gave her such a sweet smile. "We love you."

"Come here." She gave them each a big hug and told them she'd be down shortly.

"That reminds me," Andrew said. "We were out of milk so I had to use hazelnut creamer."

Ronnie smiled. "Guess we'd better squeeze in some grocery shopping later." She ate the toast, drank the juice, and flushed the cereal.

At the store that afternoon, Will picked up a dozen Hostess doughnuts.

"Now, Will, we don't need to be spending money on doughnuts. Check on the side. Pretty sure it says, 'Nutritional value: zero.'"

Will gave her a stern look and put them into the cart. "You've got to eat some fattening stuff, Mom. You're collapsing."

"Better get ice cream too. It's full of calcium," said Andrew, her ice-cream lover, label reader, and eternal opportunist. "I finished the chocolate so we'll need more."

Ronnie tried to enjoy this special attention from her sons, but it only reminded her of a darkness she could not hold at bay. If Jeff did not repeat the threat of suicide in the hospital, his involuntary commitment would come to its legal, five-day end the day after tomorrow. Ronnie would have to bring back into her home the shadow of the man who had been the love of her life, the man she was planning to leave, and the man who had threatened gun violence in that same home while their children slept—and she didn't think she had the strength to do it.

The image of him being taken away in handcuffs, which had disconcerted and then comforted Ronnie, was starting to fade.

ronnie

On Monday, before going to meet with Jeff and the hospital psychiatrist, Ronnie sat in Jeff's Altima in the driveway at the farm. She'd take his car to pick him up. She'd already wasted too much gas going back and forth to the hospital in her oversize Suburban.

She put the key in the ignition but didn't turn it. It occurred to her that beside her, in the center compartment, she might find Jeff's wallet. He never carried it with him, since it was a huge fistful of a thing.

If she took a look at it, this would be the third time she spied on her husband. The first two times had ended in damning revelations. Her fingers drummed on the center compartment. Did she really want to know what secrets it contained?

More than two years ago, during the first week of April, Ronnie needed to get a form for her taxes to prepare for the next week's appointment with the accountant. Jeff had said he'd fish the form out for her that morning but then picked up an additional day shift before the banquet he was working at the hotel that night. So while Jeff was at work, Ronnie went out to the shop, and the corner of it he used as an office, to look for her form. From the moment she opened the door, Ronnie felt like she was trespassing.

Why? she wondered. This was her property too. It was their joint tax return, her own 1099 she sought. Yet the woodworking shop was Jeff's domain. She tiptoed across the concrete floor, past the table saw and vise, and touched as little as possible on her way toward the records her husband kept private.

Receipts and papers stuck out from overstuffed desk drawers. This wasn't like him. Had he never gotten organized after moving the records out here? Hoping the filing cabinet was in better shape, Ronnie slid a drawer open as soundlessly as possible and lifted out an accordion file that suggested an orderly place to start her search. Inside were preprinted pockets labeled January through December. She reached into February, when her 1099 would have arrived. But she only found receipts, all charged to Diner's Club. She glanced toward the door before flipping to the slot for April—maybe he'd filed it there because of their tax appointment—and found dozens more receipts, all charged to American Express.

A different card's receipts occupied each slot. How many credit cards did they have?

Her senses on high alert, Ronnie flipped through the pockets, adding numbers from the most recent statements. She heard an exasperated blowing of lips. She looked up, hand clutched to her heart, but no one was there. She heard it again. It was one of the horses in the turn-in shed next door. Scanning quickly, she figured she and Jeff must owe some $50,000 in credit card debt.

Ronnie packed everything away the way she had found it, blew the sawdust from her 1099, which had been sitting on a haphazard pile of papers on top of the desk, and left the shop. After she put the boys to bed that night, she hunkered down in the living room until Jeff got home.

"Hey." Jeff jiggled her shoulder. "What are you doing in here?"

Ronnie pushed herself up from the couch cushion and squinted up at him. "I was waiting for you. What time is it?"

"Two," he said. He sat on the couch beside her and slipped his arm around her. His breath smelled like cigarettes and coffee. "It's been a long time since you waited up for me."

"That's because we have two little people who'll be getting up in five hours." She scooted farther away and turned toward him. "I had to go out to the shop and get my 1099 from the magazine. I got quite an eyeful. All those receipts—I want to know exactly how much we owe, Jeff."

"It's not like we're in trouble or anything."

"We're in a huge amount of debt."

"Why do we need to get out of debt? I always pay more than the minimum—"

"What's the total?"

A reckoning from her was apparently so unexpected that it rendered him speechless. "I don't know off the top of my head. It'll take a while to pull that information together. And I can't do it now. I have to finish getting ready for our tax appointment in the morning."

"The accumulating interest will destroy us. I want you to cut up the cards until we get these paid off."

"It's not so easy to get new cards these days. I'll just stop charging."

"Cut them up, Jeff."

"I'll keep a Visa and an American Express. We'll need them to finish the renovation."

"I'll agree to keeping them for emergencies. As for the renovation, we may have to reassess."

"Come on, Ronnie, look at this room." The walls were covered in mint green sand paint; they'd all suffered abrasions from it. An old section of carpet covered a patch of the rough subfloor. The couches looked tired and threadbare. "We only have the basement and this living room left."

"We can create a strategy once you tell me the full amount of the debt. If anything were to happen to you, I don't want to be left holding a financial mess I didn't know about."

That year, Ronnie thought it best to go along to the tax appointment, where Jeff performed a financial sleight of hand Ronnie hadn't known possible: he paid their income taxes with a credit card.

The second time she spied on Jeff was a year ago, and she was sitting right in this car, on this driveway.

She'd been walking past the Altima on her way to do barn chores one morning when something caught her eye—a bevy of Styrofoam cups littering the passenger side floor. Jeff poured himself a cup of coffee before leaving for work each night, to help keep him awake on the dark quiet roads, but he never tossed them on the floor like this.

The fact that she'd seen him flat-out drunk the night before— while celebrating Ronnie's birthday at a classy restaurant, no less— set her senses on alert. When paying the bill, he couldn't even target the line at the bottom and had scrawled his name across the entire ticket. Ronnie's anger at having to drive him home had turned to concern when she found the vial of Jeff's new arthritis medication by the sink, with its warning not to be taken with alcohol.

Finding him sprawled across the bed in his clothes, Ronnie made sure he was breathing before abandoning him for the guest room. But even in morning's hopeful light, she could not shake the image of him spilling onto the driveway when she opened the door of the Suburban for him, and the way he'd crawled up to bed on his hands and feet.

Ronnie opened the door of his Altima to have a look.

As she peeled off the lids to stack the cups, she saw the expected brown residue—but when she lifted the stack to her nose, it wasn't coffee she smelled. It was whiskey and sweet vermouth.

The accordion files, the Styrofoam cups—each discovery had snagged at the cloak of denial that protected her marriage until it had completely unraveled. Secrets always come out in the end, Ronnie knew, and they were at the end. Now, behind the wheel of Jeff's car with no marriage left to protect, she opened the center compartment.

Jeff had promised her he'd whittled down his charging to two active cards. Despite the fact that he had closed her out of their financial life, shut down their romance, and scared her senseless with that suicide threat, she still wanted to believe him. What hope did they have for joint parenting after the divorce if she couldn't trust him? Then again, what kind of wife snoops on her own husband? Before she could talk her fingers out of it, they had flipped open the wallet.

She found twelve credit cards.

Ronnie stormed back into the house with the wallet in hand, cut each credit card but the agreed upon American Express and the Visa into quarters, and stuffed the pieces back into the wallet's slots haphazardly, like so many colorful pieces to a puzzle she couldn't imagine ever solving. Rage shuddered through her. Even now he would lie. *Damn him.*

Only when she'd put the wallet back in the center compartment and put the car in drive could she start to get a grip on her emotions. Nothing new was happening, she told herself. The transgressions made with these cards were water under the bridge, and she could do nothing about them. But at least until he ordered replacements, Ronnie had erected a protective if flimsy barrier: Jeff could use the credit cards no more.

janet

One of the volunteer firemen entered the hall with a case of water bottles, which he distributed to the women at the table. "I'll just leave the rest over here," he said. "Let me know if there's anything else we can do to help, Mrs. Farnham. Me and some of the other guys are right downstairs."

"Thank you," Janet said.

The boys, along with Mr. Eshbach, made their way to the water like sojourners from the desert. Janet would have too, if it were vodka or gin. Not that she liked the hard stuff, but she could resort to it if her supply of Amaretto ran low.

She looked over Ronnie's head to the soundless lip-flapping of the women of *The View*—she actually liked them better this way—and let her gaze drop to the bar below it. She bet she could find a bottle of Amaretto back there. Not that she'd be the sort to steal any, with people watching, but she could see how it could happen. And she could also see how someone who felt lonely and misunderstood might resort to spirits to feel better.

Spirits, ha. Her own mother had been full of them. A real holy roller, Amelia Hoyer. Like Jeff, Janet preferred spirits from the known and the seen, and her rewards earthly and countable.

She heard Will asking, "What can we do?"

"I still need to talk to the corporal," Ronnie said. "Why don't you take your water bottles over to the next table?"

"And then what?" Will said.

"Why don't you pray for Dad?"

Dear god, Janet thought. Then she wondered if she had just inadvertently offered up a prayer.

"But will it help?" Will said.

The boy will be a scientist—he won't take his mother's word on anything. A smile made its way to Janet's lips.

"It sure won't hurt," Ronnie said.

Once Mr. Eshbach followed the boys to the next table, Corporal McNichol asked Ronnie to tell her how Jeff had acted in the psych ward.

Psych ward, Janet thought. *It was more like an activities room at an old folks' home.*

She didn't give a damn what this psychiatrist had to say about her son. He'd met with Jeff for all of what, an hour or two? If Ronnie couldn't handle him, she should have called Janet.

Janet had grown up believing that if you had a problem, you dealt with it. You didn't pay good money to go whine to someone you'd never even met, then leave with a primer on how to lead a better life. With an expensive prescription as a bookmark. To take the edge off, so life hurt less. For crying out loud, that's what the drinking is for.

Jeff had been struggling with a financial burden. And she'd be the first to admit he was melodramatic. But he'd always been that way. Janet's mother, who'd watched little Jeff while Janet was at work, would tell her that after disciplining him—enforcing a good pout by shutting him in his room for an hour—he'd come back downstairs with his six-shooters stuffed in his pockets. And yes, he'd threatened his grandmother with those too, Janet had seen it, but with that cute little face pinched into a snarl, it was really pretty funny.

Of course Janet had been raised by the same Bible-quoting, teeth-gnashing disciplinarian, so she could relate to Jeff's desire to arm himself with whatever he could find. Amelia Hoyer did not like to be tested.

Then there was the knee injury in high school football that "ended his career" and "ruined his life." As if football was a career. He was a better athlete on the back of a horse anyway.

Somehow they got through such dramas without calling the cops, that time or any other. Which was the right thing, because when Ronnie committed Jeff to that locked "behavioral health" unit against his will, she opened up a whole stinky sack of trouble. That kind of betrayal creates battle lines, and now he had truly armed himself.

The situation left Janet yearning for a taste of her mother's absolute faith in the unseen. Or if not that, a nip from a bottle.

Janet grabbed her purse and excused herself to use the restroom.

ronnie

Go on, Ronnie, I'm listening. I may scratch a few notes."

Ronnie had never shared this story with anyone. Some parts were embarrassing, other parts were shameful to a bar manager with Jeff's sense of professionalism, and all of it was just plain challenging to revisit. But Jeff's torment felt private—at least until today, when he took it onto a public stage.

She looked at her mother and mother-in-law. Beverly sat perched at the edge of her seat. Janet had returned from the restroom and joined them.

"I met with the doctor first, before Jeff came in. Told him about the night's events, answered questions." Ronnie stopped and shook her head. "I could tell right away Jeff wouldn't take the guy seriously. Even I struggled with it. He seemed typecast: portly, long beard and mustache, wire-rimmed glasses, tinny voice. Of course maybe he didn't take Jeff seriously either. An alcoholic bartender—cliché, right?"

Corporal McNichol offered a rueful smile.

"He suspected Jeff was a closet alcoholic, the kind of drinker who will quietly numb his pain at night, in the privacy of his home, while his wife and kids are sleeping."

"What pain? That's what I'd like to know," Janet said.

Beverly put her hand on Janet's arm. "We'd all like to know that, I'm sure, but how can we, if he won't tell us?"

Ronnie continued. "The psychiatrist said he probably remained functional for so long because he drank at night and then slept for nine or ten hours."

Janet nodded—or was she nodding off?

"So the doctor thought alcoholism was the main problem?" Corporal McNichol said.

"From what I gathered, it's hard to tell. Depression can cause alcoholism, alcohol is a depressant, and financial, personal, and professional problems can result from or cause either. Or both."

Corporal McNichol nodded knowingly.

"Then Jeff joined us."

He'd taken a seat in the far corner of the little conference room, Ronnie recalled, creating an unfortunate "us" against "him" configuration.

Ronnie relived that meeting for Corporal McNichol, keeping in reserve parts that felt too private.

The psychiatrist had begun, "Your wife is worried about you. Does that mean anything to you?"

Jeff looked at Ronnie. "Of course it does." For one brief moment, he looked at the doctor with what seemed to be sincere humility. "I know I haven't been good at maintaining our sex life. I don't know what's wrong with me. How could I not want to touch her?" He turned to Ronnie, who could only look at the floor. She was mortified that he'd brought up their sex life, or lack of it, in answer to the doctor's very first question. With emotion thickening his voice, he'd said, "She's beautiful."

The psychiatrist sat back and crossed his arms. "Jeff, there are a lot of women homelier than your wife who are having sex with great regularity. Intimacy has nothing to do with beauty and everything to do with relationship. Sex reinforces a connection that already exists. That connection is what you're not capable of right now."

"What do you mean, I'm not capable?"

"Ronnie?" Corporal McNichol prompted.

She cleared her throat. "Sorry. The psychiatrist said Jeff wasn't in touch with his feelings, and that the only way to remedy that was to stop drinking."

Janet stage-whispered to Beverly, "I wonder how many doctors she had to take him to for that diagnosis?"

Ronnie paused, noted her anger, and let it go. Without meeting her mother-in-law's eyes, she said, "I know this is painful to listen to, Janet. I won't be hurt if you get up and leave. But before you try to scratch me with more of your barbed commentary"—she raised her gaze to Janet's—"I want you to think long and hard about which one of us is sitting here speaking with you, trying to solve problems, and which one has locked himself in a room."

After a long pause, Janet said, "I'm listening."

"Jeff said he could give up drinking without a problem. That he had already done so, going without a cigarette or drink the whole four days he'd been in the hospital. The doctor told him that was because he hadn't had to deal with the pressures of home and work. That's when the tug of wills started."

Corporal McNichol looked up from her notes. "How so?"

"Without skipping a beat, Jeff started making exceptions. He said he'd only have wine if he and I were having a nice dinner, like for my upcoming birthday. The doctor said no, he'd have to stop entirely and also complete thirty days of in-patient rehab. Jeff said he couldn't do that, he had to work. The doctor said not around alcohol. Jeff said, 'I can't do rehab. I'd lose my job.'"

"Well, that much is true, in this job market," Beverly said. "And they could hire someone else at a much lower wage."

"But I'd already spoken with Norris and arranged for time off. I told Jeff that, and he looked at me as if I'd betrayed him. I explained that I hadn't told Norris why he was in the hospital. For all he knew, Jeff was having bypass surgery. Norris had told me Jeff had been a good and faithful employee, he should take whatever time he needed. He just wanted him well. And Jeff said, 'Ronnie, you know me, I'd go insane in rehab. I've got to be working.' I said maybe that's exactly what he needed: to stop running from whatever this is and sit still with it. And when he got out, he could quit at the hotel and work full-time at the farm store. He said we couldn't afford rehab, and I said I'd already confirmed payment with his insurance company. All he had to do was say yes."

All the women's eyes were on Ronnie.

"What did he say?" Corporal McNichol said.

"He said, 'I can't do it.' And while I was wondering what we were supposed to do next, the psychiatrist started gathering his papers and said Jeff was ready for discharge."

"That's it? He sent you home with nothing resolved?" her mother said.

"Just handed me a prescription for outpatient counseling, with the warning that it probably wouldn't work because Jeff needed more support than that. All I got in return for hauling my boys down there in the middle of the night and making the gut-wrenching decision to commit him? A four-day reprieve. He was coming home."

"But how could they do that when they knew the stakes?" Beverly said.

"The Patient's Bill of Rights Jeff received said they can't keep him beyond five days unless he repeats the threat of suicide or tries it while he's there—and he got out in four days because of obstinate behavior. 'We won't be able to accomplish anything else here,' the doctor said. 'Our words hang in the air all around him, but they can't sink in.' I was in a panic. I needed Jeff to get help. *I* needed help. I didn't know how we could carry on. Once Jeff left the room, I asked the doctor what we were supposed to do." Ronnie could feel the panic rise within her again. She couldn't speak for a moment.

Beverly finally said, "And?"

"He said, 'You want to know whether or not your husband is going to kill himself.' I said, 'Yes, I guess that's what I want to know.' And he said, 'We already know that he's lied to you about the finances. But the real problem is that he lies to himself. That will be the source of his undoing.'"

"I hate to say how well this supports my opinion of psychiatry," Janet said.

"So did he think you should maybe back off on the divorce?" Beverly said.

Ronnie relived what else the psychiatrist had said.

"At this point you need to protect yourself and your children," he had said. "I understand his mother is paying off the debt. His decision-making ability has been severely compromised, so make sure the divorce papers are served right after Jeff cashes the check from his mother. This will freeze his account and prevent him from spending it. When you move out, take everything that's yours. I don't suspect he'll be alone for long."

Ronnie looked up at the disco ball, too distant and fractured to mirror her lie. "No, he didn't mention the divorce."

"And nothing about the potential for suicide?" Corporal McNichol said.

Did the corporal really need her to say this? She knew how these things turned out better than any of them.

Her mother's and mother-in-law's foreheads were creased with worry, each looking to her for hope.

She found the strength to lie once more. "Not specifically."

The doctor's hand was on the door, and Ronnie's panic was rising. "Wait. What do you mean, 'the source of his undoing'? Could Jeff really commit suicide?"

And the psychiatrist had answered, "He just might."

❧

The trip home from the hospital was almost unbearable. Ronnie did not feel equal to being Jeff's guardian or whatever you'd call the duties expected of her now that he had been released from the psych unit. The air in the car was supercharged with every feeling

Jeff would never be able to discuss. How close was he to coming unhinged? How angry was he that she had committed him? And what would he do when he saw what she'd done to the credit cards? She draped her arm over the center compartment in a way that she hoped looked casual.

Jeff punctuated the silence with occasional questions about what had been going on in his absence, as if she had just picked him up at the airport after a business trip. After she parked the car, her entire rib cage clamped down on her lungs as she watched Jeff's hand move to the center compartment to withdraw his wallet.

He didn't open it until they got into the kitchen. That's when he erupted.

"What the hell were you thinking?" he shouted, holding up the worthless scraps of plastic.

Ronnie kept her voice as calm as she could, but she had never before encountered the full force of Jeff's wrath. The thrill worming its way through her chest was inappropriate, she knew. "You told me that you were keeping only the Visa and American Express active. If you aren't charging anything on the others, it doesn't matter if they're cut up."

Jeff shook with rage. He let rip a selection of profanities she'd never before witnessed, from him or anyone.

Following his example, Ronnie did him the honor of waiting out his tirade before leaving the room.

Her whole life long she'd admired Jeff's easygoing nature. He was curiously difficult to provoke. He'd once told her that his ex-wife had thrown a knife at him to try to get a rise out of him. After that, he'd thought it wise to hide the cleaver from the knife set; it was tucked away still, in a high cupboard beneath a seldom-used fondue pot, safe from the boys. Hidden, like his emotions.

Ronnie had laughed when Jeff first told her this particular Crazy Fay story. Now, her own similarity to Fay frightened her. Ronnie had taken a blade to Jeff's most vulnerable spot—his wallet—instigating an arterial pulse of passion that years of pleas and tears could not.

It turned out Jeff wasn't the unflappable man Ronnie had always depended upon to balance out her more emotional nature.

He was untouchable, except through the tender fold of his wallet.

ronnie

Ronnie took a good long drink from her water bottle and thought back over all the help she'd tried to arrange for Jeff. "I wonder if forcing Jeff into detox under the threat of jail time would even work."

"Jail," Janet said. "I still can't get over this treating him like a criminal."

Ronnie decided not to mention Jeff pointing his gun at that cop again. If Janet didn't think that was criminal, there wasn't much Ronnie could do about it. She'd also keep that morning's discovery of the twelve hundred dollars to herself. Who knew where that money had come from?

"Maybe it's a matter of timing," Beverly said. "The officer I was talking to this morning said that sometimes people who fail to commit suicide are grateful, that they knew right away they'd made a mistake. Maybe Jeff thought the same thing this morning, when that gun went off. Maybe he's confused, with all those police around him, and trying to figure out how to end this."

"That's what we hope." Corporal McNichol finished a doodle—or a paragraph—on the page. "But I have to warn you, all we can do is push Jeff into the program. He does not have to engage. He's only required to sit there for twenty-eight days. But at that point, his head would be a little clearer. Could make a difference."

How could Corporal McNichol hope to make a difference when

Ronnie and a score of professionals had already met with nothing but their own impotence?

When she took Jeff for an intake interview at the outpatient rehab center two days after his hospital release, Ronnie remembered how she'd felt in its cozy waiting area, surrounded by racks with brochures full of information on alcoholism: safe. Safer, in that public space, than she did in her own home. Information led to identifying problems, and problems had solutions. Yet when Jeff came out, he complained that the outpatient rehab was forty-five minutes away, and early in the morning at that. It wouldn't fit his late-night schedule.

"Can't you help us either?" Ronnie asked the intake counselor privately after the completion of her part of the interview. "Isn't that what you're here for?"

The counselor put her arm around Ronnie and steered her toward the door. "I understand you're leaving him. I'm sure no one expects you to support him through this. You need to take care of yourself and your children."

The more determined Ronnie was to separate herself from the threat Jeff presented, the more she seemed to be stuck with him. Maybe if he found someone he liked and respected, as she had with Anita, he might benefit from one-on-one counseling. She called their health insurance company again to explore this aspect of their mental health coverage, and by the time she hung up, she had amassed a list of counselors, phone numbers, and covered services.

She sat across from Jeff in their dining room, the pendulum of the clock above his head ticking away what Ronnie feared might be the final hope-filled minutes of their marriage. Ronnie slid the list across the table to him. "If you won't do anything else, please, at least go talk to somebody."

"I've been thinking," Jeff said, setting the list aside. "I'll do inpatient rehab, if you'd promise me one thing."

Ronnie sighed. Always exacting something from her. "What's that?"

"That you'll be there for me when I get out."

As Ronnie tried to smooth the creases in the vinyl tablecloth that had never relaxed since it left the package five years ago, she tried to imagine Jeff emerging from rehab a new person, the two of them falling into a loving embrace to reclaim what they once had. But Ronnie had outgrown her best memory of what they "once had." While writing in her journal, she had envisioned a new kind of relationship, in which she and a partner could nurture each other into becoming the best that each could be—and not one conversation she'd ever had with Jeff indicated that he had a similar goal. This demand that she be there for him after rehab seemed like another bid for time while he thought up one more way to chain her to the farm.

Yet it took no more than a moment to forgive his strong-arm technique; despite his calm facade, his desperation was palpable.

"What do you say, Ronnie? Will you wait for me?"

Ronnie chose her words carefully. "I will be there as a friend, always. I care about you. I want you to have a better life. I'm the mother of your children, and that will always connect us. But I cannot promise I'll be there as your wife."

She stood calmly. Wasting no time, per the psychiatrist's recommendation, Ronnie went to her office, called her divorce lawyer, and made another appointment for the following week.

To her knowledge, Jeff never placed a call for any kind of therapy.

∽

"Mom, they're showing the farm again," Will said. "Look at the horses. They're freaking out."

"Did you climb up and turn the TV on, Will?"

"No. You never turned it off. You just hit Mute."

Ronnie was ashamed she'd left the television on. Her boys didn't need to see any more of this. From the looks of it, more news vans had nosed up to the barrier at the edge of their property.

As she reached up to shut off the set, the camera panned back for a full view of the way their property crested the hill. The huge red barn lording over the outbuildings, the rustic split-rail fencing, the snowflake patterns in the newly thinned pick-your-own strawberry field, the brilliant yellows and reds of the fall leaves against the green yard and white stucco house—it was breathtaking. Until the line of black-and-whites in the driveway led her eye to the store. The horses paced in the pasture beside it.

Actually, *pasture* was a kind word for it. It was more like dirt with an occasional sprout of onion grass and broadleaf weed. Jeff thought the smell of earth and onions projected just the right organic image they wanted for their farm store, but Ronnie thought they should keep it looking better, with customers gathering at the fence to pet those velvety noses. The cameras focused again on the horses. The boys' lame Shetland pony, Horsey Patch, had thrust his entire spotted head through the lower two rungs of the fence to eat the grass at the edge of the road. Camelot and Daydream ran the length of the pasture, raising a cloud of dust that stuck to their lathered necks— right beneath the window of the store's office.

Ronnie could see nothing through its dusty glass.

Rob White's lips were moving; a banner said "Breaking News." How could she turn it off now, when this man had information that might have a grave impact on their lives? She found the volume on the remote as White said, "Correspondent Maura Riley has the latest. Maura?"

The scene cut to a picture of Riley standing by the barricade, her blond hair sprayed into artful layers.

"Thank you, Rob. I'm standing here with a neighbor, Karl Prout, whose house is located up the hill from the Farnham place. I understand that you aren't able to get home, Karl?"

"That's right. I work the night shift at a plant in Reading. I stopped to eat, and on my way home, I ran into this here barricade. So me and some of the other neighbors have been standing here talking. We just can't believe it."

"What's the consensus?"

"Like I said, we just can't believe it." The camera pulled back to show others nodding their heads. Ronnie recognized a few of the local fire police, pressed into service every time an accident required that traffic be rerouted.

"Tell us what you know about Jeffrey Farnham."

"I mean, Jeff is a real nice guy. About fifty, fifty-five, I'd guess. Always happy. Plowed me out a few times. His family's lived on the hill here for a long time and I know 'em all. Never had a problem with any of 'em. Real nice."

"We understand he may be intoxicated. Did Jeffrey Farnham have a problem with alcohol?"

"Well, it's not unusual if you work the night shift," Karl said, chuckling and holding his gut so it wouldn't spill further over his pants. "Look. He had no more trouble with booze than any of us do. They say he and his wife were fighting too, but I don't buy it. He wasn't like that. That stuff is all exaggeration. You know how people talk."

"Okay, well, there you have it, Rob—"

Ronnie flipped off the set. Until recently, even Ronnie hadn't realized Jeff had been an alcoholic. What did Karl Prout know about her husband? She wondered if Karl Prout knew that Jeff had once dreamed of opening a rental center for tools and party supplies. That he'd never had a cold in all the years she'd known him. That he was at greatest peace sitting on the porch on a summer evening, after a long day of work, surveying the mowed yards and growing gardens. Of course he didn't. Why on earth *Action News* would resort to a man-on-the-country-road interview during a situation like this was beyond her.

And no one seemed to get the simplest fact right. Her husband's age. She could only hope he'd make it to fifty.

"That's it." Ronnie pulled the list of media contacts from her back pocket. "Mom, let me use your phone."

"Oh, honey, don't bait them."

"This is family business," Janet said.

Ronnie left the social hall, turned right, and searched for a phone. Down the hall, she found an office where a couple of uniformed officers were manning radios. Ronnie, so removed from the police operation in the social hall, seemed to have slammed right into command central.

One officer was picking peppers off his sandwich. "My gut won't take 'em any more. It's peppers or coffee, one or the other, and you know who's winning that battle."

"Some respect, gentlemen?" Corporal McNichol said, coming up behind Ronnie. Both men stood.

Static on the radio. Ronnie caught her breath. "Scopes say Farnham hasn't moved in a while. Thought we heard him snoring, but it was a chain saw starting farther up the road."

One of the officers stifled a smile; the other cleared his throat.

"I just want to use the phone," Ronnie said. "I'll only be a sec."

The men turned down the radio. Her rapid loss of bluster left Ronnie's hand shaking on the keypad.

"Maura Riley here."

"This is Veronica Farnham." For once, Ronnie was glad for the added syllables and the gravitas they conferred.

"How are you doing?"

How the hell did she think?

"Quit guessing at my husband's age."

"We hear you're divorcing. I'm so sorry. I've been there. It's tough. Is that why he's so distraught?"

Yellow journalism 101. Delve into the emotional; befriend the interviewee. Tabloids did this all the time to make people spill their friends' stories.

Ronnie took a deep breath and tried to stay on point. "On a day where many things cannot possibly be known, it seems the very least a journalist could do is get this one fact right."

"Were your children afraid of the guns their father kept on the property?"

Go for the innocent. Oh, she's good.

"He's forty-seven."

Heart racing, Ronnie hung up the phone and ripped up the list. "Feel free to refuse all further calls from the media on my behalf," she said, tossing the torn bits in the trash and heading for the door. This was her story that was unfolding. If anyone was going to write about it, it would be her.

Ronnie agreed with Karl Prout: this was overkill. Suicide was such a big, splashy statement. So unlike Jeff, who preferred the invisible periphery of most situations. When Ronnie had been low herself, after college, the notion of self-harm had never once crossed her mind. "Suicide," with its soft, slippery sound, still felt like a mercurial threat.

She thought this even as her knuckles and jaw ached from clenching, and a nerve was zapping hot down the back of her left leg.

Anyway, the last time Jeff hadn't acted on it; he'd simply written the note. To scare her into taking him back. Now, it would seem, even the police thought this was a joke.

Yet as Ronnie returned to her family in the social hall, the tinny voice of the hospital psychiatrist grated on her memory: *He just might.*

beverly

The manhunt, the standoff, the airing of marital issues, the public humiliation—the day had pulled on her daughter like an unrelenting winch. Beverly wondered how Ronnie pushed on without snapping.

"Mo-om, we need the TV. We're bo-ored." Will always stretched the word to two syllables to underscore his point.

"I have to talk to Corporal McNichol, Will," Ronnie said. "Just sit."

"We've been sitting all morning. I want to go to school."

"Sorry, you can't."

"Then let us go over to the park," Andrew said. "You can't keep us here like we're in prison."

"Boys. Sit down. I can't deal with you two right now!"

Ah, there she blows, Beverly thought. *At least I spawned a human.*

The boys' faces went blank as they stared her down.

"I didn't mean to yell," Ronnie said. "Sorry."

"You're just going to keep saying bad things about Dad."

Will had her pegged all right. If Beverly knew one thing about her daughter, she would talk. Ronnie laughed words, cried words. Honestly, you could only stop her up so long before the words came tumbling out. Those words were going to come whether her sons wanted to hear them or not.

What her grandsons needed was a distraction—and that was Beverly's specialty.

"Come with me, boys. And, Mr. Eshbach, would you like some entertainment?"

Beverly took Andrew and Will to the far end of the room. Sure enough, her daughter was already gabbing away to Corporal McNichol. That girl could go to the end of the drive to meet the mailman and come home fifteen minutes later knowing his son was flunking history and his dog was allergic to his flea treatment. Where had that knowledge ever gotten her? Conversation couldn't solve everything.

"Let's sing," Andrew said. "Mom loves it."

"Okay, what do you want to sing, sweetie?" Beverly said, a smile always at the ready. Even when she was frightened out of her mind.

"'On Top of Spaghetti'!" Will said.

"You always say that, and you can never remember the words," Andrew said.

Yet they started in anyway, not fearing the ragged end of the journey.

Ronnie had no clue what she might be in for. Ever since Beverly had spoken with that policeman this morning, one thought kept pulsing through her mind: someone commits suicide in this country every fourteen minutes. Was this one of those minutes?

Beverly sat looking around the fire hall, so festive when decorated, now so barren. That old mirror ball had seen so many rites of passage in this room, many of which she'd attended through the years. Ronnie was ten years old when they had the reception after her brother Teddy's baptism here. Beverly couldn't afford flowers so they'd decorated the whole place with Mylar balloons. Little Teddy had untied some of them from their weights and sent them heaven bound.

Ronnie's high school graduation party had been held here too. Even though Beverly had decorated the whole front wall with tissue paper butterflies, she'd had a hard time handling her daughter's transformation. It was back then that Ronnie started rolling and blowing and relaxing her hair in order to look like her idea of an adult. Yet the mirror ball threw its colored fairy lights across faces still innocent; at their age, Beverly already had a one-year-old. She'd wanted Ronnie, she absolutely did, and no matter how tough things had gotten she'd never regretted having her, but at that party, Beverly's unlived life loomed so close that she could feel it taunting her.

Twice she'd been in this room for Janet's husband, Jerry. Janet could afford flowers. The place had looked like an indoor garden for Jerry's induction into the high school sports hall of fame and again, later, for his funeral reception. Both events were crowded. The whole town loved Jerry; as a coach, teacher, and summer playground administrator, he kept grooming new batches of admirers. Janet never seemed to bask in the glow of his popularity nor hide in his shadow, as many women would around a strong man. Beverly admired her independence.

Beverly remembered Jerry's surprise when some of his former students brought in a freestanding basketball hoop and set it at one end of the hall, then his laughter when one of them made off with his commissioned portrait and climbed up to rest it against the backboard. They reprised the prank at Jerry's funeral reception, with a black sash across the painting. Beverly had thought it was a touching tribute. Jeff had ranted about it and wanted to take it down, but the players had surrounded the pole with dozens and dozens of huge floral arrangements, creating a fragrant island to guard their beloved coach's untouchable reputation.

Celebration and letting go, beginnings and endings. Today the hall was stripped bare, as if it hadn't known how to dress. As if waiting, like the rest of them, to know what kind of event this would be.

Now these sweet boys, belting their little meatball hearts out, had brought a smile to two of the most needful faces: Janet's and Mr. Eshbach's. Beverly felt flush with warm pride. These were Dom's grandsons. The song connected them: Beverly had taught it to

Ronnie, and Ronnie had taught it to Andrew and Will, and all of them connected her back to Dom.

Beverly looked back over at her daughter, hoping all those words she was speaking were adding up in some new way. But she was thrilled to see her hair restored to its natural beauty. After so many years, Beverly had feared Ronnie had ironed the life right out of those curls.

She had to believe there was a way for her family to make it through this while still holding a song in their hearts.

ronnie

At the other end of the room, the poor meatball rolled out of the door—and the boys' voices stopped. Ronnie waited for it...and the creative verses began: "I ride on a Yeti," "My frog is named Betty," "I ate the spumoni." Will's voice: "Hey, that doesn't rhyme." Andrew's: "But ice cream is always good!" They sang with gusto, occasionally dissolving into giggles. Andrew raised his arms as if on Broadway; Will threw in a hip wiggle. From where Ronnie sat, the boys seemed up for the challenge of getting their grandmothers to smile. She couldn't imagine how Janet was managing. How would Ronnie, if it were Andrew or Will holed up in that store? She hoped that their childlike joy, which had found expression even on a day like today, would never be extinguished.

Good singers, both. Where had that talent come from? Ronnie's voice was thin, and Jeff couldn't even sing "Happy Birthday" in any recognizable fashion.

"A lot of people have been coming to see you," Corporal McNichol said after checking in with her men. "A store employee, Karl Prout, and a few others who may or may not have been neighbors. My team has turned them away. But a Lisa Schulz is here and says she can help with the boys."

Corporal McNichol's gaze flicked to the far end of the room where Andrew had just run Will through with an imaginary sword. Will clutched at his heart and fell to the floor, his tongue hanging out.

Ronnie wished Jeff were sitting beside her to listen and laugh, so they could feel their love for the boys amplified through each other. Wished he had ever felt the glory of a song in his heart. Wished his sons had inspired him to become the man he wanted his sons to be. Tears fought their way to her worn-out eyes. She had lost Jeff so long ago and was well aware she had stayed in the marriage long past its useful life. She'd done so for her boys, until she couldn't abide Jeff's role-modeling a moment longer.

The fact that this day had inserted itself into her life story was one more thing she'd have to deal with on the long, slow road to becoming Ronnie.

But it should never, ever have happened to a child.

"Ronnie?"

"Mmm?"

"This is hard enough on you as it is," Corporal McNichol said gently. "There are people willing to help. Shall we let her in?"

"Who?"

"Lisa Schulz."

"Oh. Sure."

A minute later, Lisa, who lived in the house across the street and was the mother of Will's friend Brandon, walked into the room wearing white scrubs and a pink sweater. The thought of Lisa being unable to return home after working a twelve-hour night shift at the hospital brought Ronnie a deep sense of shame.

Lisa's concern, however, was for Ronnie. She offered to take the boys to her mother Beth's house, a few blocks away. The boys were familiar with the place, a stone house set way back into the woods, and since Beth cared for a constant string of foster children, there would be plenty for them to do. Besides, Lisa said, her mother wanted to help.

"What do you say?"

Ronnie supposed Corporal McNichol was beyond done with the boys. The police had their statements, and at this point, the boys could contribute nothing but distraction.

Lisa and Beth could offer what Ronnie had wanted when she'd first called her mother that morning—for the boys to be removed from unfolding events. This wasn't their battle. They shouldn't have to witness it. And she wanted them safe.

Yet with everything in her world upside down, Ronnie wanted to hold her sons close. She wanted the distraction they provided her. While Ronnie hesitated, her mother went to round them up.

Ronnie pulled Lisa aside. "They can play video games but not on the computer. And don't let them watch TV, okay? They've seen enough." Ronnie was suddenly glad she hadn't been able to afford to buy the boys cell phones, like Lisa had for Brandon. "And if Brandon comes over—"

"No smartphone." Lisa gave her another hug. "I'll take good care of them."

"Are you coming too, Mom?" Will said.

"They need me here, sweetie. To help Dad. I'm jealous, though. You're going to have fun."

"Mr. Eshbach, if you want a change of scene, we can take you with us," Lisa said. The man wasted no time donning the jacket he'd placed on the back of his chair.

"I don't know if I should go," Will said, looking to Ronnie.

"I'll see you a little later," she said, trying to be brave. "This is good, that you're going."

"But I forgot to tell Dad we're hatching chicks at school."

"That's okay, you can tell him tomorrow."

"He loves chicks. They make him happy. Make sure you tell him, okay?"

Ronnie couldn't speak. She pulled him close and rubbed her hand across his thick buzzed hair in the same way that soothed him to sleep at night. The hairs tickled her palm.

From the folds of her sweater came Will's tiny voice. "Do you think Brandon's grandmother will let us use the trampoline?"

"Only if you follow the rules. Can you do that?"

He nodded. She kissed his sweaty head. Salt lingered on her lips.

As the group headed for the door, Ronnie pulled Andrew back. "Don't you leave here without giving me a hug," she said. She wrapped her arms around him. "Thank you for calling 911 this morning. I'm really proud of you."

He looked down at the ground, and his cheeks turned red. "You and Will were the ones that kept Dad from driving. I couldn't move."

"Whoa. Look at me."

Andrew lifted his eyes to hers. Those beautiful blueberry eyes, so much like Jeff's. "We couldn't handle this alone. We needed help, and you brought it to us. You were like a superhero." A tear spilled from his eye. Ronnie gave him another quick hug and kissed his damp cheek.

The exodus of the others rumbled through the floor as they headed down the metal staircase. Andrew looked toward the door. "Better go."

Ronnie nodded and turned back to the big room, not knowing what to do with the emptiness that now touched every part of her body.

12:00 p.m.

beverly

Once the boys left the fire hall, it began feeling too much like a tomb for Beverly's taste. She was getting hungry anyway, so she convinced Janet to cross the street and get some lunch at Perlmutter's General Store. Standing at the back counter, Beverly watched its wheezy owner, Sophie, dish up some of Janet's favorite creamy cucumber salad to go with her sandwich, then turn her back and lick the spoon. Even Sophie couldn't resist her salad's sweet, vinegary cream. After only a quick rinse under the tap, Sophie hung the spoon back on the wall for reuse.

"I saw that, Sophie." The woman screwed up her face at Beverly. Beverly had no clue how Janet could continue to eat the stuff, but today Janet needed all the love she could get, and if she wanted Perlmutter's cucumber salad, that's what Beverly would give her.

"How's she doing?" Sophie said.

"I don't know how she's still putting one foot in front of the other," Beverly said.

"I heard on the scanner—"

"Of course you did." When Beverly had lived in the apartment upstairs more than thirty years ago, the constant stream of alarming situations spewed by Sophie's police scanner had been the soundtrack of her pregnancy. Who would have thought her baby would grow up and star in one of those dramas?

Sophie reached back to turn it down, but not before Beverly heard it squawk: "That's negative. The media reports are wrong. Farnham's still alive."

Beverly looked for Janet, checking prices down an aisle near the front of the store, before breathing a sigh of relief. Jeff was alive, and Janet hadn't heard the false report that he might not be. For once, Beverly was thankful for Janet's growing inattention to detail.

Maybe a newspaper would distract Ronnie. Beverly pulled one from a pile beneath the counter. The headline: *PTSD Blamed for Harrisburg Murder-Suicide.*

Beverly shoved the newspaper back where she found it. She wasn't going to pay for that crap. What the hell was the matter with the men in this country? Teaching their younger counterparts how to kill, sending them off to fight wars that scrambled their brains with fear, bringing them home so damaged they thought they had to protect their loved ones against life itself. How were women to raise healthy kids at home with that kind of story for inspiration?

When the creaky wooden floor signaled Janet behind her, Beverly picked up a box of Tootsie Rolls and plopped it on top of the newspaper pile to hide the offending headline. Beverly couldn't help but wonder, though, what tomorrow's paper would say.

Janet set a bag of gingersnap cookies on the counter.

"Will that be all?" Sophie looked from one woman to the other. She was a tough little lady—Beverly guessed she had to be to keep her store open 365 days a year—but Beverly perceived some uncharacteristic softness in her face for her old friends. When Beverly nodded, Sophie said, "That's $24.85, girls. The pickles were free."

"Hmm," Beverly said. "For some reason, I thought the cucumber salad was free too."

Sophie and Beverly stared each other down across the counter. "Fine. $21.20 then."

Janet reached for her wallet and Beverly said, "No, honey, let me get it."

"You don't have to coddle me." Janet pulled out some bills.

"I'm not."

"You are too. You called me 'honey.'" Unable to find the change she needed in her wallet, Janet put a five and four ones on the counter.

"Okay," Beverly said. Janet had become quite the stickler about money. "I'll get the rest then."

But Janet rooted around deep in the bottom of that ridiculously accommodating handbag until she was able to add enough loose change to pay exactly half of the total. "We each have our own things to deal with."

Outside, the women paused on the stoop and looked back at the firehouse. Its featureless brick facade seemed indifferent to the tension it contained.

"You okay with going over to the park to eat?" Janet said. "I'm not sure I can digest this otherwise."

The earlier wind had died to a breeze, and Beverly watched it whip strands of Janet's gray bob across her face. One got stuck in her eyelashes and she made no effort to move it.

Beverly swept it aside for her and hooked her arm through Janet's. "Come on."

A half block away and across the street was a tennis court with basketball hoops erected at each end. A lone bench faced the high chain-link fence surrounding it, and the women sat there to eat. Janet pawed around in her handbag and Beverly looked away, knowing Janet would enhance her iced tea from a flask. Every ounce of that stuff was another hundred calories. What that woman could consume.

"Remember when we'd wheel baby Ronnie over here so Jeff could shoot hoops?" Janet said. "He was determined he'd be ready for Jerry's varsity basketball team when he got to high school."

Beverly smiled at the memory. "That ball went everywhere but in the basket."

"I think it went over the fence and bounced into Ronnie's stroller once."

"That's one way to make an impression on a girl." Beverly

unwrapped her sandwich and took a bite, recalling how hard Jeff had worked to win the admiration of his father. If Jerry had only been a little worse at his job, he would have continued to coach a bunch of small-town kids with a passion for the game, and his son may well have made the team. But once he'd turned them into state champions, expectations were raised—as were the height requirements. Jeff couldn't make the cut. Those who had made the team dwarfed Jeff at Jerry's funeral, just as they had in high school.

"So much of Ronnie's early life is a blur," Beverly said. "I felt so lost and so afraid of my future. I don't know what I would have done if Sophie hadn't let me rent a room so cheap."

Janet skipped the sandwich and went right for the cookies. "Don't say a thing, Bev. The sandwich was your idea. If the cancer's going to get me anyway, I might as well enjoy myself on the way out."

It struck her then: Janet looked old. Beverly wanted to believe age had pounced on her with the shock of today's events, but she knew that wasn't how it worked. When was the last time Beverly had really looked at her? Or really thought about how lonely she must be, losing her husband after such a good, long marriage?

Until now, Beverly had not thought of losing her ever-constant friend—whether to age, the cancer bogeyman, or the aftermath of how this day might play out. "This whole thing with Jeff is such a mess. You don't deserve this."

Janet drank down some of her doctored iced tea and said quietly, "Ronnie doesn't either."

"How can you be so calm? I want to go punch somebody."

Beverly set her sandwich aside and went for the pickle. Its sour, garlicky flavor sent pricks of pain through her taste buds. A food better suited for a suicide watch.

"I didn't see this coming," Janet said. "The second I saw that barricade today, I thought it was Ronnie."

"Ronnie? She bounces right back from everything."

"That wasn't true when she came home from college."

Janet was right, Beverly thought. But Jeff had changed all that.

"Remember the picnics at the farm? Jeff always went down to Delaware to bring back fresh steamed crabs. We'd make salads, and Jerry would ice the beer in tubs and set up tables in the side yard."

"Then cover them with Kraft paper," Janet said.

They could have spread out more at Janet's, with its larger house and property. But its stable was long empty, and its expanse impersonal. They all knew Jeff and Ronnie's six acres had the intimacy that said *family* and *home*.

"Remember that one time Jeff boosted you onto Ronnie's horse and led you around the paddock?" Janet said.

"If only I could forget."

"You were screaming and giggling and saying, 'I need a seat belt'!"

"If I'm going to leave the surface of the earth, to this day I'd prefer to do so while slung under a nylon balloon powered by blasts of fire rather than on one of those bucking broncos."

"The horse was trotting. Slowly."

"That beast was trying to get me off its back and it almost succeeded." She looked at Janet out the corner of her eye and enjoyed her smile. "I'd never heard you laugh that hard before. Or since, for that matter."

"Well." Janet rubbed her hand across her abdomen. "Life doesn't always hand you a whole lot of funny."

Beverly watched the breeze swish through the glorious red leaves in the trees at the far end of the park. "What ever happened to those picnics?"

Janet thought for a while. "I don't think they've had one since Jerry's been gone."

Once more, they had circled around to death. Beverly kicked the topic aside and spoke again.

"I'm so worried about the boys. Thank god Ronnie's a better mother than I was. I knew nothing about life at seventeen." *Or death*.

"I was only twenty-one when I got pregnant."

"But you and Jerry gave Jeff a stable home. You hung in there for the long haul."

"Togetherness is a sweet-and-sour concept."

"Speaking of which…" Beverly picked up the salad. "You going to eat this?"

"Maybe not."

"I'm craving vinegar." Beverly peeled the top from the cucumber salad and decided that her hunger for life was greater than her fear of death by food-handling infraction. Since neither one of them had thought to ask for a plastic fork, she slurped cucumbers, onions, and sauce from the side of the container until they were gone. "Do you want to get back? In case there's word?"

"We both have cell phones. If there's word, they'll find us." A sudden wind blew through the deserted park, pushing the baby swing and slapping a page of newspaper against the jail-like bars of the bike rack. "I can't stand being walled up. I feel more connected to Jeff out here in the air. As though if I keep breathing"—her voice faltered—"he will too."

Beverly nodded and stood. "Come on, hon—"

"Do not coddle."

"Then come on, Miss Bitchy Pants. Let's walk."

Beverly and Janet made a slow circle of the park before heading back. Janet took Beverly's arm; the iced tea had her wobbling a bit. Along one side was a Rails-to-Trails conversion with a lofty arch of trees overhead, and as they processed along it, Beverly had the odd sense that they were marrying.

Of course when patterns keep repeating, it's hard not to recognize them.

She'd divorced Tony when Ronnie was six. Janet had warned her not to marry him in the first place, but the pain of Dom's loss had endured, and the notion of escaping to the Massachusetts woods with a sweet, pot-smoking poet sounded romantic. Janet could have claimed her right to a big old "I told you so." But when Beverly and Ronnie emerged from the woods, Janet welcomed them back to Bartlesville without judgment and listened to their stories as if Beverly and Ronnie were swashbucklers who had engaged with every Massachusetts slug, salamander, and chipmunk.

Beverly could see the happiness they brought her in the way she was energized to suggest trips to the zoo and the library and the outlets. She and Janet were no longer student and teacher. They were friends, and when Beverly found a cute little cottage to rent within walking distance, it made them all happy.

That fall Jeff came home from college one weekend to tell his parents about his first few months at Penn State. Ronnie wanted to tell him her woodland stories, and used to Janet's undivided attention, expected the same kind of audience from Jeff, who at that age had no use for children. So she climbed right onto his lap, reached up with her two little hands, and turned his face toward hers, as if no one else in the room existed.

Beverly smiled. In light of Ronnie and Jeff's later marriage, this story had become one of Beverly and Janet's favorite co-creations, embellishing Ronnie's ringlet curls over the years with a frilly dress, petticoats, and taps on her shiny Mary Janes. Ronnie always laughed at that part, saying she couldn't imagine doing this because for one thing she'd never wear a dress—but over years of repeated telling, even Jeff remembered it the same way.

Daryl was a tougher good-bye. After Beverly had Teddy, Daryl had moved them to Baltimore to open a practice with a friend from dental school, and despite Beverly's determination to make a go of it, she was lonely for the kind of companionship only Janet had ever given her. She and Janet entered the cell phone era just to keep the long distance charges under control.

Beverly wasn't the only one who had trouble adjusting to life in Baltimore. One day, when Teddy had been crying to get up from his nap, Beverly walked into the nursery to find that Ronnie had already pulled the boy from his bed. She was rocking him, telling him not to cry, and promising that they'd find new friends in Maryland someday.

The negotiations were simple, if heartrending: Daryl would give her a nice settlement if Beverly let him raise Teddy. The bargain still sounded crass. Beverly came home without her son, and Ronnie, at thirteen, was as bereaved as if she'd lost her own child. But again, Janet didn't judge, and begged a new slew of stories from the great wide world. The money allowed Beverly to buy the cottage they'd once rented and her daughter to stay put throughout high school.

Beverly often wondered if she'd done the right thing. But Teddy turned into a fine young man, and Ronnie and Jeff...well. Beverly and Janet were even closer now that they shared two fine grandchildren.

That would have been it for marriages, if Ronnie hadn't left home for college. For Beverly it was like losing Dom all over again. For months all she could do was put one foot in front of the other out on the roads of Bartlesville. Until she found Jim on the road, equally forlorn after losing his wife a year earlier. He found Beverly fascinating, his interest made her inner fascinator spring back to life, and soon enough their neighborhood wandering turned into a proposal of marriage. Because he was willing to stay in the area, she said yes.

Identifying new distractions became Beverly's full-time work. As youngest (and let's face it, the most vivacious) in the group, she would concoct fun double dates, challenging Janet, Jerry, and Jim (he was even a *J*!) to Hawk Mountain hikes, hot air balloon rides, and bowling with fake names (the one Beverly used the most: "Jeverly"). Much to her surprise, she ended up enjoying "the college years" very much. But Beverly could only add a momentary oomph to Jim's outlook. Hikes soon required first-aid kits too bulky to carry. Hot air balloons? No way. They can snag on live wires; he'd seen it on the news. Bowling required weeks of chiropractic recovery. Beverly saw the writing on the wall and, in the end, had to admit that bonding over sadness might not lay the best marital foundation.

Janet had stood up for Beverly at all three weddings—even that first one to Tony, which was a bit of a test, conducted as it was on a Cape Cod cruise, and Janet was seasick—and when the marriages were spent, she was there to help pick up the pieces. Only once had Janet tried to lecture her about the economics of repeated marriage. Beverly cut her right off. You did not want to get into a conversation with that woman about money. When she started counting beans, the full force of her negativity sprouted, one legume at a time.

Yet when Janet suggested a moratorium on marriage, Beverly finally made a vow she could keep: she would never marry again.

It wasn't until today, when all eyes were trained on her daughter's suicidal husband, that Beverly had finally known what her life's romantic flip-flopping was all about.

She'd wanted another Dom.

He was her one true love; a connection like theirs was not easy to recreate. Since then, intimacy had seemed to require negotiations that were daunting and complex, and it was so much easier to shrug her shoulders, crack a joke, and walk away while saying love just wasn't her thing.

But it was. Love was her only thing, and she wanted to believe it had some measure of influence. She patted the hand Janet had looped through her arm. She would be the rails for her family today and steady them as they picked their way through what frightening and chaotic moments this day might yet hold.

When they emerged from the trail at the far end of the park, Beverly's newfound resolve already started to curl at the edges. Looking up at the row of trees she had seen from a distance, she saw that they weren't glorious red at all.

They were yellow and turning brown.

ronnie

Corporal McNichol asked Ronnie to draw a map of the farm property. Of specific interest, she said, were the locations of all interior and exterior doors and which of them had locks. It was like giving her a coloring book and crayons, Ronnie supposed: busywork disguised to look relevant. The big barn with all its horse stalls and the chicken penthouse they'd built onto the far end. The empty stall where Will had always wanted to keep goats. The woodworking shop with tractor storage built into its side. The milk house that now held garden tools. Should her sketch warn them of the poison ivy growing through the rotted roof of the smokehouse, in which a man wouldn't fit because it only stored yard trash for the next burning? Anyway, they'd already found Jeff; why did they need all this information about the other outbuildings?

Yet the activity calmed her. There was a sane geometry to the square corners and circular layout.

How to render the remains of the chicken shed? She and Jeff had thought its sagging floors and listing piers would have fallen long ago, but it kept weathering storms. But it had been an eyesore, leaning as it was toward its demise, and a fall-through-the-floor safety risk. No longer fit for even a flock of three-pound chickens, it had long been on the list for demolition. So, on a whim one September Saturday, while Jeff was working an all-day wedding, Ronnie and the boys had gingerly emptied it of broken cat carriers, litter pans, and warped sports equipment. Everything but a few old tires on what was left of the floor. Standing outside the building, Ronnie knocked each corner post with the sledgehammer until it clung by an inch, then looped chain around the center post and attached it to the tractor. The boys chanted, "Go, go, go!" Ronnie threw the tractor into gear...and as the last of the day's sun dipped behind the hills, the building collapsed. When the dust settled, they found the roof sitting directly on top of the floor, the tires sandwiched in between.

The elation they had felt! The high-fives, the pizza in front of the TV, the ice cream.

Jeff had been livid that they'd taken on the project without him. But for Ronnie and the boys, it was a victory. They had taken care of something on their own—something big, men's work—and it sent their confidence soaring. Ronnie felt assured they'd be able to care for the farm on their own once Jeff moved out and until she could find a new place for them to live.

Ronnie examined her drawing. Their farm was a charming mishmash of a property in transition, from old and decrepit through old and charmingly renovated to new; it suggested the full circle of life.

Only the farm store remained. She considered its layout, sketched so often earlier this year as they were trying to figure out the best way to arrange its displays. She walked mentally among the configuration of aisles, sidestepping the colorful mums, bushels of fall bulbs, and the artful arrangement of pumpkins and warty gourds spilling from the wheelbarrow.

As she moved her pencil, she felt Jeff lay his hand over hers and pull it toward the office.

She yanked away her hand, sending the pencil clattering to the floor.

After shaking off the creepy feeling she picked up the pencil and returned to her drawing. She erased the desk and chair in the office store so many times that the place Jeff was most likely to sit was marked by a hole in the paper.

It was then, as if it were ringing and lighting up, that she pictured her smartphone charging by the cash register. She wondered if Jeff had tried to reach her today, assuming she had her cell with her, only to hear the maddening ring of his own unanswered call.

⌒

One day, after she'd decided to divorce him but before she'd had a chance to meet with an attorney, Jeff had sat in the recliner in her office all morning, watching her work. He'd showed amazing fortitude, she'd thought. It's not entertaining to watch a writer write. Finally he said, "I've thought of a way for you to keep the house."

"I won't take the house from you, Jeff," Ronnie said, not looking up from her article.

"I could come back and mow, and take care of the gardens."

"Jeff," she said, now meeting his eyes. "I do not want you coming back and watching my every move. We'll be divorced. I'll want to move on. Can we discuss this later? I'm on three different deadlines, and unless you want to do it, I have to relieve Amber down in the store in fifteen minutes. It's hard to concentrate with you staring at me like that."

The next morning, Ronnie found an extra card table set up in her office.

"What's this?"

"It's my workspace," Jeff said. "So we can be together."

He'd interrupted her many times that day, about coordinating their schedules and reviewing insurance policies. After going upstairs to answer a call, he returned with the "happy news" that his mother had agreed to pay off their debt.

"Oh." Ronnie didn't know how to feel about this. Pros and cons swirled through her mind. But it was no mystery how Jeff felt about it. His mood lifted as if he'd solved every last one of their problems.

He worked with the boys on their homework that afternoon and lamented aloud that he would miss Will's next soccer game. He helped with dinner and dishes. He insisted on attending the boys' gifted conference at school the next day, exclaiming afterward that he sure was glad he went because he didn't know what a great program it was—although Andrew had already been in it for two years. He actually participated in the bedtime rituals.

Later, when Ronnie went into the master bedroom to get out her clothes for the next day, he followed her in to put away new jeans and brightly colored T-shirts he'd bought to replace the torn ones he had worn since they'd married. For a moment, Ronnie had dared to hope.

He'd then handed her a "thank you for being you" type greeting card to which he'd added the message, "I want to share my days *and* nights with you."

She looked up at him in time to catch his smile that said *I've earned this.*

"Good night, Jeff." Ronnie returned to the guest bedroom and shut the door behind her.

The next day, when Ronnie went down to her office, the card table was gone.

As she settled in to work on an article, her phone rang, and Janet's name came up on the caller ID.

"Hi, Janet," Ronnie said. "You don't usually call on this line. Is something wrong, or is this business?"

"Both," Janet had said. "Ronnie, if I pay the money you owe, will you stay with Jeff?"

Her tremulous voice begged Ronnie's empathy. It almost worked. But Ronnie had grown sensitive to Farnham manipulation, and it felt all too familiar in her mother-in-law's request.

"Oh my god. You're trying to bribe me."

"That's a horrible thing to say."

"When Jeff told me about your offer yesterday, I wanted to say yes. It sure would be easier, because I have no clue how I will possibly address half of this debt. I can't even imagine being divorced."

"Then take the money. Stay married."

"I said it would be easier, not right. Sometimes we don't get to do the easy thing. Sometimes life is tough."

"I'm in a position to help."

"But will it help? If it were my son, I wouldn't do it. If Jeff stands any chance of pulling out of this downward spiral with his self-respect intact, he needs to spread his own wings and flap like hell."

"Ronnie," Janet said with a moan. "Don't let your pride break up our family."

"I have loved you for a long time, Janet, and that does not have to end. But it will if you think you can buy me for your son. I am not a bauble. I am a living, breathing person. The mother of your grandchildren, and soon enough, your son's ex-wife. Because Jeff and I are divorcing. The marriage was over long ago. I can't tell you what to do with your money, but you will not throw it at my feet and get me to dance. Got it?"

Ronnie hung up the phone and swiveled her chair back toward the computer—and saw Jeff standing in the doorway.

"So. I guess you don't like me very much." Jeff walked through her office, adding, "I guess that makes two of us," then went out the door and down the hill to the farm store.

Ronnie realized, with a heavy heart, that she really didn't have anything more to say.

Later that day, Jeff returned to her office to ask her to make out his will. "You're a writer. You can do it."

"It hardly seems appropriate to ask me," Ronnie had said. She had the capability to do it, thanks to software she'd purchased a few years earlier. But they'd put the task off for so long the software and her computer were no longer compatible. She wouldn't bother trying to explain this to Jeff, though. Beyond the computations necessary for tracking money at the bar, he'd never joined the technological revolution. One more way in which he relied on her. "Anyway, I told you I was busy. I have articles to tend to here."

He pulled out his money clip, flipped off five twenties, and placed them on her desk. "That should cover it."

Easy cash—Jeff's ultimate seduction. She aimed her answer at the cash, hoping it would go away more easily. "I'm not writing up your damn will, and that's final."

❧

Ronnie took one last look at the drawing she'd made of the farm. If Jeff died today as a result of this standoff, he'd do so without a will. Ronnie and her sons would inherit the house and property, although that would not constitute the entire inheritance. Add two horses, a Shetland pony, a dozen chickens, a few barn cats. Max. An International Cub tractor, circa 1960. A corncrib–turned–tack room full of saddles and bridles and extra horse blankets and who knows what else they probably had never been able to afford. Six acres dotted with fruit trees whose leaves had become lace doilies, whose fruit was gnarled. A mother-in-law with no other family.

"Oh no," Ronnie said.

"Don't stress over this drawing," Corporal McNichol said, approaching. "Whatever information you can provide will be helpful."

"It's not that. Some things he said, all on different days, are kind of lining up in my head."

"Like what?"

"First, Jeff said he'd found a way for me to stay in the house. Another day he asked me to write his will. And then yesterday, when I asked him if he still planned to move out today, he said yes."

Corporal McNichol nodded as Ronnie finished.

beverly

Beverly couldn't have been more surprised to find out that Ronnie and Jeff's marriage was crumbling. Her first inkling came one night last year when she found herself sitting in the living room of her apartment across the coffee table from Ronnie. Ronnie came over from time to time, sure, to drop off the boys or share a magazine with a good article about growing patio vegetables or a photo essay of Hugh Jackman (what could Beverly say, she wasn't dead yet). But it was nine p.m. on a school night, and the absence of the boys, an article, or Hugh had Beverly's palms sweating.

"What's up, Sunshine?"

"I think Jeff and I are in financial trouble."

"Okay." Beverly rubbed her hands on her pants. Trouble was not her specialty; when it reared its mighty head, she hid. "What sort of trouble?"

Ronnie shook her head. "I think he's sunk us deep in credit card debt. On cards I didn't know about."

"Oh dear," Beverly said. "Don't tell Janet. She has no use for credit cards. She'd disown him. What are you going to do?"

"I was hoping you'd have some advice."

Beverly nodded. Boy, this really didn't come naturally at all. She thought back to Ronnie's two miscarriages and how Ronnie had been so hurt that Jeff had to leave and go to work. As if getting pregnant were a joint effort but losing a child was a solo thing. The second time, Beverly had brought over some pretzels and cheese and they'd sat up all evening watching movies, pretending Ronnie had a simple case of menstrual cramps, until one punishing contraction after another ended the pregnancy. All hope had seemed lost. But now they had such a wonderful family. Beverly hated to hear this terrible news from Ronnie.

"What did Jeff say about it?"

"He said he'd pull together all the necessary information. I'm still waiting on it."

"When was that?"

"A year ago."

"Oh, baby."

"I've asked him time and again. I feel frozen, like we can't move forward unless I know what we're dealing with here. But he keeps ordering more sheetrock and spackle, putting up new walls and smoothing over the gaps in his accounting. It's maddening."

"Are you going to leave him?"

Ronnie fiddled with her wedding band. It was thinning, Beverly knew, because she was with Ronnie at the jeweler's when he warned her that manual labor was too hard on it. Ronnie had refused to remove it, saying if she didn't wear it while doing chores, she'd never wear it. "Of course not. But I need to figure out how to get him to honor my concerns."

"I guess he either honors them or he doesn't. I don't know how you can make anyone do anything without some sort of incentive."

"My god, shouldn't human decency be enough? Let alone love? I don't know how many times I've poured my heart out to him over the past year, begging him to come clean about the finances, only to have him wait me out in silence. He knows full well that after I release my concerns to the air, I'll have made room inside to stuff more down."

"And is he right? Does that work?"

Tears streamed down Ronnie's face. "Of course it does. I love him. I love our life. I don't want to be an angry, demanding bitch. But I can't live in a fantasy world either. I need to know where the cold stone walls are."

Beverly nodded. "Oh, honey, I've got no advice. Just one fact that I've observed time and again: that man adores you, Sunshine."

Ronnie stood to go. "I just don't know if that's enough."

ronnie

When Corporal McNichol excused herself to get some lunch, Ronnie suddenly found herself alone in the hall meant to be social. How many days, since becoming a mother, had she begged for some time alone? She'd meant alone with her writing, or alone with a book.

Not this alone.

For the first time, she considered Jeff's odd note stuck to the phone this morning, with its implication that she was having an affair. Her great fear was that if she stayed in this marriage much longer, his accusation might come true.

She'd met Kevin three months ago, in August, when Ronnie set off with Jeff, the boys, and Max for their annual vacation at the Jersey shore. To Ronnie, it felt like visiting family. The house was the only legacy connecting her to her father, and her week there was, in Ronnie's eyes, the only nonnegotiable item on a cost-saving budget. Once Jeff had parked in the driveway, she grabbed a few bags of groceries and left him and the boys to pull things from the back of the Suburban. Max raced past her as, halfway up the wooden stairs, Ronnie felt for the key, hanging on an inconspicuous nail hammered into the beam supporting the decking above. She waited up by the door for the boys to catch up, savoring the narrow ocean view between the houses across the street.

Andrew pounded up the stairs and dropped his bag. Will

followed. "Ready." Ronnie compared the heights of both boys to the random-seeming nicks on the weathered door frame that had marked her height each summer of her childhood. "Beat me again, boys. One day you'll stand taller than me or your dad."

She turned the lock and opened the door. With the first whiff of wet flip-flops and sun-dried towels, all of the Ronnies of every age fused together around the spine of this annual pilgrimage that had roots sinking all the way back to her mysterious father. Here, she felt whole.

While the boys went down to the car for another load, she put away the groceries, set out water for Max, and enjoyed a quiet moment with the living room couch.

The old leather still felt pliable beneath the hand she trailed across its back. *Hi, Dad.* When it was warm from the sun and little Ronnie would lie down on it to nap, its mass accommodated and supported every part of her the way she imagined a father would if curled beside his child. Her father had loved that couch, she thought, and his parents before him, and maybe the couch loved her a little bit back. At least that had always been her fantasy, and she couldn't see how it hurt her to believe it.

What Ronnie knew of Dominic Gallagher: he loved the beach and had inherited this house from his parents after the three of them were in a car accident—one he had survived, and they had not. Since her parents weren't married, the house did not go to her mother, but even though they had little money for frills, Beverly had rented the house from its new owners for a week each summer. Even though a stepfather sometimes came along, Ronnie had always sensed that time spent at the beach house was so that her mother, Ronnie, and her father could be together.

In the thirty-five years since his death, the population of this rental-heavy beach town had turned over several times, and no one remained who could tell Ronnie more about her father. Her mother was shut up like a clam on the subject. Why was Beverly so determined to keep the man to herself, when genetics would suggest that he belonged more to Ronnie than to her?

Ronnie couldn't imagine having her family wiped out in a single moment. She would have loved to ask her father about this. Already a budding journalist in grade school, Ronnie had once written out a list of questions she wanted to ask her father and had climbed onto the leather couch, faced its broad back cushions, and asked them out loud.

1. *What is your favorite TV show?*
2. *Do you like cooked carrots? (I don't.)*
3. *How old were you when your mother first let you swim beyond the breakers? (Still waiting here.)*
4. *Did you ever have a dog? (I'm not allowed. We move too much.) What kind? What was its name?*
5. *How did it feel to lose your entire family at once?*

She then wrote the answers that came to her, pretending her father had whispered them in her ear.

1. *My favorite TV show would be whatever you're watching, so I could sit next to you on my leather couch and watch together.*
2. *Cooked carrots, blech. You kidding me?*
3. *Fifteen. You have a ways to go yet, squirt.*
4. *I did have a dog. He was a fluffy cockapoo, and his name was Max. For fourteen years, he was my best friend.*
5. *Oh, Veronica (sorry, I mean Ronnie—Veronica is just such a beautiful name). I sure hope you never have to find out.*

The interview was written on stationery decorated with a string of daisies across the top and bottom. She had lined it herself, using a pencil and a ruler, to keep the questions straight. At first she'd kept the list in the bottom of her jewelry box. A few years ago she moved it to a pocket in the front of her first journal, when she redefined what was most precious to her. It wasn't the jewelry Jeff had bought her, but the thoughts and imaginings now begging expression.

Considering the accident of her conception and the impermanence of stepfathers, Ronnie still used the pages of her journal to question why she was meant to survive. Was it for the sole purpose of renovating a farmhouse in Pennsylvania? She couldn't believe that; the next person to live in the house would swap out the Armstrong for tile, the Formica for granite. Was it to have her sons? Certainly this was true, yet in the great chain of life, she hoped to provide a stronger link. She must have some higher calling, and for a long time, it bothered her that she still had no clue what that would be. She'd found purpose in her writing, but pursuing it tugged at Jeff, who didn't understand or respect her passion for it. But it energized her—and the more it did, the more run-down Jeff appeared in comparison. Ronnie had hoped that this year, some time at the shore would restore him.

And restore her as well. This year Ronnie felt less like a whole woman and more like a mass-produced doll with different outfits. Mom Ronnie. Writer Ronnie. Farm store Ronnie. Barn Ronnie. Renovator Ronnie. Romantic Ronnie. Okay, she wouldn't even know how to dress that last version anymore, but she hadn't abandoned all hope of putting that piece of herself back into production. She was hoping for a dream vacation in that regard.

Max jumped onto the leather couch and curled up for a nap. Ronnie held the door as Jeff and the boys brought in the rest of their luggage. "Who wants to get baptized?"

She didn't wait for an answer but ran back down the stairs. The boys passed her on the way to the water. She checked over her shoulder with irrational hope. No Jeff.

The boys awaited her at the wet sand's edge. She joined them, huffing. "I don't think I can lift and dip anymore," she said. "You're getting too big."

"That's okay, Mom," Andrew said. "We'll do it like you do."

The next wave was on its way in. "Ready?"

All three of them dipped their fingers into the water, touched them to their foreheads, then pressed the remaining water to their lips.

When they got back to the house, the new owner, Kevin, was pulling tools from his pickup truck.

"Hi. What's going on?" Ronnie said.

"I noticed yesterday that the garage didn't survive the last renter. The door won't go all the way up. Sorry I couldn't get it fixed before you guys got here. This shouldn't take long."

Jeff eyed the tools, practically drooling. "Need some help with that?"

"No thanks. You relax," Kevin said.

That would be a problem. Even though this year he was vacationing with a recently strained back and a swollen knee, Jeff would never think of injury or pain as an excuse to relax.

The midday heat was building, so after she unpacked, Ronnie brought Kevin a glass of iced tea. Jeff paced above her on the deck, smoking.

"You didn't have to do that," Kevin said as Ronnie approached.

"Oh. Okay then." She lifted the glass to her lips.

"But I won't refuse it." She smiled and handed him the glass. He pressed it to his cheek before sipping.

"The mint's from our garden." Ronnie leaned against the garage door frame. "So how'd you come to own the house?"

"Hurricane Sandy," he said. "I owned my own construction business on the southern tip of the island but lost my home, my workshop, and everything in them when the hurricane hit."

"That's horrible," she said. "I guess you had hurricane insurance?"

Kevin set down the tea and returned to securing all the places where the garage door track was attached.

"That was way too nosy, wasn't it? Professional hazard. I'm a writer." She could sense Jeff, above her on the deck, rolling his eyes at the word *professional*.

"Hey, cool. I've never met a writer before. Have you written any books?"

"Who knows, I may one day. And that insurance bit just sprang to mind. My husband's family is so big on insurance you'd think they sell it or something. In this case, it sounds like it would have come in handy."

Kevin smiled, although his eyes seemed sad. There was a story on his face. "I was just trying to figure out how to shorten up the answer. Hurricane insurance is handy, yes, but it has a huge deductible. I used up my life's savings paying it and purchased this home with the insurance money." He was now slowly rebuilding his life, he explained, through rental income and the generosity of buddies willing to put him up when he needed to vacate the place. "We all kind of help each other out here."

"I appreciate you renting to us," Ronnie said. "More than you know. This place belonged to my father back in the late seventies and to his parents before him."

"Really? You'll have to tell me more about that sometime. I'm a bit of a history nut."

"You've kept a lot of the furnishings the same. Thank you. This place is all I have of him. I don't have much money, but if you ever wanted to sell anything, I'd appreciate it if you'd at least let me try to make the first offer."

"Don't worry. I'm a contractor, not an interior decorator. Place suits me fine. I was lucky to buy it furnished."

Kevin set up a stepladder and went over to the breaker box and cut the lights. He then climbed up and removed the casing for the door opener's motor unit.

"You need me to hold a flashlight for you?" Ronnie said, falling into her typical role. Jeff could never see a thing unless she positioned the light just so.

"No need," Kevin said, pulling a small headlamp from his back pocket. He slipped its elastic band right over his baseball cap and turned it on. "Ah, this is all corroded. Hey, can you pass me the wire stripper? It's that tool with the yellow—"

"I know." She handed it up to him. "If you'll let me," Ronnie suddenly found herself saying, "I'd love to write up a profile on you and try to get it published."

A sound on the stairs drew her attention. Jeff was bumping a vacuum cleaner down the steps, unreeling an extension cord behind him. *What the heck?*

"Ha! Not sure why," Kevin said. "I'm nothing special. My block alone was full of more interesting stories."

"Such as?" Ronnie almost had to shout—for some reason, Jeff had started vacuuming out the Suburban. "Wait."

Ronnie opened the front door of the Suburban, pulled a pen and pad from the front door pocket, and mouthed to Jeff the word "stop." He ignored it.

Returning to Kevin, she said, "Mind if I take notes?"

"Suit yourself."

"You were going to tell me what else happened on your block."

"A tree came down on my next-door neighbor's house and killed him, right in his bed. He hadn't evacuated. His wife had gone to check on their kids—if she hadn't, she'd be gone too. He was only thirty-four. I know it for a fact—I'm lucky to be alive."

"What happened to his family?"

"They moved in with relatives near Pittsburgh. I don't think they'll be coming back."

"But you stayed." Ronnie listened to the drone of the vacuum. "I don't think it's the hurricane's story I'd want to tell as much as the story of human resiliency. I assume you evacuated?"

"Yep. Stayed inland with my wife's family."

"I'd love to meet her. She might have insight for the article."

Jeff turned off the vacuum. In the sudden silence, Kevin climbed down from the ladder. "Not everyone is as excited about resiliency as you are." He drained his iced tea.

"Oh. Sorry."

"The toughest loss, for sure." His voice grew rough with emotion. He cleared his throat. "She couldn't face rebuilding, and I couldn't avoid it. Reminds me of something my grandfather used to say: 'You can compromise on who takes out the trash, but you can't compromise your principles.'"

Ronnie laughed at the old man voice he adopted. "I think I would have liked your grandfather. *Eek!*" Cold water sprayed her legs and splashed onto Kevin. She looked out—Jeff now stood behind the Suburban with a hose.

"Overshot," he said.

Ronnie darted him another look.

"No bother, man," Kevin said. "Felt good."

Ronnie wiped her notebook on the seat of her shorts.

"Want to see what I found when I got back?" Kevin said, reaching into his back pocket.

"Sure." He leaned in close and held up his smartphone. Despite the day's heat, a clean, fresh-from-the-line scent lifted from his T-shirt. Ronnie felt Jeff's glare boring into her but refused to acknowledge it.

Kevin flipped through picture after picture of houses collapsed and buckled, with sections displaced or missing. She flinched when she saw the tree crashed through his neighbor's roof. "My god. Jeff, you should see these."

That was all the invitation she was going to give him. He did not join her.

"See that Long Beach Bakery sign floating in this one? That store was five doors down. This was my block."

"Oh my god. Which was your house?"

"It's here." He pointed. "And here. And I think that's what was left of my roof's peak over there."

"And people complained that we were without power for five days. Were you able to salvage anything?"

"Just what I brought with me when I evacuated. I figure the sea turtles now have a pretty sweet woodworking shop set up on the ocean floor."

Ronnie didn't know whether to laugh or cry. It was one thing to see this sort of devastation on the news and another to meet someone whose loss was so complete and so personal.

"Yet this place wasn't damaged beyond a few roof shingles, the previous owner said."

"I know. Weird, right? The difference a few miles will make." He flipped to a new picture. "Everything else was waterlogged from the flooding—look at this couch floating here—or swept away. I did find one thing, though." He tipped his head, and Ronnie followed his eyes to the back wall of the garage and the nautical steering wheel now affixed to it.

Kevin took off his headlamp and flipped the breaker back on. "Finding it felt like a miracle. My grandpa made this wheel himself and was so proud of it that to this day, I still picture him standing in his fishing boat behind it. Imagine walking through a complete wasteland, like I did, and finding this one object that reminded you of someone you loved."

He ran a finger along the brass in its center. Kevin was still wearing his baseball cap. Ronnie wondered what was beneath it.

"Only had to polish it up and replace one broken handle. These were made for the weather, to be sure."

Ronnie ran her hand over the almost seamless repair. "You did a good stain match. Jeff's also a great woodworker. Over the past twelve years, we've gutted and renovated our entire house."

"Takes a lot of heart. Many think they want to try, get a room or two in, and hire me to finish up." He turned to Jeff, who was soaping up the hood of the car. "You a contractor too?"

Ronnie tensed, wishing he could say yes. Wishing he had

supported them by using his talent to help others. Wondering if he'd use the official title she preferred, "Food and beverage manager."

"Bartender."

"Ah," Kevin said. "So woodworking is just a hobby then."

"One we spend most of our waking hours pursuing," Ronnie said, to cover any slight Jeff might suffer.

Kevin tested the door. It rolled easily and fully along its track. Ronnie couldn't help but think of the big barn doors at home, heavy and sagging, and how she had to use her full weight to move them. Kevin packed up his tools.

"One last question, for now. Weren't you angry about all you lost?"

"Sure, for a while. I mean, I figure I'm human, and humans are nothing else but a big bundle of feelings. But it's not like the whole world is about me, you know? I figure I just have to keep on showing up, day after day, doing what I need to do to play my part."

"You said, 'I figure.'"

"I did?"

"You said 'figure' two times, actually."

He turned around and said to Jeff, "Damn. She must be a firecracker to live with."

Jeff looked over from where he was circling his sponge over the driver's side door. He didn't smile. Positioned as they were, with Jeff in the background, Kevin seemed to vibrate with energy.

"So it's not like you had some sort of deep knowing," Ronnie prompted.

"I think that's the entire point," Kevin said. "We don't know a blessed thing. We've just got to point ourselves in a direction that feels true, truck along at our own pace, and try to figure things out." He peeked at her notes. "Did you write that down? That was 'figure' number three." He laughed. "Anyway, if we do all that, when we get to the pearly gates, at least we can report in with some confidence."

"I heard a joke like that once."

"Grandpa had a lot of wisdom, a lot of jokes." He winked at her. "If I have them all mixed up, the joke's on me."

She offered her hand. "Kevin, I'm so glad we had this chance to talk. I think people are going to be inspired by the way you came back here and faced off against your loss. Can I reach you at the rental number if I have follow-up questions?"

He wrote his cell number at the top of her notes.

"Guess I'll go for a swim then. You know where to leave the key when you leave." Kevin picked up his toolbox and walked backward as he said, "Just don't make me out to be brave. These days, any wind over fifty miles per hour has me wanting to hightail it in the opposite direction."

Ronnie smiled. "Understandable. I'll be in touch."

More questions immediately sprang to mind and Ronnie took a moment to write them down.

Her mind was abuzz all through dinner. She was so eager to tell Jeff about her ideas for the article that she started in about it as soon as the boys asked to be excused from the dinner table. "I'll have to interview a psychologist as well," she said as she cleared the dishes. "Who knows—if I could find more stories of people who have risen above their losses, I might write a book someday."

Jeff said, "Ronnie, in case you didn't notice, while you two had your little conversation, I cleaned our Suburban inside and out. My back is sore. I just want to sit and have a drink in peace."

"What do you mean, my 'little conversation'? That's what I'm telling you. I was working too."

"Volunteer work, you mean."

Ronnie put her hand on her hip.

"Okay, what do you have to show for this work? A clean car? A sore back?"

"You know I don't."

"A paycheck?"

"That's not how freelance writing works."

"Because it's a hobby."

She set his dirty plate back in front of him. "I'm going for a walk."

"Even the IRS says so," he called after her. "If you came to the tax appointments, you'd know."

Ronnie slammed the door.

She was going to write the article, and it was going to be the best damn thing she'd ever written.

At the deck railing, she paused and felt the wood for what might be left of the day's warmth. That afternoon she'd stood in the same place with Kevin's empty glass in her hand, watching as he stepped onto the beach, pulled off his shirt and cap, and let the breeze ruffle his fine brown hair.

ronnie

We've been reviewing options," Corporal McNichol said, striding back into the room.

"Oh?" Ronnie snapped to attention as if she'd been caught doing something wrong. Her body was flush with lingering feelings of intoxicating curiosity and—she hated to admit it, even to herself—desire. Things only Jeff used to make her feel. Had Jeff seen this change in her? Is that what had him so scared?

"You may want to file a protection from abuse order. After what happened at your house today, you'd qualify."

"So after today, you suspect this will still be an issue?" Ronnie said. "Nothing will be solved?"

"I'm suggesting you prepare for all possibilities."

Ronnie trudged back down the hall to the firehouse office. The men stepped out of the room. She called the Reading Courthouse only to learn she had to appear in person to file. Though Ronnie suspected this formality offered no hope. The order might ensure that Jeff would live somewhere else, but with the state police so far away, if he really wanted to hurt them—or try to hurt himself again, on the property—he'd have ample opportunity to do so before help could arrive.

Alone in the office this time, she allowed herself a moment to relish its windows. For the first time all morning, Ronnie looked up at the sky. That blue, so brilliant you could sense its depth; was there any color more beautiful? Wanting to be closer to it, she turned a handle and tipped open the window. She allowed a long draft of fresh air to make full contact with her lungs. This was her very favorite kind of fall day, with air so crisp it made her think of biting into a sweet-tart apple. With the sun smiling down on customers coming and going from Perlmutter's General Store across the street, it was hard to believe any sort of tragedy could possibly be unfolding.

Ronnie returned to the social hall tables somewhat refreshed, certain she must have left hope for her family's future lying around on one of these surfaces. All she found was the pile of keys, which opened cars blocked in by the police.

"Did you get through to someone at the courthouse?" Corporal McNichol said.

"For what it's worth." She thought of her sons' arms, so vulnerably thin, their legs not yet muscled enough to make a run for their lives. How could she keep them safe?

Ronnie was wringing her hands again. She shoved them in her pockets. She'd worked too hard to purge the anxiety that had set in when they got home from the shore. She would not let it get the better of her now.

⟡

While absorbed in the endless list of catch-up chores that accumulated on the farm every time they went away, Ronnie couldn't stop thinking about Kevin. During early morning sessions with her journal, she tried to explain away this fascination as false intimacy created by hearing him talk about his beloved grandfather in the home that had belonged to her father. The way he took command of his situation, even while surrendering to circumstance beyond his control.

The way he seemed to be the man she wished Jeff had turned out to be.

She tackled her chores each day with unusual enthusiasm so she could get back to her journal. Her thoughts were ordering themselves on its pages as if the words painted a new portrait of her. One she was afraid to see, yet whose colors would not be ignored.

She tried to memorialize the perspective that while she and Jeff were so busy it seemed they led separate lives, what kept them together was the lifestyle they loved with the boys on the farm. She tried to convince herself that was all she needed.

Of course she would like more attention from Jeff. It had been nine months since they'd last had sex. In recent years, Jeff had relied on Ronnie to marshal efforts and morning erections to do half the work. She still yearned for his touch and the emotional fusion their lovemaking had once been, but these days, with his pillowcase stained nicotine yellow from not washing up at night and his breath sour, she wasn't sure it was worth the effort.

She wrote in her journal:

What are my needs?

Does a mother have needs? If one of the chops was overdone, Ronnie, as cook, always took it. If there was no hot water left after everyone else's showers, she was the one who'd go unclean until the water heater recharged; after all, she worked from home. She was flexible. If she was tired and needed a nap, she'd squeeze one in right after she met her deadlines or shuffled the boys to all their activities or made dinner—or, more likely, she'd just drink more coffee.

I don't know what my needs are, but my conversations with Kevin excite me. They taste like camaraderie, laughter, and emotional language—and I want more of it.

And if more were ever offered, I don't know how the hell I'd resist.

Over the next two weeks in August, at odd moments throughout the day, Ronnie would be waylaid by crying jags that had no discernible cause. She felt like someone was scratching on the chalkboard of her bones. She set out one day to take Max for one of their three-mile walks and realized, when she got home, that she'd forgotten to bring the dog. And her hands were sore and red; she'd been wringing them the whole way.

One day, Jeff came down to her office and found her sitting at her computer, tears streaming down her cheeks.

"What's the matter?" he said, his voice full of concern.

"I wish I knew," she said.

"Maybe you should go to the doctor."

"I don't think it's physical," she said. "It's more like something welling up inside of me that has to get out. I think I need to see a therapist."

Jeff braced himself against the doorway. "You're going to leave me."

Why the hell would he say that? Is my inner turmoil so insignificant that he had to add his to it?

Then again, maybe he knew her better than she'd given him credit for. Three therapy appointments later, things looked a whole lot clearer.

She may be powerless to improve the quality of her marriage, but she was not powerless to affect the quality of her life.

ronnie

The corporal stood across from Ronnie, the table between them a neutral expanse, her face expressionless. As if ready to accept her confession.

"He's doing this because I wanted a divorce."

"Divorce is tough, there's no getting around that." Corporal McNichol shrugged. "Yet people get through it every day without ending up in a suicide standoff. Humans—healthy humans, anyway—are remarkably adaptive beings."

"But I'm his whole world." It sounded at once idiotic and true. She felt heat rise to her face as she pushed her drawing across the table.

Corporal McNichol eased herself into the chair, as if not wanting to add any further stimulation to Ronnie's overwrought mind, and contemplated her drawing of the property. "You can't make a man kill himself," she said. "Even if I pointed a gun at his child and said, 'Kill yourself or he's dead.' A healthy mind will try to figure another way out. The instinct to survive is too strong."

The thought was comforting—until Ronnie considered the corollary. "And if a man really wants to kill himself, nobody can stop him." The words drifted into the quiet without rebuttal.

Corporal McNichol said, "We couldn't stop my father."

"Oh," Ronnie said.

Suicide was no longer a vague, impossible notion. It had moved right into the room with them.

Until then, Ronnie had thought of Corporal McNichol as a tough cop who got her kicks ordering around a bunch of snipers, like on TV. Someone with a function: to reach Jeff and support Ronnie. Now she saw a woman with wavy hair and hips. A mom sitting alone at a PTA meeting; a mom with a secret.

"I'm sorry," Ronnie said. "Were you close?"

Corporal McNichol smiled. "He's the reason I became a cop. When I entered the academy, he was the chief of police in Lancaster. I wanted so badly to make him proud. Instead I watched him fade away."

"What happened? I mean, if you don't mind me asking."

"He saw too much." She paused for a moment. "That's my best guess, anyway. A pregnant preteen strung out on dope. A school shooting. His first partner succumbing to ALS. We can only guess at the final tipping point."

"He didn't leave a note?"

Corporal McNichol shook her head. "Guess he didn't have anything left to say."

"He shot himself?" Ronnie said quietly.

Corporal McNichol let out a long breath. "I had to cut him down from the rafters in our garage."

Ronnie could only imagine the concrete horror of seeing your father hanging lifeless. Her own father was dead, but she hadn't seen him that way. At the beach, it was easy to imagine him forever young. She marveled at Corporal McNichol's ability to not only live through such a thing, but also somehow protect a place in her heart still capable of offering compassion to others in a similar situation.

They sat in silence for a moment. Finally Corporal McNichol said, "The sad truth is, not everyone can make it in this world."

"Sorry, but I refuse to accept that. And I can't believe they put you in charge of the SERT troops. The assignment seems cruel."

"I applied for it." The corporal's gaze was steady.

"How could you—*why* would you willingly enter a suicide stand-off? Especially knowing you might fail?"

Corporal McNichol opened Jeff's file and patted its growing stack of its papers. "Because I can't stop trying. And because sometimes, I can make a difference. Like today."

Ronnie got up and walked over to the wall before turning back toward Corporal McNichol. She needed distance, perspective. The helicopter, this SERT team, all the ammunition—it was costing so much money. "I can't put this whole police action together with the Jeff I've known who was so gentle. Could he have changed so much?"

Corporal McNichol was quiet for a moment. "I'm not so sure we change. I think that extreme pressure reveals us."

Ronnie considered the debt and how she would have consulted a credit counselor and arranged for payments, while Jeff pushed it off on his mother.

"But I have to deal in facts," Corporal McNichol said. "Right now Jeff is armed and intoxicated. That's a lethal combination. On top of that, he told you he would kill himself."

"He just said that to pressure me into—"

"Hear me on this, Ronnie," Corporal McNichol said. "Once a person has lost respect for the sanctity of his own life, it isn't much of a stretch to lose respect for all life."

Ronnie picked at some dry skin on her thumb. Hangnails always arrived with the cooler weather, like chapped lips. As if she were molting. Soon she had a tough quarter-inch of skin hanging off her finger. She gave it a good tug and watched blood fill the gap. "You think he'll do it."

Corporal McNichol spread the papers in front of her and examined them as if they were tea leaves. "I don't know. I really don't. But he threatened suicide once, with a note detailing his burial wishes, and six weeks later, it's all going down again. I think he's been trying

to work up the courage to carry out his plan. The unknown variable is whether we can intervene in time."

"Oh god." It all suddenly felt so hopeless. "What do I do?"

"Just love your boys. Fixing this is not your responsibility."

"Really? Then who the hell's is it?" Ronnie pushed off from the wall where she'd been leaning. "If Jeff lives through the day, then what is my life going to look like? He's still my sons' father. And if he dies, who do you think will inherit that mess? No matter how you define 'fixing,' it's all on me."

Corporal McNichol picked up the drawing again and said, "I think this diagram needs some fixing too." She pushed it back across the table to Ronnie.

"You probably can't tell what a damn thing is. I should have labeled the buildings—"

"It just looks too empty. You'll feel better if you add some living beings to it." Corporal McNichol smiled. "Hang on to this, Ronnie: suicidal men will often kill their wives and children too. Today worked out well for us. We were lucky to get you out of there alive."

Ronnie was grateful for their safety. Of course she was.

But what would happen when Corporal McNichol and her troops went home?

1:00 p.m.

beverly

Beverly plopped a paper bag down on the table beside her daughter. "Here, Sunshine. You should eat."

Ronnie waited until Janet walked down the aisle between tables toward the restroom. "Who paid for it?"

"Why on earth does that matter?" Beverly said. "We both love you."

Ronnie looked Beverly in the eye. "Who paid for it?"

"We split it."

"Your idea?"

"It was Jan's, but I don't see what difference—"

Ronnie unwrapped the hoagie, ripped the bun in half, and handed back the rewrapped portion.

"What's gotten into you?"

"See if I have this right. While you watched, Janet counted out her pennies to pay for this."

Apparently Beverly hadn't done too well at disguising her expression. Ronnie was right on the money.

"Well, guess what, I still can't be bought. I will not let a Farnham throw money at me again and let it stand in for love. She can keep her half of the damn sandwich."

Ronnie bent over some sort of drawing.

"All those circles in the rectangle. What are they supposed to be?" Beverly said.

"They're chickens in the barn, thank you."

Beverly chuckled. "You don't have to snap."

"I'm sorry, Mother. My armed and dangerous husband is standing off against a shitload of police with sniper rifles and my horses are frantic because they haven't eaten and my kids have been shipped off to a house deemed safer than their own home. Oh, never mind, that was the exact same situation an hour ago, when you went out for a spot of lunch."

Beverly opened her mouth to speak, then caught her lip between her teeth.

"What?"

"I can't go through this alone," Beverly said.

"*You* can't? Wow. This is truly a proud daughter moment."

"Look, Ronnie. There are some things I need to tell you." Beverly looked at Corporal McNichol. "Can I have a minute with my daughter?"

Corporal McNichol took the revised drawing from Ronnie. "I'll go check in with my men."

Beverly waited until the corporal had left the room. "You have his eyes, you know."

Ronnie tensed.

"And that same determined set of jaw that frankly scares the crap out of me. But I like to believe you have a touch of my spunk too."

Ronnie spread her hands on the table and looked at them for several painfully quiet moments. "Do you know how many times in my life I would have loved to hear more about my father?" she finally said. "And I'm not even talking about all the times I asked. I'm talking about when we left Teddy and Daryl. Or when Jeff and I married. Or when my sons were born, and I wondered if either of them looked like him. But instead you'd tell me now, when I will always associate his memory with this heartless room and Jeff's suicide standoff?" She looked up at Beverly with that determined jaw in full display. "Why?"

"Well…" Beverly was not overly eager to dive right into that part. She had carried some things alone, for so long, she didn't know if it was wise to share the burden. Yet her daughter was hurting in a way all too familiar, and Beverly knew Ronnie needed a scrap of something new to hang on to. "You have time on your hands, don't you?"

Ronnie kicked out the chair across from her. Beverly took it.

Beverly had long imagined this moment, despite her inability to bring it to fruition. She'd hoped the sharing might be more companionable, but that was the way with secrets, she supposed; the longer words stayed buried, the harder they clung to their grave. Was now the right time to exhume such a story?

Ronnie again looked at the table. "If he raped you, just tell me and I don't need to hear any more."

Beverly took in a sharp breath. "Is that what you think happened?"

"It's crossed my mind. You've kept everything about him from me, as if he were some sort of a monster. As if you feared the part of me that might exhibit the same qualities."

"For one thing," Beverly said, twirling her small diamond, "you don't wear a promise ring your whole life long from a man who raped you."

Ronnie pulled her mother's hand toward her and looked at the ring anew. "You told me it was just a trinket."

"It is a trinket," Janet said, joining them. "Look at the size."

"Now, Janet, hush. It may be little, but it's real."

"So you're expecting he still might come back?" Ronnie said. "You told me he was dead."

Beverly sighed and shook her head. When she and Ronnie had left Tony in the Massachusetts woods, and Beverly was missing Dom something fierce and needed to talk about him, she'd told Ronnie that he had died of a stroke when she was two years old. When Ronnie was a teen and questioning how such a young man had died of a stroke, Beverly had changed it to an aneurysm. Janet had called Dom's death the "ever-changing story." And Beverly had learned to keep her mouth shut. "The end's no good, so let me start at the beginning."

Janet propped her chin in her hand. "Curious to hear this story."

Beverly sank into her chair as if its metal surface had softened. This was going all wrong. She shouldn't have said anything. Sharing Dom with anyone was fraught with complication, but if their own daughter rejected the idea of him—or rejected her because of him—the tender love she'd nourished all these years would wither and be gone.

Ronnie put up an open hand in surrender, then sat back to listen.

"You remember Grandpa Saylor, Ronnie, and how strict he was. He wouldn't let me go down the shore with my friends on vacation because they were all seniors and I was only a junior. Well…I went anyway." Beverly then filled in all the missing details in the story of how she met Ronnie's father.

❧

One night, when the girls were eating dinner at Veronica's Grotto, a handsome stranger sat eating nachos and nursing a beer at the next table. Beverly kept sneaking looks at him. He had this aura of sadness that kept begging her attention. When her friends noticed, they dared her to ask him to join them. It didn't take much for Beverly to consider it the ultimate flirting challenge.

He wouldn't join their group but instead asked Beverly to join him. And once Dom pushed his plate of nachos toward Beverly, there was no turning back. She couldn't even say how long after that her friends left. She and Dom talked for hours. It was as if he'd stored all his words in a secret vault and opened it just for her. He offered to buy her a drink, but since she had just turned seventeen and was what some might call a runaway, she didn't want to push her luck. When the place got crowded and hearing each other grew difficult, Beverly suggested a walk on the beach.

At the ocean's edge, perhaps aided by the anonymity darkness conferred, Dom told her about surviving the car crash that had killed his parents. Their deaths clung to him so tightly he couldn't stop questioning why he had been spared, and before they ever touched, Beverly already knew she would be the one to kiss all his pain away. They walked for miles along the shore that night, and Beverly taught him all of the words to "On Top of Spaghetti." His voice was so warm and robust he made the ditty sound like an aria; she expected a pod of dolphins to follow along or a whale to breach. He even joined her in a little dance to the beach gods that brought him so far from that dark place and into the moonlight that he was laughing.

His laughter made Beverly feel so powerful and alive. And when they reached his house and he invited her in, and she saw the little dinette and comfy leather couch, she felt like she was home. She knew who she was meant to be. She could never make her father happy, but she could make Dom happy, and that became her new goal. She stopped by the condo to pick up her things and say good-bye to her girlfriends, and when they returned to Pennsylvania, she did not.

Her father was livid. During a loud phone call during which he invoked both God and Lucifer, he said she'd made her bed and would have to lie in it. She was more than happy to take that advice.

Then the missed period. She and Dom were so happy playing house that she didn't fear telling him she was pregnant. It was the natural extension of their intimacy. Beverly curled up on the leather couch, making lists of everything they'd need for the baby—the bare minimum, of course. It would be like camping, she told him. They could line a drawer with a blanket for a crib. Cut bibs and washcloths from old towels.

But she could not get him to join her on that couch. He came up behind it, put his arms around her, and said, "Don't worry. We'll be fine. Don't worry."

Well, she hadn't been worried at all. That's when she knew he was. Beverly assured him she'd get a job, that the clinic said she was healthy. Their two incomes would keep them afloat.

In the beginning of August, Dom lost his delivery job. With the tourist season drawing to a close, he couldn't find work. His mood grew a whole lot darker.

Then one day in late August, he returned home from the unemployment office all chipper, said he'd figured everything out. It was so good to have him back again; Beverly wanted to spend every free moment with him, but that wasn't his plan. He wanted her to go back to Pennsylvania and finish high school. But first he got down on one knee and gave her the little diamond.

$$\sim$$

"With tears in his eyes," she told Ronnie, "he told me that no other woman would ever have his heart."

"He was romantic," Ronnie said. "And dutiful. And caring. Like Jeff used to be. And the ring is sweet, Mom. I don't know why you never told me."

Oh, Ronnie. The things I haven't told you.

"Leaving him was like leaving half of myself behind," Beverly said. "But I went back home, like Dom suggested, to finish school. I was only under my father's roof for one night before he called me a tramp. Even though you were still a little notion in my belly, I figured you had ears that didn't need to put up with that kind of language, so I walked out, with no real plan of where I was heading. If a certain typing teacher hadn't found me a cheap room to rent, you might have been born on the street." She tilted her head toward Janet.

"It's a good thing my other students weren't such a handful." Janet parted her lips, almost forming a smile.

"You were harder on me than anyone else in the class, remember?"

"Of course not. I had one hundred budding secretaries each year depending on me for their livelihoods."

"You gave me a D."

"I was kind. By the end of the first quarter, you hadn't yet qualified for an F in either speed or accuracy."

"You said you didn't remember being hard on me."

"Didn't remember, trying to forget—it's all the same. What did you need typing for anyway? You can write Dear John letters longhand."

"I know enough about my mother's failed marriages," Ronnie said. "Let's get back to the romantic part. You said my father had a plan. What was it?"

A plan was exactly what Beverly had failed to have when she launched this story. She looked at her daughter, her eyes now brighter than they'd been all day. This had been a mistake. Beverly back-pedaled.

"He planned to come spend Thanksgiving with me," she said weakly.

"That's it? Mom, seriously, you have to work on your storytelling skills."

Beverly could feel the story sinking back into her. It had grown used to her innermost recesses and was not quite ready to leave the dark.

"I know that look," Ronnie said. "Don't leave me hanging. Please. Whatever it is, just tell me."

Suddenly it was all Beverly could do not to cry.

"Mom, no. You can't jerk me around like this. What did you want to tell me?"

Janet reached over and touched Ronnie's wrist. "This is the most she's said about Dom in more than thirty years. It's hard on her. Give her a bit more time."

"Just what I needed," Ronnie muttered as she stood. "More waiting."

Beverly watched her daughter lap the room. She understood

Ronnie's impatience. But experience told Beverly that it was the tension between the beginning and the end that held all of life's possibilities and the full array of her imaginings. Once the questions ended and the knowing began, there was no turning back.

And the knowing could leave you hurting like hell.

janet

For a moment, with her curls back and those bright eyes trained on her mother, Janet remembered what Ronnie looked like when she was little. Janet had been jealous of Beverly back then. She had always wanted a girl.

Like all the Hoyer family, Janet's mother, Amelia, believed in the power of women. Along with the Bible and marriage, they put their faith in a woman's tight-fisted management of her husband's paycheck—to great success.

When a few missteps had Janet threatening this matriarchal manifesto, Amelia took measures to set them right. When Janet fell in love with Jerry, who couldn't afford college, they paid his way so he could have a reliable career. And when Janet got pregnant while still in school, Amelia paid for their wedding, gave them a place to live, and nursed her after the birth so that Jerry's paycheck could be invested and put to immediate work. Although Janet tested her mother's limits by skimping on prayer, in every other way, she had taken her place in her mother's lineage and felt empowered by the way the family nest egg had grown on her watch.

After Jeff married Fay Sickler, Janet expected heirs and was surprised when year after year went by without the arrival of one single grandchild. Not that Janet cared for Fay; she hadn't liked her one bit. Jeff had met her in a barn, where she was mucking out stalls in exchange for free board, which said a lot. After all of the work it took to get Jeff through high school and into college, Fay's unrealistic demands had forced him into leaving his respectable job as a corn broker to tend bar. Janet was proud he'd advanced to manager, but those late nights and rowdy people—what kind of life was that?

Truth be told, she thought Jeff might be too skittish to have children. After he and Fay had bred one of her mares, Jeff had called Janet from the barn when the horse started pushing. When Janet got home from work, she went straight to the stable. "Oh my, twins," she said, before realizing they were still as still could be. Both females. Jeff sat in the corner of the stall, crying. He never again tried to breed.

But he seemed to set his disappointments behind him when he married Ronnie. They got right to work spiffing up the house and trying to get pregnant. They had two quick losses. Janet watched Jeff carefully, fearing he might give up. But Ronnie wanted kids, and wanted Jeff to be their father, and, well, if sheer determination can turn a sperm and an egg into a child, then she pulled it off. Then and now, Andrew felt like a miracle. A boy miracle.

Ronnie only wanted two children, so when the next one came along, Janet had one last shot at a female heir. The child took its sweet time entering the world. They'd gone to the hospital at six a.m., and when she didn't get a call all day, Janet was gripped with the memory of those stillborn fillies.

Who doesn't fear the worst when she reaches for a ringing phone after midnight? She almost swallowed the word: "Hello?"

"Mom, it's Jeff. It's another boy!"

What was with all these boys? "Is he okay?"

"Perfect. Ronnie did such a good job. She's pretty tired, but she wants to tell you something."

"Janet?"

"Congratulations, Ronnie. Have you thought up a name yet?"

"That's why I'm calling. We're naming him William Hoyer Farnham."

Janet burst into tears. She had no idea she even held so much emotion inside her.

"Janet?" The phone jostled, then Jeff's voice. "Mom, are you there? Did you hear her?"

"I heard," Janet managed to squeak out. "Thank you for using Hoyer. It means so much to me."

The next morning, before she even visited the baby, she stopped in to see Mr. Dempsey at the bank. Someone needed to ensure her grandsons' futures.

Within a month, she, Jerry, Jeff, and Ronnie all met at the bank while Beverly watched the boys. Once Mr. Dempsey had assembled enough comfy chairs so they could all sit, he said, "How much do you want to invest, Mrs. Farnham?"

All eyes turned to Janet. This pleased her. Everyone knew she was the one with the power in this meeting. "Forty thousand."

Jerry sank down in his chair and ran his hand over his mouth. For much of his career, that had equaled his annual salary.

Jeff gave Janet an approving smile; Ronnie caught her breath. "That's too generous." Jeff put his hand on Ronnie's arm.

"Forty thousand total, or forty thousand each?" Mr. Dempsey said.

"Each."

Ronnie put her hand to her chest. Janet enjoyed the entire show. She knew Beverly did not have access to such sums. Beverly didn't speak of money at all, fearing that hard analysis would extinguish whatever magic it was that had kept her family afloat all these years. When she had finished high school typing, Beverly would have been smart to take bookkeeping from Janet as well.

Janet told the banker that investing in stocks or mutual funds—yes, even eighteen years' worth, she said when he questioned her—was too risky, given the current economic climate. And since savings account earnings were laughable these days, she preferred a product you could count on. She chose to invest the money in whole life insurance on Jeff's life, with each of his sons as a beneficiary. The principal would grow slowly, Mr. Dempsey explained, but steadily. The boys could cash out the policy when they went to college. If Jeff should die before then, the boys would inherit plenty to see them through school.

"Who will you name as a second beneficiary?" he said.

"Why do you need a second?" Janet said.

"If, God forbid, something happens to Jeff while the children are still minors, the money has a clear legal path to the second person."

The question threw Janet into a tizzy. She glanced over at her husband. Jerry was not a good choice; that money had done well for generations in female hands. It was hard enough to entrust the money to Jeff, but what could she do? She had not been blessed with a daughter.

Janet felt everyone watching her. She looked at Ronnie, as close to a daughter as she would ever have. But she and Jeff had spent so much money on the renovation already, burning through their entire inheritance from Janet's brother in California on the kitchen and a new car. Fifty thousand gone, Jeff saying he'd spent it for Ronnie. Janet feared the girl didn't know how to protect her finances.

When Janet didn't respond, Mr. Dempsey prompted, "That would typically be the children's mother."

After another awkward pause, Janet decided you couldn't go around throwing large sums of money at people who aren't blood.

Jerry hung his head so he wouldn't have to watch.

Janet said, "Put my name down."

If Jeff died today, the money Janet had invested for the boys would come right back into her pocket.

And her choice had proven wise, given that Ronnie was leaving the marriage. Yet now the victory felt hollow. What good had decades of scrimping come to if it couldn't save her son's life?

ronnie

As the day wore on, Ronnie thought more and more about the distressed horses. "Is there any chance the police could throw the horses a few flakes of hay?" Ronnie said. "There's a bale inside the door on the first floor of the barn."

"I'm sorry," said Corporal McNichol. "We can't be feeding your animals."

"Horses have delicate systems. They need to eat regularly or they'll colic."

"They're right outside Jeff's window. It's too dangerous."

"But it's inhumane!" Ronnie paced in a circle and talked herself down: today was about nothing if not surrender. She couldn't control a goddamn thing. They say they won't feed the horses, the horses won't be fed. Period.

Ronnie walked until her sarcasm dissipated, her thoughts circling along with her steps. She passed Beverly and Janet, talking quietly, and wondered if and when her mother would finish the story of Dominic Gallagher, a name that always made Ronnie think of the rise and fall of her mother's laugh. She wondered if the boys had eaten lunch. If they'd been able to go outside and enjoy the glorious weather. If, like her, Mr. Eshbach was going stir-crazy.

And the poor animals. She and Jeff were so different in the way they responded to the animals. He loved them in an all-consuming, emotionally sloppy way. If a horse went lame, he'd be the one with his arms around its neck, whispering in its ear, while Ronnie would be the one out by the hydrant, morning and night, cold hosing its leg and bandaging. And when end-of-life choices had to be made, those choices always fell to Ronnie.

Ronnie recalled a time, before they were married, when Jeff had cut short a hot date so they could get home to feed the horses. How could he now watch Camelot, Daydream, and poor lame Horsey Patch through the office windows, tearing up that barren paddock, and tolerate their cries for attention? Jeff had clearly detached himself from the boys, and it made sense if he no longer cared anything for Ronnie. After all, she was going to leave him.

But the horses?

Ronnie returned to Corporal McNichol's table.

"Jeff loves animals. Probably more than he loves me."

"Okay."

A pit in Ronnie's stomach grew. She could feel the horses' hunger—and Jeff's. "He can see how upset they are. Why hasn't he come out to feed them?"

"He's drunk?"

"He was drunk. But that was hours ago. Why isn't he sobering up and responding to their needs?"

The question hung in the air, because the only person who could answer it had cut himself off from the world.

An officer came into the room and handed Corporal McNichol a piece of paper. Her brow furrowed as she read.

Ronnie looked up at Corporal McNichol. "Is it Jeff?"

"No. Your son called. I'm going to quote here, because I'm pretty sure he was speaking in code and I want to get this right: 'Princess Zartan didn't break a sweat climbing to the fifth level with the gold trunk, even though the ninja dragons tried to toast her.'"

It was in code, all right. Ronnie smiled. May they all meet adversity with the aplomb of Andrew's video game characters.

Apparently the boys were doing just fine. "Thanks," Ronnie said.

"Now if you'll excuse me, I'm going to hold a strategy meeting with my men. I'd like to see if we can't bring this standoff to a close."

ronnie

A new strategy, tenuous hope—that's how Ronnie had felt in February when Jeff came to her with his proposal.

"I've come up with the solution we've been looking for," Jeff had said, peeking his head into Ronnie's office.

Ronnie pulled her mind from where it had been happily absorbed in online research on healthy free-range practices for chicken farmers and looked at him over the top of her computer. Had they been seeking a solution? She finally, finally felt settled.

She now had this space devoted to her use, everything within easy reach. The first thing she'd done in her new office, when it was completed just a month ago: with her reference books lined up on shelves behind her as witness, Ronnie had rolled her chair across the carpet protector, from typing to reaching for the phone to switching on her new digital recorder, all in one graceful swoop. Of course Will had to try the rolling chair too.

And she could breathe again. There were times, while air-hammering the crumbling plaster to expose the stone walls in this basement office, when she and Jeff had worked just twelve feet apart but couldn't see each other for all the airborne mess. She was just starting to discover what normal dusting was like.

Organic Gardening PA magazine was now sending her assignments, resulting in steadier work.

What solution did they need?

Jeff took a deep breath. "I think we should open a farm stand."

"In our spare time?" Ronnie almost laughed out loud but was glad she hadn't when she caught the look of boyish enthusiasm on her husband's face. This Jeff—the one with the bright eyes and energized voice, whose dreams were precious to her—this was the man she'd married. She rolled her chair away from the computer. "I'm listening."

"It makes sense. Like all our interests are meant to converge. My food service experience and business degree with your knowledge of the organic food craze and connections in the farming community. Your eye for design, my construction know-how. I think we could do it."

"But selling tomatoes and peppers down on the road will not support us," she said. "Or do you mean for the boys to do it, like the Amish?"

"I'm thinking bigger—of building a real store."

"You've stayed at the hotel so long I thought you'd given up on starting a business."

Last year, when Jeff was upset about the sale of his hotel to a new chain but unwilling to tell her why, Ronnie had stopped in to see for herself—and was greeted by large flat-screen TVs blasting from every corner, as well as the flashing lights and intrusive sounds of amusements placed along the walls. The classy lounge over which Jeff had reigned for decades from his spot behind the bar had devolved into an arcade.

Ronnie could hardly take seeing him in that environment. Ablaze with the inner fire that comes from following her passion, she resolved to talk to Jeff about a change in career.

She was hardly qualified as an adviser. She was a thirty-three-year-old with a master's degree who had never fulfilled her career potential and who had only recently figured out what she wanted to be when she grew up. But if she could discover enough purpose on her journal pages to reenergize her life, Jeff could too. So she arranged for a sleepover for the boys, fixed Jeff a nice dinner, then asked him the questions she'd asked of herself in her journal.

Ronnie: "What gets you up in the morning?"

Jeff: "My bladder."

Ronnie: "What are your goals in life?"

Jeff: "I just want to get done what needs to be done. Mowing, renovating, things like that."

Ronnie: "Don't you hope that when you die, you'll have left the world a better place in some small way?"

Jeff: "It probably isn't good, but I've never thought about making any sort of contribution to society."

Ronnie: "I must not be phrasing this right. When your time on earth is through, what kind of legacy do you want to leave behind?"

Jeff had simply said, "You and the boys."

So if Jeff was finally starting to think along a more productive track, she could hardly dismiss him.

Jeff walked around the desktop to her chair and swiveled it to face him. "You once said I should be doing work I love. And it finally hit me—there's nothing I love more than you and this farm. Eventually we can quit our other jobs and work together the rest of our lives. If I invest in anything, I want it to be this land. We can let it provide for us."

"But I love my writing."

"Which is good, because we'll have to work all our jobs until we start making money at the store. It will be tough for a while. But it would be fun to start another construction project together."

Fun? At least one of them thought so. Ronnie had already left that phase of their lives behind.

Ronnie felt detached from Jeff's proposal but couldn't deny that she was the one who had instigated this line of thought. She was proud of him for thinking this through, and it was hard to deny the fire in his eyes, missing for so long.

"But we can't grow enough produce to stock a whole store with only six acres. Are you thinking we would purchase food wholesale and then resell it?"

"It would be a mix, adding in more and more of our own goods as we can. I'm sure my mother wouldn't mind if we pushed onto her land a bit. It's not like she's using it."

"But we'd need capital. Where would we get the money?" Ronnie's fears about their debt flared again. "Or are you looking to your mother for that too?"

"You think I need a handout. That I can't do this." He turned and went to the window. "I'd rather die than ask her."

"It's not like you've come clean about the finances, Jeff. I don't even know what kind of debt we're in here. You tell me how we can do this."

Ronnie wanted Jeff to have this chance to live a happier life. Every night he came home with new horror stories from the hotel, and Ronnie hadn't thought they could get worse than his decade-old story about the kitchen employee who reheated a prime rib for a late-starting wedding by running it through a soapless dishwasher. She didn't know how much longer he could hold out there.

Thinking aloud, Ronnie said, "We've worked hard on this house, so it's probably worth a lot more than it was when you bought it. And you have so many bills to pay each month. Maybe we should apply for a home equity line of credit, pay off the credit cards, and use what's left to build the store."

Jeff turned to her, the emotion he always kept at bay now rising like sunshine on his face. "That's a great idea. Let's do it tomorrow."

She joined him at the window. "So you'd want to build it right down the hill here, between the house and the road? The horses might not be too happy, with you eating up part of their pasture."

"They'll get over it." Jeff stood behind her, wrapped his arms around her waist, and laid his chin on her shoulder. "This is going to be good for us."

"I'm not saying yes yet. We'll see what the loan officer says. And

I won't give up my writing. I've made a lot of promises I intend to keep, and I like what I'm doing." Maybe she could compromise and make calls from the farm store when it wasn't busy. "And I don't want to give up our week at the shore. It's the only family heritage I have to share with the boys. So if we have to hire help to cover while we're gone, then that goes in the budget."

"Aye-aye, captain."

Ronnie followed Jeff's eyes down the hill and tried to imagine another barnlike structure where the horses grazed. With a deep breath, she fought the fleeting suffocation: the way the store would obscure the house from the road and further sequester their family life. She hoped the greater interaction with their community would counter it. "I'll have to file for a business name."

"Already got that covered." Jeff kissed her cheek. "New Hope Farms."

"Look. It's starting to snow." They watched together as tender snowflakes rested on the backs of the horses before melting.

ronnie

An early spring thaw convinced Jeff that four to six weeks was too long to wait for an answer from the bank. So they'd be ready to go when the home equity line came through, it wouldn't hurt anything for him to level the site for the farm store, build the frame for the floor, and bring in a cement mixer to pour the slab. "We'll need to open by Memorial Day at the latest so we don't miss out on all the sales at the beginning of the growing season," he said.

"What would we sell?" Ronnie said. "We won't even have any produce yet."

"We may have strawberries by then. And I've ordered a bunch of seed packets from Burpee. We could sell flats of plants and some starter vegetables."

Ronnie grew increasingly nervous. Twice she followed up with the bank for an answer, but their loan officer said she was waiting for more information from the credit reporting agencies. It would take a little while longer. Meanwhile, Jeff racked up the credit cards and convinced her to help frame out the walls of the new building.

Finally, at the beginning of April, Ronnie received the call she'd been awaiting. She rolled her office chair back and picked up the receiver. "Ronnie Farnham," she said, her voice buoyed by the enthusiasm her work inspired. "May I help you?"

It was the broker with whom they'd filed the home equity loan application. "I'm afraid your application was declined."

Ronnie was confused. "Why would it be declined? We've improved our house. It must be worth a lot more than what we paid for it."

"You may have improved it on the inside, but appraisals are done from the outside." Ronnie cringed, recalling how happy Jeff had once been at their deceptively low assessment, the affordable taxes. "But besides that, do you have any idea what your credit report looks like?"

"Not exactly, but I know we can still get credit." Her fears of impending financial doom had been alleviated last fall when their old car died. Ronnie had sat beside Jeff at the dealership when he applied for a loan to buy a new Nissan Altima. Ronnie had fidgeted, unsure of what they'd find; when approval came through, Jeff seemed to swell with the power of this new credit. If they were in deep debt, they wouldn't have extended them even more credit, would they?

"Listen to this," the woman said.

She began a laundry list of creditors and amounts owed. Instinctively Ronnie flipped on her digital voice recorder. "…Sears, $8,432…" *How could they owe Sears that much money? All she knew was that Jeff had bought a used garden tractor for $400 and that she charged about a hundred dollars of clothes for the boys on that card each fall.* "…Sunoco, $12,129…" *Wasn't Sunoco a gas card? How could it have that much on it?* "…Texaco, $5,078…" *She didn't know they still had a Texaco card. There weren't any Texaco stations around here!* "…Diner's Club, $6,854…" and on and on.

After Ronnie hung up, she sat there for a moment, stunned. She felt as betrayed as if the broker were Jeff's mistress, calling to detail all the times he had cheated on her.

Looking back, the sheer number of catalogs that came to their house should have tipped her off to the credit card purchases accumulating. Jeff had never let her recycle the catalogs without him looking first, "to see what I need," he would say, a running gag early in their marriage. Ronnie would laugh and say, "If you needed it, I would think you would know that before you saw it in a catalog." She'd lovingly dubbed him "Captain Consumer."

It was no longer funny.

Jeff walked into her office wearing his black and white work outfit, his kiss good-bye delayed when he registered the look on her face. "What's the matter?"

"I just got a call about our home equity loan. We've been turned down."

"That's odd."

"Sit down," Ronnie said, rewinding the recorder. "I have something you need to hear."

He looked at his watch. "I don't have time for this. I have to get to work."

"Not this time, Jeff." He had left her alone during both her miscarriages because he had to work. "You are not the freaking president of the United States! Be late for once. You are going to sit here and live through this like I had to."

"I can't," he said.

"You will not put me off one moment longer."

"We'll talk when I get home." He pulled his car keys from his pocket and walked away.

"You know damn well I'll be asleep when you get home."

"Then we'll talk in the morning," he said, already on the stairs.

Sure. The morning—when he'd be impossible to rouse.

His steps crossed the floor above her, and she heard the kitchen door open and close. Once again, Ronnie was left with a jumble of feelings she needed a partner to untangle. She checked the time on her computer—a half hour until the bus dropped off the boys. Desperate to engage in meaningful communication, she headed up to the guest room and pulled her journals out from underneath her bed.

ronnie

When Corporal McNichol returned, all three women rose. "It's clear that the ways we've been trying to communicate with Jeff aren't working. We want to try something new."

Communicate with Jeff. A concept doomed to failure. How many times over the past few years had Ronnie pleaded with him to talk with her—about the finances, covering the boys' schedules, or even going for a horseback ride together—to no avail? As if he'd already been walling himself off, brick by brick.

"What have you been trying?" Beverly said.

"We've been calling to him through a bullhorn. And in case he disconnected the phone, we also slid a portable phone into the store and asked him to come out and pick it up. He did not. We're running out of ideas."

Janet sat back down. Hard. Corporal McNichol turned to Ronnie. "I know it looks bad. But this could still turn around. Do you want to try speaking to him?"

"You mean call him?"

"No. As I said, he's not answering the phone. An officer would take you back to the store so you could appeal to Jeff over the bullhorn."

She was about to say that she'd already said everything she needed to say to Jeff, more than once. That she had no influence over him. That she didn't see the point.

But there was a point: Jeff still loved her. If she stayed with him, she might hold the power to save his life.

Go to the farm. Talk to Jeff. After all they had meant to each other—after all they'd accomplished, as a team—she owed him this much.

Or did she? Working shoulder to shoulder toward a distant dream, they were genial partners, but within the confines of reality and face-to-face, they hadn't had an effective exchange in—well, she couldn't recall how long.

She heard Anita saying she'd done all she could.

She remembered the psychiatrist saying she now had to take care of herself and her children.

And the alcohol counselor saying no one expected her continued support.

If only she could have one of them counsel her now. Ronnie felt she had come to the greatest test of her life and she'd have to make this decision alone.

There were only cons to consider. If Jeff died today, what kind of hell would they face? But if he lived, what kind of problems would he still cause? The operation's focus suddenly shifted, it seemed, and all guns were aimed at her.

She felt Jeff clinging to her now, his fingers laced around her neck, his full weight dragging on her as once again she was charged with a decision affecting them all. If she tried to pull him up with one last heave, at this late stage, how far might he drag her down instead?

Our words hang in the air all around him, but they can't sink in, the psychiatrist had said.

She'd already tried so many times to get Jeff care from professionals who knew much more than she did. AA. Inpatient rehab. Outpatient rehab. Individual counseling. She'd tried to talk to him, from her heart, about her own journey. She'd toed him up to the healing waters and looked right in, but in their reflection, only Ronnie saw the possibilities. She'd kicked him into the deep end with involuntary commitment, but even that didn't work. You cannot force a man to drink something life-sustaining if he thirsts for something different. Can't force him to stay afloat if he won't swim.

How much clearer could he be? Jeff had no desire to heal.

God, Jeff. Where the hell are you?

The air in the room felt too heavy to bear.

"I won't lie to him," she finally said. "Not today, not with so much at stake, and certainly not over a bullhorn with the media and all the world watching. I won't do it to him and I…" The words, so foreign to her, caught in her throat. "I won't do it to myself. I can't live for him anymore. I'm done."

Janet and Beverly turned away.

Corporal McNichol handed her a tissue. "Is there anyone else with influence? Karl Prout is saying they're good friends. He wants to try."

When Ronnie saw Jeff this morning, it seemed he'd been drinking all night. Ronnie tried to imagine what it would be like to be that drunk, that sleep-deprived. Already feeling like the relationships in his life had lost all meaning. And then some well-intentioned guy like Karl Prout comes forward to reach out. Ronnie could feel the pain deep in her own belly. For the first time, she could imagine Jeff actually pulling the trigger.

"You're the expert," Ronnie said. "But I'm telling you, Jeff forces himself to be nice to the guy. He thinks Karl is an idiot." Ronnie felt a twinge in her abdomen and bent forward to relieve it.

"Are you okay?" Corporal McNichol said.

"I'll be right back."

Ronnie felt light-headed as she walked to the far end of the hall. Insubstantial, as if the gravity that had been tugging on her so fiercely in recent weeks might release her and let her float away. In the bathroom stall, she found her underwear damp and red. A good ten days before her period was due.

Jeff was able to hold an entire community at bay, but life kept making its demands of her. When she returned to the hall, she pulled her mother out into the stairwell and asked her to go back to Perlmutter's and get her some supplies.

When Ronnie headed back to the table where she'd been sitting, she saw Corporal McNichol speaking quietly to Jeff's mother in the corner by the bar.

Ronnie strode over to them, thinking she may have missed some news—and heard Corporal McNichol ask Janet to speak to her son over the bullhorn.

"That's not a good idea," Ronnie blurted.

Her mother-in-law looked at her. "Why on earth not?"

Because he hates you. She stopped short of saying the ugly words Jeff had written in last month's suicide note. But in her cramping gut, she knew: if the police wanted to provoke violence, all they needed to do was send Jeff's mother in to console him. "He's not himself."

"Well, I hope not. My Jeff would never do something like this."

She wondered if Janet's "Jeff" was the same as hers. "He's drunk."

"Yes, yes, he's drunk, he's a drunk, he's a drunk. You keep saying that. And maybe he'd been drinking a bit last night, but—"

"No, he's still drinking." Ronnie took a moment for her thinking to catch up to her words. "He must be or else this would have ended already. But that makes no sense... We both use that office..."

"He could have taken that whiskey from the car," Corporal McNichol said.

"Janet." Ronnie took her mother-in-law's hands. "What if you provoke him? Mother-child relationships are complicated. What if he hears your voice and—"

"You don't want him to live, do you?" Janet said, pulling away.

"Of course I do. He's the boys' father. I hope he figures things out."

"And that's all you want for him? You promised yourself to him for life. For better or worse."

"Okay, so all relationships are complicated."

"Well, you can sit here with your complications, but one of us has to do something. And it looks like it's going to be me."

Ronnie turned to Corporal McNichol, silently imploring.

THE FAR END OF HAPPY

"It's worth a try, Ronnie. I know you're worried about your mother-in-law's safety, but we'll keep her behind a body shield."

"What?" Janet said weakly.

When she swayed, Ronnie steadied her. "No one will blame you if you don't do this. You've supported him his whole life—"

"And I'll support him today too," she said, although her voice lacked conviction and her face had gone slack. Janet was a listener, not a talker—and Jeff was not in the mood to talk.

"We have a squad car waiting downstairs," Corporal McNichol said. "When you're done talking to your son, we'll bring you right back here."

Ronnie felt as muddled as the room's glass block windows, which allowed some light but no clarity. She clung to the doorway, unwilling to travel any further into the shadows beyond.

ronnie

K a-POW!

The shotgun blast was louder than she'd anticipated. It had more of a kick too. Not that Ronnie had touched it—Carmelle was the gunslinger. She was always bent on keeping up with their new husbands, whether smoking, drinking, changing her car's oil, or now, insisting she could shoot. She never would have rubbed her shoulder in front of the guys, but the way she stood dazed for a few moments said that despite the padding of her raccoon coat, she was hurting. She hadn't heeded Jeff's warning to squeeze the butt of the stock tight to her shoulder. Looking particularly elfish that day, Jeff, orchestrator of these high jinks, relaxed beside Paco against the stone retaining wall at the side of the house, took a deep drag of his Pall Mall, and chuckled. Carmelle allowed a satisfied smile to spread across her face. The makeshift hanger they'd rigged to the mimosa tree was empty, and the hand-painted wedding plate had been shot all to hell.

With the house set well off the road and surrounded by neighbors inured to the sounds of target practice, no one was alarmed by what had transpired. That mix of privacy and freedom was something Jeff loved about their little farm—the perimeter was large enough to keep their animals in and snoopy neighbors out. When thrifty Carmelle couldn't sell the plate from her husband's first wedding at their yard sale—what were the chances they'd find a "Paco & Erline" to buy it?—Jeff had invited them down to shoot. Paco was all for it.

Ronnie had a couple of targets in mind as well. She buckled them together and then to the tree branch. The good money she'd made as a cocktail waitress was always offset by pain—Ronnie's feet weren't made for high heels. During the last hour of every shift, it was all she could do not to hobble. She never wanted to feel that kind of torture again.

Jeff urged her to shoot them herself. He said it would feel great. Carmelle urged her to do it too. Ronnie was coming off one decision to save her feet, though, and her guess was that Carmelle's shoulder would be purple for weeks. She appointed a surrogate, but Ronnie was the one cheering the loudest when Jeff turned all John Wayne, closed one eye against the smoke of his cigarette, trained the other down the barrel…and blew the toes out of those shoes.

"Woohoo!" They were all fired up.

"What else can we shoot?" Paco said.

Ronnie knew just the thing. "Let's get Crazy Fay's clock!"

While Ronnie usually wouldn't throw something away that still worked just fine, she'd be happy to sacrifice the clock for her friends' entertainment. She ran in to get it and strung it upside down from a tree limb by its cord.

Paco cocked his head and contemplated the odd sight. "Should we allow a slow death by hanging?" In answer, Jeff reloaded the gun and handed it over. Paco waved off the invitation. "This one's all yours, brother."

The clock exploded, reducing its mysterious inner workings to an assortment of springs and metal shards that speared right into the earth. It was a pain to clean up, but the event was cathartic as all get out.

After Ronnie was done jumping up and down—and Jeff had safely set the gun aside—she ran over and threw her arms around him. Hugging Jeff was always an incredible feeling. When pressed to hers, Jeff's body was as comfortable as memory foam; he accommodated her as if she were literally leaving an impression on him. He was her hero, unafraid to obliterate their painful memories.

They kissed until Paco and Carmelle complained, then laughed. They were goading them; their friends were always saying that Ronnie and Jeff couldn't get enough of each other.

Jeff pulled Ronnie inside the house. He'd fix cocktails, and she'd put out the appetizer platter she'd spent the day making, edged with daisies she'd carved from slices of turnip and carrot held together by toothpicks. But first, he pinned her up against the wall and cradled her face in his hands.

"You are so beautiful." He kissed her hungrily, pulled back, and looked into her eyes—through them, in fact—as if toward a potential beauty Ronnie had not yet recognized. One in which she wanted to believe.

2:00 p.m.

janet

Janet thought she might be sick in the back of the police cruiser. To concentrate on her breathing she closed her eyes, only opening them when the car came to a stop. They were at the barricade. A string of news vans stood by, cameras on tripods, microphones held to faces. Two police cars had their lights flashing as if ready to spring into action.

An officer waved bystanders aside so they could pass. Several dozen people with familiar faces stood around chatting as if they were waiting for the all clear after a grease fire in a church kitchen. These people—blue-collar workers, nouveau homesteaders, artists, horse owners, and, Janet suspected, a meth cooker or two—had their own reasons for living in these hills, on parcels sold reluctantly by the original Pennsylvania Dutch farmers. People kept to themselves; outside of township meetings, she'd never seen so many of her neighbors congregated.

And she'd never passed a police car on one of their roads, ever, let alone a news van. Among those in work boots and dungarees stood a young woman wearing a blazer and scarf whose shellacked blond hair was unfazed by the breeze. Midinterview, she pulled back her microphone and rushed toward Janet's window as if a mother's participation in her own son's life were a major news development. Janet raised her hand to hide her face. The reporter's knuckles rapped the glass as the car rolled through the barricade.

Janet put her head down between her knees and took a few deep breaths. Then she reached into her purse for a few sips of something to take the edge off.

She'd sacrificed so much to have Jeff.

In the time before Jeff, when she and Jerry first married, their passion seemed to stretch endlessly before them. Heat rose to her face now, thinking of the way her pregnant body used to respond to his. Acting on that urge under her parents' roof was always a creative challenge, even though, for a wedding gift, Amelia had divided the house in two, even adding another kitchen, so that Jerry wouldn't have to pay for a new home on top of medical expenses for the pending birth.

One day during Janet's finals week, when her parents had offered to cook, Jerry was so eager when he got home that he begged off dinner, feigned illness, and pulled Janet right up to their bedroom. She'd giggled the whole way, hoping the sound wouldn't carry.

"I can't get enough of you, Mrs. Farnham," he whispered in her ear. Her sensitive breasts yearned for his touch, her body ready to accept him. They hastily shed their clothes, and he pushed her onto the bed, their excitement growing as he rubbed his hands over her five-month belly and heavy breasts.

With the very first thrust, she screamed. Jerry clamped his hand over her mouth, laughing.

"Mmp ump mee!" She pounded on his chest. "Get off!"

He pulled out amid a wash of blood. "Holy shit."

Janet lifted her hand to the searing pain on the left side of her belly. "Help the baby." Jerry looked like he was going to pass out.

The emergency room doctor assured them the baby sounded healthy. He suspected some sort of blood-filled cyst.

"So is everything okay, since the cyst drained?" Jerry said.

"My concern is that I don't know the source of the blood filling it. Without surgery, your wife may hemorrhage. But we'll need to open her uterus. There is risk to the fetus."

"But my baby," Janet said. She hated the sound of the word *fetus*, a term used when discussing back-alley abortions. This was little Janey they were talking about. Or Jeffrey.

The doctor looked to Jerry. "Time may be of the essence."

Fighting through the fog of painkillers, Janet said, "Jerry, no, let's wait a few days," as Jerry scrawled his name on the papers.

From the time she returned from surgery until Jeff emerged by cesarean three and a half months later, Janet lay on her bed, bored out of her mind, her swelling belly tugging at her inner and outer wounds. She was tended to lovingly: Amelia by day, Jerry by evening. They took meals and drinks up and down the forbidden stairs, brought her library books and inexpensive gifts, told her stories. Jerry slept downstairs on the couch.

After Jeff was born, she held him to her breast, waiting for the rush of connection—but felt nothing. It will get better once your milk comes in, the nurses said. It will get better once you're up and moving around again, her doctor said. All that inactivity takes a lot out of you, said the gym teacher she'd married.

But Janet knew what she needed. She needed her husband to help her feel like a whole woman again.

Until then, Janet went through the motions of caring for the baby, never feeling the fierce, tigerlike devotion she expected. Breast-feeding was a chore. She took greater pleasure seeing her mother hold her child than she did in holding him herself and kept her shame hidden so deep no one would ever discover it.

When Janet was well enough to take her rescheduled final exams, Jerry had their double bed hauled away. She thought that his disposal of the bloodstained mattress was considerate and his way of coming back to her—until later that day, when the twin beds arrived.

As her angry scars faded to white and puckered the loose skin around them, Jerry began coaching basketball, and Janet got a job teaching typing. She handed her baby to her mother, bound her breasts to stop the milk, and began a career.

Teaching restored her confidence and completed the healing

process. After Jeff's first birthday party, she slipped from her bed into Jerry's and snuggled up to him. Half asleep, he'd whispered, "This feels nice." She slid her hand down his pajamas and he jolted awake.

"What are you doing?" He leaped from the bed, yanking up his bottoms.

"Is it so horrible for a woman to want her husband?"

He flicked on the wall switch, as if to better track her movements.

She nestled a finger over her scar. "You find me repulsive."

"No, no. My goodness, if that were the case, my life would be so much easier."

"Then what is it?"

"You heard the doctor. Your body won't hold up to another pregnancy."

Janet reached into the nightstand that stood between their beds and held up a square packet. "We could use this."

"Alka-Seltzer?"

Janet erupted into a fit of giggles. "No, silly." She ripped the packet open and unrolled the rubber onto her thumb. "The pharmacist showed me how to do this—"

"You have discussed our…relations…with Mr. Gregory? Have you lost your mind? He's a deacon at your mother's church!" Jerry hissed the words as if someone might overhear talk of their relations even now, as if her parents hadn't subdivided the house into halves and moved to the other side.

"Come here, honey." Janet patted the bed beside her. "I know how to put this on."

Jerry gave her a tortured look. "I've had nightmares. Did you know that?"

"About condoms?"

"About hurting you. That day… I hadn't given one thought to the baby. I just wanted you so badly and—" His composure cracked. He knelt on the floor in front of her, sobs choking off his words. "And then the ER, so much pain, your mother praying… Maybe this is God's punishment for our eagerness."

"You're invoking God? Since when?"

"Since moving here. Jesus watches us from every wall of this house. It's damnation at the ready."

Janet looked at the pale rectangle on their bedroom wall and thought of the framed Jesus face down in the bottom of her sock drawer. If God wanted to punish her for anything, it wouldn't be for loving her husband too much. It would be for not loving her baby enough.

Jerry had remained a kind, upstanding man. A decent enough provider, considering they'd never left the old homestead. And handsome—her attraction to him never died. But attraction has a way of petrifying between mates who won't touch. They had lived out their marriage as roommates, not lovers.

Love, in Janet's family, was a distant memory. But her son was in extreme danger. And she now knew, with all the fierce, tigerlike devotion that she had always longed for, that she needed this chance to try to save him.

〰

The cruiser rolled to a stop at the bottom of the Schulzes' driveway, across the road from New Hope Farms. The policeman who'd been driving said, "We're going to sit right here until the others have everything in place, ma'am."

Janet looked at the farmhouse on the hill and recalled how hard it had been for her when Jeff first took up with that Fay. They might as well have moved to Spain, for all she'd seen him. If the Fay years had caused Jeff to pull away from her, Ronnie brought them back together.

Dozens of police cars were parked along both sides of the road, punctuated with two ambulances, adding an aura of alarm to the otherwise peaceful setting. Janet relaxed a bit, though. She saw no blood on the road, no broken windows, no police tape strapped across the front door. Just the lovely facade of New Hope Farms that Jeff and Ronnie had built, so pleasing to look at with its stained wood siding and green metal roof. In front of the porch roof sat small potted shrubs, some taller hollies, and chrysanthemums in bursts of yellows, reds, and purples. The front door of the store was propped open, and inside, against the back, she could see the large wooden crates holding Galas, McIntoshes, Romes, and Delicious Reds and Yellows. Next to that, the closed door to the office.

Between two police cars, she could see the horses mouthing at invisible stubs of grass. This was all an overblown reaction from police tired of waiting at traffic lights for someone who forgot to signal. She'd have a nice talk with Jeff and he'd come out and hug her. She'd pay whatever fine they'd impose and offer a generous contribution to the Fraternal Order of Police. That should take care of everything.

Except for Ronnie, of course. That woman seemed allergic to money. Maybe she needed a break; lord knows she worked hard, what with the boys and her pet income projects. But eventually she'd come around. They were a family. They had to stick together.

"Okay, here they come," the policeman said. "Don't open the door until I say so."

ronnie

This is being handled all wrong, Ronnie thought, pacing. She should not have let her mother-in-law go, yet she still could not come up with an acceptable way she could have stopped her.

"Ronnie, sit down. You're driving me mad," Beverly said.

Ronnie paused, looked at her mother, and continued pacing. "I keep thinking, there's no bathroom in the store. I mean, wouldn't Jeff have to go to the bathroom? Especially if he kept drinking?" She turned to Corporal McNichol and asked the question she would have squelched if Jeff's mother were still in the room. "How do you know he's still alive?"

"We have scopes on the windows."

"Scopes. You mean guns."

She shrug-nodded. "And we haven't heard anything."

"He could have drunk himself to death by now. You aren't doing enough."

The corporal thought for a minute. "Do you have an answering service on your store phone, the kind that goes through the phone company?"

"Yes."

"Follow me."

Ronnie and her mother followed Corporal McNichol down the hall to the office, where she asked her men to take a break so Ronnie could use the phone. They left, taking their radio static with them.

Corporal McNichol said, "I'll leave you alone."

"Why?"

The corporal gave Ronnie a moment to think. "These are your messages. Some of them might be personal."

Ronnie nodded.

"But I think some of the voices you hear will address your concerns. We know what we're doing."

Ronnie's hands were already flying over the keypad and entering her code. When the expected automated voice came on, she flipped the switch to speaker so her mother could hear.

"You have seventy-two messages." Beverly's eyebrows shot up.

Amber: "My god, Ronnie, what's happening? They wouldn't let me get to the store. I've been trying to leave the barricade and go home, but, well, I just can't. A lot of your neighbors are here milling around. And some customers—the woman who buys one of those big sleeves of garlic every single week is over by the news van. Anyway, I'm here. Whatever you need."

"This is Mrs. Fawke, principal at Hitchman Elementary. We want to let you know we're all safe here, and we're hoping you are too. The students don't know anything yet. We told them they couldn't go out for recess because of a treatment we'd put on the lawn. I hated to lie, but there's no use stirring them up before we know how this will… Well, the wait is hard enough here so I can't imagine what you're going through. I've alerted the boys' teachers, so they understand better what your sons must have been going through lately. Let us know what other support we can offer."

"That ticks me off," Ronnie said, talking over an earlier message from Lisa Schulz saying she couldn't get home.

"I thought she sounded nice," Beverly said.

"Sure, now she does. But a month ago, my two straight-A students suddenly started screwing up—misunderstanding assignments; writing about dark subjects in their journals; Will unable to spell; Andrew freaking out on standardized testing day, which was always his favorite—and it's only once their father locks himself up with a gun that she thinks they might need support? Divorce should be bad enough to inspire offers of help. It's the death of a family."

Beverly fiddled with a curled corner on the desk blotter. "I didn't know you felt that way."

"Well, I'm sorry this suddenly got personal for you, but it's the truth. How else would I feel? My stepdads were as close as I was ever going to get to having a father, and you kept taking me away from them."

"Jeffrey Farnham?" A male voice came from the speakerphone. Beverly gripped Ronnie's arm. "Jeff, I'm one of the police negotiators. If you check these messages, I'll call back in two minutes. Please pick up." A chill infused the silent gap.

The next was from her editor at *Organic Gardening PA*, wondering whether she planned to get around to turning in the story due that morning. "If you're on your death bed or something, have your husband call so I know to fill your spot." *Leave it to the media not to watch the news.*

"Jeff." The negotiator's voice again. "Listen, I know you're facing some tough challenges. Life can get messy. But there's no reason to give up hope. Nothing has happened here that can't be fixed. You can feel better again. You just might not see that on your own. Call me back and we'll get you help."

The voice sounded kind. Patient. Confident. Ronnie would have called him back.

"Ronnie, Anita here. I just heard on the news. We knew this was possible, but, oh my, I'm so sorry it's turning out this way. Don't worry about being strong for others. Be strong in yourself. God be with you, and your sons, and Jeff."

"Anita," her mother said. "Is that your therapist?"

"Jeff." Ronnie put her hand up to silence her. "It's been a half hour, and I haven't heard from you. How are you doing in there? Maybe you feel too bad to talk right now. I get that. But there's no need to make it worse by staying in there alone. We can get you something to eat. You can take a shower and take a nice long rest in a comfy bed. No rush on the talking, okay? You can talk whenever you're ready."

That man didn't know her husband, Ronnie thought. He never took showers. He loved a nice warm bath.

"Jeff. Another half hour has passed. Maybe you've seen the firepower out here. Maybe you're afraid of what will happen if you open the door. I'm going to call you back and tell you what to do. I'll be really clear so all this talk doesn't get jumbled in your head. Focus on how good it will feel to put an end to this. I'll call back in five minutes."

Ronnie leaned in toward the phone, awaiting the instructions. Her mother leaned in beside her.

"Jeff, this is the police negotiator again. Three simple actions. Set your weapon down. Open the office door. Walk through the store with your fingers laced behind your head. That's it. Three actions: set down the weapon, open the door, walk out with your fingers laced behind your head. The outer door is propped open. We'll see you coming and take care of you from there."

Ronnie felt dizzy. She hadn't been breathing. She leaned on the desk, took in a deep breath, and exhaled as she waited for what came next.

The next voice was lower. Slower; slurred. Dripping with the black ooze of evil. Almost a growl: "Tell…them…to get…the fuck…away from me."

Ronnie and her mother stepped back as if the desk had burned them. Deep inside, Ronnie's organs started to shiver.

janet

Here we go." The officer who had driven Janet to the farm was out of the car and opening her door. He wore a vest with *POLICE* across the back. Bulletproof; she had seen enough cop shows to know that much. She just didn't know how she had become part of one.

Janet wasn't ready. She hadn't organized her thoughts; they were a jumble of loss and blood and soul-numbing abstinence and shame. What on earth would she say?

The car door opened.

"This is a military grade shield. You'll be perfectly safe behind it," an officer said. He pulled her from the car and handed her a megaphone. "This has a pistol grip," he was saying. "You can rest it right here, on this shooting platform. Put your finger on this trigger. When you're ready, squeeze."

Janet awaited inspiration. What did she ever talk to Jeff about, other than work arrangements? *Can you drive your tractor over the hill to mow my lawn? Why don't you come in for lemonade? While you're here, could you change my smoke detector batteries?* She had to admit it: her mother had known him better. Amelia had been the one to raise him while Janet taught typing all those years. It was a necessary convenience, but Janet was jealous when Jeff would run crying to his grandmother when he needed comfort. She remembered her secret joy when Jeff had tossed aside Amelia's high school graduation gift, inscribed in her hand: "To my Jeffrey:

Love the Lord above all and read this Bible, a request from your loving grandmother."

It was Ronnie who entertained them at Sunday dinners with stories about the boys, Ronnie who had planned the new corn maze with the pumpkin patch heart. It was Ronnie, not Jeff, who had poured out her fears to Janet after she came home from college, bonding them. Ronnie had needed her. Jeff was stronger; he'd never needed her at all. If he had fears, he managed them on his own.

The shame Janet had stuffed down so long ago emerged with a vengeance: she didn't really know her son. He was like steel-coated chocolate, and she didn't know how to reach the part of him that could melt.

Yet she hadn't hesitated when offered the chance to try. She had no doubt her own mother would have done the same for her, even though she would have shamed her into submission with words from a higher authority. After all these years, snippets of the Bible still came to her as if from an audiobook recorded by her mother: "My soul is exceeding sorrowful...let this cup pass from me..."

That's all Janet could remember. If she were going to summon her mother's courage, she'd have to do it without God's word at the ready. She pivoted the bullhorn on the shooting platform, aimed toward her son, and squeezed its pistol grip.

beverly

How could her daughter listen to any more of those messages? Beverly escaped back to the social hall as soon as she heard Jeff's rotting voice, but still she couldn't get it out of her head. It seemed meant to revile. It was a warning.

Fearful for Janet, Beverly flipped on the TV to see if there was any news. The scene that came to life before her was of the police cars lined up in front of the Schulz home. It wasn't a helicopter shot, yet the perspective was from above. Had a cameraman somehow approached on foot from the other side of the hill? The voice was Rob White's.

"We believe the police have brought in a new negotiator in the cruiser that just pulled up. The officer is opening the door... This is breaking news. You'll learn as we do who this is..."

Janet emerged from the backseat. Beverly put her hand to her mouth as Janet stepped up close to a shield; her frightened eyes peeked through its window.

Beverly needed to see how Janet would do this brave thing. For so long, Beverly had stowed away words she'd never had the chance to say to Dom, fearing that if she expressed her deepest desires, the very thing she'd wanted to hold tight to would be again wrested from her grasp. But what is there to lose in saying them, when someone is facing life's toughest moment?

The words swelled in Beverly's heart as she watched poor,

lost-looking Janet take the bullhorn in her hand. *Say "I love you,"* Beverly silently urged her. *Say "You are beautiful and precious." Say "Let me stay by your side and help you find joy."*

janet

J eff, this is your mother." Through the bullhorn, Janet's voice
sounded robotic. Insincere. She looked to the officer beside her.

He reached over and dialed up the volume. "Try again. Speak
nice and loud. If he fell asleep, you'll want to wake him. As a matter
of fact, hold on a sec." He took the bullhorn from her. "Jeff, this is the
negotiation team again." His deep voice could have carried through
a football stadium filled with a capacity crowd. "We have someone
here who came to speak to you." He slid the bullhorn back into the
notch on Janet's shield. "Go ahead when you're ready."

"Jeff, it's time to come out now. We've been waiting for you all
day. The boys, Beverly, Ronnie."

Quiet. All attention focused through the door of the farm store
on the closed office door.

"Look out at the horses, Jeff. They need you. We all need you."

Quiet. So quiet.

A loud thump and explosive shatter from the office. Everyone
flinched, except Janet, who fell back against the cruiser. "Oh god, did
he…did he…" She couldn't complete the sentence.

Next to her, the officer said into his radio, "Scopes, whaddya
got?" After a brief silence, a voice squawked back: "I think he threw
something against the door. A glass or bottle. He's up and moving."

The officer nodded to her. Janet's heart thrashed within her
chest, pounding again and again into her breastbone. How was she

supposed to talk? She took several deep breaths, trying to calm herself. Hoping to calm Jeff. She hated that she had no idea what was going on inside his head and heart.

She pulled herself together, took a deep breath, and raised the bullhorn to her mouth.

"Please, Jeff. Your father would want you to be strong for your boys. He loved you so much. He wasn't the kind to show it, but he was proud of you. And I...I—"

POW! Dust and splinters filled the farm store.

"That's it."

"Get her out of here, go."

"Go-go-go-go!"

Bullhorn—gone. The door behind her opened. A large hand pressed Janet's head down and back, pushing her onto the seat. The door shut as red and blue lights started to flash on a distracting number of cruisers. A sea of officers parted before them and tires squealed as their car raced away.

Janet couldn't talk, couldn't think. Her neighborhood sped past the car window at a disorienting speed. Janet's stomach lurched; either something had to go down or something else was coming up.

Without regard for subterfuge, she pulled the flask from her purse, lifted it, and downed the rest of its contents.

beverly

What was that? It seemed like Janet had said something through the bullhorn, but Beverly couldn't make it out. Beverly turned up the volume on the set so she could hear but still couldn't understand Janet's words. What was going on? What was she missing? She hit the volume button again, but it was turned up as loud as it could go.

Beverly watched for an entire minute.

She hoped Jeff would see his mother. Burst from the building and go to her, hands raised in surrender. *Come on, Jeff. Don't leave your mother. Don't leave Ronnie. And lord knows I don't need another man leaving me.* Beverly took in the entire scene, gleaning details from this horrid moment in her daughter's life to fill in gaps she had missed in her own. Why was the picture so still? Was something wrong with this TV?

POW! The camera jostled. Some sort of debris blew out the front door of the store. An officer pushed Janet into the car and sped away. *What the hell happened?*

Rob White: "Apparently the negotiation failed. We're trying to get a better angle so we can see what happened. There was some kind of explosion or shot. Can we get a better angle?"

The next view was of the front of the store. The camera zoomed into its interior, refocusing on the back wall.

As the debris settled, she was finally able to see the office door. It had a hole the size of a dinner plate blown straight through it.

ronnie

R onnie listened to message after message. Listening to them felt like speeding through a timeline, straight toward some sort of resolution. Each time the negotiator spoke, he sounded like a patient father trying to coax response from a pouting child. Only Jeff wasn't Will, whose jutting lower lip inspired Ronnie's oft-repeated phrase, "May I serve tea from that lip?" Ronnie would reach out, as if to lift a tiny teacup from its surface, and Will would bat her hand away, trying not to crack a smile. No, this was a man with way too much experience in walling himself off, now guarding his solitude with a weapon designed to kill.

The night before they'd left for the shore this summer, she and the boys had been so surprised when Jeff had followed them to the attic for a rare bedtime appearance. *He does love them*, she'd thought. The boys grabbed their blankets, opened the kid-size futon, and piled on with Ronnie as they always did, one on each side, and looked to see how Jeff would join in. He chose to wedge his rear end into the kid-size rocker Ronnie had had as a child, a few feet away. The boys had asked Ronnie to read a favorite book Grandma Jan had given them, Russell Hoban's *Bedtime for Frances*. It had "Jeffrey Farnham" written in front, angled this way and that in Jeff's whimsical little boy hand.

At one point in the reading, while thoroughly cracked up over Frances's antics, Will looked to Jeff. Ronnie had too, hoping to bond over what they found funny. Despite the extreme discomfort he must have felt with his hips jammed between the rails of that chair, it looked like Jeff was dropping off to sleep. Will said, "Dad, why don't you ever laugh?"

Ronnie and the boys waited, but Jeff didn't answer. "I fear Dad has forgotten how to have fun." Ronnie smiled at Jeff, hoping to provoke a rebuttal. But this was yet one more conversation where it seemed that Jeff wasn't present.

❧

"Hello, Ronnie, this is Peter McLaughlin from Vegan Delights. Sorry to bother you on such a day, but I felt the need to connect. Don't worry about the interview you promised me. We can work on that once your personal life resolves. I worked early this morning, came home to watch the noon news on TV while lying on the couch, and fell into a nightmare. My children were playing on their swing set, and soldiers were up in the trees watching them through their rifle sights... Anyway, if this is haunting me, I can't imagine how you're doing. Once you come out the other side, drop by the store. Smoothie's on me."

"Ronnie? Where are you?" Naked fear almost rendered her brother Teddy's voice unrecognizable. "I keep calling the house and getting a busy signal, but then no one picks up, and I don't know how many messages I've left on your cell. I've been trying to call Mom, but she isn't picking up either. You never got back to me after your call this morning, and then I got a text alert from the *Allentown Patch* about the standoff. God, Ronnie, I thought you were making this shit up! Please, if you pick up this message, call me, would you? And next time you see Mom, just reach into her purse and switch on her damn ringer."

They may have been raised in different homes, but she'd never stopped feeling close to Teddy, and his panic seeped into her now as if beneath a shared skin.

That was it. She couldn't listen to these anymore. She was about to hang up when she again heard Amber's voice.

"Ronnie, hi, it's Amber. I finally got tired of standing at the barricade, but I couldn't go home, with all this, you know, drama in the air, so I went over to put in a few hours stuffing envelopes at the township building. The office staff and a few supervisors were watching an update about the standoff on TV in the lobby. Gawking, really. But here's the thing. The office manager said, 'Jeffrey Farnham. That name sounds so familiar.' She was walking away from me so I followed and said it's because I work for him part-time at the store and she said no, it was something more. She goes to her planner and flips back through the months to July and punches her finger a few times at the writing on one of the squares.

"I ask her what's up. She says Jeffrey Farnham came to see her in July, complaining about his tax reassessment. Like, screaming at her. She looked up the records and saw that the added farm store would explain it, and he says they've been fixing the place up for over a decade without a tax hike. She said assessments are done from the exterior so any internal improvements wouldn't have mattered, and if they missed any external improvements, he was lucky. He demanded that the assessor be fired, and the collector too for slapping him with a late fee when the bill arrived late in the first place. He slammed his fist down on her desk. Sent papers flying to the floor. I said whoa, that can't be our Jeff Farnham, right? He's no fist slammer. So I ask was this guy about five ten, thick brown hair, a space between his teeth? Or wouldn't you remember? And she says oh yes, she remembers, because he was so irate she had to ask him to leave. It was Jeff all right. And here was the weirdest part. Before he left that day, he pulled out a checkbook and made a payment on the taxes. And I said that part doesn't sound weird at all, because Jeff is a straight-up kind of guy. It was the amount, she said. Fifteen dollars. On an overdue bill of more than four thousand."

There was a pause on the line. "Guess that's it. Sorry to leave such a long message. I'm glad you have one of those services because if this were a machine, it would have beeped me off four times already. And maybe you don't want to hear this today. But then I kept thinking, maybe you would. Know that we're watching here and praying. Hope to see you tomorrow."

Fifteen dollars. What the heck was that about, when he'd left twelve hundred on the table that morning?

But July 19. The significance finally struck her. It was weeks before the vacation where she had met and started interviewing Kevin and more than a month before the notion that she might leave her husband first gnawed on her bones.

Whatever torment Jeff had been keeping private had already started to swell within him, pulling him apart at the seams, and she hadn't seen it. Amber's information had damned and redeemed Ronnie, all at once.

The rest of the messages would have to wait. A familiar male voice shouted from the other room.

ronnie

I t was Rob White, Ronnie realized, when she entered the banquet hall and found her mother turning down the volume. He was saying that parents were to pick up Hitchman Elementary School students, that bus service had been cancelled, and that they should bring ID as an added precaution. The SERT troops, the state helicopter, the people who weren't allowed home from work, those standing at the barricade or glued to their televisions, feeling powerless to continue daily life, and now the hundreds of working parents who would have to figure out a way to pick up their children… If Jeff was thinking his life had come to nothing, she wished he could see the widespread effect his actions were having today.

Her mother turned off the TV. Ronnie watched as the image of New Hope Farms faded to black.

Beverly's troubled expression begged a question and Ronnie wasn't sure she wanted an answer.

"Did something bad happen at the farm?"

Beverly shook her head. Like her mother, Ronnie looked to the blank screen, as if it might come alive and offer answers.

"What did Janet end up saying to him?"

"I couldn't really hear."

"Do you think he saw her?"

Her mother shrugged. Her mouth quivered; she was breathing in spurts.

Dread constricted Ronnie's bones. Her mother was not a crier. "What is it?"

"There was this loud bang and then all this debris and… God, Ronnie, I think he shot at her."

Her mother's words sucked the air from the room. Ronnie needed fresher air. She turned to…to whom? To do what? Go where? There was no escape from this goddamn day. "And Janet?"

"They put her in a police car. I assume she's on the way back."

The words had sounded steadier. Ronnie studied her mother. "You okay?"

"This isn't some madman doing this," her mother whispered, her hand twisting the ring on her finger. "This is *Jeff.*"

Ronnie nodded. Took her bearings. Beverly here, safe if rattled. The boys with Beth. Playing, probably. Janet on her way back. And Jeff…

Ronnie pulled out a chair and sank into it.

Jeff was the madman.

beverly

T he sound of that gun.

Horror pounded in Beverly's skull. Freeze-dried her stomach. Frazzled her nerves. She felt fried in that high voltage moment, as powerless to leave as a woman strapped to an electric chair.

Dom. Beverly had never really let him go. She'd measured all others against him, as if to will him back into her life, completely setting aside his inability to deal with the fact that he was going to be a father. Ignoring that even though they had spoken in his last days, he at the Jersey shore and she in Pennsylvania, he had never revealed his fear. Had never, it now seemed, truly exposed his heart.

Beverly put her hand to her abdomen, as if still protecting her baby. For years she berated herself for going back to Bartlesville and finishing high school rather than staying with Dom. She should have been there for him. He'd needed to hold her, and Ronnie within her, to make tangible the love she'd promised. Love that would have healed him. Saved him.

If Ronnie hadn't called her—if Beverly had seen the Bartlesville standoff on television and realized it was Jeff—she would have wanted to crawl right into the set to see how it went. This was what had tortured her the most all these years, that she hadn't been there for Dom. What had he gone through in those final hours? Beverly only hoped that a lifetime of wishing to know this hadn't shifted enough energy to bring on today's terrible events. Ronnie may think she only read style magazines, but Beverly read Oprah too. She knew intention was powerful.

But if she had been with Dom that night... After what she just saw on the television, who knew if she and Ronnie would still be here today? This was some bad shit going down.

Something was changing within Beverly at that very moment. Her hands tingled as if Dom's spirit were there, holding them. Not his broken spirit, but Dom, fully restored.

Beverly closed her eyes, curled her hands around his, and told him what she'd wanted to say for the last thirty-five years. *Thank you, Dom, for giving me Ronnie.*

The tingling ended.

Beverly opened her hands and let him go. She opened her eyes and set them firmly on the future.

Looking at her daughter, with her head down on the table, her eyes closed—no doubt trying to preserve every scrap of energy she could find for what might still come on this godforsaken day—Beverly realized she was done looking to the dead and missing for love.

3:00 p.m.

ronnie

Jeff. Shooting at his mother.

When Ronnie lifted her head, her vision started to swirl. She stood and touched the end of each table to steady herself as she made her way to the restroom at the back of the fire hall.

Once inside the stall she pressed her cheek against its painted metal door. When these bouts hit, blurring her edges, the cool helped reinforce the limits of her skin. *This is where Ronnie ends; this is where the rest of the world begins.*

What a fucked up world it was.

She closed her eyes and again retreated, first to a world where she was defined by her talents instead of her relationship to Jeff, and then to one where the ocean's lullaby assured her that everything would be all right.

⁓

The last weekend in September, Ronnie had left the boys alone with Jeff. The timing was questionable at best, only a few weeks after Jeff's commitment, but Ronnie couldn't take living under the same roof with him any longer. She needed a retreat, and a Facebook post offered a way to do so while exploring new income streams. A friend from college, Dodie, had posted a link to a three-day conference in Manhattan that could help Ronnie find additional freelance writing assignments. Its price would be reasonable if she skipped the conference hotel and stayed with Dodie in Brooklyn.

Ronnie took every precaution. Should Jeff be unable to withstand the rigors of a weekend of solo parenting, Beverly could provide backup. Janet would be home as well. Her lawyer assured her that, unless there was evidence of her having an affair, her custody was secure; Pennsylvania courts were not overly fond of alcoholic fathers. She'd kissed her sons good-bye and forced herself not to look back.

The seminar was exhilarating for someone who had spent so many years locked away renovating a farmhouse. Perhaps overly so: by the end of the third day, exhaustion had caught up with her. Rather than risk driving three hours on Sunday night while she was so tired, she called Jeff to say she'd make sure to get extra rest Monday morning, then come straight home.

She lied.

The next day, Ronnie headed over the Verrazano-Narrows Bridge before the morning sun was high enough to warm her shoulders. But she couldn't relinquish her freedom. Not yet, when it was barely tasted. So instead of heading west, toward the farm, she headed south on the Garden State Parkway toward the only home that had never demanded a thing from her.

When she emerged from the car across from her father's house—Kevin's house—the warmer air greeted her. The ocean had a long memory and stored the summer's warmth well into autumn. This was the first time she'd been here off-season, and the silence stunned her into a new depth of reverence for the place.

As always, Ronnie headed straight to the beach. She felt so free walking out to it, without a thought to arranging child care, without reporting to Jeff why she was going out and then defending it three times, without leashing Max.

Max. Her thoughts snagged on her little dog and the night Jeff had left him out all night. When Ronnie had opened the front door the next morning, he'd rushed inside, shivering.

Later, when she woke Jeff to confront him, Jeff said the dog had followed him out for his last smoke. "Guess he never came back," he said thickly. "A simple mistake. Anyone could make it." She swallowed her anger, unsure who she was in this scenario: someone who deserved to defend her principles or a class-A bitch? But when Ronnie went into the bathroom to wash up, it was hard not to notice that she'd showered three times since she'd last washed the towels, and Jeff's still lay on the shelf, unfolded.

She'd been Max's sole caretaker of late, and the feeling that she had abandoned him seized her. But as Ronnie trudged through the loose, deep sand, she pushed thoughts of Max out of her mind. That rabbit hole would lead her to the boys. For just a half hour or so, she wanted what peace this setting could offer. Her footsteps eased as she reached the sand tamped by the ocean.

At the water's edge, Ronnie dipped her fingers and pressed them to her forehead and lips. Gone were the motorboats and wave runners that crashed through the August waters. The ocean was free to swell its strength again and again without the need to hold anyone else afloat. Today Ronnie needed a similar chance.

Standing there for some time, Ronnie realized she no longer felt hopelessly adrift, as she had before she met Jeff. His love had encouraged her to grow in ways neither of them would have predicted, and now Ronnie had no choice but to leave him. A tragedy, to be sure, but another she would survive.

A gust whipped sand across her face and into her hair. Before it could fully claim her as part of the setting, she ran back to the house and up the steps until her heart was thundering like the surf.

Ronnie ran her hand across the nicks in the door frame, feeling a notch taller in this unencumbered state than she'd been just months ago, and knocked on the door. No answer. Kevin must be at work.

Relieved, Ronnie sat on the deck in a patch of sun. She put her feet on the railing, lifted her face to the sky, and—her cell phone vibrated in her pocket. It took several rings for her to process the intrusion. But she refused to disturb her hard-won feeling of peace and—God help her—when she pulled out the phone and saw the picture of the tractor she used as Jeff's avatar, she shut off the phone. He had to learn to get by without her. It was no less than the divorce court would demand of him.

She settled back into the chair to listen to the surf and soak up what remained of the summer sun.

"Look what the waves washed in. Sleeping Beauty."

Ronnie startled awake and saw Kevin standing beside her, holding a bag of groceries.

"Oh my god. What time is it?"

"Eleven."

She'd been sleeping for twenty minutes. "I've got to go."

"But you didn't tell me why you're here yet. Pretty sure you didn't even say hi."

Ronnie smiled. "Sorry, I did knock, but you weren't home, so... Hi, Kevin."

"Hi, Ronnie. Well, don't keep me in suspense. Where is it?"

"What?"

"I assume you're here to show me the magazine?"

"Oh, no." She waved her hand. "Long lead time for print. That won't be out for a few more months. I'm just stopping in on my way home from New York."

He laughed. "You are not a poster child for energy conservation. That's quite a detour."

"I just needed escape, I think. And peace. And my car pointed here." Ronnie stood. "I wasn't trying to trespass or anything."

"I'll tell you whether I believe you or not after I count the flatware." He unlocked the door. "Come on in. I finished up a project this morning, and before I start the next, I thought I'd grab an early lunch..."

His voice receded as he entered the house. Ronnie lingered outside the doorway until he poked his head back through. "That was an invitation to join me."

The beach house felt at once welcoming and dangerous. As he threw some burgers on the grill, Ronnie sat on the leather couch, sank back into its bulk, imagined its arms around her. She knew so intimately this woven rug beneath her feet; she'd sponged from its surface many a sippy cup spill. She knew the dishes Kevin was setting out to serve this meal and that one of them had chipped when she overfilled the dishwasher so she and the boys could squeeze in a bike ride before sunset. She'd slept on his bed.

"Almost ready," Kevin said.

Ronnie moved to the table, laced her fingers, and closed her eyes. She didn't want to go home. Heaven help her, she wanted to stay right here. *Dad. If you could be here for me just this once. I need your strength.*

She heard the plates as Kevin set them on the table.

"Saying grace?"

Ronnie tried to smile. "Something like that."

"I'm Catholic. Got this covered." He took her hands and offered the blessing.

His halting search for the words, his cheery domesticity, the surprise of his touch—it was all too much. Out poured the anxiety she'd been holding back for so many months: for the sake of her kids, and for the sake of the husband who'd promised to move out soon, and for the sake of those who cared for all of them, and for her own sake, because God knew she was scared shitless that she couldn't handle supporting two boys on her own while caring for a farm and two businesses and dealing with an alcoholic ex.

She placed her forehead on their clasped hands as she sobbed. Kevin waited without moving until the storm had passed.

"Sorry," she said at last.

"Hey." He jiggled her hands and waited for their eyes to meet. "I've witnessed this reaction to my cooking before."

Ronnie's laugh was a gulp for air. "Guess I'm not used to saying grace. It kind of—I don't know—cracked me open."

"Grace will do that," he said, grabbing a potato chip off his plate. "That's kind of how I felt when I found my grandpa's steering wheel. I just wanted to hug it and weep. Sometimes it seems like we expect the bad things to happen, but when something good happens, we fall to pieces."

"Wisdom from the School of Hard Knocks?"

"Nah, a paragraph on page 139 of the self-help book I'm reading." Ronnie smiled and took a bite of her burger.

"So, is this about what's going on with you and your husband?"

Ronnie snapped a large chip in two. "That obvious?"

"Even a casual observer can see you deserve more."

She had to look away from the sincerity in his green eyes. The word *deserve* plucked at her taut nerves. What does anyone deserve? A chance at life, maybe, but the rest is navigation. She had some serious course-setting ahead, and she only hoped she could maneuver past whatever met her when she got home.

❧

When the Suburban made it to the top of the drive, Will burst from the house to hug her. She wrapped her arms around him and lifted him into the air, spinning, awash in relief and joy. Of all the different Ronnies inside her, this one—the mother—was the one she had never, ever compromised on, and reconnecting to her made this dreaded return feel like a homecoming after all.

Jeff and Max weren't far behind. Ronnie dealt with the wriggling pup first, letting him jump into her arms for a kiss, then turned to Jeff.

The sight of his widespread arms embarrassed her. "Come on, Jeff."

"We're so glad you're back," he said, voice trembling.

"Did you have a good time, Will?"

"Dad made up a soccer game with me, and we played in the side yard. It was great!"

"Good for you," she said, looking at Will and then Jeff.

Ronnie found Andrew inside on the Xbox and kissed him hello. "I want to hear about New York, Mom, but not now. I'm not at a good save point."

After the boys were in bed that night, Jeff asked if they could talk. On the porch, so he could have the comfort of his nicotine addiction. It didn't take him long to get to the point.

"Did you sleep with him?"

"Who?"

"Kevin."

"Jeff." She stood to leave. "We are not having this conversation."

"Please," he said. "I want to talk."

He'd stolen her line. She was the one who usually wanted to talk.

Ronnie heard her therapist: *Go get some sleep.* Heard the hospital psychiatrist warn: *This will do no good.*

She sighed. "Let me get a jacket."

"I don't understand how you could leave our home," he said when she'd returned. "We've worked so hard."

"This home is a thing, Jeff. Yes, we've made every single room exactly the way I wanted it, but in the end, it's just a house." A house that, so far, she hadn't found an affordable way to leave. "It would be much easier if you would move, at least for the time being, since my move will be more complex."

"Move?"

"Yes. I met with my lawyer again last week. These are the steps you take when you are getting a divorce."

That last word nicked her on its way out. Jeff looked like she had stabbed him afresh.

"Why do you want me, Jeff? I know you're sick of me judging you, and I don't want to do it anymore. You have the right to happiness too. To spend time with someone who shares your values." *And she wanted that for herself.*

"Don't go yet," Jeff said. "Give me some time. I'll figure something out."

"There's only one solution at this point," Ronnie said, standing. She opened the door to go back into the house.

"I read your journals while you were gone."

Ronnie braced against fury that threatened to consume her. Now, after all this time, he would try to steal the intimacy he'd refused her?

It had humiliated her to stand in the cold for so many years, knocking at her husband's door, begging his attention. That made her feel like more of a whore than fantasizing about someone new. A man who mirrored back her curiosity and passion for life and who had infiltrated her dreams; a man she'd written of in a place she deemed safe from the prying eyes of a husband who had only ever displayed indifference toward her journaling. By this time, she had filled half a dozen thick spiral notebooks. If he'd read them all in one weekend, he must have ignored their children.

When she was able to bring her breathing back to normal, Ronnie said, "And what did you find?"

"Hope."

ronnie

R onnie bent over the sink and splashed cold water on her face.
"Are you okay?" Her mother's head peeked around the bathroom door. "You've been in here a long time."

Ronnie lifted her face and her mother handed her a length of paper towel. It smelled like newsprint and felt like a sympathy card and was probably all the tenderness she deserved. "Look, I came in here to pull myself together." Before her mother could say anything else she added, "Alone."

"Fine," Beverly said, turning back to the door.

"But since you're here, can I borrow your phone?"

Beverly slipped the phone from her purse and swiped her thumb back and forth over its surface. Finally she punched in the code and handed her the phone. "Just wish you could keep your focus on Jeff today, that's all."

"But Jeff is closing off. Thinking about dying. I want to connect, Mom. I am trying to live."

Beverly slipped the phone to Ronnie gently, as if it were a weapon of mass destruction. "Please be considerate. Janet should be back any minute."

"Who do you think I'm trying to call?"

"Kevin."

"Why on earth?"

"All this divorce talk started when you began interviewing him for that article."

Ronnie leaned back against the sink. "And where did you get that information?"

Beverly shifted her weight a few times. "All right. Jeff told me. He called me while you were in New York City to see if I knew the number of where you were staying."

"Mom. I'm trying to call Teddy. He's been trying to reach you all day." She opened the phone app and showed her mother the list of missed calls.

"Oh. Well."

Ronnie hit the number and put the phone on speaker.

"Mom, thank goodness. I've been going nuts here. Is Ronnie okay?"

"Teddy, it's me. I have you on speaker. Mom's here too."

"And Jeff?"

"He's...he's..." Ronnie pushed the phone toward her mother.

"He's okay, honey, as far as we know," Beverly said. "How did you know?"

"An online news service alerted me on my phone. Ronnie, are you still there?"

She nodded. Somehow this validation from her brother was causing a meltdown. She was used to fighting for her perspective. Demanding to be heard.

"She's here, doll."

"I'm so sorry, Ronnie. I should have taken you more seriously. I feel like hell. How are the boys?"

Ronnie wet a paper towel with cold water and held it against the back of her neck. "Okay for now," she was able to say. "But what will it be like for them tomorrow? Either way this turns out? I can barely stand to think about it."

"What can I do?"

Ronnie started to cry.

"Mom, what can I do?"

Beverly looked right into Ronnie's eyes as she said, "I'm pretty sure what we can do for Jeff is at an end."

Ronnie sobbed even harder. And her mother, holding their connection to Teddy in one hand, slipped the other into one of Ronnie's.

"Call me, Ronnie. Let me know, okay? Call me."

All Ronnie could do was nod.

"She says she will, doll. Thanks for calling. And I never thought I'd be the one saying this to you, because church was more your father's thing, but maybe a prayer or two wouldn't hurt."

Back in the social hall, they found Janet leaning heavily on Corporal McNichol, her hair windblown into a lopsided corona, her eyes all but erased. Relief washed through Ronnie that she had come to no bodily harm.

Ronnie and her mother rushed over.

"Jeff…" Her son's name seemed to be all Janet could manage.

"I saw on the TV," Beverly said, throwing her arms around her friend.

When she pulled back, Ronnie also gave Janet a hug. She hadn't done so since Jerry died, and her arms told her what her eyes hadn't seen: despite those Tai Chi classes her mother had bought Janet, her mother-in-law had grown frailer. "I'm sorry you had to go through that. You did what you could," Ronnie said, knowing full well how little that could possibly be.

"Has anything else happened at the farm?" Beverly asked Corporal McNichol.

"No, things seem to have calmed back down. My men weren't too happy about that shot, but everyone was out of harm's way. Listen, Ronnie, we have another caller for you. She refused to tell us anything but her name so I thought I'd better check."

"Who is it?"

"Fay Sickler."

Ronnie looked at Jeff's mother. The name reanimated Janet's face and she lifted her eyebrows.

Crazy Fay—Jeff's first wife.

ronnie

R onnie picked up the receiver with equal measures of curiosity and dread.

"Hello, Veronica?"

"This is Ronnie."

"My name is Fay Sickler. You may not know me—"

"I know who you are." Ronnie tried to keep her voice neutral.

"Listen, I hate what you're going through. I live in Florida now, but I heard from a friend back home that it's all over the television."

"Yes, it is." Not wanting to add any of Fay's melodrama to her day, Ronnie pushed things along. "Why are you calling?"

"I'd heard that you and Jeff had sons. I know Janet thinks the Hoyers are the be-all and end-all, but I have something you'll want to know about the black sheep side of the family."

"You mean Jerry's? He's gone now, you know."

"I know. My mother and I adored that man. If he wasn't so tied to that basketball team of his, I would have stolen him right off to Florida with me."

Even Crazy Fay deserved the truth. "He still had a picture of you in his wallet when he died."

There was a moment of silence. "Thank you for telling me," she said softly. "I wondered if you knew Jerry received electroshock treatments for depression?"

"Really." Ronnie wondered whether to believe her. After all, this was Crazy Fay.

"Jerry's mother did too. I figured you wouldn't know. For some reason, that family clamped down on its stories something fierce."

"Janet told me an office fire had destroyed their medical records, so that's good to know. Our mothers are close friends, but there's a limit to what an autopsy can—"

"Wait, you're Beverly Saylor's daughter?"

"Yes."

"The loon always dragging Janet and Jerry off into the great unknown?"

The loon? She was one to talk. "Why does it matter?"

"If you're partial to Janet, you might discount everything I say, is all. I wouldn't even have married into the family if it weren't for all Jeff's weeping when I tried to break up with him. But his tears seemed to prove utter devotion, and being on the rebound, I found loyalty appealing."

Tears? Oh my god.

"Eventually I came to see all that laid-back swagger as Jeff's way of hiding one heck of a wobbly ego. That became clear when I decided to split."

"He told me you two didn't end up liking each other that well. That you were young, recognized your mistake, and divorced after a few years."

"Four long years. As for the mistake, well, at least one of us had the eyes to see it." Fay laughed. "Jeff's big plan was for us to live with his parents and pay them rent until we could afford to move out. They had a great setup for breeding horses, so hey, at first I didn't mind. After a year, it dawned on my romance-addled brain that 'temporary' was a fib—and so was 'rent.' He couldn't support a wife any more than he could support himself."

"Did you work?"

"Not at first. Jeff was queer about that, like he wanted to keep me close. After two years, we seemed no closer to moving out, but Janet still wanted us to tithe to the church when we had no money for survival."

"Yeah, he gave up on that. Janet has been donating in his name to a church they've never attended." Ronnie was too embarrassed to say how she knew this: she'd seen the name "Bartlesville Lutheran" while peeking at their tax records, where Jeff deducted the weekly contribution.

"Buying her boy's way into heaven—pure Janet. I finally told Jeff if he wanted to stay married, we'd have to get a place of our own. Janet must have realized I was serious because that's when she had the swell idea to sell us that pathetic farmhouse, whereupon we moved all the way to the other side of the hill."

"It looks a lot better these days."

"I don't know how you'd live there otherwise. Jeff put off working on it a whole year until he made some money. I got a job at the Reading airport to help make ends meet and tried to ignore all his suspicions about where I'd been. And then what does he do? He takes an entire year to fix up the attic, the only room we didn't need to use! While I had to cook in a kitchen with cheap paneling, no counter space, and neon green cupboards."

Ronnie laughed. "That kitchen was ugly as sin."

"I only lasted in that hellhole another year. Didn't want to prolong the stupidity. I started moving out, one carload at a time."

Ronnie thought of the oak cabinetry, the high-end appliances. No one would call that house a hellhole now. Yet she envied Fay's decisiveness. Ronnie was a victim of her own stick-to-itiveness. Her marriage to Jeff was like walking deeper and deeper into a web so sticky that despite her growing resolve to change direction, it seemed she'd never be able to shake herself free.

"You left behind a clock. A reproduction of an antique mantel clock with a pendulum, only it was electric. And plastic. It...got ruined." Ronnie shuddered at the thought of the clock's violent end. "I'm sorry."

"Don't worry about it for another moment. Janet bought that for us at a flea market. Couldn't have been any uglier. I'm surprised he kept it. Perhaps Jeff was clinging to Mommy Dearest."

Or perhaps Jeff had loved his mother more than he realized.

Ronnie heard voices coming from the entrance to the social hall. "I'd better get going—"

"But wait, here's what I needed to tell you. The day I moved out, Jeff came into the bedroom and waved a gun around and threatened me."

"What?" That must have been more than fifteen years ago. "Had he been drinking?"

"No, Jeff didn't drink. He just went ape shit. Like an idiot, I called his bluff. That's when he held the gun to his temple and threatened to kill himself."

The picture Ronnie had kept at bay this whole day crystallized: the cold barrel of a gun pressed up against Jeff's warm, tender skin. It was no longer a stretch to imagine her husband storming through the house with a gun as the boys hid behind furniture. Ronnie propped her forehead with her hand. "This is so unbelievable."

"Jerry was in the driveway, helping to pack the car, when Jeff followed me from the house with the gun. I always wondered if he was torn between trying to talk sense into his son or jumping into my car and making a break for it."

"What happened with Jeff and the gun?"

"I kept packing because no matter what, I was out of there. Jeff didn't end up hurting anyone that day. But I've never seen anyone go berserk like that. I felt badly for him but not guilty. That's why I'm calling. No matter what happens today, Ronnie, you aren't guilty either. He was a miserable cuss even back then."

The air went silent for a minute.

"Ronnie?"

"I'm here. Just trying to process all of this."

"But even now, I don't wish him ill. I'd hoped that you and your boys would give him the stability or whatever it was he needed. I'm sorry that doesn't seem to be the case. My family has had a suicide. The pain goes on and on."

"Maybe it won't turn out that way."

"So he's still—"

"Yes," Ronnie said. "Hey. If you knew Jeff and I were living in that same farmhouse, why did you wait until now to tell me this?"

Fay's voice softened. "You were in love. Crusty as I am, even I haven't forgotten what that felt like. If I'd told you any earlier, would you have believed me?"

Of course not. She might not have believed her today if not for her mention of Jeff's tears of devotion.

"Good-bye, Fay. Thanks for calling."

"Good luck, Ronnie. My thoughts will be with you and your kids."

Ronnie hung up the phone and the officers returned to the room with their radios.

Even as recently as May, when she and Jeff celebrated the grand opening of New Hope Farms, if anyone had predicted that before year's end her husband would be holed up in its office contemplating suicide, she wouldn't have believed them either.

ronnie

Janet and her mother were talking quietly when Ronnie returned to the social hall. Running her hand along the oak bar, her skin caught on a sticky spot. After what Fay told her, the day seemed destined to exist within a whole new story, one in which suicide may have been a constant threat. Had Ronnie and the boys been in danger all these years and never known it? And if not, what had pushed her peaceable Jeff over the line?

Ronnie wished she had a copy of last month's suicide note so she could seek clues, but the police had taken it into evidence. She'd read it so quickly and in such a frazzled state with Jeff watching her so intently. She couldn't recall much except that besides declaring his hate for Janet, Jeff had asked to be buried beside his father. As if hoping to sense, through the damp ground, the love and respect that his average stature and weak knees could never inspire from the beloved basketball coach.

How unfortunate, Ronnie thought, *to wait until death to try to share someone's life*. It had pained her to watch him squander what opportunity he had during his father's final days.

Five years ago, when Jerry had contracted pneumonia, Janet had called Ronnie and asked her to drive her and Jerry to the emergency room. Lisa Schulz was able to watch the boys. When Ronnie got to the house, she found Jerry hot, weak, and haggard-looking in a beard he'd grown that summer. He'd needed both Janet and Ronnie to help him to the car.

A specialist found a spot on his lungs as well and admitted Jerry. Jeff stopped by the hospital after work for a brief visit and to take his mother home. Ronnie couldn't believe they were going to leave.

"He's only sixty-three," Jeff said. "It's not like he's going to die or anything."

"Look at him, Jeff." Jerry lay on the bed, eyes closed, oxygen mask on his face, fluids and antibiotics flowing into him through tubes.

Jeff gave him only a quick glance, took his mother's arm, and left. When Jerry woke up on and off over the next few hours, it was Ronnie's face he saw.

When Ronnie called the hospital for an update the next morning, the nurse said Jerry was so disoriented they'd had to restrain him. Ronnie left for the hospital as soon as she dropped the boys at nursery school. She found the poor man sitting in the hallway in a geriatric chair, his hands bound so he wouldn't pull out his IV. As soon as he saw Ronnie, he collapsed forward with relief. "I'm in one hell of a mess," he said. "Where's Janet?"

Jerry rallied a bit after they drained fluid from his chest cavity, allowing his lungs to fully inflate. But as much as he seemed to want his wife by his side, Ronnie soon learned it was indeed better when Janet stayed home. She seemed to have no common sense for nursing, trying to shame him into getting better. One day he was so angry about the way she pushed food at him that he sat in bed before his untouched tray, twisting a napkin around and around his fingers, trying to rip it apart.

Ronnie suggested that a visit from the boys might lighten the mood. They were too young, according to hospital rules, but the nurses would make an exception in this case. While Jerry had spent a lifetime avoiding hospitals, it was increasingly clear that he wouldn't be leaving this one. Ronnie wanted Andrew and Will to see their grandfather one more time, but Jeff and Janet wouldn't have it. But when Ronnie showed up one evening and Jerry had again grown weaker, she made up her mind to bring the boys the next day.

It was the week before Halloween, and some trick-or-treaters were parading down the hall of the hospital, stopping in to show their costumes to bed-ridden patients. A pint-size ghost and a quart-size masked cowboy popped into Jerry's room and said, "Happy Halloween!" Jerry looked at Ronnie.

"Is that the boys?" It seemed to take all his energy to push out the words. Praying the trick-or-treaters hadn't heard him, she said yes. "I'm so glad to see you," he said, his voice full of emotion. "Thanks for coming." As they turned to leave, Ronnie rushed to cover. Since the boys were so young, she said, the nurse would only let them stay for a moment. "That's fine," Jerry had said. "I was so afraid I might never see them again."

That night, Jerry started slipping away. He no longer spoke. By ten thirty, when Janet was ready to leave, a nurse stopped in and confirmed the end was near. "What should I do?" Janet said. The nurse answered, "It depends on how important it is for you to be here when he draws his last breath."

"Oh no," Janet said, leaning on the back of a chair. "I can't do it, Jeff."

Jeff said, "I'll take you home."

"You two should stay, Jeff." When he did not immediately respond, Ronnie added, "This is your father."

Jeff could barely meet her eyes. He took his mother by the elbow and left without saying good-bye.

They would all have to deal with Jerry's loss in their own way, she supposed. But Ronnie was compelled to see it through. So she sat with Jerry through the night, until his biological shutting down was complete. He never woke up. Maybe it didn't matter to him one bit that Ronnie had stayed, but it mattered to her. In the morning, when his heart was stilled and his fever forever gone, she kissed his cool forehead and said good-bye.

4:00 p.m.

ronnie

As the day stretched on without resolution, Ronnie imagined the mirror ball spinning question marks across every surface of the boxy room. The walls let the questions gloss over their neutral surfaces, offering no answers. Time passed doubly slow.

In its corner stood the untended bar, a hulking presence in a dark mood. Even through stoppered bottles and shut cabinets, she could smell the whiskey and vermouth, spirits that were ultimately stronger than her husband's.

It was in a soulless hall like this, at the hotel, where Jeff buoyed the moods of customers twirling around the turning points of their lives, while he remained stuck exchanging booze for a plump wad of cash in his pocket.

Although not happily. Jeff's situation at the hotel continued to deteriorate. The new owner had replaced the inn's computer system with an overly complex one on the cheap. Jeff had way more practice with it than he needed as, one after the other, the new hires he'd trained said to heck with it and walked out. Ronnie could only imagine how frustrating it was for him to train someone new every two weeks.

Yet people were still getting married and having babies and reuniting with their high school classes, and Jeff didn't have enough staff to work banquets. Last November, he asked if Ronnie would fill in as a bartender.

"It's just a little extra help with the big banquets," he said, "and you won't have to learn the computer."

"But my feet. You remember what we did to my last pair of heels—"

"You can wear flats. And we have a rubber mat behind the bar. You'll be fine." He played his trump card. "You'll make good money."

With the boys' schoolwork and activities, the cleaning required to control their allergies, the renovation, the animals, and her writing, Ronnie did not need to add one more thing to her life. And if she did choose to add something, it wouldn't be bartending. She'd been determined to show Jeff she could make money from her skills and interests; she just needed more time. But she wasn't without compassion. She knew how hard he'd worked to try to get bartenders. She couldn't refuse.

The part she hadn't anticipated: she had to fill out a corporate application that included her employment history, interests, and references—as if she really wanted the job. She'd have to take the TIPS (Training for Intervention Procedures) certification course the Pennsylvania Liquor Control Board required so she could learn to deal with intoxicated patrons. She'd have to learn all those drink recipes—she'd been a waitress at the Valley View all those years ago, not a bartender. Learn all those prices. Jeff assured her the Sunday wedding he first needed her for would be an open bar; Ronnie wouldn't have to handle cash.

When they got to the hotel for the wedding, they found that the families had been feuding. The bride's family had flung generosity out the window; the groom's family would have to pay cash for their drinks. Jeff quizzed Ronnie on prices as they cut up lemons and limes and he explained the system he'd improvised: everyone on the groom's side would be wearing a red sticker. Those were the people who would have to pay.

"This is getting awfully complicated," Ronnie said.

Jeff kissed her on the cheek. "You'll do great. You always do."

Ronnie's first drink order was a whiskey and water. The guy

had a red dot on his lapel: groom's side. She could handle that. She grabbed a bottle and hoped she hadn't poured heavy. Jeff never used a shot glass and Ronnie didn't want to give away her beginner status. "Five fifty, please." The man dropped a bill on the bar and walked away. It wasn't until she got to the cash drawer that she noticed the bill was a fifty.

"I'll be right back." Ronnie strode past Jeff. "This guy left without his change."

Jeff grabbed the back of her polyester vest and pulled. "First rule of bartending," he said. "Never, ever return money people have left on the bar."

Ronnie kept up as people first streamed in, but soon customers stood two and three deep. She had no cheat sheet for prices and no scratch pad or pen for adding. At one point she had to add $5.50 + $5.50 + $8.75 (wrong price anyway) + $12.25 in her head. Jeff did this all the time, but her writing gig didn't require top-notch math skills. "That'll be twenty-eight even," Ronnie said, hoping she was close.

Due to corporate policy, Ronnie had to wear a name tag at all times, and since they didn't have one for her yet, they gave her an old one. She went through the whole long evening trying to remember to respond when people called her Suzette.

After they'd cleaned up the banquet hall, Jeff took her to an all-night diner. Over eggs and bacon, he complimented her on her bartending, although to Ronnie, the entire evening had been a strain on her skill set, her back, her arches, and her most essential sense of self. When they got home, he took a bath before going to bed. Ronnie almost wept with the near-forgotten sensation of snuggling up next to soapy skin. In the morning, it was his idea to make love. Ronnie didn't turn away the gift.

That day, he smiled at her more. She knew it was because they had resurrected a taste of the life that had brought them together. And that broke her heart: in this world where she and Jeff had met and fallen in love, Ronnie was now an impostor.

ronnie

Raised voices near the entrance to the room drew Ronnie's attention. Beverly and Janet were arguing. Approaching, Ronnie saw that they were blocking entrance to a man wearing a clerical collar.

"We don't need more hellfire from you; we've been breathing it all day." Janet's voice.

"I don't mean to upset you," the pastor said.

"Well, then you shouldn't have claimed to be from her church because she doesn't have one," Beverly said.

The pastor appealed to Ronnie as she approached. "I keep trying to tell Mrs. Farnham that she's one of my—"

"That may be a lost cause," Ronnie said. "If you want to talk to me, however, I'd like that."

The man looked around the room, empty except for its tables and chairs. "Is there somewhere we can sit?"

Ronnie smiled. She liked him already. "I have a better idea." She turned to her mother and mother-in-law. "You two go sit."

"Ronnie, don't do this to yourself," her mother said. "Think about what he's going to say. You've had enough stress as it is."

"Yes, I have, so please don't add to it," Ronnie said. "Now go on. This will just take a minute."

Jeff too would have scoffed at a consultation with a pastor. Ronnie pictured Jeff emerging from the doorway as he had in the psych ward, like a specter, his socks silent against the waxed tiles.

Ronnie actually liked that Jeff: no cigarette, no double-size coffee, no cocktail to pump some needed chemical into his veins.

Still standing inside the doorway to the social hall, Ronnie introduced herself to the pastor as the wife of the man who'd instigated the standoff. "I'm sorry about my mother and mother-in-law. They've had bad experiences with organized religion."

The pastor flashed her an easy smile. "I would have happily offered them as much disorganized solace as I could. As a matter of fact, that may be the only kind." He reached his hand forward. "I'm Pastor John. I learned what was going on when I couldn't get past the barricade. I thought I'd stop by and see if I could lend a hand."

"That was kind of you. What church are you from?"

"Considering that might be a sore subject," he said, "today let's say I am simply of God, as are we all."

"Fair enough. I don't want to distress them any further, so let's get right to the point. If Jeff kills himself, do you think he'll go to hell?" Her mother and Jeff's may not want his opinion on this, but Ronnie did. "I imagine the Great Creator isn't too thrilled when someone hands back the gift of life."

The pastor laughed. "That's not the direction I would have taken this conversation, but if you find that helpful, I won't take it away from you."

Ronnie's smile quickly faded. "I don't know what to think."

"Today, and in the days to come, you'll need strength beyond what many people will be called on to have in this life, Ronnie," Pastor John said. "Your husband's current predicament is the kind of thing that you read in the newspaper but always about someone else. Someone you don't know. But you've loved him."

You've loved him. Masterfully phrased, evoking the past without presupposing the present.

"I won't pretend. I'm divorcing him," Ronnie said, the confession spilling with her tears. But she did not hide her face; she'd take whatever condemnation was coming her way. She wanted it, she needed it, and if the man held out a crucifix and smote her with it, leaving nothing in her chest but a blackened, smoking hole, she would not have been surprised.

He lifted two fingers—was he going to invoke the sign of the cross?—and moved his hand from his chest toward hers. She could feel energy radiating through his fingertips.

"Even when you have felt alone you have never, ever been alone, and never will be."

Ronnie forced herself not to glance in the direction of her mother and mother-in-law. "But what about Jeff?" She pulled the pastor into the stairwell. "If God loves Jeff, why is he letting this happen?"

Her question took on a resonant echo. Ronnie had relocated for added privacy, not taking into account the two-story open stairwell with its metal treads. In answer, every word the pastor spoke now resounded with significance. "But Jeff is not alone either, do you see? Make no mistake. God is reaching out to him in an infinite number of ways at this very moment. As a matter of fact, I bet they have quite a debate raging."

For the first time, it occurred to Ronnie that maybe this wasn't simply a standoff between a desperate man and police as the news had reported.

Perhaps it was a standoff between Jeff and God.

"I'd better go. I'll have to try another time with your mother-in-law." As he shook her hand, he leaned in and added, "She's giving me the evil eye."

Ronnie smiled. "I appreciate you coming."

He'd descended several steps before she realized he'd left a business card in her palm. Bartlesville Lutheran—it was the same church where, in the words of Crazy Fay, Janet had been purchasing stock for heaven.

What is Jeff doing right now? she wondered as she returned to take a seat in the social hall. *Drinking straight from the bottle? Falling asleep? Resting his head on the end of a shotgun?*

Praying?

Something tapped at her memory, like a chick pipping at its shell, and finally broke through. After fearing that her last words to her husband had been about whether he was still planning on leaving, she recalled another exchange, almost lost to the fog of sleep.

Last night, late, Jeff had knocked on the guest room door.

Pulled from the brink of much-needed rest, she'd said, "What?"

Jeff's voice came through the shut door. "Does your God believe in forgiveness?"

The silence grew thick until Ronnie spoke the only words that came to her groggy tongue. "He's your God too."

Ronnie released some of the guilt she'd been carrying all day. Maybe reaching Jeff hadn't been a lone crusade after all. Maybe God was still trying to appeal to him.

If only Jeff would open the door.

janet

Janet sat stewing in the heat of her family's damnation. What could a pastor do for her now? She could sense Amelia Hoyer turning a frosty shoulder to her grandson as he fell into the crimson fires.

The way she had stood before Jeff today with no wisdom to share, no relief to promise him—it was shameful. Thinking of it now, she might say that if you take in the view all at once, life can look like a lonely journey across a long, hot desert. But she'd made the bulk of the trip and could see it wasn't so bad. If you just planned it out one day at a time, you could find a shady spot to rest, or a pitcher of something cool to quench your thirst, or some company to share a story. But even if she'd thought of it then, that wasn't the sort of thing you'd shout through a bullhorn.

She really hoped that gun had gone off by accident, but what were the chances?

Jeff had been such a beautiful little boy. Fresh from an afternoon nap, he was often grumpy when Janet got home from teaching, clinging to his grandmother and hiding his face in her shirt. It cut Janet to the quick every time: Jeffrey loved Amelia more. But over time, Janet learned that if she was patient enough while her son made the rocky transition from dream world to real, she could often turn his dour shirt-hiding into a game.

She'd crouch behind her mother's back, then pop up and shout "peekaboo"! She loved that startled look on his face right before he decided to laugh rather than cry. She'd enjoy his attention so much that—she couldn't help herself—she'd sometimes leave the room, waiting around the corner until he started to fuss.

"Janet, this is cruel. Come back," Amelia would say, always looking to add one more thing to her list of the reasons Janet wouldn't find her way to heaven. But those tears were precious to her. Because if she waited just long enough before returning, she returned the hero, and Jeff would reach out his chubby little arms to her. She'd take the boy from his grandmother and he'd wrap his arms around his mother's neck and put his cheek on her shoulder and oh my, there was no better feeling in the world. She'd bounce him and tell him everything would be all right now, Mama was here.

As he grew, every interaction was a negotiation, but time and again, Janet figured out how to win her son's favor. Once the peekaboo days were behind them, she'd bring home candy from the school vending machine for him; later, she learned that if she hid colorful bits of it around the room, their interaction would last even longer. She loved the miracle of him—the way those little legs toddled around the room, the way those chubby fingers curled around the candy and pushed it into his mouth. Her son was so smart. And industrious. She'd take him out to the garage and let him stand on the seat behind the steering wheel, where he'd drive her "coss the countwy." He loved that, offering up all kinds of joyous, little boy smiles while making car noises. And if Amelia called them to dinner and Jerry was late coaching, why risk a snit by making him come in? Janet would fix him a plate, bring it out to the garage, and spoonfeed him while he stood behind the wheel.

Of course a time came when Janet no longer knew how to make him happy. During high school, it seemed she saw him more often in the principal's office than at home, which as a teacher offered her no end of mortifying scenarios. She wished Jerry could have been more involved with him, but he was busy raising team after team of basketball players, all of whom he saw as substitute sons. Sometimes she felt it was by sheer luck that, with her tutoring, she was able to get Jeff out of high school and off to college.

Amelia died just before the end of Jeff's senior year. Janet knew from experience how disruptive it was to break away just short of finals. And her mother was dead, there was nothing to be done about it. Her son's future was on the line. So when Janet scheduled the funeral during his finals week, she convinced Jerry not to tell him about her mother's death until Jeff got home.

Jeff flew into a rage, blaming Janet for taking away his chance to see his grandmother one last time. But he had graduated, allowing Janet to achieve her goal of educating him, so she was willing to wait out his anger. She'd take his anger any day over the burden of watching her son's heart break.

Once she dared speak to him again, she offered him Amelia's side of the house as consolation.

After that, Jeff pushed Janet to the periphery of his life; she would never again be the one to make him happy. He wanted other women—a string of them, in fact. Why he settled for Fay, she hadn't a clue, since Janet felt certain she'd been the kind of tramp who'd made many men happy. Although she hadn't inherited her mother's faith in an Almighty God, she did believe in all manner of insurance, so she insisted that Fay and Jeff tithe to her mother's church, just in case their souls were in peril. Janet couldn't have been happier when Fay finally took her leave, even though Jeff went into another of his fits. Janet knew he'd get over it, and he did.

Then Ronnie. Beverly had kept quiet about their reintroduction at first, not wanting to raise Janet's hopes. But after their first date, when Jeff came over to help his father clean whirligigs out of the rain gutters, Janet saw the transformation. Most striking was that he volunteered information.

"You aren't going to believe who I went out with last night," Jeff said.

Janet had always feared the return of Fay but refused to utter her name. Her mind briefly flitted to Beverly, who looked younger than her age and was always on the prowl, but she shook off the thought. "Who?" Remembering how he looked at her, with a face that radiated such utter bliss, made tears press again at the back of her eyes.

"Ronnie."

His life was transformed, as was Janet's. She came to believe in true love. To believe that she, Jerry, and Jeff would revive as a family. To believe in grandchildren and heirs.

But then, today. Another of his fits. One that her money hadn't been able to prevent and Ronnie hadn't even tried to put an end to. And if that gun went off on purpose, she could hear Amelia pointing out, her son had been intent on breaking two different commandments.

But her biggest fear wasn't whether she and Jeff were going to hell.

It was that they may have already been living there for a good long while.

ronnie

Ronnie walked over to where Beverly and Janet sat.

Beverly made a show of sniffing her daughter's hands. "At least the holy man didn't ward you off with garlic."

"You should have talked to him," Ronnie said. "He helped."

Janet looked vacant and defeated. Ronnie wondered what she had been thinking about all day and if her expression mirrored Ronnie's own. She had to look away.

"It's so hard to believe any of this is happening when I think back to how good Jeff was with the babies. I keep picturing Andrew's little head in Jeff's big hand. Remember?"

"Are you sure about that image?" Beverly laughed. "Andrew's head was huge."

They both looked at Janet. When she didn't join in, Beverly winked at Ronnie and added, "Of course, I was the only one happy to have grandchildren. Janet here didn't want any."

Beverly knew what she was doing; Janet seemed to snap back to herself a bit. "I did too," Janet said. "I just never thought I'd get any. I didn't think he had any interest."

"He said my desire to have children was contagious." Ronnie smiled.

"I didn't think he'd make it past the miscarriages," Janet said.

"Our vision of a family carried us beyond the loss," Ronnie said. "And then, at long last, a fluttering heartbeat. I was smitten."

"I don't think you took your hands off your belly the whole pregnancy," her mother said.

"Jeff either," Janet added. "You two were a bit of a spectacle."

"Remember he took those profile pictures of me each month as my belly grew?" Jeff was always behind the camera when the boys were small. Was he recording a life he loved, as Ronnie always thought, or remaining detached from it?

"Jeff was so good with the boys when they were born," Beverly said. "He had such a calming influence. Remember how we'd find Andrew and Will, fast asleep, draped over his shoulders, chest, or lap?"

"He probably should have been a pediatric nurse," Ronnie said. "Jeff has so many talents, I wish—" She stopped herself. What was the point?

"He was so proud of them," Janet said. "That video he took of Will in the high chair, trying not to fall asleep, remember?"

"Will was bobbing his head, over and over, until he face-planted into his oatmeal," Beverly said, smiling.

"Jeff always thought Andrew had no interest in the farm," Ronnie said. "But I think he forgot the way he'd follow Jeff around, pushing his bubble mower."

Janet nodded. "I'll never forget the night Will was born. You called after midnight, and I was so scared to answer, and Jeff put you on the phone, and you"—her voice broke, but she regained it—"and you told me you'd given him Hoyer as a middle name. It meant so much to me."

"It was only fair, when Andrew's middle name was Saylor," Beverly said.

Ronnie took their hands. "We've been a family for a long time."

"They're good boys. I'd do anything for them," Janet said. "You know that, right?"

Beverly squeezed Ronnie's hand.

Corporal McNichol returned to the room with a determined

stride. "The sun will set in another hour or so," she said. "And as night falls, the situation will get increasingly dangerous. Jeff will be able to see out, but we won't be able to see in. We want to try to put an end to this before then."

Ronnie let out a long, slow breath. The logic seemed clear. She just hoped they all had the strength to face what came next.

ronnie

T here's only one reason this is stretching on so long: he's wavering. We can use that to our advantage."

"In what way?" Ronnie said.

"We want to try firing cartridges of Mace through the windows of the office. If Jeff won't come out of his own free will, he might still respond to the survival instinct by rushing outside for air. Then we could approach."

"I don't know. It sounds so harsh…"

"We'll need your permission, Ronnie, if you'd sign here. We'll aim high so we don't hurt him."

Ronnie understood that this was a last-ditch maneuver. But she had seen how far a plant's stem would bend to reach the light, and Jeff might yet be malleable. She thought it might work.

She read the paper. They weren't asking her permission to assault her husband with the Mace, as it turned out. They needed her permission to break the windows.

"Ronnie, no," Beverly said.

Janet added, "Don't. Please."

Corporal McNichol's face was kind yet resolute, her gaze unwavering. "It's worked before."

Ronnie signed the paper.

"How could you do that, Ronnie?"

"I can't live out the rest of my days in this room. You heard the corporal. He doesn't really want to hurt himself. He'll come out to get air."

"That's it? A simple decision for you?"

"If I sit here and think about it for another hour, the situation will only get more dangerous."

Leaning toward Beverly, Janet said, "Your daughter hasn't shed one tear for my son."

Ronnie set the pen down. Handed Corporal McNichol the paper. Waited for her to explain that she'd have to stay near the radios now and watched as she left the room. Then Ronnie turned to her mother-in-law and said calmly, "I have shed so many tears for your son over so many years that I don't have any left."

"Why?" Janet said. "How many times has he done this sort of thing?"

"Why don't you tell me, Janet?" She wielded her mother-in-law's name like a weapon. "Fay Sickler tells me Jeff created quite a scene when she left him, waving a gun around and threatening to shoot her."

"Really?" Her attempt to fashion her face into an expression of bemusement failed halfway up. Her eyes looked scared.

"And you never thought it important to share this story with me?"

"That was a long time ago."

"Wait, you let Ronnie marry Jeff when you knew he had pulled a weapon on someone he supposedly loved?" Beverly said.

"Boys can be slow to mature," Janet said. "He deserved a chance to try again. If it were Teddy, wouldn't you have wanted him to have a chance to find love?"

Ronnie tried to calm herself. If her mother and Janet started fighting, she wouldn't be able to take it. "You're right, Janet. Boys can be slow to mature—but so can alcoholic men. The materials I've read about alcoholism say that the maturation process is interrupted while the person is actively addicted," Ronnie said. "All day, I've been trying to figure out when Jeff's decline started, but all three of us may have to admit we don't know what his real problem was or when it took root."

"My god, Ronnie. All this harping about addiction and alcoholism is enough to drive anybody to drink."

Ronnie nodded slowly. "Fine. I for one would be thrilled to find someone to blame for this mess. But if you're going to make that person me and add dangerous secrets into the mix, don't expect to be seeing a whole lot of your grandchildren." Ronnie punctuated her point by getting up, turning her back, and walking away.

"Come back here, Sunshine. You didn't mean that, did you, Jan?"

Ronnie turned just enough to see her mother patting Janet's hand. Why didn't her mother touch Ronnie? A pair of warm arms would go a long way toward making this hall feel less funereal.

"I can't do this," Janet said. "I will not survive the day."

"Stop." Ronnie spun around. "You know damn well you will." Janet said she wouldn't live past Jerry's demise either, but the woman had a constitution that stubbornly exceeded her will to deal with life's disappointments. Janet would not succumb to grief. She'd have to face facts, as would Jeff: the comfort of the grave was not within easy reach.

"You don't want him to live," Janet said.

Ronnie looked across the table at her mother-in-law and mother. "If I didn't care about him, I wouldn't be so angry! He was the great love of my life. My husband. All I've been able to do, all day, is think about how the hell our marriage came to this."

"Tell him you'll stay, so this will all be over," Beverly said. "Can't you compromise a little?"

"Mother, you'd have quit the marriage at the first hint of rancor."

"Of course I would have. But you're made of different stuff. Better stuff."

"You can compromise on who takes out the trash, Mom, but you cannot compromise on your principles." The words, Kevin's grandfather's, tasted true on her tongue.

"But if we can get him through the day," Janet said, animating, "then maybe tomorrow—"

"Exactly. What the hell will he try tomorrow? How will he up the ante the next time he wants his way? Threaten the kids?"

"Don't talk like that. Jeff loves those boys," Janet said.

"Love is when you stick by someone no matter what. You two have taught me that, by example. Love is when you listen for what matters. Love is when you create the kind of environment in which your beloved can become the very best he or she can be. But Jeff wants to check out. He's not listening. He is not supportive of me and will not let me nurture him. Our marriage is harming all of us."

"But Jeff is an alcoholic," Beverly said, catching an angry glance from Janet. "Isn't that a mental illness? He needs our compassion."

"Unbelievable." Ronnie kicked the chair aside. "I have taken measures beyond what any professional suggested to get Jeff help, but he doesn't want it. Not AA, not rehab, not outpatient, not one-on-one, not marriage counseling. He just wants his way!"

"Maybe we can find a clue here, Ronnie," Beverly said. "What is it Jeff really wants?"

Ronnie sank into the chair and blew out a long breath. "The days when Jeff shared his dreams and desires with me are long gone. I even feared his dream for the farm store was a manipulation—he painted this vision of togetherness, then left me to run it."

"What he wants is you," Janet said.

One of the few stories Jeff had shared from his youth came to mind. After his mother let him lure a raccoon into relative domesticity with a constant supply of cat food, he'd captured it and kept it in a cage. "But a relationship is about giving too. Maybe what really scares him is he isn't sure what he has left to give." Ronnie shook her head. "Maybe if Jeff could tell me what he truly wanted, he wouldn't be in this predicament."

"Maybe there are drugs that would help."

"Really, Janet? You're going to talk treatment now, when your husband's electroshock therapy for depression—and his mother's before him—seemed so incidental that it wasn't worth mentioning?"

Ronnie glared at her mother-in-law. Janet shut her mouth.

"Don't bother denying it. Fay told me."

Beverly shot Janet an angry look. "Jerry had electroshock therapy and you didn't tell us? It is getting awfully hard to stick up for you right now."

"I'll admit, Jerry was a little upset after he quit coaching—"

"My god, wake up!" Ronnie said. "They do not administer shock therapy to people who are 'a little upset.'"

"But she has a good point about the drugs, Ronnie. They're discovering new things all the time."

"Jeff's bloodstream is already a chemistry experiment. You heard his voice today. That's not our Jeff. And even if there were such a magic potion, how do you suppose we'd get it? You can't order such a thing from a catalog. Jeff would have to go to a doctor, and he won't go. And you forget, he's already been to the hospital for this, and they sent him home." Ronnie paced.

"You heard from Jeff today?" Janet sounded hurt. Beverly shook her head as if to warn Ronnie off the topic.

"I spent too much time thinking this was an interpersonal problem," Ronnie continued. "Feeling like such an idiot that I had missed the small print on the marriage contract that said when two wounded souls have been joined, let no one ever heal. Thinking that, well, if he won't go to counseling, then at least one of us should start taking care of me. And then when it became about me, I probably missed what was going on with him. And that is a tragedy. But I don't know what more I could have done. He's a big boy."

"You're talking gobbledygook," Janet said.

Ronnie turned to her mother-in-law. "Janet, I am trying to share something real with you about my marriage, woman to woman. I sacrificed emotional connection. I sacrificed physical intimacy. But Jeff ruined us financially. What would you have me do?"

"If that was the only condition you couldn't abide, you should have accepted my bailout."

"Gee, maybe it was your delivery. 'Ronnie, if I pay off your debt, will you stay with him?' Add an 'or else' and it would have been blackmail."

"Janet, why would you say something like that?" Beverly said. "And who would accept such an offer?"

"Well, Jeff did, and look where it's gotten him." Ronnie jabbed her fingers into her curls and yanked. "I don't know. I don't know where to look for hope."

"There's always hope," Beverly said. "Look at me."

"I refuse to allow you to compare your relentless pursuit of a boyfriend to the tragedy we're facing here," Janet said.

Beverly's lip started to quiver. "Oh, Ronnie, I wish none of this was happening to you."

"Stop," Ronnie said. "Don't you dare try to take this away from me. All day I've been working to accept what's happening here. To own it. You can't wave your fairy wand and make this go away. That's the kind of thinking that got us into this mess. It's happening, and not just to me. It's happening to Jeff. To the boys. To you and Janet. To the police and our community. It's happening to my sweet little dog, for crying out loud, and the horses. It's a hell of a mess, and I'm trying to accept it so I can take whatever next steps present themselves, and it does *not* help for you to wish it all away!"

Silence stretched between them. Janet broke it. "This couldn't get any worse, Bev. Might as well tell her the rest."

"To what end?"

"Because maybe if you had been honest with Ronnie about her father from the beginning, she might have realized my son was fragile and handled him more carefully."

"Your fragile son?" Beverly shook her head. "And you get to advise me because you're the one so good at heart-to-hearts? What all did you chat with your son about over that bullhorn, anyway?"

"My god, Mom, even I think that's a low blow."

Janet turned to Beverly. "I froze up. You don't know what it was like. The situation was so tense. I have never been so frightened in my entire life. I didn't want to make a mistake, although clearly I did anyway. But why should I explain mistakes to you? I have supported you through every phase of your constant reinvention, Beverly Saylor."

"I told you I'd pay back that loan for real estate school."

Ronnie broke in. "Mom. You were going to tell me something."

"If you'd sold one blessed house, you could have paid me back already."

"The market's been slow." Beverly stood.

"The market is the market." Janet stood as well, leaning on the table. "People still need to buy houses. You're waiting for another man to come along to pay me. You're afraid to stand on your own two feet and you always have been. You're afraid to be honest with your own daughter."

"I refuse to be ignored one more moment!"

The two older women glared at each other with their toes at the edge of opposing cliffs. Ronnie dared not speak again for fear of causing a landslide.

Beverly finally spoke. "That was the only time I ever asked you for money."

"Yet it's not the only time I've supported you. Or Ronnie."

"I did not ask you to pay off our credit cards," Ronnie said. "That was Jeff."

"And if you didn't want to loan me the money, why did you do it?" Beverly said.

Janet's lips twitched as if she was working at the words. Ronnie waited—hoped—that she'd say she'd done it because she loved her mother. Love had too long skulked at the perimeter of this room and she longed for it to be summoned front and center.

"Because it needed doing," Janet finally said. "Just like the kids' loan needed to be paid off. If you all would live within your means, you'd be a lot happier."

"What loan?" Ronnie said.

"The one he used to pay for the renovation, and the store, and all the other things you wanted."

The things *she'd* wanted? She'd wanted one thing—the antique hutch in the living room—but she had balked at the fifteen-hundred-dollar price tag. Jeff insisted on buying it, saying he could make that money back on New Year's Eve. Ronnie thought of the gleam in Jeff's eye whenever he suggested an upgrade. His excitement about the way keeping so many creditors happy beefed up his credit score. He was Captain Consumer, the superhero of creative finance. "But we weren't able to get a loan. That debt was all on credit cards, some with interest as high as twenty-five percent. And most of them I didn't even know about."

Janet looked stunned.

"I see you didn't know. He lied to you, Janet," Ronnie said. "I've been trying to tell you these problems were real, but you wouldn't listen to me. Apparently you didn't know your own son."

"And apparently, you didn't know your husband."

"I'm warning you, Janet. Ronnie has been through enough today and I will not have you attacking her. You have to face the fact that your son didn't know the first thing about managing a household. You've spoiled that boy his whole life long and lorded your money over us like the freaking Bank of Bartlesville."

Janet backed up so Beverly and Ronnie could see her, head to toe. "Look at me. Really look. I wear stretch pants and sweatshirts from Kmart. The barber down the street cuts my hair for five dollars. The shoe box in my kitchen is full of coupons I clip from the Sunday paper. I have never in my life had a manicure."

Beverly crossed her arms to hide her red lacquered nails.

"I never go out to eat. It killed me to pay Sophie Perlmutter seven dollars today for a sandwich I could have made at home for two fifty.

I pay in cash only, and if I don't have the money, I don't buy it. I have scrimped my whole life long so I would be able to have something to leave Jeff and my grandchildren."

"Well, there you have it, Ronnie. Janet Farnham's keys to happiness. Hope you took notes."

Janet uttered a mirthless chuckle. "That's rich. A lecture on happiness from a woman who's worn a hundred-dollar promise ring her whole life. What are you holding out for, Bev?"

"Don't go there, Janet."

"You have discarded perfectly good husbands because they don't live up to, what, some youthful illusion?"

"You do not want to push me, Janet. I was seventeen and scared and the man I loved was never coming back."

"You're still scared."

"Of course I am! My god, aren't you?"

"Why didn't he come back, Mom?"

"Go on, tell her."

"Why, Janet? Isn't there enough suicide in the air today?"

Suicide. The word hit the mirror ball and refracted, its shards bouncing around the room until one of them sliced Ronnie's heart. Slowly, she sank onto her chair.

Beverly sucked in a breath and put her hand to her mouth. "Oh, Ronnie. That's not how I wanted you to find out—"

Ronnie put up her hand to cut her mother off. Thought of what her mother had told her about her father surviving the accident that killed his parents. Of that odd sense of survivor guilt she'd identified with and had been feeling even more acutely since being whisked from her home today, yet could never explain. She looked at her mother, who so rarely touched her. "It was because of me, wasn't it?"

Her mother trembled, not like a woman falling apart, but like a volcano whose red-hot lava was already pushing through her pores, which made her hushed tone even more frightening when she turned on Janet and said, "Thank you for your support."

Janet smiled in that self-satisfied, vacant way Jeff had in recent weeks, and it chilled Ronnie to the bone. Janet said, "And you can go to hell before I'll let you tell me how to raise my boy."

The standoff infiltrated the room. With nothing left to say to one another, the three women pushed away, each to her own wretched corner.

In the fourth stood the bar, dark and silent.

5:00 p.m.

beverly

Beverly didn't stop at her corner of the room. She went out the door and down the metal steps. More than anything she wanted to tell Ronnie everything would be all right, but she just didn't know that to be true. Anyway, she was done with sitting. She had to do something, and even though she didn't know yet what that was, inspiration rarely flew into a room and laid an egg on your head. Outside, at least, she could put one foot in front of the other and actually get somewhere.

She headed uphill because it was harder. She wanted her heart to pump and her lungs to fill with cooling air. She wanted to outdistance her thoughts of Dom, and she wanted her calves to ache in trying.

It was as true at fifty-two as it had been at seventeen: lovers kept apart can literally ache for each other. Even though they had spoken by phone each Sunday that fall she returned to high school, every inch of her body had yearned for Dom, and only in reuniting with him would she find relief.

Twenty-four times she'd called him that last day, one call every hour, to make plans to see him for Thanksgiving. When he never answered, she'd called Janet in a panic, borrowed her car, and driven to the shore to check on him. She had taken the key off the hidden hook halfway up the stairs and let herself in.

The odor in there. Food left to rot. She checked the stove, the oven, the fridge. Opened the kitchen windows and the French doors.

She found him on his bed, sleeping on his stomach. She loved the way he did that, his face turned toward hers so he'd see her as soon as he opened his eyes.

"Dom, wake up." The smell. She opened the bedroom window and returned to shake him. Something felt wrong, but her hand refused to tell her what. She rolled him over—and screamed.

No, Beverly thought, arms pumping up the hill. *I will not. I will not think of him that way.*

The pistol lying beneath him had refused to take responsibility for what it had done.

The memory of that smell lingered in her nose, and Beverly tried to clear it by pulling in lungful after lungful of autumn air, spiced with drying leaves and goldenrod and all manner of pods releasing their seeds to the wind. Finally, she sneezed.

Dominic. Oh, Dom.

How alone he must have felt as he struggled to make his ungodly decision. Nightmares—not of his ruined face but the crush of his loneliness—had tried to suffocate Beverly, who would wake up in the middle of the night, panting. Maybe that's why she'd left the beds of so many husbands. She'd needed air.

Beyond ache now, her calves burned. She relished the way a little bit of manageable pain focused her on the present. Helped her outdistance memory. Made her feel…so…alive.

Up ahead: the barricade. She recognized it as her destination.

Most of the tension still on scene was in her body. Once-curious onlookers had gone home to help their kids with homework or to fix dinner. Maura Riley, wilted inside the news van, sat looking at her phone. Beverly was surprised to see she was only dressed for the camera from the waist up; below she was wearing jeans and running shoes. She paid Beverly no mind.

Beverly walked right up to the barricade and paced. So close to Jeff now. On the other side, a policeman sat in a black-and-white with the window rolled down.

"Excuse me," Beverly said. "Anything new happening?"

He shook his head. "You look familiar. Hey, is that your husband up there?"

Beverly shook her head. *No. And yes.*

Off to the side of the barricade, at the edge of the woods, Beverly found a rock to prop herself against and took a seat on the ground. If Dom had only reached out to her, she would have been there in a heartbeat. She would have put her own heart right into his chest if it weren't for the life growing within her that depended on it.

She couldn't imagine the nature of Jeff's inner torture, which had risen to the surface and demanded control. But then again, she had smelled her lover's death. Maybe she could.

The ground's cool dampness seeped into her bones. Now that she was no longer moving, Beverly felt the familiar cloak of fear cinch around her. Smelled its mildew. She would tolerate it and live through it, for Jeff. She would not let him go through this alone.

Intention was a powerful thing, she reminded herself. In her mind, she cast off the cloak and laid it in what was left of the life-giving autumn sun. Once warmth and love had restored it, she wrapped the cloak around Jeff's shaking shoulders.

ronnie

Tension increased in the fire hall as the first round of Mace was shot into Jeff's stronghold. Ronnie had something new to cling to: the Special Emergency Response Team would start playing by its own rules, not Jeff's. She welcomed nature's deadline. The sun would set, Jeff would need to breathe clean air, and the situation would soon be brought to a close.

Expectation infused every moment with possibilities too numerous to count, too frightening to envision.

A half hour dragged by.

Ronnie wondered if maybe her mother had left for good. She'd never been one to handle adversity well, and Ronnie had an inkling of why that was true. On the other side of the room, Janet sat staring into space as if her senses were shutting down.

"Why isn't he coming out?" Ronnie asked Corporal McNichol when she returned to the room. "How can he breathe?"

"He must be quite drunk," she said. *Obliterated,* Jeff used to call it when Paco drank to excess. The assessment didn't surprise Ronnie. She'd heard his voice on the answering machine. The corporal cited instances in which people high on drugs could breathe the Mace without noticing it.

Ronnie hoped that after making his statement to Janet earlier, Jeff had stopped drinking. Or run out of booze. Or run out of ammunition. Maybe he'd fallen asleep and awoke feeling better.

Five thirty arrived. Corporal McNichol informed them that troops had fired more of the chemical irritant into the store office.

Ronnie stood at the edge of every second, peering over.

Corporal McNichol said this still might take some time and suggested the women accept the firehouse cook's offer to make them dinner. She sent him in while she returned to her men.

It seemed odd to think about eating as such dire circumstances were unfolding for Jeff, but Ronnie had to admit she was hungry. Janet looked beyond feeling anything, but she'd need her strength.

Ronnie ordered them cheeseburgers. She could hear Jeff, so much a part of her whether she wanted it or not: *That's off the lunch menu, not the dinner menu.*

The cook looked around the room. "So that's two?"

"I'm hoping my mother will be back soon. Make it three."

Jeff was so in his element in a fine restaurant, ordering food and wine for them both. He'd try her salmon and she'd sample his filet mignon, his eyes sparkling in the glow of candlelight. She felt him watching her now, ordering without him, with silent tears rolling down his face.

beverly

K a-pow.

When it finally came, the sound was muted from where Beverly sat but plenty violent; her whole body flinched. In the canopy above her, a crow screeched and lifted into the air. She sat, waiting—but there was nothing more. She heard tired voices from the police car radio, saw the lights come on, saw the car pull forward. She collapsed her face into her hands, knowing that Jeff's standoff, and his life, had ended.

Maura Riley popped from the news van and headed toward her. Beverly pushed to her feet and ran down the hill, coaxing her chilled bones into service. "Wait, I want to ask you…" Beverly strained to put distance between her and whatever question that woman wanted to ask. Her breath grew uneven as the sobs came. Tears, too long denied, wet her face. She had done what she came to do, and now she had to get the hell out of here.

She ran until the road punished her feet, the effort set fire to what was left of her knees, and the waning daylight stole the last of her breath. Beverly wanted to take the pounding and more, but her body made its own decision and slowed her step. She gulped for air.

A car pulled up beside her. If it was that news van, Maura Riley better watch out because—

"Can I give you a lift?"

It was a man's voice. Beverly slowed, wiping away enough tears to focus. It was Karl Prout.

"I heard on the scanner down at Perlmutter's and raced right up to see if there was anything I could do. I'm so sorry, Beverly. Jeff was such a nice man."

So it was true.

She couldn't think, couldn't speak. She folded her arms on top of his rolled-down window, put down her head, and sobbed.

He patted the back of her head with his beefy hand, more tenderly than she would have thought possible. "I'm so, so sorry."

ronnie

In her mind, Ronnie reached up and wiped away Jeff's tears, just as she had that night long ago, out on the hammock, on the day they'd bought Cupcake. Jeff had just asked her to marry him. With her hand damp, she'd undone a few buttons and pulled the kitten from her shirt.

"Cupcake is going to need to learn what grass is," she'd said, setting the kitten on the lawn, then she slipped Jeff's hand inside her shirt where the kitten had been hiding—against her heart. "I don't want her to get squished. Because you're going to have to kiss me now."

He touched his lips to hers, then pulled back. "Is that a yes?"

"That, my love, is a yes."

And he kissed her until the stars and the hammock and the earth fell away, and Ronnie sensed exactly who she was meant to be: Jeff's wife. Later, as the damp settled in, Ronnie shivered and reached for the kitten mewling below them. Jeff tucked his jacket around all three of them. Then, after whispering dreams between touching lips late into the night, Jeff and Ronnie let the river of endless possibility rock them gently to sleep.

The sound of footsteps near the entrance to the firehouse social hall tore her from his side.

Three people appeared at the door: a uniformed officer, Corporal McNichol, and a man carrying a zippered nylon case.

Their steps were measured as they advanced, a color guard

without a flag. Heels tapping the floor in a code Ronnie couldn't crack. She wanted them to stop. Where was her mother? Beverly should be here. She'd been here all day; they needed to be together. *Stop walking until all three of us are here. We need to see this through together. Turn crisply on your heels. Go away.* But they kept advancing. Ronnie had no authority, knew no commands.

Ronnie shot a panicked look at Janet, converging from her corner. The threesome drew near. Halted.

Corporal McNichol took the lead. "Well, I have news." She was near enough to speak quietly. Ronnie tried to conjure one more moment of hope. They hadn't had anything that qualified as "news" in hours, since Jeff blew a hole in the office door.

"Maybe you should sit down," Corporal McNichol began again.

Janet sank into her chair. Ronnie would not. She would take this standing up.

"He did it. He shot himself. Jeff is dead."

ronnie

Ronnie's legs unhinged; her knees smacked the floor. Everything went red. *My god, Jeff, no. I was just holding you and the kitten. We were just dreaming, Jeff. Come back. How could you do this while the taste of you is still on my lips? We waited all day for you. I've been waiting for years for you to come back, Jeff. The red is filling my eyes. Get up, Jeff. You know you can't just lie still in the middle of the day; you can never be still. Andrew and Will need you. Move your hands, Jeff. They're too tight around my neck. Jeff, let go. I can't carry you anymore. Get off me, I can't breathe.* Ronnie sobbed until time stopped warping and the room stopped spinning and her edges melted into the pool of her own bloody tears.

She felt her cheek against the cold floor. *This is where Ronnie ends; this is where the rest of the world begins.*

"Ronnie." A man called to her, as if from far away. Not a low ugly snarl, like she'd heard earlier, but a voice that had healed. *Jeff?*

A hand on her shoulder, gently shaking. "Hey, Ronnie?" Ronnie came back to herself and lifted her wet face. Her vision cleared, filling with the sandy-haired man beside her.

"Ronnie, this is a paramedic," Corporal McNichol said.

Ronnie looked at the stethoscope hanging around his neck. "Were you at the farm? Did you see him?"

He shook his head no. "Take even breaths," he said, his fingertips on her inner wrist, his eyes on his watch. "Not too deep, not too fast. Nice and even."

"Ronnie," Corporal McNichol said, more quietly this time. "He's here to help *you*."

He offered to help her up. Ronnie took his hand, but she didn't have to lean. As she rose, Jeff's cooling fingers slipped from around her neck, and his dead weight slumped to the floor. She didn't want to leave him behind, yet rising was easier than it had been in quite some time.

ronnie

A sound pushed through Ronnie's protective haze, like a wounded wolf that had lost the full force of its howl. Janet's lips moved. Words formed.

"How could you have done this, Ronnie? He worked so hard to fix up the farm. All he wanted was to make you happy, and you had to go and leave him. The house, the horses, the store, that beautiful property. He gave you everything."

Ronnie watched the words float past her, checking them. True enough.

But he also gave up everything.

Janet was old. Janet was a mother. Janet sought answers. Janet had to have someone to blame. But her scattershot ammunition couldn't reach Ronnie. It bounced off some invisible shield and clattered to the floor.

A mass of strangled sounds came from Janet's throat. The EMT was tending her. *She's choking*, Ronnie thought at first. She slowly put it together. *My mother-in-law, barren of emotion since Jerry's death, is crying.*

Ronnie turned to Corporal McNichol, still beside her. "I have to see my boys. Before they hear this some other way. Can you take me?"

"Not just yet," she said. "The coroner is waiting for you at the farm. There will be some paperwork to tie up first. The men have had a long day, and I'm sure they're ready to go home."

Long.

Ready.

Home.

"We can take your mother and mother-in-law over to be with the boys, if you want."

The corporal's suggestion stilled the room.

"No," Ronnie said. Janet looked at Ronnie sharply, then to the door, where Karl Prout stood at the entrance of the room with Beverly. Mascara streaked her ruddy cheeks.

"Mom," Ronnie said.

They looked at each other across a stretch of space, fresh tears streaming. Beverly moved toward her. "I know. Come here, Sunshine." Ronnie fell into her mother's arms, relishing the feel even as they cried.

Fearing she would lose herself, though, Ronnie pulled back. She still had work to do. She turned to look directly at Corporal McNichol. "Under no circumstances do I want Janet and my mother seeing the boys before I do."

"What?" Beverly's empty arms returned to her sides.

"We love them too," Janet said.

"I don't doubt it. But Andrew and Will need to believe in me right now, and you have both said some pretty ugly things to me today. You will not speak to them before I do."

Corporal McNichol put her arm around Ronnie's shoulders. "I'll take you back to the farm and leave an officer here with them."

"Like we're under guard?" Janet said.

"I'll stay," Karl Prout said, "and drive them wherever, whenever. These things make you feel so damn helpless. And you helped me, Janet, when my wife had the cancer." Janet moved her hand to her abdomen. "Let me do something for you now."

"Ladies?" Corporal McNichol said.

Beverly and Janet both nodded.

Ronnie headed for the door.

"Sunshine? Wait. Your keys."

Beverly picked up the heavy rings from where they were laying on the table. Ronnie took them—two fistfuls—and looked at them blankly.

She'd been set free, with all the power she needed to go anywhere—and she had no clue where the hell that would be.

6:00 p.m.

ronnie

In the deepening dusk, Ronnie pressed her forehead to the cool window of the corporal's car. The area had cleared out considerably by the time Corporal McNichol took the road toward the farm. The roadblock had been dismantled and the media had moved on. Police vehicles no longer lined the road. Their car was free to turn up the driveway. All of the outside lights were on at the farm store, but Ronnie resisted their glow. She focused straight ahead.

The coroner greeted her at the door to her house and introduced himself, offering his hand. For a moment, Ronnie wondered whether she wanted to touch him.

"You must be the widow," he said.

The widow. As bound to Jeff in death as she had been in life. "I'm Ronnie," she corrected.

The man had made himself at home. His paperwork was spread recklessly across her stove top. He showed her the death certificate. The facts were at the top. *Name: Farnham, Jeffrey Hoyer. Age: 47.*

His birthday was eleven days away.

At the bottom: *Cause of death: self-inflicted gunshot wound.*

Ronnie noted the time of death. She'd been ordering a cheeseburger while her husband was pronounced dead.

The coroner handed her a pen and showed her where to sign. "Because we've been on-site all day, it's a pretty clear cause of death. There won't be further investigation."

"Can we get an autopsy?" Ronnie needed answers that Jeff had never offered. Maybe his body could speak for him. Maybe his liver could tell her how advanced the alcoholism had been. Did he have cirrhosis? He had lost so much weight. How close to death had he already been? So many things weren't known. Any facts would be a help.

"I'm sorry, an autopsy won't be possible. He used a shotgun. The wound was massive, allowing a lot of interaction with the Mace, and he bled out pretty thoroughly before we could get in there. We opened the place up but couldn't stay in there long enough to do anything. The Mace was eating through our masks. We won't even get an accurate blood alcohol reading."

The coroner collected his paperwork. "We'll be taking the shotgun into evidence but will return it when we're through. I like to warn people of that. It can be disconcerting to see a cruiser pull up and watch an officer get out of his vehicle holding a weapon."

Ronnie nodded.

The coroner extended his hand. His work was done.

Ronnie went down to her office to get the boys' overnight bag. They couldn't stay here tonight with so much trauma in the air. Whether Beverly wanted them or not, she would take the boys to her mother's for a couple of days. The boys could sleep together in her spare bedroom and Ronnie would seek what rest she could find on the couch.

She found Max curled on the recliner, blockaded into her office by a ten-ream box of paper with a laundry basket on top. As soon as he saw her, he leaped into her arms, knocking over the laundry. Ronnie let his wriggles invigorate her, let his dry kisses cover her face. "I'm so sorry," she kept saying. Heard Jeff's voice: *He's your dog.* "I'm so, so sorry. I'll get you some water, boy." She filled a shallow bucket at the utility sink, put it on the laundry room floor, and went back into the office to get the duffel bag they'd abandoned earlier that day.

Sitting on top were the boys' blankets. Ronnie picked them up and held them to her lips, hoping these objects carried enough of her love to see Andrew and Will through this.

She could accept Jeff's death as her lot. She had to; she'd chosen him. But no child should have to live through his father's self-destruction.

Her gaze moved through the window toward the store's unnatural light. The back door of the farm store office stood propped open, an emergency exit with a panic bar they never used.

She saw him, chest down on the concrete floor. His face turned away from her. That full head of brown hair. The jean jacket with the tan corduroy collar. One hand cast to the side as if resting on their mattress.

Jeff.

Headlights cut through growing dusk as another vehicle pulled up the drive. Ronnie tore her eyes away and headed back up to the kitchen. Out in the driveway, Amber and a young man got out of a pickup truck. When Ronnie went to greet them, Max didn't even lift a leg. As soon as he hit the grass, he squatted and peed.

"God, Ronnie." Amber put her arms around Ronnie and didn't let go. "It's already been on TV. I just had to come over. How does anybody handle such a thing? Jeff was such a great guy."

The girl started to cry on Ronnie's shoulder. Ronnie patted her back absently, wondering how she'd already been thrust into the position of offering solace.

"Jeff committed suicide," Ronnie said. This wasn't news. But she had to put the words on her tongue so that one day she could set their bitter taste aside.

Amber pulled away and looked at Ronnie queerly. Wiping her nose across the back of her hand, she said, "You remember my boyfriend, Brad. He's good around horses. I thought we could help."

Brad looked at the driveway and rearranged a few rocks with his toes.

Drawn by what secrets the farm store held, Ronnie drifted beyond the shadow of the house, Amber and Brad in tow. The harsh glare of the store's floodlights hit Ronnie's face.

"Aw, no, Ronnie." Amber pulled Brad around in front of Ronnie to create a barrier. "You don't want to see that."

"I have to," Ronnie said, stepping around them. "To witness." Amber and Brad averted their eyes and allowed Ronnie and Jeff one final horrific moment.

Two men carried Jeff's limp, backlit form from the store and laid it on a body bag. After arranging his limbs, one of the officers zipped the bag, stopping momentarily at his head to tuck in a few strands of hair.

"Will's class is hatching chicks," she whispered.

The horses whinnied at the new activity and galloped up the hill. Ronnie let Amber lead her back up the drive.

"The animals haven't been fed all day," Ronnie said. The horses already stood at the fence near the barn, blowing through their nostrils, with little Horsey Patch bringing up the rear.

"Don't worry about that," Amber said.

Ronnie stopped and looked at her. "I've always had to worry about that."

"I mean that's why we're here." Amber had cared for their horses when the family was at the shore. She knew the horses' names and which stalls to put them in; she would know to find directions taped inside the lid of the feed bin. "We'll take care of everything."

"And we mean everything." The conviction in Brad's voice surprised her. "Don't ever feel you have to come back here again."

Such kindness.

But she knew she would come back.

Life on this farm had asked more of her than she could ever give, but it was the only home the boys had known. She felt sure of only one thing: in this time of turmoil, she would not wrench them from it. This was no time for losing one another among packing crates and yard sales and house shopping. They'd have no more energy for staging their home than they'd have for staging their faces while settling into new classrooms and neighborhoods. This was a time to confront what had happened, together. To allow their friends to help. To soothe themselves with the rhythms of chores and the comfort of their animals and the familiar roll of the landscape, as Jeff had taught her. To anchor themselves within the same passions and challenges that reflected their choices the day before the suicide. It felt more important than ever that they be fully themselves. She would not allow additional change to interrupt the reality of their loss.

If Jeff had wanted to end their lives, he could have done so, the police had assured her. The only way to convince the boys that he hadn't was to carry on with life as they knew it. Jeff had always thought this farm would be a great place to raise kids, and it would be again someday. She would not give Jeff the power to change that in absentia.

Red and blue lights suddenly flashed from the farm store drive-way. The cruiser peeled out and, shortly thereafter, its siren wailed. Life—disruptive and frightening and glorious—went on. Theirs was not the only drama, nor was it any longer an emergency.

The rest of the cars pulled away together, taking Jeff and the remaining daylight with them. A chill settled in. It would be a clear night; Ronnie watched the first stars emerge. Corporal McNichol joined Ronnie on the porch. "You ready to go?"

"I have a couple more things I need to do. I'll drive myself."

"It would be better if someone else drove."

"We'll take care of her," Amber said. "We'll go put the horses in."

"The halters are—"

"We know, Ronnie," Amber said. "We've got this."

Ronnie turned to Corporal McNichol.

"You'll want to get a hazmat team out here to clean up. Here's someone we trust to do a good job." Corporal McNichol handed her a business card. "The produce will all have to be tossed, and

ronnie

A few minutes later, Ronnie had gathered everything they'd need for a few days and put it in her mother's Blazer. Max, determined not to be left behind, had jumped onto the back gate, then sat in the front passenger seat during her trips back and forth to pack. Ronnie went back in and called the firehouse to say she'd soon be on her way to see her sons, reminding the man who answered that her mother and mother-in-law were not to see them without her.

Yet Ronnie couldn't get her feet to move back toward the car. She kept envisioning the way Jeff had acted each time she'd interrupted him the day before, flipping the pages on a yellow legal tablet so she wouldn't see what he'd written.

She had to get into the store office.

Seeing that the lights were still on in the barn, she went back to the kitchen, pulled a flashlight from the junk drawer, and left Max barking in the car as she headed down to New Hope Farms.

Twenty feet from the office door, the spicy stench of Mace hit her. The police had left the store wide open to air out. She took a deep breath, pulled her sweater up over her nose and mouth, and flicked on the light as she ran in toward the desk. One of her feet slid, and she struggled to catch her balance. She looked back. Through what appeared to be an innocuous, yard-wide circle of sawdust, she saw a dark red streak where her shoe had slid. She had just missed stepping on Jeff's eyeglasses. Reflexively, she sucked in a gasp of air through the sweater.

At the desk, she flipped up the front of her sweater to use as a satchel, stuffing in several neat piles of paper she found on top. Beside them was an open, almost empty half-gallon bottle with *G* on the label. With her throat burning, she ran back out to the grassy patch behind the store. She had been in the store a total of five, maybe six seconds, inhaling only the smallest amount of air, but she dropped everything to the ground and bent over and coughed and coughed until she retched. She could only imagine the hell Jeff must have gone through in the half hour between the first and second rounds of Mace.

Jeff's sickening voice came back to her, now explained by that jar of gin. If her experience was any indication, the Mace must have incinerated his lungs. When her airway finally calmed enough that she could breathe without gagging, she collected the items strewn on the grass and used the flashlight to examine them.

The police hadn't mentioned a suicide note, but she had to know if there was one. This whole day had been so unbelievable, she needed any possible clue that might help explain it.

She found the payment book for the Altima, the payment book for the mortgage, his checkbook. Addressed to "R" was an itemized list of all the credit cards he had already paid off and which ones would still arrive, noting that enough of his mother's money remained in the checking account to cover them.

She counted the number of credit cards. Not two, not twelve— thirty-two active credit cards. At the bottom of his accounting, he wrote, "Use the rest of the money as necessary. Everything I have here is yours and the boys', do as you wish." Beneath that, in a large dramatic sweep, he wrote the initial *J*. And beneath that, a postscript:

All taxes are paid

Dish programming is paid for one year
All ins. is paid
I think I thought this out, but who knows

More mixed signals. The note was at once thoughtful and selfish. But this accounting made one thing clear: Jeff's suicide was no act of passion. This list had been dated yesterday.

Drops of blood streaked one of the envelopes. It bore her name. Raw lungs sucked in the night air as she unfolded the yellow, legal-size pages that revealed words written with his hand.

Dear Ronnie,

Without you I have no life. Even Mother's money has no meaning to me without you. Can't even think what I would do with it.

I can see why you want out. I am not capable of bringing anything of my own to you. I have nothing positive to offer to anyone. Why else would someone spend 20 years tending the same bar. A real person would have done something more for himself and his family.

Thank God my mother had the resources and thought ahead or Andrew and Will would have no college funds. I certainly haven't done anything.

I am truly sorry that it had to come to this. This is probably the best and kindest thing I can do for you and our boys. Before I drag them down to my level.

I do love Will and Andrew more than you or they will ever know. Thanks for wanting them so much. When I think of how much fun, loving, learning, playing, teaching, sharing, comforting I've missed with the boys it really makes me sick and disgusted with myself. Thank goodness you were their mother or they would be a basket case.

Ronnie, you are the most wonderful, loving person I have ever known. *You have so much to give, but I wouldn't let you. Without you in my life, it would just be existing. I can't live like that anymore.*

If I had not been drinking as much as I did, I feel certain I would have seen what I was doing to you and our family. Now that I am not drinking, I can see that I missed out on an awful lot of wonderful things that you had to offer me and I am probably just touching the tip of the iceberg.

Thanks for giving me the best and happiest 12 years of my life, although I guess I didn't realize it until now. Too bad!

Also, thanks for sharing your family's special place at the shore with me. I had always hoped to one day buy it for you. Another chance lost.

By the time you read this, all my bills will have been paid. You will owe no $ to anyone. Don't reject my mother's money. She has always loved you, in her way, probably more than she loved me. If I can't help in any other way, at least I can help you guys a little financially and give you a home to live in.

Thanks for being there for Dad when he needed us. I will never forgive myself for not being the one that was there with him.

Ronnie, you will find love. But the thought of someone else holding, hugging, and making love to you destroys me. I don't want to die a lonely old man.

I've never been so scared in my life. This is the only way I will ever have peace in my mind and heart.

Please try to tell the boys how much I really do love them. I'm not doing a very good job by myself. See? I'm sorry, but I still need your help.

When I saw your last phone bill, with all those calls to Kevin, I knew my life was over. I would have ended it Thursday night but I promised Norris I would help him open his new hotel Friday and Saturday.

Please don't sell all my tools, I think when the boys get a little older they will really enjoy them. Try to keep the house for the boys.

You will only owe $18,500 and then it will be paid for.
I do love you very, very much—

Jeff

P.S. I do believe that you did love me, but I wouldn't share anything with you. Sorry, sorry me!!!

TILL DEATH DO US PART

ronnie

R onnie sat with the note for some time, trying to feel something for this man who wrote it. But despite the daylong wait for word, any word, she felt detached. From these particular words. This blood on her shoe.

She read it again, running her hand over his words, some underlined to make sure his meaning was heard. Ronnie knew how important it was to be heard, since he'd denied her this simple favor for so long.

Anger welled within her as she thought of all the ways he'd been leaving her these past few years. At what he'd put them through today. At the fact that he was drunk. At the fact that their beautiful children—Andrew looking so like him, Will acting so like him—should ever have to deal with his self-destruction.

Ronnie looked at the remains of what so briefly had been New Hope Farms. Shards of glass clinging to the window frames. The wood where the panic bar latched, splintered from forced entry. The dark starburst blasted through the door leading into the store.

If you were really capable of all this introspection, Jeff, why did you hoard it? And how can I possibly explain your "love" to the boys?

"Goddamn it, Jeff, argue back!"

The store absorbed her words just as its leafy greens had absorbed the Mace. New Hope Farms lay in quiet ruin.

She rolled facedown on the grass, damp with its own dewy tears, and sobbed. She'd so hoped to share with Jeff the wonder available to them every single morning just because they opened their eyes.

For so long, Jeff had been the source of her wonder.

I loved you. I tried to help you. If you had shared the problems sooner, we could have faced them together.

Even if Jeff had been running scared these last years from some diagnosis she wasn't aware of—heart disease or cancer—what she would have given to sit by his side, as she had his father's, and help him cross death's divide.

No one should feel this alone.

An owl hooted from the woods across the road. The wind that had gusted all day stroked Ronnie's cheek in apology.

Amber and Brad scooted down the grassy hill. They stopped beside her, at the periphery of the Mace.

"We heard you call out," Amber said.

Brad stooped to pick up the papers. With Amber on the other side, they helped Ronnie up, Jeff's note still clutched in her hand.

The three of them walked silently up the driveway. "Where can we take you?" Brad said.

"I'm fine. This is my mother's Blazer. She'll need it."

"Are you sure? It's no problem."

"I'm going to see my kids. I have to pull my thoughts together, but thanks."

"We'll be back tomorrow to take care of the animals then," Amber said. "Don't worry about a thing."

Ronnie could not look again at their faces, so eager to help in any way they could. She muttered thanks as she opened the car door. Max lunged toward her. Poor boy, locked one place or another by himself all day. The keys were in the ignition where her mother had left them, back when she had expected she was just stopping in to get the boys. Ronnie started the car, put on her seat belt, backed up—and heard a bang. She ducked.

When nothing else happened, Ronnie lifted her head. She'd

backed right into Brad's car, parked behind hers in their driveway. She hadn't even bothered to look before swinging around. Ronnie slid from the Blazer to check the damage and Max tumbled out on her heels. While there was only a scratch on her mother's bumper, she'd taken out one of Brad's headlights.

Ronnie looked at Brad. "I'm so sorry. I'll pay for that." *Pay for it with what?* "I-I'm sorry."

"I'm just glad it happened here and that we're all okay," Brad said. "Seriously, you shouldn't drive."

Ronnie started to shake.

Amber and Brad settled it. This time, when Ronnie climbed into the car, she was the passenger.

ronnie

Beth's awkward greeting at the door, Max clutched to Ronnie's chest. Her request for a place to share private agony in someone else's home.

Janet and Beverly were sitting on a hard bench in the foyer, jackets on, purses on their lap. Sweat beaded on Janet's upper lip.

"Don't worry," Beth said in answer to Ronnie's unspoken question. "The boys don't even know they're here."

"Mr. Eshbach?"

"They let me run him home an hour ago," Beth said. "I fed the boys some mac and cheese. I'll get them."

Beverly pulled Ronnie close. "Don't tell the boys," Beverly said. "Not about the…you know. Janet and I have already discussed this. They're too young and—"

"My god, Mom. Will was standing right next to me this morning when Jeff said he was going to kill himself. Do you think they're going to believe he wasted away of natural causes while the police stood by?"

Janet stood. "We're only thinking about the boys."

"You two have both had a chance to raise your children as you saw fit. I am simply asking—no, wait. That's the wrong word. I am demanding that you let me raise mine as *I* see fit. This is a tough situation, and I need to go with my gut. That's what a mother does."

"What is your gut telling you?" Beverly said.

At the familiar sound of pounding feet, Ronnie plastered on a smile. But those still-boyish faces, with their hopeful blue eyes trained on hers, had her gut quivering from the unanswered question.

"Maxie!" Andrew took the dog from Ronnie and Max licked him all over his face. She gave each boy a quick hug, breathing in the last moments of their innocence even as the day's violence pushed its unrelenting briars between them.

"This way," Beth said.

"Feel free to wait here," Ronnie said to her mother and Janet.

Ronnie had the length of a short hallway to decide how best to give them the news. She didn't want to hurt the boys, but hadn't Jeff already done that? She didn't know what to do. She heard footsteps behind her. The grandmothers were tagging along.

Beth showed them in to what was probably a guest room. A double bed had been pushed against one wall, and an oval braided rug lay beside it. Beth gave her a pitying smile and left, closing the door behind her.

"Let's sit on this pretty rose rug, boys. Grandmas, I suppose you'll be more comfortable on the bed."

"Can I have Max now, Andrew? You already had a turn."

Extreme politeness—a portent. Ronnie's anxiety grew.

She sat at the edge of the rug with one child on each side. Max curled up in Will's lap. Much to her surprise, her mother claimed the space beside Andrew, sitting cross-legged. Janet sat on the bed but then slid to the floor, her legs thrust somewhat defiantly into the circle they'd created. Janet waited stone-faced for Ronnie to begin. Their relationships were in shards, like the windows in the store.

Ronnie sensed Jeff in the middle of the circle, wedging them apart—and she wouldn't have it. If he wanted to instigate one last standoff, Ronnie was determined to emerge the victor.

"So, guys. You knew what this was about today, right? That your father had threatened to kill himself?"

They nodded. Beverly closed her eyes. Ronnie held still.

"And the police were trying to help him," Andrew said.

"Yes. But they couldn't. Unfortunately, your father didn't want their help. He shot himself, and he's dead."

There, the facts were out. Ronnie felt like she could breathe again.

Andrew said, "Did it hurt?"

Janet moaned. Ronnie thought of the shot ripping through Jeff's brain. She took a deep breath. "I don't think so, honey."

Will said, "Didn't you tell him about the chicks?"

Ronnie paused, her dedication to the truth already tested. "I did, Will. I told him as soon as I could."

Her mind emptied of words. How could she help her children make sense of the fact that their father had killed himself when that morning, they had seen him walking around? Death was hard enough to fathom, suicide nearly impossible. How could she explain this to her sons?

She looked at Andrew, leaning forward, eyes engaged and expectant. The same posture Janet always used to adopt when awaiting a story.

Her gut told her that's what she needed to give them. But what story? She turned to Will, his fingers working through Max's fur, wearing that stoic expression.

The image of Jeff's body being carried from the store flashed through her mind.

A story came to her.

"Remember Cupcake?"

"She was our cat," Andrew said. "We want to know about Dad."

Janet leaned forward. A story.

"Hang in there with me for a minute. Remember when she got sick?" She hoped they would remember; it had been only a year since Cupcake died. How long would they remember Jeff?

"Why couldn't the vet figure out what was wrong with her?" Andrew said.

"No matter how much we learn, some things about life and

death remain a mystery," Ronnie said. "Even if Cupcake could talk, I'm not sure if she would have been able to tell us why she was ready to die."

"We moved her out to Dad's woodworking shop," Will said, rubbing his cheek against Max's fur, "and brought her the old bed we made with our lambskins."

Ronnie's anxiety eased even as her heartache deepened. *He remembered. They would remember.*

"Dad had bought Cupcake for me when she was a little kitten and he didn't want to watch her die. He thought we should put her out of her misery."

"But to us she just seemed weak and tired," Andrew said.

"And she stretched her neck against our hands so we would pet her," Will said.

Ronnie loved the way the boys always wanted in on the storytelling.

"But even so, Cupcake's spirit was slowly leaving her body. When she finally stopped breathing, what we buried was no longer the cat we had loved, but the bones and fur that carried her spirit while she was here on earth."

She recalled how Will—only seven, yet already exhibiting equal measures of boy and man—had draped the dead cat over his arms and insisted on carrying her up to the burial site.

"That's how it was with your father. He was losing the will to live, and like Cupcake, he didn't know how to ask for the help he needed. Years of heavy drinking poisoned his body and mind in ways that we couldn't see from the outside." Ronnie looked over at her mother-in-law, who kept her silence. "And no matter how much we loved him, we couldn't save him."

Andrew said, "Why do you say you loved him if you were going to get a divorce?"

Ronnie let out a long breath. "That's confusing even to me," she said. "I never stopped wanting good things for your father. But he was making bad decisions for our family, and the time came when I had to take measures to protect us. But I never wanted to hurt him. It was a tough choice."

Will's face, neutral until now, twisted in a fight against tears.

Ronnie put her hand on Will's knee. "The only way we'll make it through this together is to share our thoughts and feelings, whatever they are." *Even if you blame me, please, speak to me.*

Will pulled himself together and did not cry. "This morning, when Dad was drunk, and I ran out to get the car keys from him…I thought I was saving his life. I wanted to save him."

Ronnie took Will's hand, which, like hers, was marked with scratches and bruises Jeff had inflicted. She wondered how long they would take to heal. Tears wet her face, but she would not let them steal her voice. "You tried, Will, and did what you could. No one can ever take that away from you." She looked at Janet. "Grandma Jan was very brave too. We all tried to help him with his problems."

"What were his problems?"

"That is such a good question, Andrew. I've been thinking about it all day. We may find clues, but all we'll ever know is that in the end, he couldn't think straight. So he made one last bad decision: today, when so much of his spirit had died that he could no longer face life, he killed himself."

Janet moaned and started to sob. "I will never survive this. Never."

Ronnie closed her eyes.

When Ronnie opened them again, she saw Will taking his grandmother's hand. "We'll take care of you, Grandma Jan. Then maybe we won't miss Dad so much."

ronnie

I lost someone to suicide too."

Ronnie's gaze bore into her mother, a plea not to increase her sons' burden.

"I know how the sadness and love can get tangled and linger."

Beverly twisted the ring on her hand.

"It was the first man I loved. I've been thinking about him a lot today. And about your daddy too, because I loved him, and because for so very many years, he made my daughter the happiest person."

"Mom," Ronnie said with fresh compassion.

Someday, when Ronnie felt they were ready, she wanted her mother to tell the boys the full story. It was their history; they had as much right to know about depression and suicide as they did about Beverly's arthritis and Janet's sweet tooth. If Ronnie had known about Jeff's medical history, maybe she could have gotten him help sooner. Maybe he would have had hope.

"When I lost the man I loved, I thought I'd never get over it. But then a little miracle happened."

Ronnie leaned forward.

"Someone else came into my life," her mother said. "Someone who made me forget the part about being all alone. Who taught me that I could feel extreme joy equal to my extreme pain and hold them both in my heart at the same time."

Janet. Ronnie looked at her mother-in-law with new gratitude.

She looked back at her mother and this time really saw her. She was transformed. The mascara was gone, her eyebrows mere suggestions. Her face looked scrubbed and fresh. But she also seemed to glow, as if from an inner source.

"And I knew that no matter what," Beverly continued, looking right at Ronnie, "I would always stay by her side. Even on a day like today. Because you are beautiful and precious to me, and"—she fought to control her voice and had to push the next words through her teeth—"because I want so badly for you to find joy."

Tears ran freely down Ronnie's face.

"And I want that for you boys too. So." Beverly wiggled free the small diamond ring. "Sometimes, when you love someone, you give them a ring as a sign of your promise. But I've always done things a bit backward, so as a sign of my promise to be here for you all, I'm going to give one up."

Beverly looked at the ring perched between her fingertips. "Boys, I will remember your father always, but I will not expect things of him he can't give. As sad as this day is, I'm willing to let him go, and while it's a little long in coming, I'm willing to let my first love go too." She kissed the ring and set it on the carpet in the center of the circle.

Beverly turned to Janet. "Is there something you might give up, Jan, as a sign of your promise?"

Janet put her hand to her abdomen. She looked forlorn and resigned, as if she'd given up on life. But what was the point in that when your heart kept beating, and yearning, and breaking?

Janet reached for her purse and pulled out her wallet, tufts of coupons visible from its bulging sides. *Oh my god, is she going to give us money?* Janet set the wallet aside, stuffed her hand deeper into her purse, and withdrew a leather-covered flask. Jeff had given it to her as a gag gift one birthday, since she never drank, saying she should try it, it might improve her outlook. Jeff had laughed, so they all had.

"I suspect there's going to be no way to take the edge off what I'm feeling right now anyway." She tossed it into the circle. Its steel top clunked with a hollow sound as it hit the ring.

Ronnie said, "Was this just for…today?"

Beverly seemed poised to answer if Janet wouldn't. Janet said, "Since Jerry's death."

"There's no time limit on mourning," Beverly said. "It could take five weeks, five months, five years—"

"Or in your case, thirty-five," Janet said. "But this wasn't mourning, really. It was regret. Forty-seven years of it."

Forty-seven? "You don't regret having Jeff, do you?" Ronnie said.

"No, I regret the quality of my marriage. But what could I ever say? Jerry was a local hero. If I walked into a room without him, someone would ask me where he was. Everyone benefitted from the love he lavished on the community. But he had little left to bring home at night."

"You're talking crazy. This day has been too hard on you," Beverly said. "You were the perfect family. You were the three J's."

"See, even my best friend won't believe me." A tear rolled down Janet's cheek. "After a while, you wonder if what you feel even matters. You want to just float away."

"You should have told me." Beverly handed Janet a tissue with a red lipstick blot on it.

"Why didn't you leave him?" Ronnie said.

"We taught at the same school, and people looked up to him. A divorce would have ruined him," Janet said. "And I couldn't do that to Jerry. I loved him."

Ronnie reached around Will and patted Janet's shoulder. She had never heard so many words from Janet at one time. She knew, from her journaling, what a relief it was to push them out.

"So I know what it's like to feel alone in a marriage," Janet said. "And I've wanted more for you, Ronnie. But I didn't know how to want that for you without hurting Jeff. And without losing you as a part of my family."

Beverly reached for Janet's hand.

"Grandma Jan, will you tell us a story about Dad?" Andrew said.

"A nice one," Will added.

Janet sniffed and thought a moment. "Back when he was eighteen, your father came home to tell us about his first year at college," she began. It was all Ronnie could do not to roll her eyes. "Your mom was only six and had beautiful ringlet curls. She had a petticoat beneath her dress—"

"She won't let us get a pet goat," Will said.

"A petticoat made your skirt full," Ronnie said, "but they haven't been in fashion since the middle of the last century. Your grandma is telling a tall tale."

"I let you tell your story. This is mine," Janet said. "Little Ronnie's skirt was stiff with petticoats, and she had on white anklet socks and patent leather shoes—"

"With taps on them," Beverly added with a smile.

"And she crawled up on your daddy's lap and turned his face toward hers as if no one else was in the room, because she adored him. And she loved him so much she had you two boys and you were happy until…until your mother…"

Ronnie tensed. Maybe mercy was too much to ask of a woman who had just lost her son. She deserved whatever Janet was about to say, but she wished the boys could believe in her for just a little longer.

Janet said, "And you were happy for as long as you could possibly be."

Ronnie broke down and sobbed. Will rubbed her wrist, the salt from his fingers stinging the scratches Jeff had left that morning. His tenderness and the pain both felt right.

Janet's unexpected generosity felt like a hug from the least likely person in the room to offer one. She thought about Jeff's hugs, where eyes were closed, heads were averted, tension was relieved, and secrets comfortably blanketed. Why had she craved them so? The tension in this circle—which required them to face one another, where comfort was desired yet not given, where escape was sought but not granted—just might hold them together.

Ronnie's stomach growled, loud enough that everyone heard. The boys erupted into giggles, then stopped short, looking to her.

"Grieving doesn't mean you have to feel sad every moment of the day," Ronnie said. "You may not know how to feel right now. There's no right or wrong. I guess each of us has to find our own way through it, however long that takes." She looked at her mother and mother-in-law. "But we have to try, because grieving is what allows us to feel everything again."

Ronnie put her hand on her stomach. "Including hunger. Mom, we'd better pick up some groceries on the way to your apartment."

"If you all can get me up off this floor, I think you'd better come to my house," Janet said. "I probably shouldn't be alone. Plus, I have more beds. And ice cream."

Andrew smiled. "I hope you have a lot," he said, already reaching for the door.

Ronnie stooped to pick up the ring and the flask.

"Mom." Will looked at Ronnie. "When will we see Dad again?"

The question took Ronnie's breath away. Hadn't Will understood what death meant? Hadn't he understood the story she'd shared?

"I think I have some old albums at home with pictures of your dad at about your age," Janet said, putting her arm across his shoulders. "How about we'll look for them tomorrow?"

"That'd be cool," he said.

"Give it time, Sunshine," Beverly whispered and slipped her arm around her daughter. "We've got a bit of winter ahead. But summer will come around again. And who knows, maybe next year, you could talk me into coming along to that beach house you like so much."

Ronnie opened her mother's purse and dropped in the flask and the ring. Then, with her family around her, she headed out into the night.

reading group guide

1. Do you relate to Ronnie's determination to honor her marriage vows and stay with Jeff despite the challenges of their relationship? How did she cope? What makes a vow worth breaking?

2. How do Ronnie, Beverly, Janet, and Corporal McNichol differ in the way they respond to the stresses of the standoff?

3. In her voice mail on the day of the standoff, Ronnie's therapist says, "Don't worry about being strong for others. Be strong in yourself." What do you think she meant by this?

4. In what way do you think Ronnie's and Jeff's characters are an outgrowth of their mothers' issues, and how did they each differentiate themselves from their mothers?

5. Where do you see Ronnie, Janet, and Beverly five years beyond the end of the book? Who do you think will have the hardest time adjusting to Jeff's loss, and why?

6. At one point, Janet makes a crack that she doesn't believe in genetics. The genetics are bleak for Will and Andrew: on one side, their grandfather and great-grandmother received electroshock therapy for depression and their father committed

suicide, and on the other, their grandfather committed suicide. Do you think these children might go on to lead emotionally and mentally healthy lives? What factors beyond genetics might influence their development?

7. Tension between the three women feeds on secrets kept and truths revealed. Even Ronnie, who thrives on the truth and who suffered from secrets kept, sits on some information. How do you feel about others withholding information to protect you? What might influence your decision to withhold information from others?

8. "If a horse went lame, [Jeff would] be the one with his arms around its neck, whispering in its ear, while Ronnie would be the one out by the hydrant, morning and night, cold hosing its leg and bandaging." What do Ronnie's and Jeff's differing approaches to the care of animals say about the way they loved other people? How do you think each would define love?

9. Discuss the role that setting plays in this story. In what ways do Ronnie and Jeff's house, New Hope Farms, and the firehouse social hall contribute to the story? How do these settings play a different role for Ronnie and Jeff?

10. Corporal McNichol says that fixing Jeff's problems is not Ronnie's responsibility. In what ways do you think this is or isn't true? Did you find it relatable that Ronnie picked up Jeff's slack as his drinking and depression worsened? At what point does "helping" start to hurt? At what point must you allow a loved one to face the consequences of their actions?

11. In his final suicide note, Jeff asks Ronnie to teach the boys that he loved them. If you were in this situation, would you be

able to teach this message to your children? How would you go about it?

12. Beverly and Janet concocted a family story about Ronnie—dressed like Shirley Temple, she climbed on Jeff's lap to command his attention—and have told it the same way for so long that they've changed the family's collective memory. Ronnie uses a similar technique when she recounts the kitten story for her sons to replace the horror of the suicide. Has your family ever told a story in a way that bent it over time, while also capturing an essential truth?

13. Janet consciously decided not to tell Ronnie that Jeff had pulled a weapon on his first wife. If it was your son, and you saw how happy this new woman made him, would you give her this information before the wedding? Or would you, like Janet, think your son deserved the right to try to mature and be happy?

14. In what way does Ronnie's story complicate the well-intentioned notion that we should be more compassionate toward people who are depressed and get them the help they need? In what ways did the system let Jeff and Ronnie down, and what can be done about it?

15. In response to her final attempt to get him help, Jeff wants to strike a bargain: he'll try rehab if Ronnie is there for him as his wife when he gets out. Do you think she should have tried this additional measure? Why or why not?

16. By the end of the standoff, Ronnie wonders whether she had ever really known Jeff at all. Do you think we can ever really know another person? What did Ronnie's marriage teach her about relationships—and about herself?

17. Several times in the book, a character signs a legal document authorizing an action that will have a significant impact on another character. Ronnie commits Jeff to a psych ward; Jerry signs for Janet to have fetus-threatening surgery; Ronnie authorizes the police to break her windows with canisters of Mace while Jeff is inside the building. Discuss these decisions. Would you have made the same ones? Have you ever had to authorize help for someone else, and how did it feel to take responsibility for that decision?

18. At several points, Beverly compares her relationship with Janet to a marriage. Do you have friendships that sometimes feel that way? What are the benefits and challenges of maintaining such a close relationship with a friend during life-changing events?

19. Ronnie and Jeff were deeply in debt. Although Jeff was in charge of the family finances, in what ways was Ronnie culpable for the state of their financial affairs? Did she deserve to pay this price for her mistakes?

20. Ronnie and Jeff, Beverly and Janet: both couples have a substantial age difference. In what ways do you think this feeds and/or challenges the relationships?

21. *The Far End of Happy* takes place over only twelve hours. In your opinion, which character exhibits the most significant growth arc, and why?

22. Throughout the day, the big challenge for the characters is to try to sustain some sort of hope. Do you think the story ends on a hopeful note, despite the obvious tragedy? Do you, like Beverly, think it's possible to hold extreme pain and extreme joy in your heart at the same time?

a conversation
with the author

This is a novel based on true events. Why did you decide to fictionalize? What is true, and what is made up?

Before writing this novel, I had spent several years drafting a memoir, mining the events that led up to my first husband's suicide standoff for aspects of story. I did so to create a record for my sons and me. Even while writing memoir, though, which relies on "facts" and naturally occurring story arcs, I always realized my version of those "true" events would differ significantly from someone else's. Both memoir and fiction, however, are ways of arriving at what is true for that writer. By freeing me from the constraints of fact, fiction ultimately gave me the leeway to tell an engaging story while still bringing my personal truth into full emotional bloom.

As for what is factual, other than an embellishment or two, most of the police action is as I remember it. As for what feels true, I'd answer the same way I would about my first, entirely fabricated novel: all of it.

Do any of the characters play themselves?

Yes, but they were all four-legged: Max, Daydream, and Horsey Patch. In memory of my therapist, who was struck down on the streets of Reading, Pennsylvania, by a hit-and-run driver after offering free counseling at Berks Women in Crisis, I named Ronnie's therapist Anita.

This was sensitive material and must have been hard to revisit. Why did you decide to write a book about it? What did you hope to accomplish?

While sharing my story through the years, verbally and on paper, I learned that the events that led up to the standoff's tragic outcome were relatable to many women. When our country's economy crashed in 2008 and so many lost the hope and security that comes from a lifetime of saving and investment, I felt more strongly than ever that sharing my story might help provide hope to others who had to start over and rebuild.

Interaction with death almost always invites us to reassess how we are spending our lives, but what made my husband's suicide so troubling were the persistent, unanswered questions. When did everything start falling apart? How did I miss it, in what ways was I compensating for it, and why did I ignore the signs? There are no clean lines in a story like ours, only endless shades of gray, and a lot of questions about relationships and life that are well worth asking. Without a doubt, that's why I wrote this book.

But I also realized, even as we were experiencing it, that death did not have dominion over the day of my husband's suicide, which contained within it the full range of life's emotional content. Joy and pain, tragedy and victory, togetherness and aloneness, beauty and revulsion, faith and despair, the known and the unknown—it was all there. A tragedy is always unfolding somewhere, whether we know it or not—during the time it takes to read this interview, at least one more person in the United States will die at his or her own hand. Yet despite my family's focus that day on a loved one determined to die, for those of us who chose life, it was a day worth living.

How did you decide to rename yourself for the novelized version of your story?

First, I want to be clear—while we are a lot alike, I am not Ronnie.

As happens in many novels, each character carries some spark from the author's personal fire.

My perspective is closest to Ronnie's, though, and naming her wasn't easy! I wanted a masculinized version of a female name to suggest, subtly, that she was functioning as both mother and father to her children. I began with Mick/Michelle, which I loved right up until the backstory referenced "Mick and Jeff," which sounded so much like "Mutt and Jeff" that I had to abandon the choice. I switched to Bennie/Benicia until "Bennie and Jeff" became "Bennie and the Jeff."

After that, further naming felt too random. My first husband's name was Ronald, and his mother and coworkers called him Ronnie. A lightbulb went on—I could name her Ronnie/Veronica—and the entire project clicked into place for me. By naming her Ronnie, I could achieve that thing story does best: create meaning from chaos. Oddly, I latched right on to the notion and never grew confused during the writing. It was healing for me to write about the standoff in a way that allowed someone named Ronnie to experience the end of the marriage, the financial disaster, and the day's events, yet still choose to embrace life.

How did you choose your point-of-view characters?

Even on the day of my first husband's standoff, when all was fresh and uncertain, I knew that the events of that day affected many more people than just my sons and me. A single point of view seemed disingenuous; I wasn't even the only mother involved. By creating points of view for the mother who lost her son and the mother with hidden secrets who had to share her daughter's trauma, I was able to spread the pain across the broken shoulders of all who were left behind, as does suicide.

It made no sense to presume to know Jeff's heart by giving him a point of view. His actions silenced his voice. If this character wanted his perspective known, he would have fought harder to stay in the story.

Telling the story in twelve hours is a technique more often used in suspense and thrillers than in women's fiction. Why did you decide to tell the story this way? What specific challenges did this structure present?

To my way of thinking, the standoff symbolized the stalemate that resulted when all efforts were spent at the useful end of Ronnie and Jeff's relationship. All marriages exhibit moments of miscommunication, lack of connection, and disappointment, but this high-stakes scenario electrifies Ronnie's look back at what might have led to this moment in time with the undercurrent of imminent harm.

For all three women, the deep shame that comes when private matters are exposed publicly is blown sky-high when governmental resources are tapped to save the community from Jeff's actions. Keeping the war at home within a tight frame seemed the best way to keep the reader focused on the fact that the way we lead our family lives can at any moment become a high-stakes game.

Yet a standoff, for the most part, is really a lot of high-tension waiting. My challenge was to include enough story events during those twelve hours so that the three women's private thoughts about what might have brought them to this place in their lives didn't outstrip the ongoing standoff action. To do so, I moved true events from elsewhere on our real timeline into the fictional frame of that day's events.

What advice might you have for others considering a novel based on true events?

I'd say take a lot of notes and don't be in a rush to publish.

Difficult life events require time to process. Do that work. I recall someone wise saying that the best literature about the 9/11 attacks would start to come out seven years after those events. Maybe that's a random number, but it's not a bad one to keep in mind. Although it is all about human emotion, literature is more than an outcry of grief or anger. Your reader has no interest in being dragged through the muck and mire of your existence unless they are going to gain new perspective about life. When you can offer that, you are ready to begin.

READ ON FOR AN EXCERPT FROM

The

ART

of

FALLING

BY KATHRYN CRAFT

AVAILABLE NOW FROM
SOURCEBOOKS LANDMARK

CHAPTER ONE

*M*y muscles still won't respond. It's been hours since they promised a doctor, but no one has come. All I can do is lie on this bed, wishing for some small twinge to tell me exactly what is wrong. My body: a still life, with blankets.

I'd settle for inching my foot back beneath the covers. I command my foot to flex. To point. To burrow beside its mate. It ignores me, as do my hands when I tell them to tend to the situation.

Why has someone covered me so haphazardly? Or—could it be?—that in my dreams, I had somehow moved that foot? I will it to move again—now.

It stays put.

This standoff grows more frightening by the moment. If my focus weakens, I'll fall prey to larger, hungrier questions. Only motion can soothe me; only sweat can wash away my fear.

From somewhere to my right, I hear an old woman's crackling cough. My eyes look toward the sound, but I am denied even this small diversion; a flimsy curtain hides her.

I close my eyes against this new reality: the bed rails, a constant beeping over my shoulder, and the device clamped to my index finger. In my mind, I replace the flimsy curtain with a stretch of burgundy velour and relax into its weight. Sink. Deep. I replay each sweep, rise, and dramatic dip of Dmitri's choreography. My muscles seek aspects of motion: that first impulse. The building momentum.

Moments of suspension, then—ah, sweet release. When the curtain rises, I will be born anew.

"Is time. *Merde*." The half-whisper I remember is intimate; Dmitri's breath tickles my ear. With a wet finger, he grazes a tender spot on my neck, for luck, then disappears among the other bodies awaiting him. My skin tingles from his touch.

The work light cuts off, plunging me into darkness. On the other side of the curtain, eleven hundred people, many of them critics and producers, hush. We are about to premiere *Zephyr*, Dmitri's first full-evening work.

I follow small bits of fluorescent tape across the floor to find my place. The curtain whispers as it rises. Audience expectation thickens the air.

Golden light splashes across the stage, and the music begins. Dmitri stalks onstage. I sense him and turn. Our eyes lock. We crouch—slow. Low. Wary. Mirror images, we raise our arms to the side, the downward arc from each shoulder creating powerful wings that hover on an imagined breeze. One: Our blood surges in rhythm. Two: A barely perceptible *plié* to prepare. Three: We soar.

Soon our limbs compress, then tug at the space between us. We never touch but are connected by intent, instinct, and strands of sound from violins. I feel the air he stirs against my skin.

Other dancers enter and exit, but I don't yield; Dmitri designed their movements to augment the tension made by our bodies.

I become the movement. I fling my boundaries to the back of the house; I will be bigger than ever before. I'm a confluence of muscle and sinew and bone made beautiful through my command of the oldest known language. I long to move others through my dancing because then I, too, am moved.

Near the end of the piece, the other four dancers cut a diagonal slash between Dmitri and me. Our shared focus snaps. Dissonance grows as we perform dizzying turns.

The music slows and our arms unfold to reduce spin. Dmitri and I hit our marks and reach toward each other. We have danced beyond the end of the music. In silence, within a waiting pool of light, we stretch until we touch, fingertip to fingertip.

Light fades, but the dance continues; my energy moves through Dmitri, and his pierces me. The years, continents, and oceans that once held us apart could not keep us from this moment of pure connection.

Utter blackness surrounds us, and for one horrible moment I lose it all—Dmitri, the theater, myself.

But when the stage lights come up, Dmitri squeezes my hand. His damp curls glisten.

Applause crescendos and crashes over us. Dmitri winks before accepting the accolades he expects.

I can't recover as quickly.

No matter how gently I ease toward the end of motion, it rips away from me. I feel raw. Euphoria drains from my fingertips, leaving behind this imperfect body.

I struggle to find myself as the others run on from the wings. We join hands in a line, they pull me with them to the lip of the stage—and with these simple movements I am returned to the joyful glow of performance. We raise our hands high and pause to look up to the balcony, an acknowledgment before bowing that feels like prayer. My heart and lungs strain and sweat pushes through my pores and I hope never to recover. I am gloriously alive, and living my dream.

The dance recedes and the applause fades, but I'm not ready. My muscles seek aspects of motion—where's the motion?—I can feel no impulse. Momentum stalls. I am suspended and can find no release.

The curtain falls, the bed rails return, and I am powerless to stop them.

acknowledgments

It wasn't long after my first husband's suicide standoff that I knew I'd one day make a story of it, and now that I have, the words "thank you" don't begin to cover my indebtedness to those who have brought this novel to fruition. My agent, Katie Shea Boutillier, contributed the enthusiastic vision that helped define (and title!) this project. By acquiring it for Sourcebooks, Editorial Director Shana Drehs allowed me the chance to share it. Associate Editor Anna Michels rolled up her sleeves and asked just as much of herself as she did of me as we shaped it into its final form. Eileen Carey designed another dynamic, meaningful cover.

I'd like to extend thanks to *Mason's Road*, the literary journal of the MFA program at Fairfield University, for publishing "Standoff at Ronnie's Place," a memoir essay from which some of this material is taken, and to my editor there, Elizabeth Hilts. Suicide facts came from the American Foundation for Suicide Prevention website, www.afsp.org.

Jane Hull, Pam Byers, Lisa Leleu, Amy Barnett, Rachel Trauger, and Kathleen Hoy listened to drafts of my memoir material and consistently encouraged me to share the story. Linda Beltz Glaser helped me wrap my head around what it would mean to fictionalize true events. For all manner of end-game support, I must thank my first reader, Janice Gable Bashman, as well as writing pals Tori Bond and Donna Galanti.

It isn't easy to stand beside someone through the trying events that inspired this novel. To every family member, friend, neighbor, and stranger who reached out to us, my deepest thanks. For their exceptional support during and immediately after the events in this story, I want to recognize Ellen Gallow, Scott Graham, Dr. Peter Klugman, Jennifer Zelenak, Stephen Brassard, Phyllis Graham, Lois Martin, and Bally Mennonite Church, to whom I was a stranger; sadly, John Graham, Robert Graham, and Anita Freedson did not live to see publication. To my surprise angel, Dierdre Smith Dabney: I wish you could have lived long enough to realize how very much your role in this story meant to me. I only hope you knew.

To my husband, David Craft: not every man would hold up as well while his wife spent a year with her former husband. For all the ways you are remarkable, not the least of which was proofreading at the rate of one hundred pages per day as my deadline loomed, you have my love.

Jackson and Marty: thank you for your generous permission to build this novel from aspects of our shared experience. You are courageous, exceptional men.

And lastly, to Ron: I hope you found peace. I finally found mine, in allowing someone named Ronnie to walk away from this standoff with hope in her heart.

about the author

Author photo by Jackson Williams

Kathryn Craft is the author of *The Art of Falling*. Long a leader in the southeastern Pennsylvania literary scene, she loves any event that brings together readers, books, food, and drink, and mentors other writers through workshops and writing retreats. A former dance critic, she has a bachelor's in biology education and a master's in health and physical education from Miami University in Ohio. She lives with her husband in Doylestown, Pennsylvania, and spends her summers lakeside in northern New York State. You can contact her through her website, www.kathryncraft.com.